The Black Cross

By Omar D. Rios

ISBN 978-1-7771486-1-4 (e-book)
ISBN 978-1-7771486-2-1 (hardcover)

Published by Kallpa Publishing Inc.
Visit us at www.kallpapub.com

Rios, Omar D.
The Black Cross

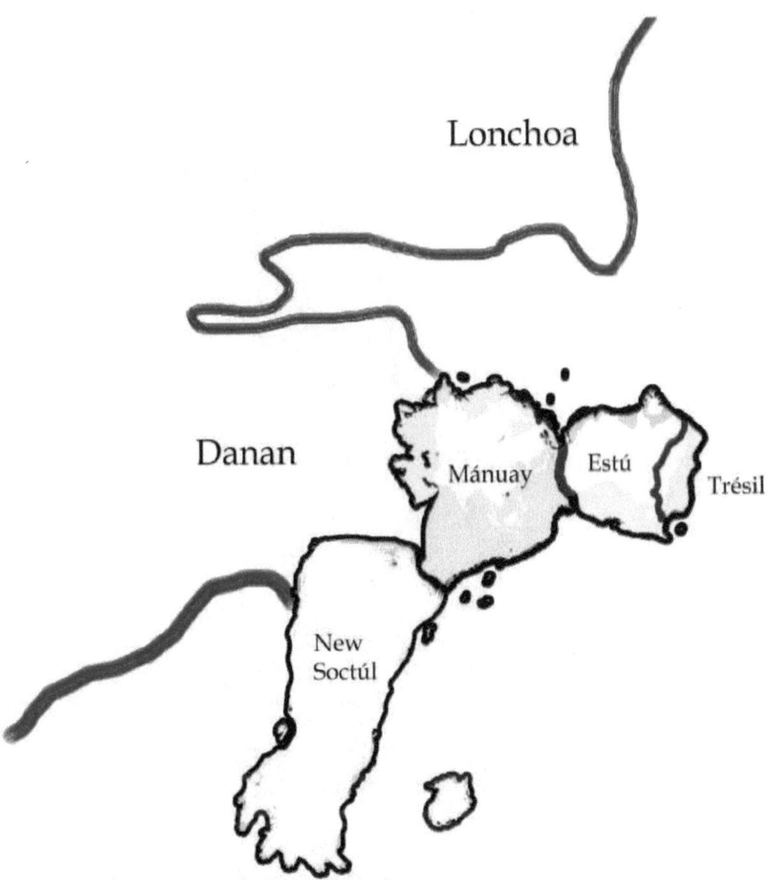

Danan

Znta
Klofia
Platae
Drilia
Rimac
Soctul
Peruvia
Nogalia
Chilinia
Las Esbirras
United Kingdoms of Panthea
Villavia

Panthea

For those who never stopped believing in me

Prologue

Those eyes. They always look at me.

They follow me everywhere.

Ever since I fell and scraped my knee, I have felt them on me. Silent like a turtle. Evident like the Sun. What do they want? Whose eyes are they? Why me?

Every time I looked back at them, they would simply disappear. Dad often told me that it could be mom, watching me from beyond. I don't think that's the case. Whether I'm at the garden, the wine cellar, or the rooftop, there they are. Fixed on me as if I was the only person on the planet.

I'm scared. What did I do? How is it even possible?

Even when I play with my dolls, or my tea set, or my bike, they look at me. Don't they ever grow tired of it? Will they ever be? I'm too afraid to tell anyone else.

Nevertheless, I know I will meet the owner of those eyes. They wait for me. So, I will wait for them. One day I'll know the truth.

One day, I'll be complete.

Torment of
Reminiscence

|

"PLEASE… SPARE ME… I have four children… please. I want to see them again… I beg of you!"

In response, a maniacal laughter resounded throughout the dark and blood-stained aisle as the intruder looked into his eyes. Then, alongside her cruel smile, she raised her weapon with her right hand and plunged it right into his head as his screams of agony lived and died along with him.

The light sound of her steps approaching was everything Doctor Kelvin needed to hear to realize he had to leave the facility as fast as possible. Being the first, and possibly the last, Rolve director of Sanatorium, Kelvin pulled documents out of his desk as quickly as he could.

"Tom, Hank… I'm so sorry… there was nothing I could do…" he murmured. "I will make her pay for this… I swear it… but first… some things must come with me!"

The last scream from down the hallway had become increasingly louder. Closer. She'd be there any second now.

"Where the fuck is it?! Damn it! C'mon! C'mon! I don't have time for this!" he ranted as he nervously opened all the drawers of his desk, as quickly as he could, shuffling around the papers inside them until he finally found what he was looking for. Sighing deeply in relief, he placed the document in his briefcase and ran out of his office. The relative darkness of the place made it hard to discern the forms that arose from within the shadows in the aisle. And yet, he could easily observe what lay down there in front of him: mutilated corpses and limbs. Some of them would look back at him with lifeless eyes, their expressions fixed in a macabre fashion; their mouths open as if trying to warn him about something. Indeed, a warning arrived at his ears, in the form of an acute laughter, as a shadow loomed at the end of the hallway.

"It's you!" he exclaimed at the sight.

She walked towards him, calmly, smiling. Her deadly weapons were dripping a trail of blood as she looked at him… into him. Kelvin, knowing what she was planning to do, dashed down the hallway, getting to the end of the aisle. Then, he pushed open the emergency exit door and ran downstairs as fast as his legs could carry him. As he descended further down the building, he heard the door upstairs being torn to pieces. Given the deep darkness all around him, he could only guess it was a miracle he hadn't tripped and fallen to his death. He only wished his hurried steps and the echo they produced didn't disguise those of his pursuer and her approaching maniacal and acute laughter.

"Please be here! Please be here!" Kelvin begged looking at the sky through the windows as if it could hear him. He had called the police five minutes ago, or so he thought. They had to be at the front gate by now. They were his only hope.

Once he managed to get to the first floor, he pushed the emergency exit door open with so much force that he fell flat on his face out in the main yard. The approaching laughter coming from the stairs above made him get back on his feet in one second and keep running, realizing that the fact that she was chasing him only meant one thing: everyone else in Sanatorium was dead.

"I'm sorry! I swear for Kothat I didn't take part in this!" he screamed in vain. His reply came in the form of mocking mirth, one that sounded closer and closer as the seconds passed by. "Damn rain! I can't see well!" he ranted as he kept his speed as steady as he could towards the main gates. Then, he heard the emergency exit door he had just opened being torn to pieces.

I've gained quite a distance… I can still make it! he thought with a small smirk appearing on his face.

He looked up as his legs started to hurt and saw several lights by the main entrance. Those lights made him smile in hope as they were the right colors: red and blue. He was so close, and yet so far.

Or so he thought when he tripped on a loose stone.

The asylum was an old building, indeed. Maybe it was the wisdom and history of the asylum that had allowed such an incident to occur. Maybe pure luck. Kelvin thought of both as, somehow, this inconvenient accident had become a convenient lifesaver because, as he fell to the ground, a giant black object passed flying right over his head.

He looked over his shoulder as he reincorporated. There she was, the woman with yellowish skin and raven black hair, showing that malicious grin. Kelvin simply set his eyes back to his escape route and, jumping over her weapon now lying on the floor, he continued on his way to the gate, turning around several times to see if she was about to throw her other remaining horrendous thing, hanging on her right hand. Nearing the main gates, he looked back once more just to realize she was about to do just that.

"C'mon! C'mon!" he begged the skies once more as he reached for the main gates: two big steel-bar doors which he pushed open, taking advantage of his speed, and exiting successfully. The doors closed automatically behind him as his heart slowed down in relief. There were heavily armed officers just outside the gate, aiming at him. There was still hope to stop her!

"Freeze! Freeze right now or we'll open fire! Raise your hands above your head and walk slowly towards us! Now!" said one of said officers behind a van through a megaphone. Said action only perplexed the Rolve man who didn't know whether to obey him or to keep running.

"Please help me! She's right behind me! She'll kill me! I can't stop moving or she'll get me! I BEG OF YOU!" pleaded Kelvin, his feet trembling and willing to step forward. The officers looked around the surrounding area, skeptical. They didn't care, even though they could see the terror in his face, the sweat from all the running, his whole body shaking, and his eyes pleading.

They still didn't care.

"Follow our orders and everything will be fine sir! Now come towards us in a patient and calm manner!" continued the same man behind the van.

Their carelessness contrasted with their cautiousness. Kelvin didn't have time to play their games, no matter how serious they were. Thus, as there was no other choice in the vicinity, Kelvin was forced to comply, reducing his pace as he approached the authorities. He knew that the armed officers would shoot him on the spot if he did anything wrong, but there was *that* other pressing matter.

That nightmarish matter right behind him.

That insane woman was getting closer, he could feel it. Her light steps, even though barefoot, echoed in his ears. In his mind, he wanted to look back, but he couldn't. As his body shivered more and more, he felt how her steps had begun to accelerate. The beating of his heart accelerated accordingly as if pacing along with them. Each step he heard behind him turning into a hammer, hitting his core harder and harder. If he waited any longer, he wouldn't be able to tell the tale.

He couldn't bear it any longer.

The steps, louder and louder with every passing second, produced a fear beyond control in Kelvin. Fear he had never felt before. What if she was about to throw one of her lethal weapons at him while he couldn't turn around? What if her weapon was already travelling towards him in mid-air? What if she was right there, a meter behind him, while he made up his mind? There was only one option left.

"Stop! Stop right there or we'll shoot!" requested the man behind the van. This time, it was Kelvin who didn't care. He'd rather get bullets inside his body than being smashed by one of those damn lethal things. So, he rushed into one of the police cars as the officers opened fire, getting his right leg and slowing him down. However, there was little else they could do to stop him. The adrenaline moving through his body worked as the perfect fuel, and as a painkiller.

Sure enough, his luck couldn't be better: the car was already on. Probably because the officers weren't expecting to be there for long. He thanked his lucky stars as he stepped on the accelerator and the engine roared. Caring little for the officers still shooting at him, and taking advantage of the armored car hull, he dashed at full speed, almost hitting two officers on his way out.

As quickly as he had appeared, he had disappeared.

"Phil Yang reporting here! A Rolve man took one of our vehicles and is heading south!" said the man behind the van in a slightly irritated voice onto a walkie-talkie. A Lurn in his forties. He smiled at the response he received from the device. "Very well, over." Then, he frowned at the next instruction. "Under-understood, sir. Over and out."

"Do we chase him down, sir?" asked one of the operatives nearby over the radio.

"We can track that moron with GPS. He won't get far," answered Yang. "Other than his address, there's nowhere else he can go." He then pointed his rifle towards the entrance gate. "Let's focus on the actual task at hand… on *that* woman."

"She's just a woman, sir. We should be able to wrap this up easy," said confidently another officer nearby. All of them seemed to be relatively calm. "Can't wait to get home already!"

"Never underestimate your enemies, son," replied Yang trying to prevent his nerves from getting the better of him. Being the commander of an operation was never easy, especially when the monster they were about to face had already killed several people before Sanatorium. Fellow officers who had tried to stop her, in vain. Maybe it was because of the characteristics attributed to her by central command, over the radio, that seemed out of this world that made the whole situation completely absurd. While Yang didn't believe them wholeheartedly, these details just made the hunt more thrilling, scary, and unexpected for the youngest officers. Yang just wanted it to be over with.

"Everyone, attack positions! Now!" instructed Yang through his handy megaphone. "Here she comes!"

All the officers placed themselves behind their respective vehicles, aiming at the Sanatorium's main gates. Even though they had had a hard time believing the reports, mostly due to their lack of conclusive evidence about the information they had been provided with, the officers had an idea of what was waiting for them. And even within the vague abilities that were said to be real about this woman, one thing was certain: no mercy could be shown on their behalf. Shoot to kill was what their attack positions meant. Their laser sights pointed at a height where a human head would be as they waited, focused on searching the target with their infrared visors while the cold pouring rain kept hammering them like a giant showerhead. Even with that equipment, the darkness was quite endearing and made the search harder than usual. Their focus had to be absolute, and focused they remained. At least until an acute laughter from within the garden made them lose it.

The reports had been clear. She was to be shot down for the operation to be a success. Any other emergency could wait for later. Thus, alerted, their laser sights looked for their target within the garden in darkness, like fish looking for an exit from their fish tank. Fortunately for them, the dim light provided by nearby lampposts allowed their infrared vision to work in acceptable conditions, as too much light would've been disruptive.

"There she is!" exclaimed one of them, pointing at the middle of the garden with his weapon.

And there she was, picking up the weapon she had thrown at Kelvin in a slow and calm fashion, as if she had all the time in the world. As she did so, a random lightning lit the yard for a few seconds, allowing them to make out perfectly her horrifying features. They could feel her lack of empathy and utter insanity just by looking at her face for that brief time.

"Everyone! On my mark!" announced Yang as he joined his comrades in the discovery. The intent of killing she emitted crawled into their bones, as if the underworld itself was taking over them. They couldn't stop feeling that they should run away and never look back. Some of their laser sights could hardly keep aim, shaking all over the place. Still, they resisted, and, even though their urge to flee increased steadily as the demon walked towards them, both of her weapons dripping a continuous stream of blood, their feet wouldn't budge an inch. Her ragged, torn, and blood-covered white dress stood out in the garden coated in darkness. She didn't seem scared of them at all.

They took the safety of their weapons off and placed their fingers on the triggers. Yang raised his right hand, ready to issue the command, when the woman stopped on her way out.

She simply stood there, motionless. Something had caught her attention to the point of making her focus completely on it.

"What is she looking at?" wondered one of the officers out loud as they followed her gaze, finding perplexing what she was looking at: a very small fountain near the entrance gate. Oblivious to the laser sights showering her body, Carmen de la Cruz, as that was her name, kept staring at said fountain. The men wondered what she was thinking of. Whatever it was, it had to be important. Yet, they didn't have a single hint as of what it could be. Unbeknownst to them, Carmen had entered the innermost of her core.

Her memories.

As she chased them around inside her mind, she extended her right hand towards the structure as if holding a cup. The fountain had a similar shape to one, after all. The darkness of her past, as well as the light, was appearing before her very eyes. It was just the cup and her. The rest of the world didn't exist anymore.

She had taken a trip down memory lane when times were happier. Better. It was a cup of wine, in the end, that had engraved itself in her memory before everything started going downhill.

II

"THERE IS NOTHING LIKE A GOOD RED WINE," she said, looking embezzled into the cup in her right hand.

As usual, she deeply enjoyed one of her favorite wines down in the mansion wine cellar. An *Alegre Crianza 1976*. Its flavor and texture, still cradling within her cup, enhanced her reading experience, a quite lovely one at that. The darkness of the wine cellar always felt welcoming, its silence teasing, and its smell rewarding. It was quite elegant, and unrefined, at the same time. The loneliness it provided was, actually, way too comforting for Carmen. Something no one truly understood about her, or her voluntary confinement, even though the explanation for it was simpler than they thought. If they would've just noticed the date when this new habit of hers had started…

Every servant in the mansion knew that all the La Cruz family had died off in a plane accident when going to a family reunion before Carmen was even born. At least almost all of them. The exception being Don Fernando de La Cruz, Carmen's father, who could only watch as his wife died during childbirth. However, because Don Fernando's health had been deteriorating quickly in recent years, the thought of becoming the last of the La Cruz on the planet often crossed young Carmen's mind.

As she flavored the delicious and dry wine, feeling its soul with her tongue, as she liked to put it, her sixteenth birthday came to her mind. Indeed, by the time she turned sixteen, she had already been tasting and differentiating the different types of wine around the mansion for at least eight years. A family tradition she wanted to keep alive. As one of the last owners of the renowned La Cruz Vineyards & Wines, in the country of Estú, Carmen often felt compelled to continue said legacy alongside her family trade. Sure enough, making her father happy was also an important factor to keep her compelled, especially since she knew her father would be gone before she'd be able to assimilate the truth of his *departure*. Given that her duties included having to be prepared for her future tasks as the mansion's mistress, and to become the head of the family business, the burden of such future responsibilities and her current problems were lifted off her shoulders simply by tasting wine. In her own words, it prevented her from crying in despair. Nonetheless, it wasn't like she had no other sources of distraction…

Being homeschooled all her life, Carmen had learned all she could by being an avid reader. Like the wine she enjoyed, the large family library was pretty useful at making her problems vanish for a while, too. By reading and studying subjects she didn't understand at first until mastering them, Carmen also became aware of her fascination for that which she couldn't understand. A never-ending quest of enthrallment, as she liked to put it. Ironically enough, she didn't care much about questions impossible to answer, such as the origin of everything, or the end of everything. As per human interactions went, she couldn't thank her servants enough, especially Pablo, the closest one to her age, for helping her with such an important subject in her future role. For instance, Carmen would practice business discussions with them, even though they couldn't truly understand the subject at hand most of the time.

Carmen wished they were the only ones willing to talk to her, though.

As her family tragedy became widespread, several pretenders made their appearance out of thin air. Sometimes, literally before her front door in expensive and lustrous limousines. Carmen's beauty and fortune were a magnet for many young men, albeit some not so young, who wouldn't hesitate in trying their luck with the last La Cruz. Like her mother, she had inherited her raven-black hair, thin complexion, and rosy lips, and like her father, she had inherited his raven black eyes, his pronounced cheekbones, and his tall forehead. Added to her white as marble skin, as expected from a Frisk, and tender face, Carmen would often provoke quite the insistence in the men mentioned before. Nevertheless, her pretenders and their propositions were always declined. Carmen often said she'd have none of it, and that there were more important tasks at hand. Among several activities, she considered the most important there were the management of the company, her father's decaying health, or her favorite one, the celebration of her birthdays.

She had always celebrated them accompanied by her loyal servants, her father, and Spunky, a small furry dog she had had since she was eight. However, her most recent birthday had been quite different than usual as her father couldn't be there with her anymore. He had to stay in bed that very day, which didn't allow Carmen to fully smile during the celebration like she used to. Thus, along with the servants, Carmen brought her party, usually held at the main hall in front of the La Cruz seal, to her father's bedroom. Seeing him trying to sing "Happy Birthday" for her, barely able to breathe, broke her heart. She had managed to withhold her tears, smiling for him at all times, though. Afterwards, as soon as the celebration was over, she went down straight to the wine cellar, looking for her usual forgetfulness. As she wondered how she had managed to keep smiling the whole time, a single answer always came on top: had it not been for *him*, her life would've already become hell itself.

He, who manifested himself only through letters, was one of the pillars Carmen knew she could always count on. The way his calligraphy was executed invariably made her keep making wild guesses as per who that could be. Was it Pablo? No way he could write like that. Was it one of her pretenders? She hoped not. She knew quite well what the *true* goal of any of her pretenders was. This was completely different. The way this man directed his wishes to her couldn't be that of a man interested in money or fortune. She could feel tingles down her spine every time she opened one of his letters. Eventually, she had come to expect them, feeling quite depressed when they didn't appear below her bedroom door. It was because of a letter from him that her last birthday hadn't been a complete bust. Besides his sweet words, there was also *that* gift...

Over her lifetime, she had gotten many gifts from different people, most of them unknown. Although she deeply appreciated all sorts of gifts, even those her father's acquaintances considered poor or disgusting, none of them held the same meaning as this gift. The sweetest one she could have ever hoped for: a teddy bear she eagerly named Derzú. It appeared before her door that awful night, once her father had passed out from being unable to sing for her birthday, with a note on its forehead. The handwriting told her right away who it was. She tightly hugged Derzú as she thanked her secret admirer in silence while reading the note, which was quite simple, and yet meaningful.

"Every time you feel sad, I'll be there. Happy birthday, Carmen."

Ever since then, Derzú had been her companion during her solitary reading sessions down at the wine cellar. Now, she could truly feel happy for once. Now she could properly forget her problems for a while as the small bear would look at her with innocent eyes, prompting her to smile back at him, or so she liked to think.

Spunky wouldn't stay far behind on the matter, as he also allowed her to forget her problems when they played outside. When left alone, he'd go downstairs to see Carmen when she was reading, eager for her to caress his head while wagging his fluffy tail. It was a cute little fellow. His soft brown fur always reminded Carmen that she wasn't alone, not even in the darkest dungeon. Fortunately for her, the cellar wasn't as dark thanks to a small lamp she brought with her every time she went downstairs. Her cellphone had an integrated flashlight as well, but it would never do. If at least technology was just as good a companion as her books, maybe she wouldn't be able to read at all, distracted by the lights of the screen like a moth drawn to a flame. Thus, even though she also had a laptop with a battery that lasted for at least three hours, with the newest five-by-four processors that allowed it to have quite the processing speed and power anyone could ever ask for, she still rejected the whole idea. Besides, she also hated the feeling she got from staring at the screen in the dark. It reminded her of herself in the near future. That of being the last La Cruz. This behavior drove her servants to believe that she would be against anything that didn't mean complete absorption from reality, as her reading sessions lasted several hours on end. And yet, unbeknownst to them, somehow this behavior made her more connected to her father.

Like her father in his better days, Carmen enjoyed poetry quite a lot. Her favorite poems had been written by a man known as the "Bard," a famous playwright that had been given said nickname three centuries prior but was known everywhere around the world as a master of Stony's literature. Those beautiful verses kept her away from reality, not completely, just enough, to help her forget about her problems, and enough to remember that her father was still there by her side, regardless of how ill he might be feeling. Given that his illness had been diagnosed as unknown by the top specialists available in Estú, and that the cure for his sickness was also unknown, Doctor Wright, the family doctor, would often say there was little they could do to help him.

As the new official La Cruz family doctor, after his father--Doctor Henry Wright--had passed away a few years ago, Jason Wright was the only one allowed to examine Don Fernando. Thanks to the well-earned trust his father had gained towards Carmen's family, Fernando de la Cruz would ultimately believe every word he said, blindly. As a citizen of the United Kingdoms of Panthea, or Panthean, as he would often point out, he had a thick Stonian accent, which prompted Don Fernando to laugh at him sporadically from time to time. No other doctor would suffice for him, though, something Carmen agreed with completely.

Thus, Carmen said nothing when the doctor made a decision, regardless of how harsh it could sound. Besides not wanting to go against her father's will, the other reason she agreed to such exclusivity was that she often thought of the doctor as handsome. Albeit he was seven years older than her, not really a problem to her, especially since he had a good image on behalf of her father, this thought would rarely leave her mind. The same couldn't be said for Spunky, who would bark ferociously at him every time he came to the mansion. Unlike him, the servants could tell that the young maiden had set her eyes on him since she was twelve. What they didn't know was whether a relationship with him was possible or not given the circumstances. Still, she liked to dream about that possibility. Besides, if her feelings were not reciprocated, she could always turn to her secret admirer.

"Thus, thou shalt not dismay... For I doth enter the fray..." she read out loud. The echo of her voice resounded within the darkness of the cellar. She felt quite silly identifying herself with this line as she drank a sip of wine, as if a knight in shining armor would appear out of thin air, right there, to rescue her from her ordeal. She often dreamt of it, and she often forgot about it right after. Purposefully, most of the time.

As she turned the page, Pablo swung open the door, bringing in turn sudden bright light into the cellar forcing Carmen to close her eyes and focus them on him, getting them used to the invading light. Once set, she wished they hadn't as the young servant's face only brought distress into Carmen's very core. Her heart shrunk at the sight as it could only mean...

"*Señorita* Carmen! *Señorita* Carmen! Don Fernando has woken up! Please come quickly!" said Pablo, taking off his straw hat and looking at the floor. "He-he… he's not looking good…"

Carmen's eyes widened at the sound of those words. She immediately got up and ran to her father's chambers, as fast as she could, almost tripping on the stairs, begging for it to be just a scare. Her heart pounded so heavily inside her chest at the thought that her worst fear would finally come true.

Not yet.

She opened the two big doors leading to her father's bedroom in one push. And there he was, lying on his bed, looking at the ceiling into emptiness. As he had only gotten worse with each passing day, Carmen often compared his health to an old building that was quickly losing bricks. One day he'd lose ten bricks at a time, the next, twenty, and so on. Thus, seeing him like this always had the same effect on her: that of wanting to fall down to her knees and cry in despair. And yet, a smile was all her father would get from her.

Upon a closer look, she realized that not even her wildest imagination could've produced a picture like the one she was watching right there: lying down on his bed as a corpse, kept away from the sun he loved so much for four months now, Fernando de la Cruz turned his emaciated face to the left and looked at her. Although his face showed nothing more than utter serenity among the shadows of his grand bedroom, it only reinforced Carmen's silent despair. The powerlessness she felt at that moment was more potent than usual, causing her to clench her fists as she approached him.

This wasn't supposed to happen now. It could happen at any other time, but not now. She wasn't ready. She could never be ready. He couldn't go now. She wouldn't let him go.

Fernando de la Cruz looked at her gently, smiling slightly. Despite having difficulty breathing, he managed to hold his daughter's hand tightly as she knelt beside his bed. His soft skin and warmth felt as if he was not sick at all. He was going to be fine… He would be fine! And yet, she could feel how she was trading those droplets falling from her eyes for complete resignation. She could only wonder why. She could only wonder if it was truly the moment she had feared for months now.

Pablo stood by the door looking at the scene, holding his straw hat down as a sign of respect. He could only remember the moments he had shared with his boss. He had known Don Fernando his entire life as he had been taken into the La Cruz mansion when he was abandoned by his parents at the age of three. Don Fernando was the father he had never had, which allowed him to relate to Carmen's pain, yet he never cried, not even when he was completely alone. Men weren't allowed to, at least according to Don Fernando. Something that gave him an easier understanding as to why his 'sister' was so different and rebellious to his 'father.' Carmen thought of that custom as archaic and often encouraged him to defy it. However, since Pablo wanted to be like Don Fernando, he'd simply ignore her, especially now, as many memories started to flood his mind. Many memories that would keep him away from what he was seeing through sheer abstraction. It worked until Carmen's voice broke him out of his inner thoughts.

"Call Doctor Wright! Now!" requested Carmen to Pablo as she snapped out of her own trance of sadness, too. "There is no time to lose! Do it now!"

Pablo took his cellphone out of his pocket as fast as he could, almost dropping it on the floor, and dialed Wright's number. They had called emergencies already, even though they knew that the nearest hospital was way too far compared to Wright's home. They also knew it was completely useless from the start, still, if by some miracle the ambulance got there on time... then just maybe...

Even Carmen was aware that there was little Doctor Wright could do for him, other than administering painkillers to make his future departure from the world more comfortable. It was still better than seeing him suffer like this. Any means of soothing his pain was better than nothing.

Carmen stood by her father's side, unable to tell what she should do next, deep in thought when he, almost inaudibly, uttered some words. "Carmen... my little *ángel*..." Carmen could tell he was no longer able to see her as he stared somewhere else instead of her eyes. His lips had become thin like silk and his eyes had sunk like teabags in hot water. His skin, though soft, had become extremely delicate, getting blisters from a simple touch. The illness had consumed his youth almost entirely.

"I'm here *papá*! Everything's fine!" Carmen replied in a positive tone, with all the energy she could muster. "You will be fine!"

She didn't know whether she was trying to comfort him, or herself.

"You are so... beautiful..." he continued weakly as he caressed her face.

"Don't worry *papá*, Doctor Wright will be here any second now. Just hold on!" continued Carmen as she approached her face to his, trying to hear him as well as she could. "Please don't speak! Keep your strength!"

"I know... the truth... my little *ángel*... I'm done for... don't worry... it's... okay..."

"No! Don't say that! You were following Doctor Wright's prescription verbatim! You will be fine! Trust me! Please!" Carmen encouraged him as she felt her heart burning with grief.

"You... have... to be... careful... my... child... the world is... a bad place... for those... who don't... adapt to it..."

"What are you saying?! After all this time together, you can't go! I don't wanna be alone! Please! Please!... Please... don't leave me..." cried Carmen in a sadder and less energetic voice. Pain and darkness clouded her mind and heart, after all.

And just like that, as she held his hand, his breathing stopped. She pushed his body with both of her hands, trying to wake him up, trying to undo the inevitable. It didn't matter, for his eyes closed forever that very moment. She could only scream her lungs out, feeling her heart being ripped off her chest. Now she was truly the last La Cruz. Now, she was truly alone.

How does it feel? It looks amusing...

The main mansion doors opened as Doctor Wright arrived and ran upstairs. However, when he was about to enter the bedroom, Pablo stopped him by patting him on his right shoulder. He immediately understood why as he saw Carmen bent upon her father's bed in evident grief. Both could only watch and keep silent. They could only witness how Carmen finally released all the tears she had held back all this time…

The young damsel grieved for an entire week. She wouldn't see anyone. Not even her secret admirer's letters were allowed into her mind. As her thoughts came back to order and pain became a memory, her father's last words came back to her thoughts. What did he mean by them? She hated herself for not being able to understand his message. At that moment at least, those words meant the world for the young girl. However, no matter how hard she tried, she failed in figuring out anything that made sense. After her thirtieth attempt, she decided it was time to stop grieving. She became content with having heard them so that she might be able to understand his message someday in the future. She also realized that, opposite to what her father had once told her, time didn't heal everything. The pain was always there and presented itself inside her heart each time she looked at his empty bedroom or lonely office. At the realization, she forcefully changed her numerous habits, trying to go out of the mansion as often as she could. Crying sporadically here and there, when completely alone. Her remaining 'family', or her servants, would often help her in this regard as, if they managed to spot her crying, they would crack a joke or talk to her about something positive. They might not be her blood-related family; however, they were the only people she had left, and they knew it. On the other hand, Doctor Wright's visits became less and less frequent as he didn't have any real reason to come to the mansion anymore, although he did come when Carmen would get colds and such. During one of these visits, he mentioned there was always a small chance that Carmen could get the same sickness that had taken her father away. Contrary to what he expected, that possibility didn't scare her in the least. Reuniting with her father, wherever he was, didn't sound that bad.

And, before she knew it, one month had already passed. Accordingly, the executive board contacted her requesting her to become the new official CEO of La Cruz Wines & Vineyards. For such a meeting, she was to carry all related documents to the meeting. As the notice had come to her when she least expected it, she had no choice other than looking for all concerning papers the day right before said meeting, and shuffling through the papers, she found it.

"That letter… I had forgotten I had it in here…" she said in a moment of revelation. "How rude of me…" she continued her self-reflection as she opened it. She had always considered bad manners if a person didn't read a letter someone had made the effort to write. As expected, its contents brought a smile upon her face:

"I wish chivalry was still alive so this letter wouldn't sound so old-fashioned because, in a moment like this, I would like to be your knight in shining armor. Whether nowadays it might be considered corny and such, it matters only for those who don't vouch for it. I wish I could be there by your side. I wish it was on me on who you would abide by. I wish this letter written in this fashion will always remind you that you are not alone, for, without you, I would be long forlorn."

Reading it, even though she didn't feel as sad anymore, was still quite alleviating. She hugged the letter close to her chest and stored it where she kept the rest of his letters: in the drawer right beside her bed. She did so since, at times, she would read them when she was feeling down, or before falling asleep. And so, while looking at the ceiling, about to sleep, one thought often invaded her mind…

Who was he?

The next morning, as she exited the mansion to go to her meeting, she decided to go to the family chapel behind the mansion before leaving. It was always the same feeling every time she entered it. The coldness of stone, and the dry fall air, provoked fear and marvel within her mind while she could never avoid admiring the black marble structures in that place, the very symbol of her family. As it had been done for generations within the La Cruz family, heavy black marble crosses were on top of each of her parent's tombs. When the airplane accident happened, all of the La Cruz family members were buried in their respective households with the same tradition. Her father had once told her that it had been that way since the Middle Ages. She often found it funny to remember that a battle in a valley called La Cruz, due to it being an intersection of two valleys in Estú, resulted in victory and provoked two brothers, named Paltro back then, to change their last name to La Cruz.

By the time she arrived at the company meeting, she was quite late. Somehow, it didn't seem to matter for the rest of board members as it was as if they were expecting someone else, entirely. Once she occupied her seat, at the head of a long table, the meeting proceeded as Carmen had expected. Nothing farfetched, mostly graphics about the company's rising sales as well as one or two projects she didn't care to listen to. Over time, she realized her meetings weren't going to be any different, prompting her to wish to trade her position to someone who actually cared. However, she knew her father would never forgive such an attitude if he were there. Thus, every time that wish came to her mind, she quickly dismissed it by remembering just that. And so, as the months passed, as well as her meetings, and way too many pretenders she cared to count, she became more and more eager to actually know who her secret admirer was. As his letters kept coming, sometimes she would purposely miss a meeting just to try to spot who was the mysterious sender *in fraganti*.

At first, she thought he sent the letters through regular mail, and that then they were carried to her room by her servants. She was deeply mistaken. The letters, one after the other, would appear directly below her bedroom door without the servants' knowledge. From the behavior of the sender, Carmen could only assume he knew the mansion like the back of his hand. The same would be true for her work schedule.

She could only deduce that he was quite careful, as not even fingerprints would show up. Given that there was no way to contact him, and that the whole situation had started to become increasingly strange, Carmen started to think the worst scenario: from being her prince charming, he was quickly becoming prince creepy.

That was until she actually caught a glimpse of him. Ironically, it was by accident. She hadn't planned to do her, by now, usual surveillance that day. And yet, she saw a shadow moving away from her door as she approached her bedroom after she had brushed her teeth. She quickly chased him down to no avail, following him into a closed room, used mostly for storage near the attic, just to see an open window within. Deducing he must've jumped out, she glanced out the window to see if he was still within her sight, and to her shock, he had vanished into thin air. All of her bravery vanished in a single breath as well as her knees, which trembled uncontrollably. She fell onto her back. *Who the hell was he?*

This situation was now way out of control, or at least that's what occurred to her during the first minutes. If he was truly her admirer and all that, why all the secret? Maybe he was just a serial killer or a criminal of the sort. She thought of calling the police, but with all the letters she had received, and how well he knew her behavior and her household, he would simply be more careful while the police would only tell her what she wanted to hear, and do nothing about it. Or worse, that she was in league with him due to the insane number of letters in her drawer. Thus, all the fondness she had developed for this mysterious man had suddenly transformed into utter terror. She could now relate to those who were about to get killed in a horror movie. So, biting her nails in desperation, she stood up and went towards the door to get out of there. It was locked.

"Oh no... no, no, no..." she said as she frantically tried to open it, knowing full well her efforts were useless. It wasn't long until she heard loud steps coming behind her that she banged as hard as she could on the door with the hope that one of the servants would come to her rescue. Her blood pulsated faster than a bullet train as she tried to scream in vain while a hand covered her mouth and turned her around. The darkness of the room only increased her terror. This was it!

"Easy there. It's me Carmen…" he said.

His voice sounded familiar, and yet Carmen tried to hit his face in confusion and despair, just to get her hands caught into his. "Leave me alone!" she ordered, also in vain. She continued her struggle to set herself free when the man eventually let her go on his own. Carmen saw him calmly get away from her and sit down on a chair nearby.

"Easy there, child. It's me, Jason," he said in a tender voice.

Carmen collapsed onto the floor, looking at him directly into his eyes. "Doctor Wright…? why…? why are you doing this…? did someone send you?"

"I thought the reason was already obvious," he continued while looking at the full moon outside. "Look, I'm sorry for breaking into your mansion, but it was the only way to keep it a secret. No one would look upon me as a righteous man if they saw me writing love letters to a young damsel… You know what I mean…"

Carmen's bloodstream had slowly come back to normal. She had known him for a long while, and yet she could have never imagined that he and her secret admirer were one and the same. Deep inside, it made her quite happy. At the same time, she felt betrayed. Thus, her fear quickly transformed into rage. "You think it's funny to toy with a girl's feelings this way?! You think this is a game?!" she reprimanded him in an increasingly higher voice. "What is wrong with you?!"

"It's all my fault. I understand," he continued, now looking at her with a glistening gaze she had never witnessed before. "But you gotta understand that this isn't a feeling that I developed over a single night. Your father's sickness was destroying him inside out and having known you for a good chunk of my life, and seeing you broken, even if you didn't cry… let's just say that it awoke something inside of me. Seeing you so frail and sad is what started this whole mess… I just… I just wanted to make you feel better…" He placed his head between his hands as Carmen's iracund gaze started to quench. "It was then that... it happened... that... I fell for you..."

"Get out of here... please..." she commanded to his surprise. "I don't want to see you ever again!"

He looked into her eyes, but she turned her head to the right, avoiding his stare. So, he stood up, unlocked the door, looked at her one last time, and left. As for the young damsel, she felt onto her knees, looking down onto the old wooden planks decorating the floor.

Are you satisfied?

The next day, she felt like burning all the love letters. However, and going against her very own will, she ultimately decided to store them in the attic. She couldn't understand it at first, but she felt strangely happy while, at the same time, she also felt an increasing hatred for them. Jason had hidden his intentions from the start. He was no better than any of her pretenders, and yet, her heart wouldn't agree with that reasoning, something that bothered her constantly with each passing day, especially since his letters had stopped coming. As those days turned into months, she turned eighteen, and before she knew it, she found herself in the attic. Once again, and against her better judgment, she took out all the letters and read them one by one, from start to finish. Why was she even doing this? She couldn't tell. Studying the word choice, structure, and semantics like a literature specialist, she arrived at a single conclusion: he had been telling the truth all along. His feelings for her showed themselves and evolved in front of her eyes with each letter she read. Another sign of it was the fact that he was a doctor, a rich one at that, which meant he didn't really have a need for her fortune. On top of that, she had known him since she was twelve. Her heart pounded with force before her new conclusion. The letters only served her to make something clear in her chest: whether she liked it or not, she missed him. She missed his letters. She missed having someone that cared for her in *that* way. She missed not feeling alone. Not that she was truly alone, but this was a different type of loneliness. Jason had always known what to say, and yet, that was not enough. She needed something more.

She knew that her servants would leave her side one day. She knew they were workers held in the mansion by a contract, that her bond to them would be easily severed the day they were no longer happy with their pay, or any other reason. That mere thought scared her to the bones. She needed a true family, one of her own, and Jason could be the answer to that.

Did she truly love Jason? She had read hundreds of books at this point, and yet none of them would show her what defined what the symptoms for falling in love were. As the stories and testimonies were so varied, she could only guess. The happiness she felt in her heart should be clear enough, right? Why else would she feel this way? She had liked him since what felt like an eternity. She could trust him. She could bet her life on him. So, there was just one thing to do…

"I was wondering if… you would like to… ehmmm…" said Carmen on the phone.

"Surely. I'd love to see you on your birthday… and about that night…" he answered on the other side. The mere sound of his deep voice made Carmen tremble to her very core.

"We'll talk about that once I see you," he continued, seemingly aware that she was flustered by his confidence.

"Until then," she hung up with a cold voice. She knew the answer to her feelings, and she didn't, at the same time. It was quite evident at this point, to everyone who saw her, even to herself, that she wanted him back into her life. Deep inside, she knew he at least deserved a chance…

He arrived at the mansion that very evening dressed in a white suit. Once there, he celebrated Carmen's birthday in a calm and happy fashion, contrary to what Carmen had been expecting as she didn't utter a single word. The servants could easily figure out what was going on with the maiden as her behavior wasn't her usual self. She would stumble here and there against furniture for no reason, for instance. The older servants could at least assume the obvious, which only caused jealousy in young Pablo's heart.

After having a delicious dinner in complete solitude, and

in silence, in the main dining hall, Carmen invited Jason over to the balcony on the second floor. Her latest favorite place in all her mansion as she loved to look at the full moon on her free evenings. How could something so simple calm her heart was beyond explanation for the people surrounding her, yet, the peace it generated on her countenance was good enough not to question it. It was definitely better than staying down in the wine cellar reading books in utter loneliness and darkness.

"You know? I have always been wondering how many pretenders you must have by now," Jason said jokingly, breaking the ice. The fall breeze caressed Carmen's hair as she dared not look into his eyes, even though it had been her who had asked him to join her there. An open red *Constanto 1968* was calmly served by Jason in two cups which were placed upon a small round table on the balcony.

"You have no idea. None of them seem in the least interesting. I wish they would just give up," she replied casually as she approached the table to take a sip of wine. "Nobody understands how hard it is to make vital decisions for such a company on a daily basis like to have the time to think about men. At least, thanks to my father I'm not making a mess out of it… I still have so much to learn…"

"Look, I'm sorry if what I did was out of place back then," he said realizing Carmen was clearly avoiding the topic. "I guess this type of thing just happens…"

"I… I studied them…" said Carmen nervously. "You know… the letters… I know your feelings are sincere… it's just that… I… I…"

Jason approached her and looked directly into her eyes, "Carmen, it's simpler than you think. Please answer me this question. What do you think about the stars above us?"

Carmen's train of thought stopped short. What kind of question was that? She loved to look at the moon, however, she hadn't stopped to think about the stars in a long time. Why was she even thinking about the answer to such a stupid question? It made no sense. Yet, by thinking about it, she realized she had been so busy with her new position at the company that she had almost forgotten about their existence. She had been neglecting them for a long time, focused on her earthly issues and completely ignoring the big picture. Thus, she looked up and saw them. Since the vineyard was far from the city, the light contamination wasn't so bad, and the stars were clearly visible to the naked eye. Despite having seen them a million times already, it felt like the first time in ages. They were so sublime that she lost herself into them until a confession came to her mind. There was more to life than just loneliness. There had to be.

Or so you'd like to think.

"You know…?" Carmen replied after lowering her head. "I have always guarded a little secret… I guess to you is no secret at all."

"What secret is that?" asked Jason, curiosity invading his voice.

Carmen took out an old teddy bear from her purse, one Jason immediately recognized. "I have been hugging him for a while now. Every time I do, I remember the day you gave him to me. It must sound quite pathetic for the owner of the La Cruz vineyards, but it's the truth." She was blushing as she remembered that she had kept hugging Derzú despite knowing the identity, and 'betrayal', of her secret admirer.

"Well… there's a confession I have to make, too," Jason said with a shy smile and looking down. "Although it's no secret to you at this point, either."

"I expect all kinds of confessions by now. Go on," said Carmen in an increasingly confident and curious voice.

"Haven't you always wondered why I became your secret admirer?"

"Actually… I have always wondered that question…" she replied while looking at him, emitting increasing interest in listening to his words.

"You'll see… Ever since I left Panthea, I have been on my own. When I met you, you were twelve. Forgive me if I offend you, but I thought of you just as a mere brat that I was forced to see from time to time."

"Not quite the romantic confession I was expecting..." she said in momentary disappointment.

"But over the years, as you grew up, I started to realize the person you'd become. I could see the respect you had for your father, and for your servants... something I had never seen before in other people out there... You know, people who happen to have a similar status to yours. Your treatment was the same for me. So, I stopped thinking of you that way and started admiring who you would turn out to be in the future. I guess I wasn't wrong to do that... "

"And what were you expecting...?"

"Well... in summary... *you*'re what I've been expecting all my life... and that's why I have a request in mind for you..."

Carmen had never heard words of the sort, but, although she had read them in books a million times, her eyes kept looking at him in expectation. "I'm listening."

"I think my request is pretty obvious at this point, but I'll ask it either way. Would you like to be with me? No, scrap that... Would you marry me?"

Carmen truly didn't know what to say. She wasn't expecting those words. Nevertheless, all those months of loneliness had taken their toll on her. She truly wanted to have a real family again. She wanted to feel the way she did years ago. Loneliness had been carved into her bones and she needed to get rid of it desperately. And at the same time...

"L-let me think it over... I'm sorry..." she replied nervously.

Jason smiled sweetly without a hint of sarcasm. "It's okay. Take all the time you need. I'll be waiting."

Later, he said good-bye and left the manor. She saw him driving away in his old Ghuzzo. A car manufactured in the co-continental country of New Soctul. As he disappeared into the distance, she was still trying to assimilate that something that actually made her happy was truly happening. Everything she had dreamed of so far were nightmares compared to what was going on before her eyes. Was it even possible? Was she even in love with him? How could she know that?

Dreams are treacherous, you should know that...

The next morning, she armed herself with courage and called Jason. Pablo could only watch in utter sadness as he understood he would never stand a chance within Carmen's heart. The rest of the servants felt his pain; however, they also knew that was part of growing up. Pain and maturity could often go hand-in-hand.

"H-hey there!" said Carmen in the most cheerful voice she could pretend.

"Hi, Carmen. How are you doing?" replied Jason calmly.

"I'm fine, thanks..." she replied in a shy voice. "You know... about t-the proposal you made..."

"I'm all ears, my dear."

"I have been thinking that... we should..."

"Live together before making up your mind?" he guessed. To Carmen's surprise, he was correct. Even though she didn't have friends of her age, it was her house maidens who had advised her about this. Most of her maidens were over forty years old, and most importantly, married.

Carmen cleared her throat. "Yes. I think we should see if... you know... we're compatible and all that... stuff..."

Jason laughed out loud. "Just as I expected from the girl I admire so much. Very well, it shall be done then!"

Carmen remained silent for a few seconds, unable to decide what to say next. "When would you like me to go there?" continued Jason happily.

The very next day, he arrived with two big suitcases.

Almost every servant in the mansion approved of this new relationship, except for Pablo, who constantly declared Jason as a menace to the peace that had reigned for years in the manor. As the powerlessness he felt each and every day was eating him inside out, he voluntarily quit after two months to Carmen's regret. Regret for not knowing why he had actually quit in the first place.

As for Carmen and Jason, both of them seemed to get along pretty well. Her first kiss didn't take long to arrive, as well as other intimate activities. And thus, without noticing, a year had come and gone, and Carmen had turned nineteen. By now, she could easily say that Jason was indeed part of her life. No matter the problem or situation, he was always there. Every time she needed support, he was always there. Even when the company was about to go bankrupt, he was still there. If he had a role to play, he was doing it perfectly. Eventually, Carmen would just smile just by seeing his face which told her that there was little else to think about… now she was finally ready to answer Jason's proposal.

"Yes!" she said to him out of the blue one day.

"Huh?" He looked at her perplexed in the living room, without rising from the sofa where he liked to work on, typing on his laptop.

"Yes, yes! I will marry you!" she continued.

Jason lifted her into the air and spun her around like a madman. Her happiness knew no limits that day. Carmen could see his broad smile as a beacon of hope. A beacon for the right direction to get back what she had lost, to have a family again. The news spread around the mansion like wildfire, raising a party within it alongside Carmen's closest friends. The soon-to-be-weds raised a cup of a *Tintado 1929* each to celebrate the future that looked on them with brightness before all their self-invited guests.

Like humans say, the road to Hell is paved with good intentions...

The ceremony was held after three months. The three-story-tall cake, the music, the cathedral… everything felt like a living dream. Jason was the one who insisted on having a religious wedding, to which Carmen didn't really oppose. She didn't consider herself a Dahsitian, unlike Jason who carried a pillifix around his neck twenty-four-seven. However, since his family wouldn't be able to make it, she thought that that was the least she could do. Once the whole celebration was done, the couple travelled throughout Danan in what felt like the ideal dream trip. Different languages, climates, and cultures felt as if they had fallen from the sky right before them. The cherry on top of the perfect dessert. After one week, on their last day of honeymoon, Jason asked what Carmen had been suspecting all along.

"Would you like to come with me to the United Kingdoms of Panthea?"

It was no wonder such words came out of his mouth. Estú had just entered a period of recession, which had been felt especially hard by the company. As it stood, bankruptcy could just be around the corner for the country, again. Many economists had named it the explosion of the "real estate bubble," as the lack of security measures when granting loans for common folk to buy houses had put the banks all over the country in a dire situation. Carmen knew it would be a difficult transition, but she also knew that it was a necessary change for the survival of the company. It struck her heart often when thinking about that decision. The world she had always known was there in Estú, after all. Nonetheless, there was a big difference this time: she was no longer alone. She felt as if she could eat the world now. At the same time, the survival of the company was the only thing left she could do to honor her father's memory. Every time she thought the company taking a dive in the stock market, with possibilities of never recovering, was excruciating enough. Even her chest hurt. This couldn't go on any longer.

"So?" insisted Jason as Carmen's eyes were still looking into nothingness while seated in the living room, on Jason's now favorite red leather sofa.

"It's not something I truly want, but I see your point." Carmen could only look down this time. "I guess we don't really have a choice… you know what? Let's go!"

Her final exclamation gladly surprised Jason who embraced her and kissed her. And yet, unbeknownst to Jason, a small tear rolled down her left cheek. They started packing the next day after Carmen had explained the situation to the board of directors, who turned out to be very supportive to her surprise. They could also smell the imminent economic fall of the country. Besides, everyone knew the economic demise of Estú wouldn't last forever, yet the company might not be able to survive until the nation came back to life. Full of good news on that front, she told Jason and together they went to explain the decision to the mansion servants. Some of them, to Carmen's sadness, renounced right there. It tore her heart apart to, what she felt, would destroy her father's work and family. Some others decided to remain, going as far as going to the U.K.P. with them. Jason opposed the idea at first, however, Carmen convinced him otherwise. Hiring new staff that needed training was always cumbersome, especially for a company that had to basically start over in the logistical department. Thus, with their minds made up, they went to the embassy. Thanks to their union, residence papers were easy to obtain. Even Spunky obtained a small "Yellow Card," or so it was called.

The first days within the Kingdoms, as the U.K.P. were also known as, were mostly Carmen traveling around looking for providers and customers for the new company. Being the new contender was never easy, even though sometimes it wouldn't look like it she would just relax inside the car after driving for days. Renting motel rooms had become a habit at some point. Jason would often go with her as he was also on the hunt for a job. While travelling together all over the country, Jason happily answered all of Carmen's questions regarding his home country. He often said that it was known as the land of liberty, as well as the most powerful country on Earth, in all aspects. They possessed the strongest military, the strongest economy, and the strongest influence. If new laws or technology were created there, it would usually be followed by other countries as well. Jason explained that the country on its own was a union of several kingdoms, ruled in unison by a constitutional monarchy. Each kingdom had a governor, a parliament, and its own ministries. Thus, in each kingdom, the prime minister had all the executive power and had to be elected every five years, along with his cabinet. Although Carmen had read the history of this country many times over, it wasn't as fascinating as when Jason told her about it. Extremely proud at that. Carmen soon realized he wasn't the only patriotic one as she could see the national flag waving on several rooftops.

Eventually, Carmen chose the outskirts of Las Esbirras city, within the kingdom of Friornia, to set up the company, as well as her own home. A kingdom known for its sunny climate all year long, next to the sea, and lands perfect for agriculture. In order to establish La Cruz Vineyards & Wines in the kingdom, Carmen had been forced to sell most of her properties in Estú, thus at least she was happy when she tried her competitors' products and discovered that their wine wasn't very good. An advantage, no matter how small, was always good news. Unfortunately, she would soon discover that the quality of the grapes of the area was the cause of it, more so when she finally produced wine from her own vineyards and realized that her wine wasn't as good as the one made in Estú. At least she was relieved to be able to compete on the same field as the others. As for her parents' grave, she ordered the construction of a small chapel along with a new mansion, which looked exactly the same as the one she had in her old mansion back home. There, she placed the coffins within along with the whole structure that defined them. It made her sad to have to do such a thing as her father would've never approved to do so with her mother's corpse. Fortunately for her peace of mind, Carmen was quite busy and wouldn't give too many thoughts to it. A peace that wouldn't last long given that Jason started considering even the smallest mistakes done by Carmen's former servants as a reason to fire them. Many were dispatched due to his new demeanor over the following months. A demeanor Carmen couldn't understand at all. Without wasting any time, he started to replace all of the employees as soon as he could, despite Carmen's complaints. Over time, she understood why: it was just a matter of time until they resigned on their own, or at least that was Jason's reasoning. Nevertheless, by this point in her life, losing them wasn't as painful as she had once imagined. Her husband had just accelerated an inevitable process. Still, for the first time in many years, she felt alone, again.

You must be careful about what you wish for...

Eventually, after hard work and sleepless nights, her vineyards did a full recovery. It was amazing! People did enjoy her wine in a way that orders doubled every month. Carmen was happy. She hadn't let her father down. She could feel him smiling upon her from beyond and relieving her stress, in turn. Besides, she had another reason to be happy. It didn't take long for Carmen to have a new surprise of her own: she was pregnant.

And so, nine months passed like a bliss when she found herself in the hospital. As she called that day the happiest of her life, she gave birth to her son. His name would be Juan Fernando Wright, to honor her father. Jason couldn't stop looking through the hospital window when Juan Fernando was placed in an incubator. Congratulations were given all over the place, from the employees to her newest circle of friends. Even Spunky seemed to be more alive than ever, wagging his tail when Juan Fernando arrived home in his mother's arms. Carmen felt that she was back on the right track after a long time, that she was finally recovering her long-lost family.

All that glitters is not gold. You'd be wise to remember that...

III

INDEED, the glittering lights were that of the police cars who had fixed themselves into Carmen's eyes, breaking her immersion.

They would've been intimidating in another time, another place. She had faced so many dangers at that point that even the most powerful weapon in existence wouldn't make her think of retreating or flinch. The men outside were clearly disturbed as even their shadows were trembling in fear. They wouldn't tremble so much had they not known about the feats the Dire One, as they had nicknamed her not long ago, had accomplished before.

"Freeze right there! Come out with your hands over your head! Now!" Yang ordered through his trusty megaphone. Unbeknownst to them, she could sense their tension miles away as she felt the adrenaline running through their bodies. The fear of the unknown. Due to his training and overall experience, Yang didn't join his men in said emotion and kept a cool head, even though he could understand their reaction. If the reports were true, they were indeed in dire danger. Although they all knew about the countless officers dead by her hands, a part of them still resisted to believe this information as fact. Most of them were actually expecting some sort of ambush where the actual killers showed up to back the

Dire One up. Thus, their actual nervousness came from not being able to tell where the true enemy was, or where this enemy would shoot them from. Still, there was yet another doubt in their minds, including Yang's, as some claimed this wretched woman was one of *those*. A supernatural.

Yang knew, as he shared the same perspective as the officers under his command, that it would be better to be finished with it as soon as possible and take as few risks as necessary. Supposing that she had no backup and that she was actually a supernatural, a possibility Yang had too much trouble thinking of as real, then she couldn't be given any chances. If she had backup, the same would apply. Otherwise, the Black Cross, as many claimed she called herself, would do another mass slaughter with them, or in other words, with no survivors. Yang was one of the few who got to witness the expressions drawn on the faces of the corpses of her victims in a past raid. Countenances with despair embedded into them that caused Yang to feel terror himself to the point of choking right there in front of his senior officer. There was no choice in the matter, she would get one last warning. That was it.

Thus, as the demon walked slowly towards them and exited the entrance gate, Yang issued said warning. "Drop your weapons now! You are surrounded, Carmen de la Cruz! If you don't surrender, we'll shoot to kill! Surrender now! You got nowhere to run!" However, the Dire One wasn't stopping in her undisturbed pace. Her calm and slow steps just increased the tension the men were feeling already. Whether she was doing it on purpose or not, it didn't matter much. It was her life or theirs.

As the safeties in their guns clicked and their fingers were placed on their respective triggers, the Dire One grinned maliciously at them while keeping her graceful strides steady. Her long and messy hair covered her intense red eyes and insane gaze partially, but that didn't help the officers in their quest for courage. "The stones might try to stop the river... but the latter will always bypass them... order will perish if faced against Death... order knows what's evident... withdraw... and order will endure." The men looked at each other in disbelief and confusion: she had actually spoken. They expected some sort of ghoulish or scratchy voice, but it was all the opposite. Her voice was maternal, soft, and sensual, unlike her acute and insane laughter which was the only sound they had heard from her so far. After listening to it, the tension in their hearts started to appease. She was just a woman, wasn't she? Her bony cheeks, her red lips, her delicate hands, and her raven hair gave away the answer. She was a human being, just like them. Maybe that should be reason enough to have nothing to fear. Maybe not.

So, the officers smiled at each other in relief. Some of them even lowered their weapons and watched as she kept advancing towards them with her malicious grin. Given that they had also confirmed that there was no one backing her up, thanks to Lieutenant Ramirez, who was done with the reconnaissance of the surrounding areas and had returned with them, a sentiment of peace started to extend among them. The people inside the asylum were all dead according to the reports, yet, how did they know if someone else had done it and this woman was just one of the escapees from that lugubrious place? Their thoughts came and went as more and more of them lowered their guard allowing the Dire One to get closer and closer. Nevertheless, unlike the rest of them, Yang hadn't changed his mind. He still wouldn't take any chances. For him, the reports were real enough, even more so since this woman had escaped this very same building a year ago.

"Hey there! Don't worry gal, everything will be okay," said one of the officers condescendingly by the time the woman had approached him less than one meter away. Upon hearing his words, she stopped. Now, under the lamppost lights, they could observe her in more detail. Her weapons were enormous and seemed to be quite heavy on her hands. Thus, by logic, she would hardly be able to lift them or do anything with them. This prompted the rest of the officers to approach her while some of them still aimed their weapons at her.

"You see? Nothing to fear here!" continued the same man

as he extended his hand towards the Dire One, tapping on her left shoulder and smiling. "Let us help you." However, his smile disappeared when a bullet went into her head, spilling blood and brains on the ground. She fell limp to the ground as the officers saw the scene in terror. There was only one gun smoking, and that was Yang's. Angry looks met his own as he lowered his weapon in alleviation.

"She was resisting arrest. It had to be done," he argued. As his defense wasn't convincing enough, the complaints of his men didn't wait to be voiced. Nonetheless, as they were discussing the repercussions of shooting a, seemingly, defenseless woman, one of them couldn't stop looking at her.

"Guys... guys! She's alive! She's alive!" he yelled terrified.

They all turned around and locked their eyes onto her, unable to understand what was going on. Indeed, she was getting back on her feet as the bullet inside her head popped out of her skull and fell to the ground. The clinking sound it did upon contact with the asphalt felt like an alarm bell that was waking them up from a sweet dream. Unable to react on time, the closest man to the Black Cross fell prey to her deadly weapons. Sure enough, they watched in horror how, without a sweat, she severed his head from his body in a single swing. The rest of them kept looking at the scene petrified, unable to decide what to do next. Thus, she proceeded uninterrupted in her slow and confident pace towards the next officer. It was this man's screams of pain that made their brains finally assimilate what had just happened. So, they turned around and prepared themselves to run for their lives when the voice of the Lurn stopped them in their tracks.

"Shoot to kill! Now!" commanded Yang, who, following his own order, started to shoot the Black Cross until his clip emptied. Seeing that the Dire One couldn't advance due to his rate of fire, and the barrage of bullets penetrating her body, keeping her in place, his officers turned around, obeyed, and rained fire upon the wretched woman. A simple and scary female would not defeat them. Not on their life... or so they thought.

After one minute of constant shooting, all of them had emptied their clips. As they reloaded, they noticed how the bullet caskets had created an improvised carpet upon the road around their feet. The corpse of their decapitated colleague surrounded by the empty steel shells quickly reminded them of what could've happened to them. Whether they liked it or not, the reports were correct, they had always been. However, the little relief they could've attained didn't last long…

"What in the world?" mentioned one of them as they watched in bewilderment how even several bullets to her head had had no effect. She was still standing, bleeding streams of blood from the bullet holes showering her body. Smiling viciously. Such a sight made their just regained confidence and peace quickly turn to dust. Their faces changed from perplexity to horror as she resumed her way towards them, popping their bullets out of her body which fell in a cascade of tinkling sounds around her. Even the teeth she had lost due to some bullet pulverizing them were growing back as well as her eyes. She was indeed a monster of the worst kind.

"What are you doing, you fools?! Reload and shoot again! Now! Don't let her get any clo-," the Lurn couldn't continue his phrase when the demon used both of her weapons to crush the body of the immobile officer closest to her. The unfortunate man had been too slow to run away from the Black Cross as horror had taken over his will. His blood gushed out of his eyes and mouth as his internal organs and bones were crushed under her swings. Thus, as the corpse fell limp to the floor, the Black Cross continued her slow pace with her devilishly grin renewed.

"Fuck this! Every man for himself!" screamed one of the officers as the demon charged towards them with all the speed her legs allowed her. This, in turn, developed into mass hysteria provoking the rest of officers to imitate their fleeing comrade. Even though Yang stood his ground, he couldn't avoid sharing their feelings once again. Even more so, his own fears worsened when he witnessed how the monster ran at the same speed as them, catching them in mid-flight. The first to run became the first to die as the Black Cross buried the officer's head into his body by hitting him vertically with the weapon on her right hand. His torso was now swollen as his body fell to the ground. The remaining officers stopped short at the sight, realizing they had dropped their weapons during their flight to reduce weight. However, it was the ones that tried to reach for their handguns, still in their holsters, the ones to be struck down by the Dire One right after. And so, one by one fell to her blunt weapons. Some of them would have the mercy of dying quickly. Some of them would see their own body completely mangled before their eyes as the next blow would finish their agony. Others would just die from being unable to handle so much terror, being torn to pieces either way in their stillness. In the end, the last one standing, the Lurn, hadn't been able to move his body during the entire massacre. His legs wouldn't obey him while his index kept pressing the trigger of his bulletless gun. His eyes, now dilated to a great degree, could only watch as the Black Cross finished the last one of his officers and made her way towards him.

Yang's mind could only hold so many thoughts. In the end, his team's only achievement had been that of adding more bloodstains on the monster's massively ragged dress to the ones she already had. Was she some sort of unstoppable force of nature? She looked completely undisturbed by all the death and blood she was producing. Was she capable of feeling pain? Could she feel guilt? Was she even human? It didn't matter. Torsos, limbs, or plain pools of blood, with crushed bones splattered around, littered the floor as if a firehose had been spreading viscera all over the place. Their deaths had been quite painful, indeed, as their agonizing voices had been the most powerful witnesses of the crime committed. It could be said that the street still resonated over with their cries of terror. Their faces still carried the horror and pain with which they had been killed, at least on the heads that were still intact somehow. Yang couldn't avoid shaking at such a sight. His legs, now bathed in his own piss, still refused to listen to his orders as her deception dawned on him.

She perfectly knew what she was doing, Yang concluded in his mind. Her weapons looked extremely heavy, and indeed they were, as whatever made contact with them ended into pieces. Nonetheless, she had concealed this fact by walking slowly, seemingly struggling to carry those damn things when exiting the asylum. It had all been an act from the start, and he could only regret not realizing it sooner. The shock value when she decapitated her first victim had also been effective as they weren't expecting something so out of reality, even if they happened to believe the reports. She had wanted to strike fear at their very cores from the start, and she had succeeded.

As his thoughts revolved around this realization, an intense pain forced him to come back to reality. He realized he had fallen to the ground and looked at his legs: he no longer had lower legs. The burning sensation coming from his knees, now releasing blood all over the place, was too much to bear, causing him to scream in pain. His entire life flashed before his eyes as the Black Cross lifted one of her dreaded weapons up in the air. Only one additional thought came to him.

If I'm going to go out, I'll do so bravely. I owe that much to my family… and myself, he thought.

"You were never hurt by our bullets… you dropped on the ground as an act! You tricked us, didn't you?! Didn't you?! Damn you!… Damn you monster! I may go down, but you will go down as well! You hear me? Bitch!… Someone else replace me and you will never find peace! Hahahahahaha!"

"Nothing like transition… from tranquility to fright… in the heart of a hominid…"

She stared into his eyes, still showing her insane smile, almost as if mocking his words. Words that stopped coming out of his mouth as soon as he realized they didn't affect the demon in the least. Thus, prayers in low voice appeared instead, probably hoping to get reincarnated into someone, and somehow get back at her someday. Most Lurns believed they could. And so, as he prayed, it was all over.

The demon crushed his chest into the ground. Yang's mouth spewed a jet of blood as his slightly greenish skin bathed in red. Yet, contrary to the rest of his team, his facial expression wasn't that of horror, but that of resignation.

The Black Cross simply laughed hysterically at the scene as she picked up and shook her weapons, splashing the crimson liquid in which the corpses were soaked in around her. She simply looked around and kept on laughing and laughing, unable to stop.

"Death's bliss endures undeterred under the aegis of coarseness," she murmured as her laughter gradually came to a stop. Then, she looked up into the dark sky, grinning at the pouring rain which slightly washed her skin and hair. The same couldn't be said for her soulless victims maimed on the ground. Thus, without giving it further thought, she approached the nearest vehicle to her. Regardless of its lights being splattered with blood, and the possible issues that that might create for her later on, she kept her choice steady. She opened its door and smiled when she spotted the keys still in position to turn it on. Details like these told the Black Cross how confident these men were on defeating her. With the sea of darkness surrounding her little island of red and blue lights, another thought invaded her mind. A thought backed up by her past experience. The equipment and weapons they had used didn't seem to come from regular police officers. She could only assume they belonged to the city's elite police force. Looking at the insignia on their chests, there was the strong possibility of them being from the Special Arms And Strategies branch, or S.A.A.S., for short. The best unit of trained policemen the country had to offer. At the same time, there was also another possibility.

It could also be *them*…

Once her own explanations satisfied her curiosity, the Dire One placed her bloodstained weapons on the passenger seat and proceeded to turn on the patrol car. The open, or broken into pieces, window allowed her to feel the cool waning rain and the fresh breeze, a feeling she loved quite a lot. She couldn't actually remember when it had been the last time she had been able to feel it this much. As she kept looking outside said window, accelerating down Highway 13, she spotted several ads pointing towards the now lifeless asylum. "Thanks for having visited Sanatorium! Hope to see you again soon!" said one of the panels. She could still remember it. It was the same place a year ago. The same style. The same design. Destroying it would be meaningless as she had nothing to gain from it. And yet, she smiled viciously at the thought. To think that her most recent visit had been her last one…

The visibility of the road was becoming blurrier and blurrier as the intensity of the rain augmented, and the windshield wipers had stopped working. Thus, while looking around the car panel for the headlights to alleviate said problem, she couldn't avoid checking around for anything else that might prove useful inside the vehicle. After a quick inspection, outside of a pair of cuffs inside the glove compartment, there was nothing else. She assumed there were probably weapons in the trunk. Not that she would ever need them, but it was nice to keep in mind. Her eyes kept examining the contents of the vehicle until they stumbled upon a small picture next to the odometer. A man in his mid-thirties carrying his son on his shoulders while hugging his wife. All of them smiling back at her, happy, without a worry in the world. A picture that reminded her what was once hers: a husband, a son… a world forever gone.

IV

"DO YOU THINK IT'S GONE?" asked Juan Fernando.

Carmen saw him standing by the door and asked him to come in. It was the second rabbit gone that month. Somehow, they always managed to open their cage and get away, after which she knew that the odds of finding them were pretty much nonexistent.

"Don't worry honey, we'll find it," Carmen replied comfortingly alongside a sweet smile. Then, she hugged him tightly, to which he answered reciprocatively. He was almost four years old now, and Carmen couldn't feel any prouder as he had been doing quite remarkably in kindergarten. The stars he brought home were quite consistent in quantity, almost five per week. His most recent award had been granted to him after building a small projector out of some crêpe paper and a candle. Along with some drafts, he had even managed to make a 'short-film' about a magical strawberry and its adventures. Ever since then, Carmen would give him *Pum* chocolates every time he arrived home, his favorite brand. She could only imagine what he would become in the future, like how many lives he would be able to save, or how better the world would become just because of his existence in it. Dreams she was certain he would eventually achieve. "Of course, he had to inherit my natural intelligence! Hohoho!" Carmen would often brag when visited by her neighbors, or the staff.

As she couldn't take him to school, nor could his father, and because the school bus didn't make it all the way to the mansion, Erik, a friend of Jason's, would usually pick Juan Fernando up. Along with his two children, Nestor and Luke, they would wait for Juan Fernando at the mansion's door and then rush to school as if there was no tomorrow. To quench any anxiety Carmen could build inside herself, Erik also always provided her with the GPS location of his vehicle.

Thus, once Juan Fernando arrived home, the same tradition would repeat over and over as he would usually go straight running for the attic where he'd find his mother, who would normally be managing the finances of the company, and give her a kiss. Seeing him storm into the attic made Carmen always keep a happy face just for him. Having him there also prevented her from feeling like a mole, all day surrounded by darkness, as she loved to work with her laptop screen as the only light source. A habit that still brought her pleasant, and unpleasant, memories.

"Have you seen Dad? He said he would help me with my homework…" continued Juan Fernando with his little blue notebook among his hands, happy to have heard Carmen's promise to find his rabbit. Jason would usually help him out with math homework while Carmen would do so with languages and grammar, or so they had agreed on. Sometimes, she wouldn't be able to help him at all, not because she couldn't but because she would be entranced when watching him and her husband having fun together. It never failed to make her smile. It all felt like a utopia…

And that's pretty scary…

"I think he's at work honey," she replied. "I think he'll be here by dinner time. Go give him a kiss on my behalf when he arrives." She then sweetly kissed his forehead causing Juan Fernando to blush slightly.

"Then… I will go to the living room and draw… uhmmm… something! See ya mom!" he replied with a wide smile.

"Hey! Don't forget about my kiss!" demanded Carmen, pouting affectionately. Juan Fernando kissed her cheek shyly in response to later run downstairs. She saw him off and continued to work. It was at those moments when she couldn't believe how much her work had absorbed her. She could swear that she had spent almost her entire weekdays in the attic, including some weekends. Jason had told her to relax a little bit, and that her laptop wouldn't go anywhere unlike the days when Juan Fernando was still a baby and she could barely remember where she had placed it. Yet, she would simply laugh at the remark and kept at it as she had two very important reasons to work as intensely as she did this time around.

Before meeting Jason, the justification would've been to continue her father's legacy. Now, she also added Juan Fernando's future to the 'excuses mix'. A mother's sacrifice was never too great, she would usually tell herself. A quote she had often heard from one of her maids, Carolina--the only one she ever wished was her mother. It was this maid who always reprimanded her for not spending more time with her father instead of secluding herself in the cellar back then, a mistake she would not repeat with her son... even though she felt like she was.

Fortunately for her, the company was booming beyond her wildest dreams, and that allowed her stress to go down quite a bit while granting her more free time. The way she made the wine stand out prompted a surge in popularity for her production in a manner she had never witnessed before. Many companies within the field were eager to know her secret, which became apparent to Carmen when she discovered how they had tried to research her company through corporate spies. They couldn't find anything extraordinary, albeit, in reality, Carmen was using a different sort of grape. One she had brought from Estú that was able to grow in the Friornian climate. Such a tactic had given her a considerable edge among her competitors as new purchases of said grape seed had increased considerably along with market demand for La Cruz wines. Carmen had even used the company's most recent earnings to buy the adjacent lands to the main production plant and increased production. She knew that their competitors would eventually figure her secret out, but she trusted her company to be way far ahead by the time it had to come to that.

"We're in our longest *enhorabuena!*" she would frequently say when talking to her employees whenever she visited the production plant. She would often say the same Estúan word whenever questioned about her utter abstraction, when working in the attic, by Jason, as well as whenever questioned about why she wasn't taking any breaks. Although she was having the time of her life, she couldn't avoid looking out the window from time to time. Indeed, seeing her son and husband playing through that very window didn't always bring a smile to her face...

At least Jason had been lucky as doing his usual job gave him enough free time in general. He had easily landed a nice job in the General Saint Rain Hospital as head physician, which he was quite happy about. This was one of the reasons why he often bragged about how he always made the right decisions as, even though he studied at Cetep University, located in another kingdom within the same country, his diploma was valid and recognized in any territory within the U.K.P. Given that Cetep University was also pretty well known around the world, his diploma was also accepted in, pretty much, every nation.

"Not that I needed one..." answered Carmen begrudgingly whenever Jason made his remarks. "Someday I'll also get one... just you wait and see..." she murmured to herself.

Over time in this new country, she learned quite a bit about its society and culture, even more so as she had made several new acquaintances over the years. People felt more attracted to gold, so to speak. This feeling became more present in her mind as not a single one of her original servants remained at her service by then and trusting her newer servants had proven to be a difficult task. Since she had no one left to talk to as a friend, she felt blessed to still have her family lawyer, Eliana Tapia.

"How come you don't remember that, girl?! We were both five! I've always suspected you had a chicken's brain! Haha!" she would often remark mockingly at Carmen's lack of long-term memory. She hated her personality when they had just met but wanted to see her more often than not. Eventually, Carmen learned to deal with her and to appreciate her company, or so she liked to think. "I don't know what I'd do without you..." Carmen would often say on the phone to her after a long day of work. Being the daughter of the servant she would've wanted as a mother, Carolina, Eliana also served as a bridge to her 'former family', now in Estú. Hearing her lawyer over the phone, on a casual conversation, made Carmen remember how she had won the hardest deal of her life: that of convincing Eliana to join her in the U.K.P.

"Maybe Estú is in recession... but to go away just like that? I have my entire life here, girl..." Eliana explained upon hearing the request. "I doubt you can change my mind, girl. And by the way, don't even try to change it or I'll hate you...! But in good faith, eh!"

As no other offer would do, Carmen proposed her to become her company's exclusive lawyer with a fixed income that had the chance of increasing depending on how well the company was doing. "I donno girl... to depend on just one source of income is always unwise... let me think about it, girl..." However, her rhetoric changed when Carmen was about to depart as she capitulated without resistance. Carmen assumed it was because her mother was coming, as well as the growing unemployment in Estú, that had finally convinced her. Nonetheless, the La Cruz maiden was wrong. When she heard the actual reason, she cried and laughed at the same time.

"You see... this little fella here asked me to come with you guys and... you know my weakness, girl! I can't resist innocent beings asking me for stuff! I bet you made little JF do it in your place! This is emotional manipulation! I hate you so much...! But in good faith, eh!" In the end, it had been Juan Fernando who had made the little push that Carmen was missing to achieve her goal. She just couldn't believe how she hadn't thought of it sooner, especially when she remembered that Eliana was constantly broke after visiting terminally-ill kids at her nearest hospital; a habit she had started since her little brother died from terminal brain cancer in that same building.

And so, as promised, Carmen found a nice apartment for her lawyer in the nearby city of Las Esbirras, and the very next day, after signing the contract, Carmen announced her as the company's official lawyer to the meeting board. Of course, Jason didn't pass this up as he tried to fire Eliana several times, but she wouldn't budge. She would have none of it and she would tell Jason just that to the face. Carmen was happy about it, although by then she felt as if Jason was trying to get everyone she knew away from her. Jealousy maybe? Still, that didn't make much sense when applied to Eliana...

Besides her personality preventing Jason from succeeding, there was also Carmen's need for her counsel. Carmen, being always haunted by her father's advice, often tried to keep everyone around her happy, or like her father used to say, to be in peace with good and evil. Yet, Carmen still had a hard time to do so, making Eliana's presence more of a blessing in that regard. "You know, girl? I'm good at doing the 'talk' and all with your clients, but sometimes I miss prosecuting actual criminals..." she would mention when Carmen came up with questions regarding somebody infringing her trademark. Truth be told, Eliana's field of expertise was mostly within criminalistics and homicide cases, as that had been her main source of income back in Estú. Regarding these, Carmen would often ask her about her past cases or experiences since she found them quite intriguing. However, something Carmen didn't tell her was that she actually loved Eliana's company more than her stories, mostly because she was one of the few who could speak to her in her native tongue, unlike her son who wasn't interested at all in learning Estúan. It was during those enjoyable chats that she would often remember why she hated being alone so much.

"Have you ever felt... observed?" Carmen asked Eliana casually one day at the mansion's dining room. "Like... eyes looming over you?"

"Again with this, girl?! I thought you were an adult now!" Eliana replied mockingly, as usual. "Maybe if we were five, but still with this?"

Those eyes... the other reason Carmen wouldn't tell anybody the reason why she looked for constant abstraction was just that. That weird sensation she had had ever since she was a child. Being alone, and yet, not being so. Although she had learned to ignore it over time, the feeling would always come back to her during her long hours of solitude in the attic.

"Finally! Done for the day!" she explained while stretching her arms over her head and folding her laptop. "It's past eight o'clock... damn it..." She turned off her computer and, as usual, went to check on Juan Fernando in his room. As she kept going downstairs, she noticed that there was utter silence all throughout the mansion. Usually, Noria, the recently hired head maid, would be gone by seven o'clock, and so were the rest of the servants. Given that they used to inhabit the mansion every day of the week, Carmen ordered them to take a break from living in the mansion on Soldays, the seventh day of the week. Thus, not a single one of them remained on that day. And, since every sound in the mansion was no longer disguised under the sounds people made there every day, the sensation of loneliness was slowly encroaching around her in the empty building.

Even though the mansion was well-lit overall, it contrasted with the creaking sound her every step yielded, making her feel as if she was walking into a killer's den. This was the first time she ever felt genuinely uncomfortable for just being alone in her own house. So, out of this uneasiness, she unconsciously started walking faster towards her son's bedroom. She opened her son's bedroom door slowly, as silently as she could. Since the inner lights were off, she assumed that Juan Fernando might've already fallen asleep. He knew bedtime was at eight after all. Nevertheless, he wasn't in his bed. "Juan Fernando?" she asked in a low voice, trying to make sure he wasn't there. Then, she quickly glanced around the room, but he was still nowhere to be found. Maybe he was playing a prank on her. So, she stepped into the room, prepared for the scare with her eyes closed. Notwithstanding, after waiting for a few seconds of apparent cluelessness, thinking her son's prank might be triggered at any moment, nothing happened. She checked under his bed, inside the closet, inside the bathroom. With his absence looming all around her, she finally turned on the lights and looked around once more, in vain.

"Juan Fernando?! Where are you?! It's past your bedtime!" Carmen called in a high voice. No answer came back. Subsequently, she got out of there and went downstairs, slowly at first, guessing he might be just around the corner, thinking he was still playing an elaborate and genius prank on her. Again, no matter what she did, nothing happened. Finding him would've been easy... if it wasn't Solday...

"Out of the seven days of the week, he had to pull a prank when no one was around to find him," ranted Carmen. "Clever actually." She couldn't avoid feeling silly for a while there. At the same time, she cursed the day she had implemented that policy for her servants. She utterly regretted it while a fear she had never felt before, yet familiar, started to crawl into her bones. It was a fear like that when her father was about to die... that of becoming, once again, the last La Cruz on the planet.

By the time she checked her wristwatch, it was ten past nine. Had time gone so fast? The worst started to come to her mind. What if he was trapped in the wine cellar? Or... what if he was in a place he wasn't supposed to be?

As Friornia was a land subject to small earthquakes, unlike the entirety of Estú, she had designated an underground chamber that had enough water and food for one month. Of course, in the case of a powerful earthquake occurring, or the direct hit of a nuclear warhead, she would take her son there and survive until help arrived, even if that meant sleeping under the ruins of the mansion. As a way to reduce the time for rescue in such an emergency, Carmen also designated that the four pillars in the main hall, the one where the La Cruz family seal was displayed, similarly to her former mansion in Estú, were to be the main supporting structures of that section of the building, which would easily withstand an earthquake up to level nine in the Richter scale. Thus, if they were to break, which they weren't supposed to, the main hall would collapse immediately on top of the chamber's entrance, in turn making a rescue all the harder. Besides this mechanism, there was also an emergency exit that would allow her to get out from under the chapel's tiled floor. Since this chamber wasn't supposed to be easily accessible, it needed a special key Carmen, as well as Jason, always carried around. Although there was no other way to open it, one could force his way inside by operating the emergency lock, which needed a four-number code that only Carmen and Jason knew. Of course, Juan Fernando wouldn't be able to do such a feat... right?

Thus, she continued her way to the main hall, regardless of that possibility being next to impossible. Even if Juan Fernando had managed to see her entering the chamber, Carmen remembered she had only used the code once when he was at school. But... what if he had seen Jason entering it with his code? With questions swirling around her mind, her steps slowed down when another question popped inside her head. What if he had been kidnapped? If that had been the case, the perpetrators could have been just about anybody. From the servants themselves--onto which Carmen never got to fully trust--, her company competitors, to plain common criminals looking for ransom. When would they call? How much would they ask for? Who hired them?! She stopped short and started to pull out her hair. She wanted to kneel. She wanted to scream. How could this be happening to her? As despair started to sink in, she ran everywhere while calling for her son several times to no avail. Her calls had quickly become shrieks as insanity started taking over her.

"No... not again!" she screamed repeatedly while breathing deeply, trying to calm herself down. If the criminals wouldn't show up, or wouldn't send any sort of message, there was only one thing to do. She opened her flip-phone and dialed 611. As the phone started ringing, a voice behind her startled her.

"Carmen, what are you doing?"

She turned around and saw Jason with her son sleeping in his arms. She felt her essence coming back to her body at the sight as the voice of an agent answered her call, just for her to hang up. She ran up to Jason and hugged him strongly, waking up Juan Fernando in the process. Followed by her intense gesture, tears of joy started to flow down her cheeks.

"Mom... what's wrong...?" Juan Fernando said in a sleepy voice, barely opening his eyes. After Carmen delicately kissed his forehead as an answer, Jason put him down and embraced his wife. Their son looked at both of them, puzzled, rubbing his eyes and keeping still as his mother wouldn't stop crying out loud. Eventually, she calmed down thanks to Jason hugging her against his chest.

"Everything is okay..." he said in a soothing voice. "I'm sorry I didn't hear you before. You know sometimes I turn up my music player quite a bit when I'm relaxing..."

Once Carmen had completely calmed down, and having put Juan Fernando in his bed, Jason explained that he had found him asleep in the surprise room, or so Carmen liked to call a small room next to her office in the attic. Juan Fernando had simply sneaked in there while Carmen had gone straight to his bedroom on the floor below. Thus, it was no wonder that he hadn't been awakened by her screams as she had never raised her voice in the attic. The rooms within the three-stories mansion were incredibly good at keeping sound away, which had been a suggestion Jason provided when building it from the ground up. As he was not fond of listening to anything when going to sleep, he wanted the whole place to be soundproof, otherwise, he would wake up at the sound of a needle falling to the floor. He also explained that he had climbed up the attic window, as he used to do before their marriage back in Estú, in order to surprise her romantically. However, as he entered the surprise room, he found his son sleeping there, which prompted him to cancel his plans and join the little one in his nap. She could only laugh at the event while feeling completely stupid. Jason kissed her lips and comforted her by swearing to never do such a surprise again. He also told her not to be desperate if the same thing happened again because it was the worst thing she could do in such an emergency. In addition, he proposed that the servants were to stay during Soldays as well to prevent future problems of a similar nature. Thus, obeying his advice and placing new rules, the following month proved to be way better mostly because the possibility of repeating the same event became nonexistent. As she continued her working days in this newfound peace, she realized an important date was coming soon. On September twenty-second, the seventh month of the year, and the middle of summer, Juan Fernando had been born. Usually, like in past years, they would celebrate it privately, which meant that no servant was to participate in it, so they were to be dismissed just for that day. It had been that way ever since the first celebration, as per Jason's decision. According to him, these new servants were only hired people who didn't deserve to have a part of the joy his beloved family was having. Carmen would often remember how he had fired her 'family' when he mentioned it to her but wouldn't say anything about it.

On that special day, Carmen would wake up at six in the morning and go straight to the kitchen. Contrary to anyone who knew her might've believed, including Eliana, she always chose to do all the work related to the preparation of the party during that day and completely ignored her duties to the company: cutting vegetables, baking, cleaning, among others. As the servants often told her it wasn't her job to do so before leaving the mansion, their words fell on deaf ears and sunk deep into the earth. She took no breaks, looking like a machine, rendering impossible for anyone to be able to truly understand why her gaze seemed lifeless and her concentration at the tasks at hand unbreakable. It was just a party, wasn't it?

By the time she was done, it was seven o'clock. Just in the nick of time! She admired her work as she wiped the sweat off her brow. The cake she had made had a design from a cartoon Juan Fernando loved to watch, The Toadman. She had even dressed him like that for Halloween last year, mostly because he had persisted on it for weeks on end. "I... I think I would like to... save people..." Juan Fernando said shyly when Carmen asked him why he had been so adamant to get that costume. She often wondered if that was why he would usually go to great lengths to help his classmates when they had a problem, a feature of his that his classmates thanked often through gift cards in the mail, sent every time he missed class when sick. That day, Jason would arrive two hours later than usual due to an unexpected case at the hospital. As she knew that he wouldn't miss his son's birthday no matter what, even if the work at hand were to force him to stay at the hospital for the rest of the night, she wasn't feeling anxious about the possibility of something going wrong with the party. He would always find a way to be there.

Funny... maybe?

Once everything was ready, Carmen went upstairs looking for Juan Fernando. She called his name once. Then twice. No answer came back. This time she went straight to the room next to her office, but he wasn't there either. Maybe he had fallen asleep in another room. Given the size of the mansion, the task at hand would be too time-consuming for her on her own. So, she proceeded to take out her cellphone and to call her servants, apologizing for doing so outside their work schedule, and asked them if they had seen the kid. The answers were mixed, which was expected. Each one had seen him in a different part of the mansion at some point during the day. Seeing the uselessness of calling them, the increasingly anxious mother hung up and continued her search. After two hours, the same fear she had felt a month prior started to resurface. Even if she was able to keep her head cool this time, that dread would eventually catch up with her judgment once again. Whenever her mind started to wander away from her control, she simply remembered Jason's advice. So, she took deep breaths and kept looking incessantly. Juan Fernando had to be within the mansion limits, that was for sure. While thinking about getting into the emergency chamber, again, Carmen remembered the only place she hadn't searched, yet: the rooftop. Tired from having traversed the entire mansion back and forth, she weakly opened the hatch in the attic and went upstairs.

Out there, the breeze of the night comforted her nerves as, with the help of the moonlight, she could look around properly. After a quick search, it was quite obvious he wasn't there, either. Besides, why would he even be there? He was an obedient boy in that regard, and the rooftop had always been off-limits. Carmen had momentarily forgotten how Jason's scary stories about ghosts hunting this place had done a good job at keeping the child at bay.

As she kept walking around still looking for him, just in case, she heard him. Faint moans coming from the garden below that reminded her of the time Spunky died, of how he was suffering. The dog had moaned in agonizing pain as cervical cancer slowly finished him, ending his life in that very same garden. Later, he was buried near the chapel.

Such horrifying sounds were the more reason for her to feel disturbed beyond measure. Upon a closer look, her eyes widened as she found what she had been looking for all that time. She couldn't believe her eyes as she steeled her nerves and covered her mouth in horror.

So, it finally happened...

She ran downstairs as fast as she could. Was she imagining it? No way. This couldn't be happening to her. Not again. Definitely not again!

She stumbled upon furniture on her way down, falling flat on her face. "Damn side table," Carmen swore as tears wanted to come out of her eyes, but she wouldn't give in just yet. She remembered that feeling all too well... "No... no... NOOO!"

screamed Carmen on her way down, cursing time for not stopping, as she hurried her steps chaotically causing her to slip here and there, increasing her despair. After running for around a minute, she finally arrived at the garden. She still had a glimmer of hope, that little possibility that would mean everything would be alright. At least until she saw what had actually happened…

Juan Fernando was lying there, on the grass. He had to be sleeping. Yes! He had to be! That had to be the answer! Maybe a prank! Yes! He was probably joking! Once she got close to him, she would just lift him up and bring him back to his room! That would be all! However, by the time she finally felt relieved due to her own explanations, she was already right beside him. Juan Fernando still laid there, prone, hiding, not moving an inch. "Get up sweetie! It's late and we have to eat cake! I bought you an action figure that…" Carmen said in a nervous voice as she pushed him gently to make him react. Due to his lack of response, she picked him up and it was then that she finally saw it.

A bloodsoaked knife fell from him to the ground.

She felt her hands wet as she held him by the belly. She turned him around to see him face to face. He was very pale and his white t-shirt was now red, near the liver. The grass below was also crimson red. Carmen trembled as she felt his blood dripping down her hand. Still keeping control of herself, she quickly placed him on his back, his head on her lap, and checked his breathing. He was hardly doing so. At this point, she felt like screaming, losing it, but she couldn't. There was no time to lose. She quickly opened her cellphone up and proceeded to dial 611 when two flashlights appeared in the garden and aimed at her, blinding her and forcing her to cover her eyes with her left arm.

"Freeze! FPD! Raise your hands now!" said two men in blue uniform behind said lights. She felt her tension go away at the sight as she started to thank her lucky stars.

"Please help! Help my son! Someone has stabbed him! He needs urgent medical attention!"

"Get away from him, now!" ordered one of them, ignoring her pleas. "If you don't comply, we'll be forced to open fire! Do it now!"

"I'm his mother! Help him for the love of-"

A taser interrupted her, making her convulse on the floor as the current traversed her body, leaving her defenseless on the ground. Notwithstanding, she resisted unconsciousness, although she wished she couldn't, as she watched how Juan Fernando's eyes grew lifeless, powerless to stop it. Unable to scream, only tears cascaded down her cheeks at the scene. One of the men got close to the boy and checked his pulse. "He's a goner," he said. "We were too late…"

Carmen's heart stopped at that very moment. She wanted to die, wishing with her whole heart that the earth would just swallow her and make her disappear forever. She could only moan in sadness as she was carried and cuffed into a police car by one of the men. From the distance, she could only watch how the other one, who had stayed behind, placed a black bag upon her son. A familiar sensation came to her for the first time in ages, being able to look into the nothingness once again.

"You have the right to remain silent," said the man who had brought her in, now in the driver's seat. "Anything you say can, and will, be used against you. You will now be taken to the Friornia Federal court for prosecution and…"

Carmen wasn't listening to him. By the time she was put in a cell, she hadn't noticed it, still looking into emptiness. The next day, this event had taken over the media by storm. The shares of the company dropped substantially as the judgment was finally appointed a date. Not that she cared about any of it at this point. She had enough problems on her own having to deal with her new cellmates in the temporary court jail, who happened to hate rich kids. Some of them tried to bully her as they couldn't stand the fact that she wouldn't fight back, or even show a glimpse of anger at their provocations. "Just let her be. That bitch is like a breathing corpse. Way too boring," said one of them after trying in vain. As she wouldn't eat, nor drink, a doctor had to be called in once she fainted. However, this all changed after her first visit…

"My love… w-what happened?" Jason said nervously to her, both sitting at the opposite sides of the visiting table. Carmen tried to get up to kiss him and hug him, but she was cuffed to the chair, making it impossible. At the display, Jason approached her instead and did just that. Then, he knelt beside her and looked into her eyes while holding her left hand. He could clearly see the desperation and torment she was going through. His face also showed clear signs of anxiety and disturbance. Carmen could tell so because of the additional new wrinkles on his forehead. And yet, he wouldn't cry a single tear. Still, Carmen could feel his pain by his tight grip when he hugged her.

Oh dear, you'd never even imagine what's going on…

"I-I don't know… Jason… my Juan Fernando is… he's…" Carmen couldn't arrive at the obvious conclusion as she shook in horror. Jason caressed her as she threw herself onto his chest to cry inconsolably. After a few minutes, she was able to continue her tale. "Some bastard killed him…" she continued furiously. "We have… we have to get him… we have to prevent more innocents from…" Her anger changed back to pure sadness as the tears from her eyes flowed out again.

"Don't worry, I'm sure we'll get him," answered Jason in a soothing voice. "That is why we're here, right?"

"What do you mean? Why am I even here? We're wasting time!" Her voice became exalted again, to the point where Jason jumped up slightly. "I have to get out of here!" she continued as she shook Jason by his shirt uncontrollably. She then realized what she was doing and released him while looking at her palms. Was she finally losing it?

"You see… someone called the police because of the screams they heard…" continued Jason, looking mildly confused. "One of the servants had forgotten her coat and went back to the mansion to recover it when she heard them… by the time the police arrived, you were the only one there… the murderer's weapon has your fingerprints… Carmen, please tell me. I won't ask more than this. Please tell me why… that's all I want to know." His voice sounded like he was about to break down.

For the first time in a lifetime, Carmen didn't know how to respond. She was looking right into him, while not at the same time as her constant state of shock kept her away from reality, unable to assimilate the situation. This immersion, however, ended when Jason softly grabbed her by her shoulders, saying words she could listen to, but that didn't penetrate her mind. She felt in a trance no drug could ever allow her to enter.

Who knows...?

By the time she came back to herself, she already was back in her cell. Her cellmates gave her a disgusted look as they now knew what was going on, and for them, there was no crime worse than that of killing your own son. It was useless to try to convince them otherwise. After a few hours of withstanding the other cellmates' incessant harassment, the guards had to transfer her to solitary confinement. There, she spent three days that felt like an eternity, awaiting her next trial. She wondered why she was even waiting if there was no hope. No one would be willing to help a monster, or at least that was what she thought.

"Carmen, please tell me what the fuck is going on here?!" asked Eliana in shock when she visited her. "How is this even possible in the first place?!" Her rude words and challenging voice awoke something else in Carmen. She knew Eliana would be slapping her face if there were no security cameras. However, she had seen this behavior before. She only swore when there was something dangerous nearby, like a time when she swore in order to make her react and run away from a pack of wolves back in Estú. Carmen understood, and yet she still had the same question in mind: did Eliana actually believed her?

"I didn't do it," Carmen finally answered. "I don't know what happened to be sincere with you. The fact of the matter is that... that... I think I was framed. I'm not sure by who, but I have some guesses..."

Contrary to what Carmen thought her childhood friend's

reaction would be, Eliana smiled. She seemed truly happy to hear those words. Maybe she still saw her as a person, not as a monster, unlike what Jason's gaze pointed at. As Eliana took out some papers from her trusty purple briefcase, her face changed into that of utter seriousness. "There is a problem," Eliana continued, still looking at her, changing her happy gesture to a worried one. "All the knives and utensils in the mansion have your fingerprints. This is good, and bad, at the same time." Carmen frowned at the assertion as her lawyer continued. "The good thing is that, since this is the case, we could demand more conclusive evidence. If everything has your fingerprints, it will be easier to make a case of someone framing you for this. The bad thing is, there are no other fingerprints at the crime scene, which places you as the main, and only, suspect. Even if someone else were to claim he's known you all his life, and that he knows you can't even kill a fly, that wouldn't matter much. Anyways, don't worry, we'll get you out of this one before you know it!"

Carmen cried again, even though she felt she wasn't supposed to. Maybe there was a solution to all this mess. At such a sight, Eliana hugged her trying to calm her down. "No more crying, okay?" she asked politely. Carmen nodded and wiped away her tears. "I'm sorry about the funeral, though. It will be held tonight. It was Jason's decision..."

"I-I understand..." answered Carmen, trying to withhold her frustration. "I wouldn't want to see his body degrade, not even by a little bit. So, I think it's okay. He would also understand if he were in my shoes... I hate myself so much... I could've prevented all of this..."

"It's not your fault," Eliana said to later check her watch and quickly pack her documents back into her trusty purple briefcase. "Just remember... we're gonna rock the show tomorrow girl! Trust me on this one!" Eliana winked at her with a confident smile, referring to the judgment to soon take place. As she left, Carmen was reminded of older times. Better times. Eliana had said the exact same thing every time she was about to perform a little closet drama for Don Fernando back in the day and was nervous beyond repair. Despite her nervousness, her plays always went well. Actually, it went beyond her own expectations. Besides, Eliana had also said the same phrase before winning three different lawsuits for the company a few months ago. Thus, a surge of confidence and security hit Carmen which, in turn, prompted her to smile and stand up as well. Determination took over her eyes.

"That's my girl!" Eliana said to her from afar, by the exit door. "See you tomorrow!"

Carmen was conducted back to her solitary confinement cell. There, she started to think about the possible strategies to be used in court. Even though Eliana's confidence had rubbed off on her, she was still nervous. She still felt a black storm was looming ahead as she changed her clothes. Fortunately, some had been brought in by one of the servants. According to said servant, her husband had been the one to order so. This tiny detail gave Carmen further hope that Jason still trusted her. He had to be aware that this was all to make the company fall down. He was quite smart after all. He had always been. As her newest acquaintances wouldn't show up at the visiting table at all, the feeling of inhabiting a solitary world slowly crawled back into her core. Thus, as the black storm kept raging inside her mind, she fell asleep.

Oh yeah, time to rock the show...

It was ten in the morning when she was forced to wake up and conducted to the courtroom, flashes from the press showering her as she was taken to the defendant's table. Flashes so intense that blinded her beyond measure. "The famous La Cruz case is about to commence," declared one journalist near the court's door. Nevertheless, no matter how much the cameras blinded her, she was still able to see who the prosecutor was. "Jason?" Carmen muttered in shock. He seemed grieved and confused, and yet, she could understand why he was there. Despite his doubts, she knew he would be the first one to stand up and embrace her once she won the trial. She would put her hands on fire betting on it if asked. As their eyes met, full of regret and sadness, Carmen sat down on her respective chair.

"We are here to proceed with the case of first-degree murder by Mrs. Carmen Wright," the judge said as he put on his glasses and proceeded to read the paper given to him, lying before him. "On September 22th of this year of our Lord, Mrs. Carmen Wright was sighted by two enforcers of the law with the victim lying on her lap, along the murderer's weapon, which contains her fingerprints..." He kept on reading after cleaning his glasses with a small tissue. Then, he stopped and raised his head. "These two officers are present here in the room. Are you ready to testify about what happened?"

One by one, the two men presented their case. Their consistency and serenity about the issue made Carmen shudder a little. Were they there to help her? Would their testimonies sink her even lower? As their words entered the ears of the judge like an awakening sound, Carmen could only focus on what her argument was going to be. Eliana had explained little about her strategy, which meant that she had been all night long making it up. As for her, there she was, sitting beside her, looking intently at the men giving away their testimonies to the public. Given that both of them were sitting with their backs facing the rest of the courtroom, Carmen could tell there were a lot of people behind her just from the sounds they made. A lot of press. Faceless individuals making their own assumptions, and conclusions, with whispers that only fed her tension. Jason, on the other hand, seemed composed. He had always been able to, and yet, he also seemed as spaced out as herself. What could he be thinking about? She could only guess. She wanted to talk to him. She wanted to be alone with him. She wanted his worried gaze to go away.

"Carmen, up you go girl," Eliana said, snapping her back to reality. "But first, take a look at this." Eliana handed her a manila folder for her to open. Within it, the first page was written in handwriting. Carmen read it and looked at Eliana perplexed as she tapped on her shoulder. "Just follow my lead." She couldn't be serious! This was her master plan? A bad feeling about it was an understatement.

Isn't that what we all wanted?

Thus, she walked calmly to the witness stand. "Your honor. I declare myself innocent of these charges. When I found my son, he had been stabbed already and there was nothing I could do for him..." stated Carmen with slight despair in her voice. Eliana knew it was too hard on her friend, but she had told her explicitly to hold out her feelings and to not explode in tears, especially since she didn't want her to look like a desperate criminal to the jury. As the judge and the jury didn't seem impressed in the least, Eliana's stance of confidence told Carmen everything was going according to plan. Whatever that could be. Besides, Carmen had restrained herself quite a lot to avoid accusing the agents for their obvious negligence. If they hadn't acted in such a manner, at least she could've spent the last seconds of Juan Fernando's life in peace. If she could've at least had that, maybe her core would've been in more peace compared to how it was now. The rest of the people surrounding her showered her with the same eyes all around: those of pity and fear. Jason also looked at her in a similar fashion. His gaze made Carmen tremble as what he would declare was now within the negative range. Whatever it was, she hoped it'd be helpful. As her mind wondered about the possibilities, the lawyer for the prosecution stood up and approached the witness stand. "Your honor, it's imperative to assert that a case of this nature isn't seen daily," he said elegantly as if he was completely unaffected by the current situation. He had probably seen way worse. "If I remember correctly, Mrs. Wright has always lived a life in the countryside, in Estú. Needless to say, if you allow my intrusion on the subject matter, this lady is used to killing stock animals." Carmen felt her heart come up to her throat upon this declaration. Eliana could only see it as a low blow as such a declaration only threatened to step on the judge's most ignorant cords. "Although the defense might argue it sounds far-fetched, we must make clear that a person who's accustomed to killing living beings is less sensitive when killing in general," he continued. By the way Jason was looking at him, Carmen could see certain regret drawn on his face. Probably the regret of telling the prosecutor that part of her past, who was now sinking her even deeper than an anchor already falling to the bottom of the ocean.

"I've never killed anything or anyone!" exploded Carmen, trying to control herself in vain. The anger and powerlessness upon hearing such conjectures almost prompted her to cry.

"No more questions, your Honor," said the prosecutor, smirking as he returned to his seat beside Jason. He seemed quite confident that Carmen would soon break. Even Eliana realized this as Carmen was exhibiting small shivers. Jason remained silent, confused. His eyes couldn't meet Carmen's. Probably the reason why the prosecution had stopped its attack was because they no longer needed to stab upon the same wound: Carmen would do the rest of the job for them. Thus, seeing her imminent collapse, Eliana proceeded to use the ace under her sleeve. She stood up and walked to the front as well.

"Your Honor, please allow me to present to you several facts which point out that the criminal in question is still walking free, out there, and that, of course, said criminal is not my client." The judge nodded and Eliana continued with a linear voice. "It's certain that the evidence points towards my defendant. However, there is a point to be made about said evidence. Even if my client was the one whose fingerprints were found upon the weapon, it's also worth noting that all the utensils in the mansion, belonging to the same bladed weapon type, had them on them as well. Additionally, she was on her way of preparing a party for her son, which she has done ever since this latter was born. The situation seems just... way too convenient, if you don't mind my saying, for a crime of such a horrendous kind to occur." Eliana took out a small envelope and handed it to the judge. "If you read the report, you'll see that the La Cruz Wines & Vineyards has always been the target of constant verbal threats from different sources. Ranging from death threats to general insults, some companies have even joined this sentiment by showing their support of said individuals on social media, added to propaganda aimed at smearing this company."

Carmen realized how little she had cared for those issues as she didn't know they were so many. Her eyes widened when she saw that Eliana's file was quite thick. The eyes of the judge paid special attention to these papers, and after sifting through them, he looked at Carmen. Her puzzled look gave him what he was looking for. Carmen, in turn, also found what she was hoping for. "With this evidence presented to me, the possibility of purposeful framing the defendant is no longer out of the question. Therefore, I would like to continue this session when more conclusive evidence has been found regarding this issue." The judge said as he placed the file next to him and was about to use his hammer and close the session, as Carmen couldn't avoid smiling for the first time in a while when a man whispered something to the judge's ear. Afterwards, he placed the hammer back to the table without hitting it to Eliana's surprise. "New evidence has been delivered by an anonymous source," he resumed to everyone's surprise. "It's a videotape recorded from the security cameras at the La Cruz mansion. I still wonder why these haven't been checked first. Regardless, without further ado, and according to the Royal Decree 17.4 that allows any sort of evidence to be presented to the jury in cases of homicide, this evidence shall be examined within this courtroom right away. Please proceed." Eliana was about to protest due to the high irregularity of such a procedure, however, Carmen showed her left palm to her, signaling her to stand down. Eliana didn't understand as she looked at her friend, still at the witness stand, with a puzzled face. A court guard took the videotape, turned on a projector available in the room, and played it. Carmen couldn't believe her eyes. Why hadn't she thought of that? The real culprit would show on camera! It was perfect! She was eager to watch. Even if it would destroy her remaining sanity to see her son being stabbed again, that was a price she was willing to pay. Thus, she watched it with great intensity as it unveiled its contents. There, Juan Fernando appeared walking across the great hall, towards the garden. Once there,

there was a raven black-haired woman who received him with open arms with a knife in hand. Then, everyone watched in horror as she stabbed the kid repeatedly. The child's cries were silent due to the camera not having sound recording capabilities. Despite being an audio-less black and white film, its effects were still hard-felt as one of the members of the jury couldn't stand it anymore and collapsed, ignored by the rest who were still focused watching the tape. The judge, realizing the evidence was too much to bear, hammered the table, breaking everyone out of their immersion and signaling the guard to stop the video short. "Due to the gruesome and grotesque nature of the evidence," he continued with clear tension and anger in his voice. "This session is to be resumed within a week. One of the members of the jury is now indisposed due to it. Session closed."

"No… it can't be…" muttered Carmen in shock.

Everyone directed a gaze of disgust towards Carmen. The guards came to her and grabbed her by the arms. This time she could feel the anger in their movements with the way she was being handled. As she was dragged back to her cell, she could see Jason's face. The horror was also embedded onto it. It didn't take long for him to collapse his head in his arms and look down. He definitely wouldn't have been able to speak after watching that, contrary to his lawyer who tried to comfort him in vain. That was the last Carmen saw Jason as she was looking again into nothingness. Not even Eliana was able to talk to her without a clear horrified expression drawn upon her face. Carmen couldn't believe it, and yet, the cameras didn't lie.

The culprit was indeed in the video, and it was her.

V

"IT'S HER!" said one of the men on her tail. "Don't let her get away!"

They had been following her for a while now. Being so close already made them stop caring if their intense headlights gave them away. Still down Highway 13, the longest one in the Friornia Kingdom, also the one traversing the entire country from West to East. Although, initially, they thought they would fail from the start due to the unknown nature of the target's capabilities, they were quite surprised since, being unable to know if their target could attack them with guns or not being a definitive factor, they had managed to get pretty close without suffering any casualty. So far, she had proved to be no menace to them as she seemed to simply ignore them. Whether it was because she didn't want to engage or not, they wouldn't let her get away.

Their mission was clear: to neutralize the target, for good if possible. Nevertheless, they knew what awaited them in a face to face combat. They were the auxiliary reinforcements that were to back up the first S.A.A.S. team sent to Sanatorium. As calls for reinforcements never came from said team, they had wrongly assumed their teammates had been successful in taking down the monster. The protocol demanded them to receive confirmation that they were actually needed before departing. As news from the first team sent were still absent after the appointed time, and with no reports of success either, they tried to reach their comrades first instead. Something felt wrong as no one answered the radio, as if they didn't even exist. In the worst-case scenario, the first team had been instructed to call for help, even if it was the last thing they could do. "This whole thing is getting on my damn nerves. We're moving out!" ordered Captain David Brown. "Second Division is to move out with me in T-10."

By the time they arrived at Sanatorium, they could only watch with horror the mutilated bodies of their comrades carpeting the ground. The gravel had become crimson red with their blood. Some of them only puked at the sight while others did their best to recover what little intel they could find. Fortunately, or maybe unfortunately, they were able to watch what had happened thanks to a body camera still intact on one of the corpses. The rest of the body cameras had been destroyed along the bodies themselves. Recorded into said device was the slaughter caused by the Dire One, from beginning to end. The only intact camera had belonged to the man first to fall by her weapons; Seamus McDougall was his name. He had been well known in the force. On the other hand, the rest of the corpses were so mutilated that it would take days, if not weeks, to verify their identities regardless of their bodies having ID cards attached to them. The forensic team didn't take long to arrive, fortunately, and once they were deployed on the field, Brown ordered his unit to continue their pursuit of the suspect. They were expectedly irate. Some of them would've gone straight to fight this demon without any backup, or any thought for that matter. As experience had taught them better, the veterans in the unit helped greatly in controlling the younger officers who were in disarray at the gory scene. They were also the ones in charge of the vehicles pursuing the Black Cross while the rookies sat in the back seats, eager to fire. They would tell the youngsters over and over that their orders were specific. They were to wait for further orders and more reinforcements from the department if they were to successfully neutralize the fleeing vehicle. Then, hopefully, they could neutralize the Dire One, or at least that was what one man in the back seat claimed he could do.

A chestnut-bearded man had made his apparition right there, at Sanatorium's main entrance, before they could depart and start their chase. Approaching them silently, he introduced himself as the best opportunity they could ever hope for in order to catch and destroy the Dire One. He had a Neo Soctulian accent and spoke some Soctulian words from time to time. He seemed to be in his late forties and wore a black and white stripes jersey, one Brown recognized as the one worn by the Viellentus soccer team that played in New Soctul. He also wore gray sweatpants, white and blue running shoes, and a light brown leather jacket. His voice was harsh and unforgiving, and yet, it reflected great hatred for the Dire One. Said hatred was possibly equal, if not greater, than that of Brown's division.

"Look, pal, we don't need any civilians involved in this," answered Captain Brown dryly, looking straight into his eyes. "We're dealing with forces beyond our understanding. I appreciate your bravery, nonetheless."

The man gave away a wicked smile. "You truly think you stand a chance against her? Don't make me laugh, *sciocco*. Here you see a man who has faced her and survived to tell the tale… Are you willing to give up the chance I'm giving you so easily?" His confidence burrowed deep into Brown who couldn't avoid wondering if he was actually telling the truth. However, looking into the captain's eyes was enough for this weird man to realize what was the question he had in mind, so the weird man continued. "What if I showed you this…?"

Brown's eyes widened when the mysterious man showed him a finger protruding out of his neck. Said finger went back into his neck as quickly as it had come out. The captain froze for a second, unable to decide if he should shoot him or not. If reports were to be believed, and all evidence to be considered, this man was just like the Dire One, after all. A monster. Seeing his evident confusion, the weird man continued. "If you don't want my help, I'll be on my way. I'll be sure to bring flowers to your funeral once she's done with you, *piccoli poliziotti*."

"Wait!" Brown said, realizing he wouldn't be able to capture this man even if he wanted to. Sure enough, if he was a monster like that wretched woman, there was no telling what he would actually do just because of being rejected. The unexpected was no longer a chance Brown was willing to take at this point. He had quickly concluded that it was better to keep an eye on him instead of letting him loose. "Very well. I accept your help. Mister...?"

"Creature. You may call me the Creature," he answered sympathetically, extending his right hand to shake Brown's. He had a firm grip and his voice didn't quiver in the least, even though his 'name' produced a perplexed reaction in the officer. It would've made him burst into laughter had he been in another situation. Brown didn't know if that was a good thing. "I know that you will take measures to ensure the safety of your men, I presume?"

"Yes, exactly. You will be handcuffed for the duration of this operation. Any intel you may provide us will be greatly appreciated," continued Brown slightly relieved, without letting go of his weapon holster. "Unfortunately, I can't guarantee you a part regarding the neutralization of the suspect. Civilians aren't supposed to be a part of an operation of this kind. You'll be an exception I hope I won't regret." To his surprise, the Creature laughed to his heart's content. This reaction of his made Brown's chest ache for some reason.

"Whatever you say, officer... whatever you say..."

It's not that I actually care anyways. I have a personal score to settle with that cagna. If she's to fall, it will be by my own hands, and mine alone. It's her fucking fault I'm in this situation. It's her fucking fault my life is a living hell. From being a king to being no one. Oh, she'll pay for this... I can guarantee you that much, grullo.

Unfortunately for the captain, he would need way more than mere deductive skills to even catch a glimpse of the Creature's past. If someone would've told him that he had just handcuffed the former king of crime of New Zesl city, he wouldn't have believed it. Probably even laughed at such a statement. The *Padrone*, as many had nicknamed him, used to run several operations regarding drug dealing and human trafficking within the Big Pear, as New Zesl city was also known. No one dared challenge his power as he ruled with an iron fist as the slightest show of disobedience would be quelled with a show of brute force. That was, death and disappearance.

Oh, che bei tempi...

Having grown up in Nichia, one of the poorest neighborhoods of the city, and abused by the circumstances and the people around him, the Creature had always strived for power beyond measure. However, in his quest for a better life, he had often thought that maybe there was no way to achieve such a goal. Maybe he would simply get a job unloading docks and arrive home late at night until his retirement came. Nevertheless, that would change forever upon meeting Don Fabo, who became his aspiration and his mentor as the young man continued to grow within New Zesl's underworld. At the same time, Don Fabo would've never guessed that it would be his own protegé the one who would eventually betray him and take over his huge criminal empire as the new King. A power no one had had the gall to challenge. No one, that is, until the Black Cross happened.

It all started when a monthly shipment of cocaine was to arrive at the city docks, as usual. Officers were to be bribed with their lives for silence while the boys were to take the merchandise in, disguised in fine Neo Soctulian wine bottles. The *Padrone* was to receive his money on time for the 'protection' provided. Nothing out of the ordinary.

As the *Padrone* lit one of his Shift Strike cigarettes, his favorite brand, covering the fire with his hand from the sea wind, he realized that buying his fifth mansion was going to be quite time-consuming this time. The new mayor had proven a little too 'idealistic' for his taste, which prompted him and the boys to take care of the matter immediately. No position of power was superior to his. It was his city, after all. No one was safe from his wrath.

With the largest shipment of cocaine in his records finally at the docks that night, a sudden issue arose without his knowledge, which he learned from the next day. All his men had been butchered and his biggest shipment exposed to the press. Of course, the figurehead he had placed as scapegoat did his job, so no attention was given to the King while his *capro espiatorio* was sent to prison. His man would be out of it soon enough. Still, he would've let it pass as a minor mishap if it was intended to be such. Normally, they would purposefully leak some minor shipments to fulfill their part of the agreement with the local police. Nonetheless, this time he had just lost billions of wollars in the process, something new to him. The humiliation he'd face would be overwhelming as other groups could take this loss as a sign of weakness. Things that fed revolts against rulers were never good. Thus, the *Padrone* wanted to know who it was, although he just wanted his head. Luckily for him, one of the boys had barely survived the slaughter. He was missing his right arm and had lost a lot of blood. He was still terrified to talk about it, even as he agonized right before his boss. A silence that didn't last long when the *Padrone* pointed a gun to his head, and talk he did.

It wasn't what the *Padrone* had expected, as it sounded more like a horror movie to him. He even laughed at his tale, asking harshly for the truth in the process. He had always hated *le bugie*. After the third time repeating the same story, the King lost his patience and put one between the boy's eyes. He wouldn't give further thoughts on the subject afterwards. He assumed the tale he had just heard was a product of the drugs his men consumed on a daily basis. Even so, assuming this tale was pure fiction or hallucinations, he wasn't one to let his grudges go, especially not for someone who had challenged him to a power contest. So, he looked up online. What he found were mostly tales made up by conspiracy theorists, which he found what he could only describe as *ridicola assurdità*. The most nonsensical out of all of them was a tale about a woman who held two extremely heavy black marble crosses, one in each hand. Vicious and savage. Uncaring of human life. Also described as a demon from hell. Nonetheless, that was the best hint he had to get his payback as this woman was the only one who fit into his, now deceased, boy's description. As no official data could be found about her, as if it had been conveniently erased out of existence, he had no choice. So, he had to make a call.

"So, Patrick, what's up? How are the kids? Everything going alright with you *mio capo*?" Carmello Barbieri, as this was the name of the King of the city, said in an amicable fashion. Upon receiving his response from the New Zesl Police Department chief in command, Rodard Stheno, the *Padrone* proceeded. "I'd like to know what you know of this… *croce nera*. Any information will be deeply… appreciated."

And information he got. It took him a while to assimilate it, mostly the fact that the chief had been 'warned' regarding its disclosure by upper powers, which prompted Stheno to tell it to him in code. It didn't take long for the *Padrone* to learn the concept of the supernaturals, individuals with abilities out of common understanding and of unknown origin. It didn't tell him much while telling him a lot at the same time. Now he knew this was no ordinary challenger. And yet, it pissed him off even more to think that this 'Black Cross', or whatever her name was, would get away with it. Thus, he ordered some of his boys to inform him if they caught sight of the wretched woman and her location. Then, he would go personally to give her the *coup de grâce* once the boys had done their job. Within two days, his informants had already found her, as well as the direction she was going towards. "As per custom in the *famiglia*, you know how it goes… the perfect *imboscata*… nothing else, nothing more," the *Padrone* said to his henchmen with a wide smile, causing the boys to smile as well.

It would take place at an old abandoned school in the outskirts of the city. Whether the King liked it or not, he wouldn't get kids involved. It wasn't part of his code of honor, or so he called it. Kids were pretty unlikely to seriously challenge his power, anyways. Besides, thinking about executing minors brought him painful memories as he had to put down a child once. His boss, the former King of the city, had ordered him to. An experience that he'd rather not repeat. Thus, the Old Saint Marin school building would be the ideal stage: abandoned years prior and now rigged to the core with explosives. The police knew what the boys were up to when they spotted them setting up the charges, however, they simply continued their way upon knowing this was a *Padrone*'s mischief.

After a few hours for the *Padrone* waiting up at the top of a water tower nearby, the Dire One appeared on the horizon. Said horizon and the setting sun behind her did little to hide her disturbing features, especially those dreaded crosses. The King of New Zesl watched comfortably with binoculars while lighting his cigar, something he loved to do before watching a nice spectacle of fireworks. "You're done for, bitch. You'll regret ever crossing my path!" he said to himself as he laughed to his heart's contempt. Three minutes later, she was in position. Of course, the *Padrone* never had any soft spot for those who challenged him, regardless of gender or age, that was, if said challenger was over fourteen. The plan was simple: once she was shot down and carried to the school, where she would be 'properly punished', then her body would blow up along with the school. He smiled at the fact that the school was also an insurance policy to be used if the shooting didn't work in neutralizing her. It was a foolproof plan! His plans always were! However, something was amiss…

Upon closer inspection, the King realized she had a devilish grin drawn upon her face while walking slowly and calmly as if she owned the place. Even though the *Padrone* took it as a show of force, he smiled confidently as everything would go according to plan. Then, he realized what *was* the problem.

As she continued her way, he wondered why in the world hadn't the boys started the spectacle yet. He turned on his walkie-talkie and tried to communicate with his men, to no avail. "What the fuck is going on?! Start this fucking shit already!" he screamed as the silence on the other end was his sole answer. He took out his binoculars once more and looked for them. Sweat rolled down his face when he looked at the monster as she had stopped walking and realized she was now looking directly at him. Her red eyes made her all the scarier. Then, he understood.

Her damned crosses were dripping blood in streams. Fresh blood. Blood drops galore that had made a small crimson trail behind her. The *Padrone* couldn't believe his eyes as he dropped his binoculars to the floor and desperation started to take root within his heart.

"Is everything alright boss?" said one of the two men accompanying him.

"That fucking wretched bitch! She has killed them all! Fuck! Fuck! Fuck!" he replied furiously to his men's surprise. He drew out his trusty *Codeo 50* revolver and pointed at her with it. "The one who gets her gets a fucking million wollars! You hear me?! Go at her now!" The eyes of his men widened in expectation and their faces enlightened. Thus, they eagerly ran down to combat the Dire One. Nonetheless, the emerging hope drawn upon the King's face soon became despair as he saw his men fall like flies. Mutilated. Unrecognizable. As he watched the spectacle, his legs could only shake in terror. His body froze...

Soon enough, she was right in front of him.

"The family may have chosen a direction..." she said, still grinning maliciously, almost mockingly. "Like the birds looking for water... thinking themselves hunters... looking at themselves... as something other than what they are..."

The *Padrone*, confused at first, took advantage of her temporary inaction and quickly placed a bullet between her eyes. However, his recently gained confidence disappeared when he realized the same bullet was coming out of her head as fast as it had gotten inside, with her wound healing so fast she might've never had one to begin with. But, more importantly, she was still standing.

Terrified, the *Padrone* tried to retreat with haste but tripped on his own feet like a child learning to walk. The Black Cross approached him as if she had all the time in the world and crushed his left leg with her right weapon. "Aaarrrggghhhh!" he screamed as she crushed his right arm right after that. He didn't need to look where he was being mutilated realizing that supporting onto any of these limbs would be painful was enough. Contrary to him, the expression she wore on her face described utter satisfaction and enjoyment. Not even he had been able to feel such a thing when doing similar activities. Even after countless executions and killings, he had always felt bad for the poor bastards, even if it was just a little bit. He realized that compared to her, he was a little boy killing an ant when it came down to who was truly evil. Indeed, she was a whole new level.

"WHAT THE FUCK ARE YOU?! WHAT ARE YOU?!" he kept on yelling as she crushed his remaining limbs. "WHAT THE FUCK ARE YOU?!" As he was about to pass out because of the pain, he heard her speak in a maternal voice.

"A human… maybe..."

Then, everything turned black.

"*La notte buia*… always reminding me of my failure..." he muttered to himself. "Keep reminding me all you want… *il potere* will be mine again… I'm certain of it." Even if it had been a very long time since then, every time he looked at his legs prompted him to feel the pain that monster had inflicted on them back then. As he accommodated himself in the backseat of the accelerating police car, checking on his cuffs, he looked out the window into the moving trees.

Notwithstanding, this was far from over. Once he'd eventually make her pay, there was also *him*. If he hated someone on the planet more than the dreaded Black Cross, that was *him*. If he at least knew *his* name, he would've tracked *him* down already and be done with it. It was thanks to *him* that he finally understood the lesson about why knowing who you are screwing up in advance was very important. He gritted his teeth as he remembered how his own desperation had played with his mind; how it had made him sign that fatidic contract.

A contract with evil itself.

The Black Cross had said the truth back then. Little did he know that was all there was to her message. Had he known that the fear that had paralyzed him, at that moment in time, the worst one in his lifetime, had been caused by the unknown, maybe everything would've been different. Just maybe…

By the time he opened his eyes, he realized he was in an empty white room, feeling as if he had been hit by a truck. He slightly smiled as the possibility of having just woken up from a nightmare had started to increase. Nonetheless, this possibility went down to zero when he saw his wife and son there, right besides his bed. "He's finally awake! Call the doctor!" said his wife with tears covering her face. "I'm so happy… I love you so much!"

Once the doctor was done with some minor health checks, his wife told him that they had been coming to see him every day over the past month. He didn't know how to respond at first, yet, words started to flee his mouth when he looked around and realized his limbs were missing. "No… no…" he mumbled as his eyes released tears unconsciously. Many thoughts ran through his mind while his wife and son joined him with tears of their own. As they hugged him, only one thought came to the surface: his life was over.

Over the next few days, and as rehabilitation started, he was finally informed that all his limbs had been actually amputated, not lost. The bones in his limbs had been completely pulverized, so it was an impossible recovery and the surgeon had had no choice. His wife's cries, when the doctor recounted the story, only made him feel worse. Not because of guilt or sadness, but because he felt bothered by it: he couldn't talk to the doctor properly with all her noise. He wanted her to shut up but could hardly remember her name. "Adelaide…? please be silent… I can't hear the doc…" he ordered, to which his wife promptly followed. As he looked at her and her saddened face, he remembered he had bought a small clothing store for her downtown so that she had something to distract herself with, mostly because he simply wanted her out of his sight. He then realized he couldn't remember why he had married her to begin with.

"So… not everything is bad, sir. You'll see, now we have several types of prostheses that will help you into a complete recovery. Don't worry, I'm sure your family will be there to support you all the way," said the doctor while smiling uncomfortably, after which he left in a hurried pace. His wife approached him and kissed his forehead, something she hadn't done ever since they met each other. "Why?" he asked her, to which she simply smiled back as a response.

The next day, he felt truly happy for the first time in a lifetime. Truly blessed, and at the same time, truly cursed. This time it was his son, Italo, who came to visit him during his rehabilitation session. He seemed angry at him as his gaze was intent onto his. His clenched fists reminded him how he had hardly ever spent time with him. "If… if… if at least you would've come to the championship finals to watch me play soccer before… before any of this happened…" Italo said in anger and regret. His words made the King realize that, besides the matches he didn't watch with him in them, there would be also soccer matches he wouldn't be able to play with him. Italo's eyes looked as if they wanted to get out of their sockets. The King wanted to reach his hand, but couldn't, even if he wanted to. As his eyes tried to meet his son's, a new perspective opened before him. Even if he were to accept being stuck to a wheelchair for the rest of his life, there was still something he could do: if he was going down, he wouldn't go down alone. Nobody had taken so much from him before. This had gone way too far. He'd destroy the Black Cross one way or another. The only problem was the fact that now he was a sitting duck, not only for the Dire One but also for his innumerable enemies, eager to take his crown for themselves.

Then, as his anxieties started to get the better of him and prompted him to rant in despair, a blond man in a black suit made his appearance one day, with the answer to all his problems. "Mister Barbieri, I presume?" he said when meeting him at the small garden at the back of the hospital. He wore sunglasses and seemed to be in his early thirties. The nurse left them alone as he squatted next to the King so that their eyes were at the same height. "I have a proposition that only you can accept. A proposition that you will surely agree to," he continued. "From what my reports tell me, you faced and survived the woman known as… the Black Cross."

Barbieri trembled just by hearing that name. The man realized this and smoothed the tone of his voice. "That is a feat that is, certainly, on-demand."

"I assume… I assume you want to have some information on the matter?" Barbieri answered, still unsure of what was going on. "Un-unfortunately there is little I can tell you…" he continued. After looking at him more carefully, he realized this man could be a cop. No wonder how he knew about that demon. Since he didn't know what division he was in, as he could be a high ranking officer for all he knew, or in other words, outside his sphere of control, he decided he didn't want to jeopardize his business any further, even if that meant abandoning the destruction of the Dire One, at least at that point in time. Thus, he returned to silence.

As soon as the *Padrone*'s words stopped coming out, the man approached his face to his even more by hanging his right arm around his neck. "I can guarantee you that our proposition goes beyond anything you can think of," he continued, smiling. "After all, we know what you do for a living, Mr. Barbieri." These last words made him jump on his chair. "Allow me to introduce myself. My name is Ethan Pint, and I'm a representative of the United Kingdoms Air Forces, UKAF for short. One of our branches is researching, what we bluntly call, regeneration for soldier enhancement. A regeneration that would undoubtedly get you back on your feet, in all senses of the word." The blond man took out a small black card and placed it in his wheelchair pocket. "If you're interested, please do not hesitate to give us a call." Then, he approached his left ear and whispered, "we can also help you if you wish to get payback from… you-know-who." Afterwards, he left.

It took the *Padrone* several days before he could make up

his mind. Even if he knew that it was only a matter of time before someone else would snatch the power away from him and that the longer he waited, the more his enemies would be prepared for an assault, experience had taught him who to distrust, and that blond man belonged in said category. Eventually, and realizing there was little else to do he could do, he decided to accept the deal. Could it get any worse? He would soon learn so as he had to pay a generous sum of money to them for their secret. He was accessing classified information, or at least that was how they liked to put it. Of course, he thought this was no matter for women to handle, so he didn't tell his wife.

On the other hand, new considerations started to appear in his mind. For some reason, he didn't want her to see him like this. A few days ago, he wouldn't have cared at all to let her know. He couldn't really understand why…

After just one phone call, the blond man didn't take long to show up with a piece of paper for him to sign the next day. According to this contract, he was to pay the whole fee in two halves. The total was a whopping ten million wollars. Not that he was thinking about paying the whole amount as, for him, these losers had no idea who they were messing with. For the *Padrone*, they were simple tools giving him the means to threaten them. Thus, the plan was quite simple: once the contract, and soon himself, became clear evidence of their deeds, he would soon be free of its terms the moment he showed this to the media. If they dared expose him, he would expose them. Trade in its most basic form, or so the King liked to put it. "They won't know what hit them after challenging me…" he muttered to himself when departing to the appointed place.

The place itself was a tiny office in the middle of the New Zesl slums. Once he exited the car they had provided, a black Hepfu SUV, he was escorted by men in black suits as mysterious as the blond man. Curiously enough, the site was surrounded by hobos, prompting the *Padrone* to wonder if *they* picked them up for experimentation as well.

"Welcome to our facilities Mr. Barbieri," said gently a young woman who opened a thick metallic door for them on what looked like an old and tall rusted steel structure.

Whatever the King had thought at first melted away once he saw the interior of the building. A metallic, clean, cold, machine-like circular room with a big human-sized pod right in the middle of it appeared before his eyes. It looked like something out of a science fiction movie. And so, before he knew it, *they* injected him with some sort of blue serum and strapped him into the pod. "You're allowed to ask some questions before we close the pod and perform the experiment, Mr. Barbieri," said the blond man who had approached him without the King noticing.

"So, what's gonna happen to me now?" Carmillo asked, nervous deep inside, but maintaining a calm voice.

"Well... This serum will just modify your DNA." The reaction drawn upon Barbieri's face prompted the man to continue in a soothing voice. "Don't worry. The tests have proven successful... so far. We used to have another type of serum for regeneration, one way more effective, but-" the blond man was abruptly interrupted by a man in a black suit that whispered something to his ear. "Unfortunately, I can't tell you anything else... We're about to start after all. Let's hope for the best!" Before the *Padrone* could open his mouth for his next question, the pod was closed. As he felt the air being drained out of his temporary prison, various red rays appeared before his eyes and bombarded his body. It burned right into his bones, and into his every cell. He thought he had experienced death before, but he was sadly mistaken.

There were no words for the experience he was going through. He felt his body dividing itself into its basic elements to then reassemble itself. And so, an eternity of painful torture later, the pod finally opened. The blond man closed in on him and smiled. "The process has been successful! It seems there will be no issues with your new... gained 'skills' Mister Barbieri," he continued as he removed the restraints. Barbieri could hardly move. "Right now, you should be feeling as if you just got out of an oven. Don't worry, that's normal! You've been bombarded by ionizing radiation just now!"

"I feel like I've been run down by a *furgone*... again..." Barbieri said as he sat up. "How am I even alive? This makes no sense whatsoev-" he continued while rubbing his eyes. Then, he noticed he was indeed touching his face... with his right hand.

His surprise overcame the burning pain he was feeling as he jumped out of the pod stepping on his recently lost feet. He couldn't believe it. As tears of happiness rolled down his face, he kneeled and thanked Kothat for the miracle he had just experienced. However, as he was doing so, the scientists looked at him in a strange fashion to then take pictures of him from various angles and write notes. "It seems there have been some unregistered side effects, mister Barbieri," said the blond man with a look of amazement and slight disgust. "I think it will be better to study you for the next few days..."

"What's wrong? I feel great! Greater than ever!" declared happily Barbieri. He, then, raised his right fist in victory and realized there was something else to him: a third arm had come out of his chest and was mimicking his right one in the gesture. "What the fuck is this?! What have you done to me?!" His anger festered from his pores as he grabbed the blond man by the neck and started to shake him violently. Almost immediately, several men in black suits came onto him and reduced him by cuffing him and fixing him in place under their weight. Barbieri struggled uselessly until the blond man approached him again, this time crouching on the floor. "It seems you have gained a special skill besides great regeneration, mister Barbieri," he said as he placed his glasses up from the tip of his nose. "Fortunately, it seems you can control those new extra limbs you can produce. This is indeed a scientific breakthrough! We made it!"

"Get off me you bastards! I wanna get outta here now!" Barbieri complained, which went completely ignored by them. On the contrary, the blond man produced a syringe and took a sample of his blood out of his neck before the men on top of him let go. "What the fuck is wrong with you?! I'll sue you! I fucking swear it!" continued the *Padrone* until he was eventually released. As he stood up, he realized he no longer had that third arm. He touched his chest in disbelief as the blond man approached him again, wearing a smile. "You see, it's not that bad, mister Barbieri. I hear your favorite team is Viellentus. It's mine, too!" he said in a sympathetic voice. "I hope we can become good friends... for your sake."

He still remembered that day as if it were yesterday. The day he thought his old life would come back... the day everything changed.

As the officer driving the car announced that they were getting close to target, the Creature started to tremble with excitement. That wretched demon was there, right in front of them! He could hardly wait to lay his hands on her neck and choke her to death. She'd finally pay for all the misery she had caused to his life!

"Any information could be useful right about now," said Brown, who occupied the co-pilot seat. "It's time to spit it out... how do we defeat that monster?!"

"It's actually simpler than it seems," the Creature answered eagerly, along with a smirk. "The crosses she holds... They are the source of her power. If we get rid of them, she'll be defenseless, and her capture will be *un gioco da ragazzi*."

"And to kill her?" Brown replied, unconvinced as he cocked his pistol ready.

The Creature smiled widely. "Unfortunately, I don't think that's possible..."

"What the fuck do you mean that's not possible?" Brown grew rapidly impatient. He turned around and looked into the Creature's eyes, thinking if he had made a mistake in bringing this mysterious man with them. "There must be a way... for your own good, pal."

"*Credimi* on this one," the Creature insisted, looking back at Brown and grinning slightly. "I can tell you that much. Besides, I'm the only one who can survive her among your *scemi*. In fact, I have done it at least *twice*." His answer baffled

Brown and the officer next to him, driving the vehicle, to the point of almost losing control of it. When the Creature had mentioned he had survived before, Brown had simply assumed this man had survived once, and by accident. His statements made him sound insane. "Easy there *amico*, we don't need to lose more lives for stupid reasons," continued the Creature looking at the driver.

"How... how is it even possible to survive this demon?!" said Brown, no longer trying to mask his surprise this time. As the men started shooting at the wheels of the car the Dire One was driving, thus provoking it to lose control at such great speeds, the Creature smirked back at Brown.

"Well, let's say I'm exactly what you think I am... a monster." The Creature had learned to cope with this concept by force. A force he had only imagined existed in the past. Brown's exalted eyes of disbelief and condescendence reminded him of that...

He could still remember when he left that mysterious lab right after the experiment and got home. He sat down on his favorite leather sofa in his living room and promptly watched the *Sequenzia A* soccer league on TV. Viellentus was owning the game, and just when they were about to score the winning goal, the King received a phone call. He hated interruptions, especially when it came to matches, so much, that he almost destroyed his cell phone against the floor.

It was the blond man. "... so, when will you pay the rest of the sum, Mr. Barbieri?" he said, smiling over the phone.

"I believe... next month..." replied the *Padrone*, with a frustrated voice due to the goal he had just missed. "The contract says specifically that the payment is due in the next five working days," the man continued, slightly pressing on. "If you read the fine print, it clearly says that if you-"

"Look, pal, I'm grateful and all." The *Padrone* wanted to hang up as soon as possible as he considered that paying only half of his attention to the soccer game on TV was unforgivable to his own standards. "But I'll be honest. Even I can't pay that much in that amount of time. You know my *line* of work and-"

The man on the other end cut him off with a friendly voice. "Just remember. The fine print is clear. Please don't disappoint us, Mr. Barbieri. See you soon."

He hung up before Carmello could think of a proper answer to that. The King just slammed the phone against the wall in response and pressed his hands against his head. After taking deep breaths, he forced himself to calm down as he was planning a big surprise for his wife, who didn't know anything about his miraculous recovery, yet. A big comeback for the man who had survived the unstoppable demon, as he liked to put it. While he breathed deeply, he also remembered *that* other pressing matter. He had used up all his money to pay the, now slaughtered, men at Saint Marin school and the little he had left had been used to hire new ones into an attack that would make the monster pay in the near future. It had to work! He knew, in turn, that if successful, he would kill two birds with one stone. Other kings, that was, from other cities, wanted the demon dead as well as she hadn't been messing around just with the *Padrone*. They contacted him upon hearing his survivor story and decided to lend him a hand. Thus, with their reinforcements and funds, the *Padrone* would get payback for his core and would pay his debt to the other kings by handing her head over to them on a silver platter, and to the motherfuckers who had cured him in no time. Everything would be perfect. His big comeback. His big resurrection.

This time the location changed. This time, the plan was truly foolproof, and the boys would be placed on the rooftops. None would wait for her at ground level. The wretched Black Cross would pass right down Hawk Avenue, in the poorest part of New Zesl City, the Csepy district. The neighborhood next to the one the King had grown up in, Nichia. There was no way in hell for failure to show her ugly face! This time, he would be victorious!

He had even checked his newly gained powers by cutting his left arm just to see it grow back, which it did. Of course, this scared the hell out of the boys, but they dared not run away. Additionally, his own men were ordered to shoot his head and chest. Hesitant at first, they emptied their entire clips into his body once one of them found the guts to begin and the rest simply followed. To their surprise, all the bullets came out of his body as it regenerated completely after one hour. He laughed his lungs out once he was back to his healthy self, his men cowering in terror at the sight. They even knelt before him as a show of respect and fear. He had become an immortal god. The owner of their lives forever.

Thus, he stepped into the middle of the avenue, waiting for his victim, or so he liked to think.

Indeed, it didn't take long as, on the horizon, she appeared walking confidently, exactly like last time, carrying her crosses. This time with dried blood on them. As she approached the King, he stood still with his arms crossed, and, exactly like he had planned it, he was the only one greeting her that night. "Hey there bitch! I bet you remember ME!" he greeted enthusiastically, with his voice showered by an effusive tone and his body showing the abundant confidence he had gained recently. "This won't end like last time! My powers are just like yours now! Hahahahahaha!" Surprisingly for him, her expression remained unaffected. She didn't look surprised in the slightest. She acted as if he wasn't there at all, not even preparing herself for battle. Such an arrogant attitude blew up Barbieri's wires. So, he quickly drew out his weapon and aimed at her skull.

"Open fire, you idiots!" he ordered and all the men surrounding him promptly obeyed as projectiles rained upon the Black Cross. Her body shook and danced as the bullets penetrated and destroyed it in wounds galore. Barbieri couldn't stop his laughter, grinning just like the demon he was butchering while also shooting all his bullets into her. By the time they were all done, the Dire One fell on her back along with her heavy crosses. The *Padrone* approached her and kicked her in the face repeatedly. "So now what bitch?! Now what?! Hahahahahaha! I showed you who's boss! Hahahahahaha!" After the fifteenth kick, he ordered his men to come down and handle the corpse.

"It's finally over… I overestimated you bitch…" he concluded while sneering at her. "Now to blow you up and- what the fuck?!"

Sure enough, as his men descended from the rooftops, the corpse started to tremble and make sounds, like that of cracking bones, as her flesh regenerated beyond their wildest imagination and all the lead came out of her bloodied body. Not even the King of the city could regenerate that fast with his new body. All of them watched the spectacle in disbelief. Some of them just ran away right there while others remained frozen in place by the fear of the unknown.

"Impossible!" Barbieri said unable to move as well. Within less than a minute, the Black Cross was back to her feet and holding her dreadful weapons at chest level. Her malicious grin had never vanished as her teeth grew back into place. She looked straight into Barbieri with her crimson red eyes, full of madness and complete damnation. As their eyes locked onto each other's, she started laughing insanely. "What are you idiots doing?! Shoot her down now! NOW!" ordered Barbieri as his men were now also on the ground level near her. However, this time the monster wouldn't let them. Swift as the wind, even though it was still average human speed, she swung her lethal weapons against the men who had made the mistake of staying. The mutilation and the horror drawn on their faces made Barbieri realize that he was living the fear of the unknown once again.

He even started to doubt if he would survive this time while watching how his men's limbs were amputated, as well as their heads. The suffering around him felt as if it lasted for a thousand years as he tried to move and run away, in vain. Once the agonizing screams of his men died down, the Black Cross approached him and hit him with her left cross on his chest, sending him flying with a broken ribcage, and smashed organs, towards the nearest wall. The force of the hit was so strong that his right forearm was severed upon impact. "I'm… I'm still alive…" he muttered as he tried to get up while she approached him at the same pacific pace like last time. Even though his arm was growing back slowly, a familiar pain to him was still there... The pain of utter defeat.

"Dominance... the game no one ever gets tired of..." she said in a vague voice, almost whispering. "The wind of despair and joy... struggling to rip cores apart..."

"What the fuck are you on bitch?!" Barbieri managed to speak, still trying to stand up. "Now we're on the same level, demon! You won't get rid of me this time!"

She simply smashed him again with her crosses to a pulp through repeated swings as a reply, with her devilish grin being the only constant in her body. By the time she stopped, the *Padrone* was nothing more than a piece of clubbed meat on the ground. All he could remember was her leaving while humming a lullaby.

Several hours had passed when he opened his eyes. He looked around as soon as he remembered what had happened, but there was no one nearby. He touched himself and started to cry in joy realizing he was intact, that he was indeed immortal. Notwithstanding, even if he had been granted the power of a god, he was no longer the King, and the Black Cross had proven it to him. Still, being alive and all, he laughed, celebrating his apparent victory, among the remains of his men. He laughed and laughed, thinking of the countless possibilities this new power would allow him... until he remembered he was deep in the abyss of ruin. His most recent investment had gone to shit as he no longer could pay those people who had made him become a freak in the first place, nor his most recent benefactors. "It doesn't matter! With these powers nothing matters!"

Or so he thought.

"*Amore mio*! I'm home!" he announced as soon as he entered his mansion. Only silence came back as a reply. "Where are you?! This isn't funny!" Silence kept coming at him in a flow of despair while he ran everywhere looking for his family. Then, he arrived at the main hall and finally found someone. It was the blond man, drinking tea, sitting on his favorite sofa. "Welcome home mister Barbieri! How have you been my dear sir?!" he exclaimed after putting the cup on the small table next to said sofa. He then stood up and he approached him as if trying to hug him. Barbieri pushed him away and looked around. He quickly realized he was surrounded by men in a uniform he had never seen, and they were all armed to the teeth.

"What the fuck is going on?! Where is my family?! I still have a week to pay you motherfuckers!" Barbieri exploded. Yet, none of them even flinched. "WHERE ARE THEY?!"

The blond man returned calmly to the sofa and picked back the teacup. "You see, we know what you have just done. We *know* that you won't be able to pay us on time. Actually, we've always known. We even predicted what your plans were from the get-go. So, as predicted in our plan, the fine print, which you didn't read, implies we must take certain *measures*... I hope you understand..."

Barbieri tried to go for his throat when the men shot at his knees and feet. He tried to get up and resume his attack, but his legs wouldn't budge. "You shot me with stakes motherfuckers?!" said Barbieri realizing he was now pinned to the floor.

"You'll see... We're specialized in the supernatural field, which now includes people like yourself, or that demon you seek... what was her name again...? oh yeah! The Black Cross," continued the blond man while cleaning his mouth with a small white napkin. "You see, the fine print was pretty specific... specifically, if this particular case were to happen... well, let's say that now... you belong to us."

Barbieri looked at him enraged as he, effectively, hadn't actually read the fine print and he had no idea what it truly entailed. The blond man took out the contract from a folder beside him and showed it to the King's face to then read it comfortably out loud. "If payment were not possible for diverse reasons, the contracted party will be required to issue a guarantee to the contractor, whether it comes in the form of private property, confidential information, the fulfillment of a new contract, or family members until the payment is done."

Barbieri listened to him in disbelief as the blond man continued. "In this case, mister Barbieri, we can arrange a special contract for you since you already survived the Black Cross twice. You see, we need an insider to track her every move, meaning, a man who can't be killed by her. The serum we used on you, unfortunately, can't be replicated at this time, so you're the only one with such capabilities we have right now. Your mission will be to hunt down this woman. You may use any methods you deem necessary and we will provide you with all the necessary intel to do so," he went on as he accommodated his round glasses with his right hand. "Were you to fail this task, your family will have to be, what's the word…? uhmmm… oh yeah! Executed. Plus, you would have to be taken in to become our new testing subject for new upgrades regarding our newest programs. Do you have any questions?"

Barbieri growled like a caged lion, still trying to break free from the stakes while the blond man and his company left his house. "We expect nothing but progress from you, Mr. Barbieri. We have trust in you!" he said with a big, and almost cruel, smile. When he closed the door behind him, Barbieri finally broke free and went directly for it, breaking said door to pieces in the process. He looked everywhere, but there was no one outside. They had disappeared as fast as they had appeared. He fell to his knees, sunk in despair. Sad, defeated. He cursed his destiny as the days of being the King and Lord of the city were gone. Now, he was nothing more than a mere slave…

"We got her! Everyone ready on my mark!" Brown commanded, preparing his assault rifle and breaking the Creature out of his immersion once more. "She crashed her car against a tree on the side road! Don't allow her any chance of defending herself! Our very lives are on the line here! Mistakes are not allowed! Am I clear?!"

Such an inspiration you're, cap, Barbieri thought while watching them put on infrared visors and walk towards the crashed police car near the road, surrounded by forests, with extreme caution, pointing their laser sights everywhere. *That cagna knows exactly what she's doing… she's always known,* concluded the Creature given that luring them inside that army of trees, in the middle of the night, was quite smart. They were making the same mistakes he had made back then: underestimating the opponent and assuming the nature of someone from only observed behavior. It was clear that they assumed she was a monster who couldn't think of anything intelligent while the Creature didn't, at least not anymore. She was a supernatural, after all. A cold and calculating one, to that effect. *I guess I forgot to tell these scemi that this is a trap… my bad,* remembered the Creature, showing a wide grin without realizing it. *I guess I can't say they don't deserve it, but they do cause me some pietà.*

"Captain! She's not inside the car! She's definitely inside the forest!" said one of the men after checking the crashed vehicle. "Her footprints lead towards the East! Following target right now!"

"Don't overdo it! We're dealing with a freak of nature here! Think of your families and the future all the time! Wait for Newman's reinforcements before engaging!" Brown ordered, following them as well. Yet, he stopped short when he heard a knock from the car window. "What do you want now?!"

Brown lowered the window to hear the former King properly with a remote control, impressing Barbieri slightly. "Since these are your last moments, would you like to say some final words?" the Creature jokingly said, causing the annoyance of Brown who simply ignored him and kept on going after closing the window shut. As he got further away, the Creature smiled like a shark in dark waters about to bite its prey.

"We must separate into pairs to cover more ground! Be careful!" a voice claimed, coming from the integrated radio available in the car.

"This is so ironic…" whispered the Creature realizing they weren't obeying orders anymore as they were obstinate with their petty hunt. *They remind me so much of myself,* he thought while accommodating himself onto the seat. Had he become a monster just like her? Maybe he had always been one and never realized it.

A few minutes later, and as he had expected, their screams were all over the place. Fortunately for the Creature, their despair didn't disappoint him. He could hear perfectly well as the demon's crosses ripped their flesh apart. "Ahh… the cycle anew," sighed the Creature, enjoying his personal orchestra over the radio inside the car. They would beg for their lives just to die anyways. It was beautiful! And her accompanying laughter was just the icing on the cake! "Wow… half an hour… I could've sworn it was just ten minutes…" said the Creature after checking the clock near the steering wheel once the screams ceased completely. "I guess time goes faster when you are having fun," he added as he kept rocking his torso back and forth in ecstasy on his seat. "*É giunto il momento di agire!*"

He produced two right legs out of his chest and kicked the car door open alongside his real right leg. By now he had experimented with the advantages of added strength to normal hits by multiplying his limbs against a surface. Once open, he made his extra limbs go back into his body and unlocked the driver's door from the outside. Then, he sat down and pressed the button below the driver's seat and opened the trunk from which he took out a gun with a new left arm, produced from his chest, to later shoot his cuffs and break free. "I guess it's time to have some *divertimento*, finally!" he said as he tossed the gun away. It was quite obvious that weapon was useless on its own for the enemy he was about to face. Knowing the most likely path the demon was to take, he quickly hid behind Brown's car and waited. Some minutes later, just as he had expected, the Dire One appeared and seemed to be going to open the door of the car next to the one he had been imprisoned in. As always, she was wearing her wretched and unchanging expression. He hated it so much. In addition, she had some fresh blood stains on herself which the Creature doubted were her own.

"Hey there bitch! Missed me?!" he greeted as he charged against her who reacted by quickly swinging her weapons towards him. He received the full brunt of it, however, this time he produced extra limbs to cushion the strength of her attack. The pain was almost unbearable, but he decided to ignore it completely and quickly produced even more limbs to the point where his face couldn't be seen by her as he kept running towards her.

"Now!" he exclaimed as he grabbed her with his many remaining arms by the neck, wrists, and torso. Then, by using the momentum gained from his charge, he pushed her deep into the forest. A few seconds later, he had her pinned against a nearby tree, rendering her unable to use her deadly weapons. "You're done, whore! I've got you right where I wanted you! Hahahaha!"

Or, so he thought.

He took back the arms he considered unnecessary and looked at her confidently, captive as she was of his might, and grinned devilishly just like her. "Finally, *cagna*, you're mine! There's nowhere to go! No one to save you! Breathe as much as you want before your reign of terror ends!"

As expected, her expression never changed, not even for a second. "A child that does not understand the world… cannot hope to understand an associate mortal…" she said, her confidence wavering that of the Creature's.

"What are you on this time whore?! It ain't matter! This is over!" he replied showering himself in reassurance. Then, he looked at her hands. "Where the fuck is your other fucking cross?! WHERE?!" he continued, now in increasing confusion, as she was holding only the cross on her right hand, replacing his confidence abruptly with fear. Silence was the only answer he got in return as her other cross fell from the sky right into the arms he was using to hold her down, breaking and butchering them, making the Creature scream in pain as well as release her. He could tell his screams were quite similar to those of the men now dead in the forest.

"When did you throw it upwards whore?! WHEN?!" he

yelled, his brain being unable to withhold such an input of pain. Distracted as he was with that unbearable sensation, the Black Cross quickly picked up her recently landed cross, with her left hand, and hit him in the chest with her right weapon, sending him flying and crashing him into another tree nearby. Said tree fell down when his head broke it in half. He tried to stand up, with his head now dented and bleeding, but his regeneration wasn't as fast. While trying to get up as quickly as he could, he was struck down to the ground by her left cross. His head was quickly flattened, as well as the rest of his body by the continuous strikes of his opponent. By the time she stopped, what remained of his body was nothing more than a fresh carcass surrounded by a pool of blood, like the rest of the men before him.

"Join the air… and dispose of," she said in a dreamy voice. Without any further mention, she went back to the car she was initially about to take and turned it on. Before departing, she looked back at his body, still trembling due to the regeneration taking place, as his muscles and bones went back into their former position. By the time he opened his eyes, she was already gone and the promised reinforcements from the S.A.A.S. had finally arrived. They were quick to aim at his head and to order him to surrender, and so he did. Cuffed again, and pinned to the ground by three officers, he looked towards the horizon where the wretched demon had gone to.

"Fuck… *maledetta donna…*" cursed the Creature as he was taken into custody for questioning. His, now ragged, clothes had several bloodstains on it which made him a prime suspect of the mass killings on the road. On his way inside the patrol, he kept on thinking how he could convince these bozos with the information he held. Information which sooner or later would be discovered anyways. He knew, at any rate, that he could easily get out. These idiots didn't know who they were messing with, after all.

"Take this idiot away, now! We got a witch to pursue!" ordered Commander Newman.

VI

"I SAID take this… 'woman' away! Now!" ordered the judge having a hard time assimilating what he had just watched. "Don't make me repeat myself over!"

The same assimilation issues happened to the others present in the courtroom while Carmen couldn't stop watching the film in horror, now paused in the frame where she stabbed her own son, over and over again. It was impossible! How in the world… Had she gone insane? Was this an elaborate trick? Whatever it was, even she was falling for it. The evidence was clear and her chances of getting out of this one were definitely over. She could only look down as the guards dragged her out of the courtroom rudely while the jury booed her to no end. In the same fashion, the guards threw Carmen back into her cell. Then, the door was closed and locked with an enormous and loud clout. They probably wished for her death sentence to be carried out right there. Once locked up, they left with a hurried pace, as if they didn't want to share the air they were breathing with the likes of a monster. Carmen simply hugged her legs and waited for the inevitable. She knew it. Everyone knew it. The death sentence was guaranteed, there was no sugarcoating it… at least she had a week to live.

Isn't that convenient?

Eliana appeared the next day with her face showing the

same astonishment as the day before. She simply sat in front of Carmen and asked a single question while looking straight into her eyes, anger spilling out of hers. "Tell me the truth... Did you do it, Carmen?" The coldness in her voice said it all. The indignation drawn upon her face reduced Carmen's already almost nonexistent hope. While keeping her eyes connected to Eliana's, which was hard on its own merit, Carmen decided to answer from the bottom of her heart. "No, I didn't." Did she believe her? Carmen could only assume she did as she wasn't going anywhere.

"There's only one solution... and you won't like it a single bit," Eliana continued. "Since all hope has been lost regarding you being free and all... I took the liberty of bringing over a psychiatrist. You'll be mentally evaluated, and, if my theory is correct, he will diagnose you with a mental disorder. If you catch my drift... that way, the judge will be forced to send you to an asylum until you're fit to go back into society," she sighed and continued. "Do you have any questions?"

Carmen couldn't avoid rolling down some tears. "Eliana... I don't know what to say... I'm at a loss of words... I thought you... you had..."

"Abandoned you?" Eliana completed her sentence in a serious voice. "I might have. Actually, I'm still considering it. But you know me, when my guts tell me something I just follow 'em. I've always trusted my guts," she stood up and placed her chair closer to the table. "Whatever happens, I hope it's for the best. Just trust me on this one, okay?" Carmen showed a genuine smile in response. Eliana showed none. With their conversation over, she left in a hurried pace while Carmen was taken back to her cell. Thus, as she sat down in the shadows of her imprisonment, she wondered what her lawyer was really thinking of. Could she trust her old friend? It wasn't like she had any other choice, anyways. However, the fact that Eliana was betting, not only her job, but her entire reputation trying to save her life calmed her innermost fears. There was only one thing to do. Whether she was sane or not, the psychiatrist had to be absolutely sure he was talking to an insane woman.

Quite hilarious.

As promised, the next week, Doctor Gupta showed up all alone and met Carmen in a special chamber designated by the judge for psychological evaluation. His questions were quite different from what Carmen had anticipated, yet, her answers only went in one direction. Not that she was a big fan of horror films, but she was able to draw important characteristics from the psychopaths she could remember. At least, the fact that she was just 'pretending' tranquilized her beyond her imagination. After two excruciating hours of interrogation, and nodding his head several times, the doctor left without saying another word. Carmen could only imagine, or wonder, if she had done a convincing job or not. As she waited for an answer, the days passed by like the steps of a turtle. These days made her realize that her acting had been quite good as the guards now feared her. They probably believed she was indeed insane. Whatever the case may be, it was good for Carmen given that an extra safety net was always welcome.

While reading an entire book in a single day, the only source of entertainment she was allowed to have in the cell, thoughts of her possible future flooded her mind. Her life, as she knew it, was indeed over. Whether she succeeded or failed with Eliana's plan, she would no longer enjoy the caresses or affection of her husband or her son. She would no longer be able to keep the wine company afloat as, in the best-case scenario, it would take years, if not decades, for her to be free again. Years of her life that would never come back. The mere thought of such a destiny was enough to make her consider hanging herself with a rope made of her own clothes. However, something always stopped her. A small bug itching inside her mind always told her that she should find the true culprit of the crime, that her son needed justice of her own.

As her husband had stopped his visits altogether, it was quite evident that he believed the film presented in court and not her. But, why wouldn't he? Any sane person would do the same. What if Eliana was the one who was actually insane?

What if she was helping her due to that very insanity? If she was, Carmen was quite grateful for it. And if she wasn't, at least she was performing her duties as her lawyer, and as her friend. Maybe the insanity Eliana was suffering from was just that… a convenient truth.

As the day for the final judgment approached, Carmen noted that her hands had started shaking out of the blue, more and more, over the days leading to it. She'd also cry from time to time, moaning in regret and sadness, as if begging for someone to listen to her howling. Indeed, the diagnosis from Gupta was still unknown, along with her only chance, and it was killing her inside out.

Get on with it already!

By the time the dreaded judgment day finally arrived, her days of isolation had taken their toll on her. The bags under her raven black eyes and messy hair told the whole story, especially since it was the story Carmen wanted to tell the judge. Unfortunately for her, as soon as she entered the courtroom, she realized that the judge wasn't buying it just by looking at his eyes. His cold and steel-like stare said it all. Carmen could only sigh as it was now all on Eliana's hands, again. To her surprise, Jason was called to be the first to declare before the court. This alone made Carmen shiver throughout her whole body. "I don't know what to think… I can't understand any of it… whatever this is… that's not the woman I fell in love with…" he said as his voice, breaking and showered in sorrow, broke Carmen's heart to no avail. She felt the betrayal he felt. Since his was the last missing declaration, Carmen was glad that was all there was to it. She closed her eyes as they released tears of resignation. It would all be over soon.

"Very well, we shall continue with the session interrupted due to reasons of *force majeure*," said the judge after hitting his table two times with his mallet. "So far, a sentence has already been decided if no further evidence that may prove the defendant's innocence is shown."

Carmen looked at him with watery eyes. It all sounded

like a cruel joke. As silence increased her tension, and no one seemed to be willing to break it apart, Eliana spoke up. "Your honor, here I possess evidence that shows that my client wasn't acting under proper mental faculties," she said as she stood up and handed in a folder which the judge looked at closely. "As diagnosed by the renowned Doctor Gupta, head of the Panthean Psychological Association, my client here suffers from bipolar personality. This unfortunate incident was indeed done by herself when she was having a personality takeover, which can be further corroborated by this other piece of evidence I present to you."

Carmen was surprised at how Eliana had tuned down murder from a hideous crime to an 'incident'. She was even more surprised when she saw that Eliana had brought a videotape taken from the same surveillance camera a month prior to the assassination. Within it, Carmen could be seen pulling her hair out in despair and walking aimlessly throughout the mansion with nobody around. The jury, and especially the judge, seemed to grow more and more convinced of Carmen's fake mental problem. As for Carmen, she clearly remembered when this tape had taken place: the first time that Juan Fernando had gotten lost within the mansion and her despair had taken the best of her. She looked towards her lawyer while being unable to stop admiring her as some sort of genius for pulling this one out. Not even her wildest imaginations could have prepared her for the awe she was feeling upon witnessing such a move. Eliana, even though expressing a serious face, couldn't avoid transmitting her radiance towards her client. Much needed radiance.

The judge, contrary to Carmen's initial assumptions, changed his expression to one of sadness and pitifulness. He carefully placed the documents in front of him and continued. "Upon the reception of such an important piece of evidence, I shall announce that this case is no longer ready for sentence as circumstances have changed the entire perspective we previously had. In sight of this development, I shall declare a fifteen-minute break after which the sentence will be defined."

The judge used his mallet, and everyone was allowed to leave the room for the time being. Carmen couldn't avoid looking at Eliana with a slight smile but didn't dare talk to her for fear of messing it up. Regarding Jason, he simply stayed still, seemingly confused, unable to look at Carmen. Before they realized it, the judge was already back at his seat and the room in order. Thus, he continued, "due to the piece of evidence just provided by the defendant's representative, proving a mental disorder, changing, in turn, the context and nature of the crime, this tribunal sentences the defendant to be committed to a mental asylum. Once her treatment is complete and she's deemed fit to go back into society, she shall be freed. Case closed." He used his mallet once again and stepped down as the guards came for Carmen and took her back to her cell. On her way there, she glanced at Jason and their eyes met once more in what Carmen thought felt like a moment in the midst of eternity. His eyes, on the other hand, showed nothing more than disappointment. He was probably asking himself the same question over, and over. 'How could I have been married to this insane monster?'

As she was being dragged back in, Carmen still blamed the men who had cuffed her back at her garden inside her mind. The ones who could have saved Juan Fernando's life. New feelings, as she would describe them, started to take shape within her heart as the prospect of her life was one of utter losses. Once locked up, she sat back in the shadows of her cell and planned how she would get her revenge.

Now we're talking!

With several hours coming and going, waiting for her transfer to the asylum, her memories emerged right before her eyes. Juan Fernando's laughter and joy, when he spent entire afternoons playing as if he was one of the Knights of the Triangular Table, a popular kid's show, came to Carmen's mind. Times she would do anything to get back. With her body falling limp onto the cell's bed, she wondered if she would be able to sleep at all. Her dreams hadn't been pleasant ever since that day.

Juan Fernando, running towards her begging for help, trying to reach her just to fall into her arms with a knife through his chest. Carmen screaming in pain and unable to do anything as a shadowy figure behind her got away. Then, in a burst of rage, Carmen grabs the figure's shoulder and turns her around just to see herself smiling devilishly back at her. Carmen puts her hands onto her own mouth, unable to believe what she is seeing. She steps back as her other self advances towards her with a mocking smile drawn upon her face.

"NOOO!!!" Carmen opened her eyes, panting deeply. "The same thing… again…"

Her cell was still showered in shadows as the sunlight bit into them from her tiny window. She rubbed her eyes, hugged herself due to the cell's lack of heat, and prepared herself for what was to come. A guard then came to inform her that her lawyer had paid her a visit. Upon seeing her, Carmen couldn't avoid hugging her with all her strength, rendering Eliana unable to breathe. "Let go of me… cof cof cof!" she said while recovering from this 'surprise attack'. "You'll be departing in… around three hours. Yeah, I know, quite quick, isn't it? Blame these new quick trials! Just remember, I'll go see you there, in this asylum… let me see here…" she continued while looking at some documents, "this one! Sanatorium! I'll go see you there in a week! Don't worry, everything will be fine! Just keep playing along with the craziness…" she said, whispering those last words. However, her worried expression was promptly copied by Carmen.

"What's wrong?" Carmen asked. "I guess that's a stupid question on its own… you know, seeing how messed up everything already is and all…"

"You know… I think… I think I…" Eliana replied, having a hard time uttering her words. "I think… that you're not the murderer."

Carmen's eyes bulged in surprise, yet she still wondered why. "You saw the video. How could you not believe it?"

"I'll explain it from a logical point of view, girl," Eliana continued in a warm voice. Carmen's spirits grew to a great length without her noticing, just because she had said *that* word of old. At the same time, she couldn't tell why she was so worried. Thus, Eliana continued her explanation. "First, you had no real motive to kill your own son. If you had any, which could be anything, you'd have done it way better. Also, there's the fact that you're pretending to be insane. Since the only possible motive, your insanity, doesn't exist, that leaves me with one sole conclusion," she stopped to gasp for air, still doubtful about her next words. "Doctor Gupta told me the true diagnosis. You're NOT insane, girl... that makes me think that there is something fishy about this whole situation... but I can't grasp what..."

"But... that's not what his report sa-" Carmen replied surprised when Eliana reached her mouth with her left index, silencing her. She immediately understood and promptly whispered. "How is that possible?"

Eliana winked at her. "Let's say that he owed me a favor." Her face remained unchanged as they were being filmed by security cameras. "It doesn't change anything. Not one bit. If my supposition is right... you might be in grave danger, girl." Carmen looked at her as if asking for more information, yet none came out. "I gotta be on my way, girl. Take care, okay?" Eliana left the room while Carmen sat still, completely nervous. A guard approached her and conducted her back to her cell. As she walked down the hall, she could hear the flashes and clicks from several cameras on the outside. Clearly the press couldn't avoid asking all sorts of questions when Eliana got out, who decided to be silent on the topic. Little did they know that the lawyer would jump in joy once she got home. Carmen's life had been saved. For some reason, whether it had been a good idea or not to achieve such a feat never crossed her mind.

Later on, the transfer to Sanatorium happened as it was supposed to be. Still, she felt quite uncomfortable, maybe due to the rudeness on the guards behalf, or maybe to the cold steel that cuffed her wrists, or the cold steel on which she had to sit on while on her way to her rehabilitation center, or the way the men escorting her looked at her, or the way she was received at

Sanatorium's reception. She could only look around, searching for any familiar face she could find, yet none would show up. As she was wrapped with a straitjacket, foreign hands touching her everywhere, her thoughts drove her mind to see Jason running around it as fast as he could.

Who could blame him? It should be quite obvious by now...

She could only look around once the guards placed her within her new cell. A padded one. One that Carmen had only seen in movies, usually horror ones. Lonely, but strangely comfortable. There, she was presented to her doctor, a Rolve man dressed in a lab coat with black pants, black shoes, a blue tie, and a light blue shirt. His eyes were startling, at least for Carmen. He only presented a faint smile while the guards left the cell, staying near the door seemingly not out of fear.

"Greetings Mistress Wright," he said, breaking the ice. "It is my pleasure to welcome you to Sanatorium. I hope that the treatment you are about to receive here will be considered as a good experience for your rehab back into society." He took out a small notepad alongside a blue pen and wrote something down. "I'm aware of the circumstances that brought you to me. So, I'll have to make an examination pertaining to your mental health. I know that you have been examined already, however, it is the protocol of this institution to do so on our own. Pardon me for any inconvenience that this may present to your person. Rest assured that you rest in good hands." His haughty speech and mannerisms gave Carmen much-needed confidence. To her eyes, he seemed like a qualified professional. Eliana's words were still ringing inside her head, so this doctor's performance was more than welcome. Whether he meant it or not. "My name is Peter Kelvin. Although everyone here calls me Doctor Kelvin. You may call me however you like, though." The friendly tone in his voice further soothed Carmen's spirit. He seemed to be someone she could trust. She knew better, though, at least following Eliana's piece of advice.

Does it matter at this point?

"I guess you know my name already..." Carmen said nervously. "I-I don't know what to do doctor..." she said, fully aware that her acting role wasn't over yet. If Gupta had seen through it, it was better not to repeat the same mistake with Kelvin, as a rebuttal for her sentence could come at any time if her cover was blown. Thus, she added a certain growliness to her voice to improve the desired effect. "I know I didn't do it..."

Kelvin kept on smiling. "Of course, you didn't, Mistress Wright, of course you didn't," he said in a soft voice, the one psychologists always used in order to infer an inoffensive stance towards their patients. After writing something else on his notepad, he closed the door. "I hope you have a pleasant stay at our institution. I'll see you soon." Then, he left.

Carmen felt the lock on the door creaking through her core as she realized she was still a sitting duck. If her enemies were coming here, there was little she could do, so she decided to stop stressing herself over it, or at least to try to do so. As she accommodated her body to the straitjacket, she wondered if Eliana was doing okay. It wasn't like she had something else to think about as the padded walls of the cell did little to entertain her. As time passed on, and boredom started to take over, she approached the seemingly harmless stall next to her and decided to figure out how to activate it, which she discovered to be automatic in the end given that she could wave her feet near it to flush. The straitjacket didn't help at all in this discovery, but at least it was easier than it looked. While it flushed, she looked around the ceiling and realized she was being constantly observed through a camera in one of the corners of the room. Said camera also meant that her privacy within her cell was nonexistent. Its watchful eye reminded her of stories she had heard before about asylums, albeit all of them came from horror stories where patients were abused with no one on the planet knowing about it. And, even if the patient got to get his words out, his supposed mental inability, along with his lack of reliability, would render him to have no one willing to believe him. Indeed, anyone could do anything they wanted to her and go unpunished. The possibility of it happening to her as well scared her to death, quenching her desire for vengeance in the process, ever so slightly. Still, Eliana's warning was taking a sweet walk inside her mind, adding to the convoluted paranoia cocktail she was experiencing while isolated from the world. Fortunately for her, those fears were over within a month to the point where she could only wonder if they were trying to torture her with the food served there. Simple, tasteless, and almost solidless. Such a display prompted her to miss those afternoons of wine in solitude. That wine bitterness that had always accompanied her during her best and worst moments. She felt incomplete without it. The closest thing to it she was allowed to have was orange juice.

"I hate orange juice..." she would usually mention to herself every time she drank it. Every sip brought her the image of herself spilling out the juice through her nose due to Pablo scaring her just at the right moment, at the right time. He'd laugh incessantly and loudly as he ran away from her. Of course, he did, she wanted to strangle him right after. How was he doing after all this time? Did he think of her? Or, more importantly, would he be willing to help her if given the chance? She knew that the news of her imprisonment had gone far and wide. He probably already knew about it as well.

What about her 'family'? As her solitude became increasingly hard to ignore over the next few days, she wished they would visit her at least once. It wasn't too much to ask. Their laughter, now engraved in her memory, only resonated along with the bells of Sanatorium. She guessed the bells were there because nobody was allowed any watches or phones. Due to said bells, Carmen often felt like she was trapped in a monastery far away in the mountains, and in a certain abstract way, it was because of how far this facility was from the city. Given that she couldn't enjoy the landscape outside her cell either, she often imagined it. She often pictured it as a definitely better, and more beautiful, sight than the one she 'enjoyed' every time she opened her eyes to her padded walls. Once she had closed her eyes to see this landscape within her mind, the screams of her neighboring patients would pull her out of her immersion every time. And yet, thanks to them, she was able to tell that she hadn't gone insane. Not yet. She wanted to ignore them, but it was impossible most of the time. And so, the days passed on…

By December, or the tenth month of the year, boredom took over her patience, as well as constant regret. The thought of getting back out there and finding the true culprit of her 'crime' flooded her mind more and more, even more so as her powerlessness and desire for vengeance didn't mix pretty well in such a confined space. Sometimes, she would even join her fellow neighbors in screams of despair at that point. The pain wouldn't go away, no matter how much she tried to ignore it, especially since she had gotten wind of the situation outside thanks to Eliana's visits, who had managed to see her twice that very month. These visits were deemed unproductive by Carmen since she could only see her lawyer through the small door slit she was allowed to use, constantly watched by Tom and Joe, her assigned nurses. Said surveillance didn't allow them to talk as they desired, or needed, making Eliana's visits the more frustrating. Carmen had to keep faking her insanity as Eliana talked to her in a code they had created back when they were kids. Every 'ula-ula' meant danger, and every long, or emphasized, word was meant to be taken only by its consonants and reordered. They had made up this complicated system in order to go unpunished if they broke something back at the mansion, like those expensive collection vases Carmen's dad loved to acquire, and they were caught *in fraganti*. Their versions of an 'unfortunate accident' had to be the same when interrogated separately. Thanks to it, Carmen had avoided quite a lot of confinement in her room, and so did Eliana. Thus, as her lawyer spoke to her in this complex code, Carmen could tell that, regarding her reports, her lawyer seemed to be getting closer to crucial information.

"I found a 'deal' to get the 'cliparts' you were looking for!" she said enthusiastically while showing Carmen some cartoons on a cardboard.

So, she found a lead to get the real culprit… I can't wait!

thought Carmen while pretending to listen to her in the most absent-minded fashion possible.

Unfortunately, as Carmen's nurses were there the whole time, Eliana couldn't give her more specific information, which made Carmen's curiosity kill her from the inside. By the time she had decided to 'lessen' her insanity to be let out of her cell for privacy with Eliana, it was too late as her lawyer wouldn't show up anymore. Eliana never explained why. She simply stopped coming. True despair was just starting to show its ugly face…

At least not everything was bad news as none of the staff seemed to realize she wasn't insane. The discovery of her acting skills made Carmen grow overconfident in them, becoming a new hobby that she had been forced to learn to enjoy while her very life hung by a thread. She didn't know if she enjoyed it because she had nothing better to do, or due to the thrill of being discovered. She didn't know which reason was the worst one…

Go ahead… make my day.

"How are we doing today Mrs. Wright?" Kelvin said one day with his usual broad smile, staying near the cell door. He always referred to her as 'we' after his first visit to her cell more than six months ago. "Today it is *that* day of the month…"

Every month she was to be examined as indicated by her judgment sentence. "Sure… doctor," Carmen said shyly, looking down.

"Very well…" Kelvin said as he raised his eyebrows at her. "But first, I would like to share this story with you, if you don't mind." Carmen nodded and Kelvin took out a small piece of paper onto which he started writing as he paced back and forth. This time though, the tone in his voice was different than the usual tranquility it distilled. "Depending on the reaction you show, we'll see if there's an improvement or not…" Something was wrong. He never abbreviated verbs when speaking, and his voice was extremely cold. What was going on? "Is something the matter, Mrs. Wright?" he continued, looking at her from the corner of his left eye. Her subsequent reaction to this sudden change in his character didn't need a performance on her behalf to be real enough. She was truly frightened.

"No… no problem…" Carmen felt cold sweat down her cheeks. She would've never imagined that such a simple change in his tone could have triggered such a nervous reaction. "Wh-what's the story about?" she said, trying to sound insane again, with a shaky growling voice. Kelvin's face didn't change at all.

"This story is about a little bunny. I love it a lot," he continued. "It's about a little bunny that entered a wolf's den. Of course, the little bunny didn't know what she was doing, or *who* she had been messing with," he paused and approached Carmen to talk closer to her right ear. "And… it didn't end well for her…"

Carmen got away from him in terror as he continued. "Unfortunately for the little bunny, Mr. Wolf wasn't hungry and… not wanting to let his prey go to waste… set her body ablaze." His words only increased the discomfort and horror in Carmen's eyes as she shied away from him without realizing it. Her body was now close to the wall, shaking as if she had been put into a freezer. Somehow, such a sight pleased Kelvin greatly. "The sad part is… the bunny had a friend who had been a big liar… do you want to know what the bunny's name was?" That last question made her thrill as she knew the answer already. The answer was given away by her eyes as he smiled broadly and devilishly. She had seen that smile before; she was sure of it.

Kelvin approached his right hand to her face and touched her cheek. "Why are you crying Mrs. Wright? This is just a story…" Her eyes widened as he looked into her eyes and put his hand away. Carmen had never felt so scared. She hadn't even realized tears were streaming down her cheeks and her breathing had become deep. Yet, Kelvin's smile of satisfaction was still there. It had always been. "At any rate, this just confirms my diagnosis regarding your case. Normally, a person in your mental state would not have shown any sort of empathy, which is a big improvement." These latter words terrified Carmen.

Kelvin went back to his helpers, who stood just outside the room, keeping the door open. "It seems that we must proceed with a new experimental treatment I like to call... 'Human Approach'. I'm sure you'll love it. It is part of our new 'Back Into Society' program, or BIS for short," the doctor continued as the unfamiliar tone in his voice rang all sorts of alerts within Carmen's nerves. "Oh, by the way... the bunny's name was... Eliana."

His last sentence made Carmen spring up to her feet and throw herself at him, just to be shoved away by Tom and Joe. Carmen fell on the floor as they locked the door. She got up and tried again, in vain, hitting herself hard against the padded gate. "Don't get stressed before time, Mrs. Wright. You seem eager to receive your treatment, so it will start tomorrow. Until then."

Kelvin's words felt like a dagger covered in alcohol, stabbing her repeatedly in the same spot. Once back on her feet, she tried desperately, and uselessly, to release her arms from the straitjacket just to sit down on the floor and look into the emptiness. For the first time in ages, the darkness provided by her cell felt comfortable and soothing. As loneliness closed in on her, she realized it didn't make any difference anymore. Her only hope and friend left was now gone.

History may take its course... but only myth can modify it...

The next day came as fast as the last had finished. Kelvin showed up at her door at eight o'clock in the morning, along with the nurses. The main difference was that, this time, Tom and Joe wore similar smiles to that of the psychiatrist. Unlike the past three months, when their faces showed seriousness and professionalism, now they displayed some sort of twisted happiness. The cruel kind. They opened the door in a single swing, almost slamming it against the wall as if trying to prove a point. Regardless, Carmen was already awake, ready for them. They approached her and grabbed her by her arms rudely, despite her resistance and protests, and took her outside the cell. They didn't care if they were dragging her feet around as Kelvin walked right behind them, patiently.

"Powerlessness... the worst human emotion, isn't it Mrs. Wright?" he mentioned as they approached a double-door room at the end of the aisle. "That is why humans fear... and SHOULD fear... the unknown."

He seemed quite happy as his lips released those words. Although Carmen had already assimilated what Kelvin had said the day before regarding her best, and only, friend, there was still a little bit of hope that everything was a lie. A dying hope, nonetheless. She tried to use her newfound bitterness to numb her heart for what was about to happen. What exactly were Kelvin's plans? For this once, she'd rather keep her curiosity instead of exchanging it for knowledge.

By the time they opened the doors at the end of the aisle, she understood.

She struggled and fought with all her might. It was useless. They promptly released the straitjacket and strapped her to a bed within that room, while Kelvin closed the doors and produced a syringe with some substance Carmen hardly had the time to discern. They had cuffed her wrists and ankles just tight enough to restrain her every move, even her neck had been strapped to the bed. Kelvin ticked on the syringe with his right index while approaching calmly towards her. "Very well Mrs. Wright, this is our new treatment. The one I mentioned yesterday... I'm sure you will cooperate accordingly." He placed the needle on her left arm and injected the substance. "Hopefully, your mental state will improve even more from now on." Once he finished, he turned to the nurses. "You may proceed guys. Please don't be *too* rough on her... she's our fastest-improving patient." His voice felt cold and mocking at the same time. What in the world were they planning to do to her? She was about to find out as she felt number and number by the second, even though her sight and brain were still active and aware of everything around her. As this new sensation took over, she felt hands descending upon her body without warning, taking off the small envelope she had been wearing as clothing. Indeed, Tom and Joe looked like hungry wolves as they took off the straps holding her in place and sat her down on the bed. Carmen wanted to get their hands away from her, but no matter how much she tried, she couldn't move. She could only feel while they took a razor blade and shaved her head. She could only observe as her body wouldn't react, being at their mercy. She had become their toy.

Afterwards, they laughed at their heart's contempt as they took her near a horizontal beam hanging from the ceiling and cuffed her wrists to it. Once she was secured in place, she felt the sound of a whip. Sure enough, she could tell they whipped her back for at least ten minutes. Even though she could barely feel any pain, she was aware they were enjoying each hit quite noisily. A few minutes later, the drug administered to her wore off and she slowly began to feel the burning pain. She imagined her back, red like a tomato and slashed everywhere. She would've cried if her eyes would've been able to. Contrary to her countenance, Tom and Joe's faces showed extreme satisfaction, and yet, not content with their work, the men washed her back with ice-cold water causing Carmen to shiver and shake quite visibly. She was then released and strapped back onto the bed in the same fashion as before, without offering any resistance. This time, however, she was also muffled. The pain she had been subjected to was starting to take control as she felt her back burning intensely, and the contact of it with the bedsheets only worsened the situation. She looked around, unable to speak, looking for anyone else who could help her, but she only found Kelvin standing by the doors. He had never left the room, looking at her with a wide smile. She could feel his pleasure as the nurses took off her clothes. And smiling, he quietly watched as they played with her body.

The defiling of her entire sanctuary lasted for what felt like an eternity. She could only close her eyes, trying to forget her helplessness, as tears of despair and sadness cascaded down her face. Once they finished, they took her out of the straps and washed her intimate parts with the same ice-cold water they had used before. Carmen wouldn't say anything, nor complain. The water felt just like the nurses' hands, traversing her entire body, making her feel dirty, sick. No matter how cold the water was, she could still feel them on top of her. Nothing would ever shred away those horrible memories.

With the process finished, the nurses dried her with white towels without missing a single detail. Her body felt like a rag they had just used, and they were cleaning it before reuse. She could hear them laughing at the whole situation, mockingly. By the time they brought her back to her cell, the effect of the drug was completely over. She could only cover her face with her hands and cry away the pain...

The straitjacket was no longer necessary.

And so, the process was repeated over and over during the next six months. Kelvin would even create new additions to her 'treatment', one of them included the use of a taser to make her dance by electrocuting her legs. At the beginning, her resistance had been as fierce as the first time. However, as the routine and her helplessness started to sink in, she gradually gave in. Begging didn't work, so, since nothing changed, she no longer fought. She no longer talked. Her only relief was being able to rest every Solday, as if she had just gotten into some sort of rotten contract. For all matters, hope was the last thing she had up to that point.

The official news of Eliana's death arrived a month after her initial treatment. Her body had been found burned, along with her entire apartment. Carmen could hardly react to it, as Kelvin and her nurses were watching her every move, eagerly waiting for tears to appear on her face. The only thing she wouldn't give them. It was the least she could do between her new sessions of torture as for them, it didn't matter if she bled or not, they would keep going by touching her shaved head. Her defiled body. The thought of finishing it all by herself once and for all, by cracking her head open against the doorknob, started to loom on the horizon of her mind quite often.

Nonetheless, as she never had the gall to do it, she often

hoped for them to do it instead. This want for death increased tenfold as Juan Fernando and the killer appeared within her dreams every now and then, reminding her of her failure. Reminding her of her powerlessness. However, her thoughts were always interrupted by the same sound, that of a click on the lock of her door that always made her tremble in fear and contract her body into a fetal position. No matter how long it had been, they never showed any sign of wavering in their determination... as if they truly wanted her to become insane. Maybe they had already succeeded as her silence contrasted to that of the screams in Sanatorium. At that point, Carmen thought that those very screams were due to a similar treatment to hers. Still, their screams had more will to live than her entire heart. At least she wasn't pregnant, which only prompted her to deduce that the drugs administered to her included some sort of anticonceptive. That little relief didn't stop her from getting her nerves, though. Every time any clicking sound stalked her from the outside, usually from the doors next to hers, she felt like wanting to die. That clicking sound would always come with the same question to her mind: why?

Seriously? Is that the only question you should be asking? You could do better, you know?

A question she was never able to answer, comforting herself to answer it by screaming in silence, the despair of loneliness and helplessness taking over her senses. She would even pray for Jason to come and rescue her. She no longer cared to get his forgiveness. Whoever could rescue her was good enough, but then, as her hopes flourished galore, the truth would dawn on her every time: did anyone remember she even existed?

She wondered if the press had already forgotten about her case, or if the world had forgotten about her. She wondered if that was the reason why she often wanted to talk to the other inmates, regardless of their insanity, or to talk to someone. Anyone...

Maybe this was her destiny: to die for a crime she didn't

commit. To die alone as a fucktoy to be tortured for the rest of her days. However, as she assumed her fate in silence, the thought of giving up always disappeared when her will to avenge Juan Fernando came to her mind. A tiny fraction of strength that could make her keep going regardless of all the torture she was experiencing. It felt like a vicious cycle she couldn't avoid resetting every day. Perhaps it was this little desire that had allowed her sanity to stay alive for so long.

Just... for how much longer would that be the case?

No evil lasts forever, nor a body that can resist it... I think that's how it goes...

If Carmen had been counting, she would've realized she had been already there for a year. By now, Kelvin didn't even smile anymore while watching her 'treatment' unfold. He and the nurses would simply continue with the process like machines following orders. Carmen often thought that it was because she never gave any sign of suffering in front of them. Whether she had gotten used to it or not was something she'd rather not think about.

On the last day of Sixtillus, the sixth month of the year, however, Kelvin seemed more pleased than usual. A pleasure that angered Carmen greatly, even if she wouldn't show it. Within her mind, she could only picture herself killing him. Stabbing him in the neck. She didn't care if she was insane or not anymore.

As usual, she was being dragged to the 'treatment' room when Kelvin spoke to her in a joyful, yet sarcastic, voice. "I like your recent increased cooperation with us, Mrs. Wright. We are truly in debt to you. You are helping people! With this new treatment, we will save thousands of lives!"

Carmen chose to remain silent. Them thinking they had absolute control over her had made them overconfident, which in turn had made them lace her straps not as tight as the first times. She had planned it for a while by then. That day was the day when she'd finally release herself and use their own damn syringe and plunge it into them. She smiled to herself on her way to the end of the aisle. She knew it perfectly well by now.

"Oh… I forgot to mention… Mrs. Wright, we will return to lacing your straps as tightly as before! Isn't that exciting?" Kelvin said, enjoying the despair suddenly drawn upon Carmen's face. "You thought you could escape? Tch, tch, tch… Wrongthink is something we don't tolerate here…"

Realizing the obvious, Carmen made a run for it and tried to free herself from the nurses' grasp. Tom simply slapped her with the back of his hand, with such strength, that she felt dizzy and felt almost unconscious onto the usual bed. In a last effort to fight, she tried to hit him, but Joe placed his hands around her throat and started to strangle her. Seemingly unable to stop his grip from tightening, and Carmen starting to get a blue face, Kelvin intervened. "What are you doing savage?! Do not get on my nerves, am I fucking clear?!" he yelled as he injected the hated drug once more into her bloodstream, making Joe stop and cower away. "You're always full of surprises Mrs. Wright," he continued softly alongside a gentle smile. Then, the rest of the glorified ritual took place, once again.

Ever since then, they would drug her right within her cell to avoid these 'inconveniences'. This reduced even more her almost nonexistent chances of escape. This time, she'd only keep silent and close her eyes to prevent any extra satisfaction to be gained by them. Both of her arms were now full of punctures from the constant injections, and the pain they brought her had become excruciating. She could only tell herself that, if she were to die, it would be at least under her own terms. If they had to kill her, that would mean a small victory for her as they would've failed to drive her insane. Until death knocked on her door, she had decided to resist. Whatever came first, it was okay for her. However, reality often snapped her back to reality given that even she knew she would break eventually. Her mind could only take so much pain and despair, something that became evident when she realized she had stopped acting a long time ago. Her snap was closing in. The fact of not having any escape or hope only increased her wish to lose her sanity voluntarily and join the insane inmates around her. As she couldn't kill herself, her core would die in her stead and she would cease to exist in the world. A dead woman walking... maybe that wouldn't be that bad.

By the end of the next month, Carmen was dragged in there again, although by then Kelvin no longer bothered to show up. He would only come to her cell to see her off and let the nurses take care of the rest. The process was about to start once again. Nothing would be different. She would no longer fight nor resist as she had assumed her new reality. She knew that she would be gone that very day or the next. No one would help her. She was all on her own... or so she thought.

Please... someone... anyone... save me... Carmen thought, feeling her remaining sanity slipping away, looking up into the white ceiling and having its indifference as a response. She couldn't cry, even if she wanted to. So, one more time, she simply closed her eyes and prepared her consciousness to die forever.

Meanwhile, the nurses had just finished strapping her to the bed and unzipped their pants in order to start the 'treatment' when the speakers of the asylum issued a warning that pounded Carmen's ears as well as the nurses'. "Warning! Warning! An intruder has entered Sanatorium! An intruder has entered Sanatorium! This isn't a drill! I repeat! This is not a drill! He might be armed! Extreme caution recommended!"

"Great! Just great...!" complained Tom zipping his pants back up. "You know how much I hate it when I get cockblocked man!"

"Easy man. We'll get to eat this bitch soon enough. That idiot will get caught in the blink of an eye," replied Joe. "I feel you bruh. I can't get it on with all this fucking sound all over the place either."

Tom was still holding the syringe when the alarm had gone off as, somehow, its horrible sound had made him stop just in the nick of time. The sound might've bothered them greatly, and yet, it was also a screeching sound of peace for Carmen. Maybe this was the signal she had been waiting for all along. She hoped that this intruder was a psychopath who could potentially kill her. Perhaps, this intruder could finally end her misery. If this was the case, this intruder had become her new hope. Her hope of saying goodbye to that world once and for all. However, after a few seconds of nothing happening, and despite the incessant annoying sound, the nurses decided to resume their activities, probably because they had other 'treatments' to grant. A fact they let Carmen know every time they defiled her. She wished she could scream to at least guide the intruder to her...

"Don't worry bitch. We'll start your treatment right now. We'd wait for the clear signal... you know... institution protocol... but fuck that," said Tom confidently. "We know how much you enjoy us inside of you! Hahahahaha!" He then proceeded to take off his clothes with saliva coming out of his mouth, syringe on hand. Carmen, as usual, kept her eyes closed and shut herself in, trying to forget the world. Trying to forget her fate and the sensations she was about to perceive. She would usually focus on the different sounds she could get to hear, like the birds chirping outside, or anything else that was better than the sound of zippers opening. Tom proceeded to puncture her arm, in the usual spot, and was about to press the plunger when hurried steps emerged just outside the door, followed by several clicks from several doorknobs failing to open. Finally, the double doors of the nightmarish room opened wide and a youngster entered. He quickly turned around and locked the doors with a sigh of relief, pressing his back against them.

"Oh boy that was *cerca*!" he said breathing agitatedly, looking first at the floor, panting. Then, his gaze rose and looked at Carmen and the nurses. The horror and indignation took over his face once his eyes met the scene that was about to happen. "What in the world..." he uttered, unable to contain his surprise. Carmen looked into his eyes begging him to react as Tom secured his pants back to his hips.

You've got to be kidding me...

Notwithstanding, the so-called dangerous and potential

killer seemed to be nothing more than a Mizelas teenager. He had raven black hair, like hers, and a slim body, along with a copper-toned skin. His expression changed from shock to anger in a matter of seconds as he seemed eager to fight the nurses. She had forgotten the last time she had seen similar anger… powerlessness… then she remembered when she had had access to a mirror.

"What on Earth are you *monstruos* doing?!" he demanded in a commanding voice. His eyes described a lack of fear she had never seen before. Even though he was small in body mass, his presence inspired great confidence and security. He was clearly smaller than Tom and Joe, most likely weaker, but he didn't seem intimidated at all.

"Nothing of your concern! Now get outta here before we get to deal with you, fucking wetfeet!" replied Joe while bumping his fists against each other. Tom, on the other hand, closed in on the youngster, ready to grab him while also getting closer to a fire extinguisher hanging on the wall. Since he was holding the syringe, half full, it seemed to Carmen that they intended to capture the Mizelas boy by using the same drug they used on her. Carmen wanted to take advantage of the situation, yet her straps had been placed so tightly that she could barely move. And, even if she could move, she had been injected half the dose. She wouldn't be able to do much. Besides, her overall treatment had rendered her weak enough to have troubles in the locomotion department, something she discovered in her padded cell as she could barely walk ever since her disgrace had started. There, unable to move, she just watched her last hope of freedom take a stance. A stance she had forgotten existed months ago.

The Mizelas boy exhibited what her father had talked to her about during his final days. He called it the Stance of a Lion. When surrounded by hyenas, a cornered lion would fight with all his might regardless of the odds of winning. The fear of death would be gone from his being and he would fight until life abandoned his body. The hyenas would then laugh at him, or his corpse, but wouldn't eat him, nor touch him. She later realized that her father was talking about a metaphor as she never found any evidence that such behavior ever took place. Thus, she concluded that he was referring to the concept of bitter respect. A hated fierceness strong adversaries always saw as an annoyance in their prey. The same fierceness she was witnessing in the body of the Mizelas teenager. His every move, his every step, were solid as if he owned his space in the world. At the same time, the teen had posed his body in a seemingly martial arts defense form. One Carmen thought only belonged to action movies. A few seconds later, Tom had finally taken the fire extinguisher off the wall and prepared to attack.

"Don't worry whore, we'll be back quickly," said Tom looking back at Carmen to then charge against the youngster along with Joe. "This will be a piece of cake!"

Torment of Rebirth

FABIAN HOOVER had seen many disasters before in his life. Ever since an earthquake hit his hometown, where he lost his wife and daughter, nothing else would impress him, or so he thought. Over the years, and thanks to his feats in the force, he had been promoted to head in chief in the Las Esbirras County police department. As such, he was supposed to lead the reinforcements to capture the dreaded Black Cross and to support Newman. However, the whole situation didn't make any sense, at least according to simple logic. In his eyes, the whole thing seemed too stupid to be true. Despite the footage found within the portable cameras of the dead men lying on the ground at Sanatorium, where the Dire One had been spotted last time, seemed quite convincing, Hoover would instead attribute it to some conspiracy, or some well-arranged plot to cover something up. His paranoia had been one of his curses within the force, as well as his main talent. Without it, the big corruption scandal the police department was facing wouldn't have come out to public knowledge as his lack of trust had led him to investigate everyone around him. As such, no one showed any sympathy for him, nor expected any from him.

As the case files laid on the desk in front of him, he often wondered what he considered the most important question of them all: Why was that woman killing people in the first place? He had seen some messed up serial killers before, yet, there was always an underlying reasoning behind their deeds, and this was no different. As the reason for it remained unknown, and so was a way for Hoover to explore her criminal mind through deduction, he was glad to have at least one witness who had been captured *in lieu*. A hooded middle-aged man who seemed furious, frustrated, and sad at the same time. He called himself the Creature. Such an attitude and ridiculousness prompted Hoover to go into his standard stance of paranoia. Whatever this weirdo was on, he probably was part of a conspiracy as he was the only survivor they had managed to find in the entire area. Given that all the officers laid dead on the road, the chief felt there were just a few dots left to connect, waiting to be discovered by him. If he did, he would be finally unveiling a real conspiracy! Not that the others weren't real, of course! Big Hands, among others, existed for sure! But he'd finally have irrefutable evidence that he had been right all along! Nonetheless, no matter how hard he tried, the witness wouldn't give him what he wanted as his mind wouldn't crack, no matter what.

"I don't have time for your bullshit. Tell us all we need to know, now! My patience isn't a very enduring one, I'm warning you!" he said while lighting a cigarette and leaning closer to the Creature, the latter remaining sat in the backseat of the police car, handcuffed and smiling. "You don't seem to know what the consequences are for being complicit in a crime, my friend," Hoover said as he hit the car's roof with his fist, trying to intimidate the man in question, however, the Creature simply laughed out loud. Even the most fearful criminals he had faced before would've jumped, at least a little bit, at the provocation. It seemed the one reading the mind of the other was the man in custody.

"You're wasting your time. You're letting her escape and keep murdering. You're bad at your job, ain't ya?" taunted the Creature.

Hoover wasn't falling for it. "How the fuck did you

survive?" the chief pushed again, looking into his eyes intently.

"Let's just say that... I survived... miraculously," answered the Creature sarcastically. "Just let me go and I'll help you with this, I swear. You can see it even in the footage. I'm completely innocent, *poliziotto*. I warned those guys over there... you know, the dead ones."

Hoover frowned. Whether he liked it or not, the hooded man wasn't lying. He could tell as he couldn't fathom why was this man so calm after witnessing something so horrific. Nothing made any sense... unless this man wasn't really a man, at least not of the ordinary kind. There was only one way to find out. "I want the recordings! Now!" Hoover ordered his men, even though he was aware that there was only one intact camera. The reports had indicated that the blood showering said camera had almost messed up its electrical components, however, the SD card had survived unaffected. Once it was cleaned thoroughly, the data was saved into the police precinct main systems. From there, it was uploaded into the projector room where Hoover had brought the Creature, surrounded him with his officers, and proceeded to watch the slaughter. The ones who had watched it prior were glad the recording was so short as the screams of despair of the officers shook their very core. Notwithstanding, its shortness wasn't helpful regarding the capabilities of the attacker, or attackers. The only crystal-clear information they managed to pull out was her insane laughter, which caused goosebumps to the entire unit. As they kept silent, watching the video, the Creature laughed ever so slightly at every cry of agony.

"Kothatpillist... This might be more than what I had in mind..." said Hoover realizing the extent of the problem. Nevertheless, panic couldn't take over his unit if he was to stop such a dangerous being. So, he encouraged the boys in the room. "It's okay boys, we've handled worse... individuals..."

"Is that even human, chief? Is that woman not some sort of demon from Hell?" asked one of the men still in shock. And, indeed, it was still hard to believe. From the looks of it, she was bashing her victims with two heavy crosses with ease, as if they weighed nothing in her, seemingly, frail hands. As Hoover kept watching the powerlessness of Brown and his men, as they died in the video, a radio call coming from one of the cars was quickly transferred to Hoover's personal cell phone. "Hoover here, report!" the chief answered. His face turned pale as he heard the other side full of screams. Screams that ended quickly afterwards, accompanied by a hysterical female laughter. "It's her! It's her!" said one of the men in the room that had managed to hear his phone as panic started to take over. "She got Newman's unit! We're next!"

Hoover hung up quickly to regain control.

"Boys! We've come this far! We have to avenge our fallen brothers! She'll kill more and more innocents if we don't do anything! Remember that it's our duty to protect the citizens of this beautiful country! We've all signed up for this! And so we'll do!" Some of the men regained some composure, yet, it wasn't enough.

"Chief, I think we should let the *royals* or anyone else deal with that monster," suggested Terry Blossom, the newest recruit. "She's obviously out of our league. We'll only die if we go for her." Hoover hated to admit it, but the kid was right. Still, this was something his unit was supposed to do. Besides, the call he had received had come from the boys guarding the road towards Kelvin's home. Newman's death was pure speculation on his men's behalf. Maybe not.

"In all my years, I've never been unable to see through a conspiracy," the chief murmured. He looked into the projection screen dumbfounded. It seemed that nothing could stop her, and soon she would be engaging the guys who had been sent to make a blockade at the entrance of Kelvin's neighborhood.

"Hey *capo*, have you ever wondered why she left only one camera intact?"

Hoover looked at him surprised, realizing this had also happened to Yang's unit at Sanatorium. "If you wanna get the *donna maledetta*, you must understand her fucked up mind... so, I got a suggestion for you guys," said the Creature in a relaxed fashion, standing up calmly from his chair. "What if you take me with you and we defeat that bitch *tutti insieme*? I know how to defeat her."

Only a part of Hoover's mind listened to the ex-mobster. Despite his want for recognition, he still cared for the men under his charge, at least more than what he considered acceptable. There were also the possible, and horrid, consequences of having all of them killed. On the other hand, he wasn't sure if he could trust the hooded figure. As his mind wandered around the odds of bringing him along, the chief considered four possible options regarding this man's survival: One, he had faced the demon and survived unscathed due to his own skills, which was hardly believable, so it was probably a lie. Two, he had watched everything happen from afar and had a guess as to how to defeat the Dire One, which was extremely risky to rely on. Three, he was an amateur journalist with the chance of a lifetime to cover a crime in progress to publish online, risking his own safety to get a quick buck, which was quite possible. And four, that he was in league with the monster and this was a trap. Every one of them was just as bad. Therefore, there was only one way to go, even if he would regret it later. "Blossom, Erikson, take this clown out of my sight. The rest of us, we'll reinforce the boys at the blockade."

"But chief..." Erikson complained.

"No buts. We might be their only chance of survival. We must go and help them! Is that clear?!"

"Yes, sir!" said Erikson without hesitation. Following suit, Blossom and Erikson, with the latter being the driver, got into a police car alongside the Creature and cuffed him to it. Erikson was quite aware that when Hoover said the word "clown," it usually meant one thing: they were to take said individual to the holding cells, located in the Esbirrino Lows district, for further interrogation. Hopefully, useful information would flow out of his mouth with more 'complex' techniques of persuasion. As they closed the vehicle doors, Blossom watched the weird man through the rear-view mirror. The Creature was looking down, his hood hiding his face, however, he raised his head causing their eyes to meet. Blossom looked away. "Trust me, this idiot is merely an appetizer compared to the rest of good-for-nothin's you'll ever see," mentioned Erikson after realizing what had just happened. Unlike Blossom, who was a rookie, Erikson had been two years with the force. Although he still had problems asserting his confidence over how the law worked, regarding the rights of a citizen, he had won the award as officer of the month, twice. Blossom, on the other end, had studied hard on his own regarding law and order as the eight-hour-long training they had received hardly covered any theory. Both were in the blue in that aspect.

"*Ragazzi*, why are we leaving? Are you a bunch of *codardi*?" the Creature broke the ice. Blossom was about to answer him but was stopped by Erikson. Not because of the procedure, but because of fear. There was something intimidating about that man, especially because they didn't know what those words in another language meant. "If you don't mind my asking… *le arme* are legal everywhere here, right?" the Creature continued his teasing without any response whatsoever. "I've always thought everyone had the right to bear arms, including me," continued the man in the backseat, sneering. "Or you…"

As both of them listened to this man, Blossom unconsciously checked his weapon holster. "What the-?!" he said as he looked around the surrounding areas next to him.

"What's wrong?" asked Erikson glancing at Blossom, quickly, as he couldn't take his eyes off the road.

"I can't find my gun! Damn it! The Sergeant will kill me!" replied Blossom in complete despair as he kept looking.

"Are you perhaps looking for this?"

Blossom looked through the rear-view mirror and his body petrified like a statue. "H-how-" he said as he saw the Creature holding his gun in his hands and aiming at the back of his head. "What the hell is going on Blossom?!" asked Erikson. His answer came in the form of a gunshot, after which he only saw his comrade fall onto the car panel, blood covering his head. Erikson immediately took out his gun just to fall dead on his back with a shot to the head, too. The car, now driverless, went onto the right side of the road and crashed against a tree.

"That was way too *superfluo* for my taste... that car would've been useful, but whatever," the Creature claimed as he used the gun to shoot the locking mechanism of the door and break free. Then, once outside, he opened the passenger's door and took the keys for his handcuffs from Blossom's body with an arm that he produced out of his belly. "I should've taken the keys from the get-go... oh well," he realized as this extra arm unlocked the handcuffs. Although the car was a wreck, he counted his lucky stars because it was out of sight due to the limited vision the night provided, and the slope it had fallen into the perfect cover. "*Molto bene...* there's still a monster to catch..."

He went onto the road and, luckily enough, a few cars were passing by, which, judging by the time being, were probably late partygoers racing to the city. Such a sight made him go back in time when he was still single, young. Careless. Times when nothing, and no one, could threaten him. Sometimes he wished this organization, or whatever it was, would've taken his parents instead. Given that his father would beat him up regularly while his mother was constantly seduced by alcohol, he wouldn't have missed them at all. Thus, as soon as he became the King, he sent them to a so-called fourth-world country, a sub-Panthean kingdom to be precise, to never be heard from again.

He gave one last look at the crashed car before making up his mind, just in case there was any hope of using it. "*Qualsiasi or qualunque cosa succeda,*" he said as smoke started to come out of the engine. Realizing it was a hopeless endeavor, he looked for help on the road instead. Indeed, help came sooner than he expected as a blue SUV stopped nearby. "Hey there buddy! What's in the zich?!" said a young man with a red cap from the passenger seat. "Do you need help?" continued the same man, probably thinking the Creature hadn't understood the first question. Upon closer inspection, the Creature realized there were four youngsters in the vehicle. *Easy peasy*, he thought as he approached them. "I do need help, actually. My car crashed and I got lost here in the woods..." he said while looking down, hiding his malicious grin from their view thanks to his hood. Somehow, what was going on in his mind got him excited, or in other words, what he was planning to do to them got him excited. *Fortunatamente, these idiots should only be able to see the smoke from the engine from here and not realize it's a police car*, he thought in relief.

"Oh boy! I'm sorry to hear that. Your crummy needs fixing?" the man continued, showing concern on his face while the rest of his friends were fooling around with cell phones. *I guess this is their way to get away from the world*, thought the Creature as he was never able to truly understand that kind of drug, as he used to call it, even if his son would often do the same thing himself. "I think it's beyond repair. I don't know what to do..." answered the Creature in a seemingly desperate voice, avoiding purposefully words in his mother tongue. He knew the bad reputation his country had, given that, as a stereotype, his countrymen were usually thought of mafia-related people, or at least that was how Carmillo liked to put it. "You wanna tag along then? We'll be passing by the city," continued the youngster. "You might get some help there."

"Sure."

While the Creature got inside the car and sat in the backseat, Hoover arrived at the first barricade. What he saw paralyzed his core. Seeing it for real had a completely different effect than seeing it on video, even if the scene was the third of its kind in the same night. Nevertheless, this time, besides the butchered men spread all over the road, not even the cars were spared from the ordeal as they had several dents all over them, seemingly made with a blunt squared surfaced object. Hoover could easily guess the reason why. Fortunately, it was three o'clock, and the travellers going towards Kelvin's neighborhood were few and far between, which made their rerouting an easier task compared to what he expected. "Who was commanding these men?!" asked Hoover to the officer near him, who simply shrugged. As Hoover was about to yell the same question to the rest of them. In response, a thumping sound made its appearance.

He looked up into the sky and saw a helicopter that watched over them like a scared eagle, unsure as to whether land or not. Judging by the designs it bore, it had to be the Royal Police. Judging by the hierarchy of power in the Friornia county, it was most probably Augustus O'Connell who was coming down to verify what had happened. After a few rounds over their heads, the chopper landed on the road near the former barricade. Three men came out of it, one in his mid-fifties and the others in their mid-twenties. All of them were shivering slightly as Hoover approached them, trying not to lose his hat due to the gust created by the propellers. "Augustus O'Connell, I presume?" Hoover said, reaching his hand out to him. His hand was left hanging in the air, though.

"I-I'm sorry... I just don't know what to say... I've never seen anything like this... so... inhumane..." O'Connell replied, forcing himself to calm down as quickly as he could, knowing that this kind of attitude tended to be contagious among the men. "If demons do exist, then we have found one..."

Hoover had heard of O'Connell many times. He was usually referred to as 'War Hero' ever since he was condecorated with three Silver Eagle medals and the Pillar of Freedom. His heroic actions had led him, not only to survive, but to gain the eternal gratitude of those he had commanded as he had killed an entire enemy bunker, and saved his platoon, all by himself. However, his most recent failure was too hard to bear. Given that some of the men he had saved during the war were the fathers of the officers that had recently been killed, he couldn't forgive himself. And yet, his amazement surpassed his anger, although just momentarily. In all his years in the force, and the army fighting abroad, he thought he had witnessed everything that could be considered inhumane. Now, he knew how wrong he was. His best men had been decimated by a crazy woman with two marble crosses. It was ridiculous. It didn't make any sense. Nevertheless, he knew what course of action to take whenever something seemingly unexplainable happened.

Whether the rest of the staff might have called him superstitious, or just plain wacko, he knew better than messing with that which wasn't within human understanding. Probably the only reason why he was still alive after the war. He could remember how, back during the war of Wiospan, he would often avoid facing enemies with unexplainable might. And by might, he meant the power they possessed to kill their enemies without the logical means to do so. He would usually prefer a war of attrition in those cases, and, needless to say, he had always succeeded so far…

In this situation, he guessed this enemy wouldn't stay in one place since this foe was an invader. Sure enough, invaders were never sedentary in order to succeed in their mission. "I guess it's my turn to act as a defender and not an invader," concluded O'Connell. Indeed, his duty was to protect the citizens of the United Kingdoms of Panthea, which he had always exalted above anything else before his comrades. A duty that had to be fulfilled no matter what, even if that broke his 'avoiding the unexplainable' tradition. But, how could he stop something like this? By the looks of Hoover, it seemed this latter didn't have the answer, either. At least he knew that monster would definitely go to Kelvin's house. It was quite evident. She had probably dug out information about him before attacking Sanatorium, otherwise, the attack at the asylum happening at the same exact moment Kelvin was present, and her knowledge regarding his home address, couldn't be explained.

"What can we do, O'Connell?" asked Hoover, realizing the road had become slick with blood, almost slipping on it and falling. "Newman is gone along with the whole unit barricading this place he was supposed to reinforce. We're out of options. Needless to say, the only one with experience regarding these… things, is you."

"It's quite evident," O'Connell said, finally free from shivers. "We must send a new elite squad to support the boys at the second barricade down Highway 13 and get this damn monster for good..."

"I think we should rather prioritize the main barricade, even if it's at the expense of the others," said Hoover in a spike of phosphorus.

"Main barricade?"

"Yes, chief, the main and more powerful barricade I ordered to be built around Kelvin's neighborhood. This is our golden chance to get that woman once and for all. The boys there are armed to the teeth. There's no chance we can lose!" affirmed Hoover with increasing optimism just to be looked at in amazement by O'Connell.

"No chance we can lose you say... like we did here?"

O'Connell's remark was answered with silence and a gaze of powerlessness. Besides, Hoover could even feel the anger in the eyes of the War Hero. Of course, he knew each and every single one of the men who had died on this barricade. At the same time, Hoover could tell that O'Connell had just traded fear for vengeance as his, now almost nonexistent, shivers were replaced by clenched fists.

That damn woman must pay the price, thought the War Hero. Not every police department had a similar view on events such as this, but for O'Connell and his men, these crimes were punishable outside the law. No judges, no lawyers. Just plain justice. Thus, as it was his custom, O'Connell took out a little black notepad and a pen. He drew a house on it along with a bunch of squares and exes. "Sorry, I didn't get to catch your name... Sergeant Hoover, right?" he asked.

"Yes, sir!" Hoover answered in a determined fashion, which was also contagious for his men.

O'Connell continued. "By logic, as you have already deduced Sergeant, she will be looking for Kelvin at his address," he took out his glasses to clean them with a small tissue and continued after placing them back on--they were tarnished by his own body heat. "Right now, your men and my reserve are the only ones standing between this monster and the blood of innocent people. Our topmost priority will be to evacuate all the civilians from the area. Even more so if we'll be using high-end weapons this time. Fortunately, I wasn't so bold as to place all my eggs in the same basket... I mean, into this failed barricade right in front of us."

Hoover rolled his eyes at the middle-aged man's attempt at humor. Whatever was the case, his eggs were all but in a good state. O'Connell continued. "We must reach Kelvin's household before this demon, or whatever she is, arrives. We're in a race against time Sergeant. We must move. Now."

"I couldn't agree more, sir," said Hoover, struggling to smile in hope, as he looked at the destroyed barricade covered in blood and limbs. A scene that caused his desire for recognition to diminish significantly, mostly because he could see O'Connell's reaction. Even he knew these men were like family to him as he treated them like his own children. Luckily for his own good, he saw vengeance as a petty desire that wasn't worth the hassle, however, he knew this feature of his didn't necessarily apply to O'Connell.

I know how to defeat that bitch... The Creature's words resounded in Hoover's head. Maybe he had overestimated his own logic and underestimated his own instincts. If he wanted to take the demon down, he had to consider otherwise. Thus, he would trust his guts on this one. "I think I know how to save the Kelvin family, chief," he finally said after deliberating with himself for a few seconds. Such an answer earned him a hopeful look from O'Connell. "But... I don't think we can stop that monster," he added.

O'Connell looked at him perplexed. "Explain yourself, Sergeant."

"We must limit ourselves to buy enough time to let the Kelvin family escape. We can't risk the lives of our men any further. This is clearly out of our league," Hoover continued, trying to sound as convincing as possible. "Even if we plan to stall the demon, it'd be useless. We can't keep repeating one failure after another. Let's let the army take care of this... thing."

These last words somehow hit O'Connell's pride, and Hoover knew it, the reason for which he had said them in a low voice. Still, the words had been said, and the old War Hero was having none of it. "Then what? We let that demon out there, killing everything that crosses her path? Is that what you want son?" O'Connell retorted in a calm, yet reprimanding, fashion, reaching out for Hoover's shoulders and looking straight into his eyes. "How many more innocent people will have to die? It's our duty to pursue this monster and finish it before she causes more harm. Is that understood, son?"

"Yes, sir…" Hoover answered, resigned to his decision. He knew *that* gaze pretty well. Indeed, O'Connell had completely renounced the very principle that had allowed him to survive so many battles in the past. He was sure of it.

The War Hero's calmed and cold blue eyes were fueled by vengeance to the point of becoming contagious to Hoover. Feeling his drive, even Hoover started to feel hope that they could be able to win. *So, this is what's like to be an effective leader, heh?* he thought. "What's the plan, chief?"

"Asprey! Come here!" commanded O'Connell. One of the men that had been in the chopper with him approached them. He still showed signs of shock as his nervous steps almost made him trip on his way there. "Do you remember which car was taken?"

"Y-yes, sir!" he affirmed, trying to sound composed. O'Connell reached out to his shoulders and reassured him. "Don't worry son. We'll defeat this monster. Far from avenging our fallen brothers, we must fulfill the duty we were entrusted with. There's a family out there… actually, there are a lot of families out there waiting to fall prey to that demon. We can't allow that."

Ryan Asprey, who had joined the force a year ago, found some comfort in his words. Sometimes the War Hero and him would talk for hours on end inside O'Connell's office about different contexts and worldly hypotheses. What it meant to be a hero, among other topics. So, greater words couldn't be said by anyone else other than him to the young officer. *He is a hero because he is clearly looking for the well-being of the country*, he often thought. One day, he would be just like him.

"It had the plate 1AAA003 and was going north," Asprey finally answered in a small voice. Although O'Connell's words had calmed him down, and even inspired him to stop shaking, deep inside he still didn't want to see that demon again. A part of him told him that that plate number was like a key to Hell itself. A key that would open the doors of intense agony for those bold enough to enter. "Why did I tell him...?" Asprey muttered a second later in regret.

"Can you activate the GPS on it?" asked O'Connell with clear contentment on his face.

"Yes, sir... the car is still going down route 13," answered Asprey timidly.

O'Connell rapidly made some notes and formulated a plan by drawing the whole neighborhood in his little notebook. "This is Kelvin's neighborhood. We must take any shortcuts available and get there A.S.A.P. Then, we'll place our men here... and here..." O'Connell explained while using his pen to pinpoint some positions within his drawing. Albeit childish, Hoover was somehow impressed while Asprey simply looked away.

"With all due respect chief, are you serious?" asked Hoover in disbelief. Yes, he was impressed, but at how O'Connell was managing to keep calm and joke at that moment. Hoover was just making sure he hadn't gone mad himself.

"Hmmm... I see... listen, son. Everyone seeing me doing this reacts the same way. So, don't worry. I happen to have lived in that neighborhood back in my thirties, and I know it like the palm of my hand," said O'Connell smiling sweetly. "I've always done my sketches before taking on any enemy. A custom I got from my days in the frontlines. Right, Asprey?"

Asprey was still looking down. "Right, sir," he said with the utmost resignation. The first time he had seen his chief drawing sketches for an operation, he couldn't believe it himself. It proved to be effective, though. Maybe it was the way in which O'Connell explained his plans, he didn't know for sure. Either way, seeing him drawing eased him a little bit, just a little bit.

"Very good then, on we go!" commanded the War Hero. "I've already instructed my reserves and should be on their way to Kelvin's household to help as reinforcements in case everything goes downhill. I'll need your officers as well, Sergeant. Do not spare a single one away for this operation, is that clear?"

"Sure…" said Hoover.

The officers thus departed towards the main barricade. Fortunately for them, they were lucky enough to have an important shortcut through a barren path down the forest. As O'Connell and Asprey mounted back into the helicopter, Hoover entered his car, still wondering… still hesitating…

Without them realizing it, another car was following suit. A car with a bunch of dead youngsters inside. Of course, the Creature would let the cops lead him to his prey and deal with the frontal assault, which was assured to fail, and then take advantage of a hopefully weakened Black Cross. It was perfect. Had they been more cooperative with him, maybe he would've managed to let a few of them live. He had already told them the trick to defeat her. To the fools at the prior barricade where he had been 'slain'. Those idiots didn't believe him, so why would these new ones?

As he drove behind the police cars down the soulless passage among the trees, with his headlights off not to be discovered, he couldn't avoid feeling a little bit bad for the dead guys with him in the car. The former driver was now sitting on the front passenger seat, with a broken neck, his head still turning left, looking at him with empty eyes. The others were on the back seat, looking emptily into the car's ceiling with an open mouth, still carrying the surprise death left on them. The Creature had never done something of the sort, that was, killing people with his bare hands. That was a privilege he had reserved for the Dire One. He had always relied on weapons otherwise. Any weapon. The sensation of warmth leaving their bodies on his hands was something quite different from how he had imagined it before. Even in times when he was the big boss, he had never had the chance. Not that he had never wanted to. He had initially thought of using the gun he had concealed before, but the panic that would ensue onto them, as they would've been killed one by one, would've ended in the loss of control of the car, and a possible and undesired accident that would've destroyed the vehicle. So, he simply produced a bunch of hands in every direction. Two per neck, and one extra for the steering wheel. Needless to say, it worked flawlessly as they never knew what hit them and died at the same time. By producing a leg from his belly, he pushed the dead driver's leg, still on the accelerator, and placed it on the brakes, almost crashing against the car in front of them. After that, the rest was quite simple, as, having also brought the police radio from the broken patrol car he had gotten out of, he could easily tell what O'Connell's plans and path were to follow. By the time he arrived near the main barricade, after following the cops for two hours, he saw the chopper that had departed from the prior barricade watching the entire neighborhood safely from the black sky. Their jabbering on the radio made it easy to deduce what they were after.

He couldn't avoid laughing out loud at what was about to happen, that was, their horrible fate. Most of those idiots were going into the slaughterhouse blinded by revenge. He knew better, or even much better, by now. *When you push a man too far, he stops fearing la morte itself*, he thought. It had happened to him, and now it was happening to them. Whenever he saw his life being replayed in this fashion by others, a smile would never fail to come to his face. As if he was in a competition to see if they would be alive after facing the Dire One, as he had done after trying to kill her twice. As if his feat of surviving her made him somehow special.

Thus, he kept listening to the radio and jumped in joy when it looked like shit was about to go down. He stopped at the edge of the forest, left the car there, and continued by foot to what looked like a small neighborhood. He could imagine the inhabitants of this place having achieved the Panthean dream, or so they used to call it. A nice house, a nice lawn, wife, and kids. Perfection that was about to be hit by calamity. *I wished I had brought some popcorn…*

In the distance, some new armed guys joined the ones he had been following and placed themselves throughout the buildings after adding a new barricade with their cars with more men behind said cars. They wouldn't enter the houses. The Creature had to hold his laughter with all his might--it was too funny to watch. So much respect and correctness would be their undoing. On top of that, how in the world would something that had clearly failed before work this time? Then he remembered he had done the exact same thing against the same enemy, and his laughter went away.

Thirty minutes later, the protagonist of the *opera* made her entrance driving at full speed, charging against the barricade with her own brand-new stolen police car. The men behind the barricade opened fire without hesitation as the chopper high in the night sky watched and illuminated the scene with a bright spotlight. The Creature was glad he had never had to pay to watch a show of this caliber, even if he was covered by the shadow of the trees nearby and his seat wasn't comfy, it was good enough. "*Un spettacolo* you don't see everyday…"

"Fire! Fire! Kill her!" ordered O'Connell from the safety of his helicopter through a megaphone. "Don't let her get any closer!"

Easier said than done, thought Asprey, also watching the scene, seated beside the pilot.

All the bullets glimmered upon the charging car. However, contrary to what they were expecting, the Dire One looked as if she was enjoying it, and for good reason: the windshield was made of armored glass. Her eyes showed nothing short of utter excitement as if fear didn't exist. Asprey, watching from high above, could only wonder why, or how, she managed to display that disgusting grin the entire time, even when she had been shot at in the past and failed barricade. Realizing their mistake, when the bullets wouldn't go through, the men aimed at the engine, but it was too late. The charging car kept on racing, tilting to the right, while the Black Cross opened the driver's door and stood on the vehicle's body. Asprey could only deduce she was using her crosses as some sort of counterweight to pull it off. Asprey could see the same scene replaying: the same barricade, the same slaughter.

After a few seconds, the car crashed against the barricade as the Black Cross jumped upon the officers waiting for her. A half a second later, she was claiming her first victim. Then, her second. Then, her third. All of them with their skulls smashed to bits. Yet, they kept fighting, shooting, and retreating. Her acute and insane laughter only increased the extreme panic the men were hardly suppressing. In a matter of seconds, most of the officers at the barricade had been exterminated as the remaining brave souls still breathing were further back, along with the ones who broke the law and were now hiding in the buildings. All of them, designated as the last line of defense, were to shoot the demon with high-end weapons, hoping for her destruction. Hoover was among those, preparing his rocket launcher.

This has to work... please work! thought the Sergeant as he loaded a rocket within his weapon.

"This is it! Or we win everything, or we die trying. Ready boys?!" Hoover cheered, aiming at the wretched monster running towards them. "Don't you dare miss a single shot! Fire now!"

At unison, the orchestra of missiles played along. Some of them inevitably failed while some of them hit the ground at her feet spawning a dense cloud of dust all over her. Hopefully, some of them would've actually hit the target. It was a war after all. Everyone was trying mostly to scare the enemy off, killing by chance, not by intent. Such had been human nature for centuries until the most recent training in the army of Panthea solved this issue by using reaction-related aiming. It was thanks to this that a group of eight Panthean soldiers wiped out 200 enemies when a chopper was downed in Tenumiu, also known as the White Nightingale incident. While those 200 were shooting at them aimlessly, trying unconsciously not to kill them and scare them into submission, the Panthean soldiers nailed every single shot they could. Unfortunately for Hoover and the remaining police force, they were not in the army. Their very humanity would prove to be their undoing against death itself.

"Hold your fire!" Hoover commanded, trying to see if the Black Cross had been obliterated as the cloud of dust was too dense to confirm it. To his horror, he soon realized that wasn't the case as her devilish eyes reappeared amidst the mist and her laughter recommenced to echo within their hearts and minds.

"Everybody reload and shoot! Now! Now! Now!" ordered Hoover with despair in his voice. Some men couldn't take it anymore and repeated the same mistakes prior barricades had made: running away as the demon emerged from the smoke unscathed. Her big and triumphant grin, accompanied by her red crimson eyes, was like a vision of the apocalypse. Her yellowish skin and her black veins, visible even from that distance, started to sink in Hoover's mind. At the sight, the men who didn't run away didn't wait for his order. They shot her once again as soon as they could. This time, however, the Dire One used her crosses to deviate the missiles that would have otherwise hit her as she continued her charge towards them with a viciousness drawn upon her face impossible to describe. Hoover, like his predecessors that night, also wanted to run, but, also like his predecessors, his legs wouldn't obey him. "Now I see what you saw… Newman… Yang… I guess this is it…" he said as he closed his eyes in order to accept the inevitable. Surprisingly, the demon went right past him and the men nearby. Hoover soon realized she had done so to chase the men who had chosen to flee the battlefield. She threw her crosses at them, amputating their legs, just to finish them off with the same cross she had used once they were within her reach. It took her around one minute to do it to every single one of them. Hoover couldn't let this chance go to waste.

"Retreat! She's distracted! Retreat now! Now!" The men were happy to hear it. Albeit feeling guilty for their comrades being slaughtered as a distraction, they knew their lives mattered more, including Hoover who led the massive flight. Thus, they obeyed and started fleeing when a motherly voice from behind them spoke. "You had a choice... you forced me to do this... what is your personal gold worth when despair hits your very door?"

They wouldn't answer. They kept running instead, ignoring everything, including the screams of one of them far behind. As they kept running, Hoover ran out of breath and was forced to stop. "This is... impossible... we can't win..." he said as he turned around just to see the man behind him in the process of being maimed to death. He fell to his knees when he looked around and realized he was the last survivor of the team, tears falling down his face, looking at the grim figure approaching him with her two deadly weapons.

"Why... WHY?!"

As he saw the monster getting closer to him with a big smile, empty of empathy, and full of sadism, Hoover could only look at the night sky and close his eyes.

I am so sorry guys... I truly am...

||

PLEASE HELP ME… please… kill me…

Carmen couldn't think of anything else as Tom and Joe charged against the youngster. They knew that approaching slowly would've given the Mizelas time to think of a way to get out of the room. They had called him 'wetfeet', hadn't they? How did they know that was his status? Did he have it stamped on his forehead? The simple fact that he had a thick Estúan accent and that he was running away from the authorities said it all, even to Carmen, still held against the bed and watching in silence, feeling pity, hope, and fear at the same time. Would he be okay? Was he the one to end her life of torture? If so, how would he kill her? How quickly? Despite her need to discover her son's true killer and the culprit of her misery, those thoughts were always there. Sometimes the balance would incline on their favor, and sometimes it wouldn't. Maybe it was true. Maybe she had finally gone insane.

Regardless of her thoughts, the fight was going in one way. The young man could evade the nurses' blows easily, as if he knew where they would hit next. Then, he would hit them back with great efficiency, making the nurses tremble on their feet. As her captors grew tired without getting any tangible results, and constantly failing to land any hits, the difference between them and the youngster became even more evident. He was in top shape and was hardly agitated by the commotion, unlike his attackers. Not to mention, the Mizelas boy didn't look tired at all. Thus, seemingly not going anywhere, by using a distraction provided by Joe, Tom tried to punch him in the stomach in desperation, but the Mizelas evaded him by jumping as high as he could and hitting the nurse in the face with his right knee, knocking him out and breaking his nose. Even if he had just scored a small victory, the youngster didn't let his guard down for a single second and stayed in a defensive stance before his remaining opponent. Joe tried to grab him with a hug, possibly looking to catch him and break his bones with mere force, to which the youngster simply ducked, and by placing his feet onto Joe's stomach, used the nurse's arms as a lever to throw him against the nearest wall, in part thanks to Joe's own kinetic impulse. Joe fell hard on his head against the floor and was out of combat for good. Then, the intruder looked around the room as if looking desperately for something. Carmen assumed he was probably verifying if there were no more enemies. Once done, he approached Carmen. He looked into her eyes, and so did she into his. His calm face changed completely when he took a good look at her into one that displayed pity and sadness. "This is beyond bad..." he said as tears rolled down Carmen's face without her realizing it. Her body trembled in fear as the boy's hands started getting near her body. Seeing all that power, exploding in each punch and kick, made her feel so insignificant she knew he could crush her if he wanted to. In the worst-case scenario, he would have her body first, just like Tom and Joe. Carmen closed her eyes as the bitterness of her inability to defend herself appeared before her once more, waiting for the expected. Thus, she waited, with her heartbeat racing, her nerves ready. She prepared herself to feel his filthy hands on her body. The darkness her eyelids provided made the waiting all the worse. Then, she felt his hands on her wrists...

He was untying her.

"I donno what those *imbéciles* were doing to you, but

whatever it was, even I can tell it's *inhumano*. Come here, let me help you," said the Mizelas youngster, extending his right hand to Carmen once he was done releasing her ankles. Some of his words penetrated her very core as he spoke them in her mother tongue. Something she hadn't heard in ages. Those words alone brought her back to happier days. The warmth of understanding and feeling exactly what he meant compared to the cold Stonian language. He was dressed in white t-shirt and white sweatpants. He was also younger than her, probably in his late teens. His youth prompted Carmen to wonder in astonishment how was a kid like this one able to overpower such powerful men. She had read about delinquents in her books, or in other words, young people becoming gangsters with dire consequences. Was he one of those? Or, had he been paid to come for her head? Any of them was possible and said possibilities struck Carmen as different fears started to converge into her heart. She could only stay seated still on the bed, frozen by dread, not knowing whether to take his hand or not. Apart from all those possibilities, there was a worse one: whether it was him, or someone else, the fact that someone might be trying to save her was too good to be true. Why was he even there? Another cruel joke made by fate? She had so many doubts, so many questions, as her hand stayed petrified in mid-air just a few millimeters away from taking his. What if he had been hired by the real killer of her child? He definitely could have killed those two men and had the potential to be a professional assassin. She felt he could break her neck without too much effort, despite his age, and especially given how weak she was. Her mind created all sorts of scenarios where he would deliver the final blow, and as these played over and over in her mind, she was brought back to reality by sounds of people pounding on the door.

"You're surrounded filthy wethands! You got nowhere to go! Surrender peacefully and open the door!" cried the men outside as they kept on hammering the structure with all their might, louder this time. Said door wouldn't last very long.

"I guess I got no choice..." murmured the youngster to

himself as he approached Carmen and took her hand. Due to her reactionless body, the teenager pulled her towards him forcefully and carried her on his back. She was so weak that, even if she would've wanted to resist, she wouldn't have been able to fight back. Deep in her heart, something told her that this was it. Whatever fate he had in store for her, she'd rather not know given that, if she were to die, at least she would do so free of that cursed place. *In any way you kill me... Thank you,* Carmen thought as the Mizelas boy moved around the room looking for a way out while she could barely tell what was going on. What she could tell, however, was that he'd use her body at some point or another. She had come to accept it at this point, and even her body was just expecting it as well. All mankind was the same. First Jason, who had abandoned her, then there were those monsters in the asylum, and now, there was this youngster.

A mind full of regret? That's it? ... I expected more...

The youngster grabbed a metallic chair and managed to break the nearby window with it after several tries, even though the glass was reinforced. "*¡Qué suerte!* We're on the first floor!" the boy said, smiling slightly when he stepped onto the window frame and opened the curtains. Sunlight hit Carmen's eyes strongly with its brightness, prompting her to squeeze her eyes in response. "Fortunately, you're not heavy at all!" he continued as he reassured her body onto his back with his left hand. Carmen could barely move, feeling like a rag, but hearing how the door was about to give way. And so, before she knew it, the Mizelas teenager had jumped out the window. Carmen didn't know what was going on anymore as the door behind them was finally kicked open by men in black suits, and sunglasses, with handguns. They ran to the window, but it was too late. So, not wasting any time, they started shooting at the fleeing couple immediately. They were trying to kill them and didn't seem to care about a kidnapped patient. As she could hear the bullets hitting the ground around them, she could only conclude that their aim was only surpassed by the youngster's agility. She could feel him moving from side to side, getting closer to trees to get cover to then move on and get behind the next tree. She remembered then how big Sanatorium's garden really was. Eventually, and surprisingly, the boy went the opposite way to the main gate and climbed the fences of Sanatorium by jumping on perpendicular walls on the facility's corner. When he stepped on the sidewalk outside, he accelerated as if there was no tomorrow. It was then that Carmen remembered that Sanatorium was outside the city near some suburbs.

As he ran down the streets, she could tell about his small, yet powerful muscles by the way he had grabbed her body and kept her firmly onto his back, his sweat impregnating her nose and clothes. It was clear that he was in top shape, powerful. However, it was probably because he was just as tall as herself that he didn't look all that threatening. Instead of danger, she could feel great determination in every step he made. "We're almost out of their reach!" he said while barely panting and keeping up his speed. His calm and confident voice made Carmen wonder several things, even if she was on her way to meet death. Who was he? Why go through all that trouble just for her? Since he looked like a minor, even if he were to be a killer, why would someone use lethal force on him? Nothing made sense. And yet, hadn't she seen some nonsense herself before?

After running across the suburbs until the armed men could no longer be seen nor heard, the teenager got into a backyard with a bush-made fence surrounding it. Since they had made it in one piece without any interruptions, Carmen assumed that the men chasing the youngster had been bluffing: they had never actually surrounded Sanatorium. Were they the royal authorities? Thinking started to get stressful as the teenager gently placed Carmen on the grass.

"I hear *them* coming. *¡Escondámonos!*" he said as he opened a small window leading into the basement of the house the garden belonged to. Unable to move, feeling once again like a rag, Carmen was dragged inside it by the Mizelas boy. Just after a few seconds of making it inside, the steps of four furious men could be heard outside.

"Where is that wethands? Where the fuck did he go? Damn it!"

After some fumbling, their steps sounded farther and farther away until they went completely silent. Only then did the youngster sighed in relief. "That was a close call," he said happily. He then looked at Carmen from head to toe, helped by the dim light coming through the very same window they had used to enter. "I think you should get something else to wear," he muttered as he continued to look around the place on tiptoes. The basement was quite dark, yet not so dusty, which prompted the teenager to assume it to be in regular use. For Carmen though, even if it were extremely dirty, it was a million times better than Sanatorium. "Nice!" the youngster said happily when he spotted a drying machine. As Carmen observed him, she realized why the youngster was so happy. It seemed that the owners weren't of the hurried kind and had left their dry clothes inside. He took them out, and after choosing for what it felt like a minute, he came back with a white t-shirt, loose blue pants, and grey socks and handed them to Carmen. Was he that cruel as to raise her hopes before killing her? Otherwise, why was he doing all of this? What was his deal? What did he want from her? She wanted to ask all these questions, and yet she remained in the same stance, frozen in place by fear.

Upon seeing that Carmen wasn't moving, nor trying to change her clothes, and looking at him with empty eyes, he realized something. "Oh! *¡Lo siento!* I'll turn around so you can change. Don't worry," he said, turning around and staring at a wall. Not that it mattered to Carmen, she was in his hands anyways, but she appreciated the gesture given that her weakened body only allowed her to change at a turtle's pace. After around fifteen minutes, she was done. "Can I turn around now?" he asked patiently, still fixed on the same faded wallpaper.

"Uh-huh," said Carmen with a voice still bathed in fear. The Mizelas youngster turned around and looked pleased at the sight, nodding with a smirk. Carmen looked into his eyes once more, yet, no matter how she did it, she couldn't find what she was looking for. Instead of killer instincts and a sadistic nature, his eyes displayed a certain peace and calmness. Who the hell was he? Carmen could have tried to utter words; however, she had been silent in the asylum for so long that… maybe she had forgotten how to speak. No matter how much she wanted to, words would not come out. This lack of response earned her a perplexed look from her captor, prompting him to approach her little by little, reaching out to her, which in turn made her stick closer to the wall, away from him. She covered her face with her hands, waiting for whatever his sick mind could be planning, and yet, nothing happened. Carmen opened her eyes just to see him crouched before her and keeping his distance, his hands on top of his knees, his expression relaxed. Not knowing what he wanted, or what he planned, started to build despair in Carmen's very core. She was ready to burst when he finally spoke.

"Look, I donno what those guys did to you. Whatever it was, it seemed horrible. I get it," he stood up and walked away a few feet from her. "Just so you know, *señorita*, I'm not one of those guys." Nevertheless, Carmen's eyes showed her disbelief and utter fear of him. The Mizelas breathed deeply and continued. "What I'm trying to say is that I won't hurt you, okay? Now, we must go. Those guys might be around somewhere looking for us. I see you aren't doing so hot, so I'll ask you to please bear with me." Carmen's eyes relaxed as the tension in her body also went down a few notches. She tried to stand up but instantly fell to the floor. Fortunately for her, the youngster caught her in mid-air before she made any unwanted noises that would alert the owner of the house he had uninvited guests. The Mizelas boy handed her a rag. "Cover your head with this. Until your hair grows back you might be drawing attention we don't need. Oh! Before I forget, *puedes llamarme* Nico."

He helped her up and both of them proceeded to leave the place through the same window they had used to get in. By the time they were out, a lot of police cars could be heard in the distance. They were surrounding the asylum, probably on the lookout for them. They had to get out of there as fast as possible, but how?

Have you considered... crime? So much for a knight in shining armor...

"Although I hate to do this, but a faster way to get outta here is by taking someone's car," said Nico. "Do you know how to drive?" he continued, even though he regretted his words as soon as he had said them after looking at Carmen's decaying body once again. "Okay, maybe there's a better idea..."

At a traffic light, they sneaked onto the back of a small pickup truck waiting for the red light to turn green. Of course, there were no vehicles behind it. As planned, the night didn't allow too much vision for possible unassuming witnesses, otherwise, seeing a shaved woman being carried by a young man would've meant trouble, especially in Panthean society. Once on the truck's bed, Carmen kept her distance from Nico, even though that distance wasn't much due to the narrow space they were clustered in, among rusted electrical appliances. She kept at it during the entire trip, even though the youngster didn't try anything nor tried to approach her. In her temporary moment of solitude, Carmen closed her eyes and felt the wind blow her way, enjoying every fresh breath of freedom she could draw. *Free at last*, she thought as she opened her eyes and saw Sanatorium getting lost in the distance. At the same time, she would casually look at Nico, watching his every move.

To her surprise, he wasn't looking at her. While his eyes lingered into the night sky, he was constantly moving his arms and legs, whether by tapping his fingers on his knees or tapping his feet softly against the truck's bed, which he kept doing for the whole duration of the trip. What was he thinking? Was he this anxious? Somehow, the thought of him killing her started to become more and more unlikely. He could've killed her if he had wanted to go back in that basement and left her corpse rotting right there. She knew she was a burden for him, and yet here he was. In that case, what had he done to deserve such a pursuit? Was he a human trafficker? Either way, the innocence in his eyes said otherwise. Nevertheless, Carmen had learned long ago not to trust such simplistic characteristics. Maybe he was older than what he looked like. A trait like this wasn't hard to find among the Lurns, the people who vastly populated the West of the globe. Nico had somewhat slanted eyes, which mean that he could have some genetic relationship with them, something not hard to find in a Mizelas, either, as these latter tended to have several race mixtures within them. She had met some of them before, for instance, some of her workers at the company who came from Chilinia. Although most of them had different faces and a similar skin color, and possibly similar ancestry, that wasn't the case for all of them. Some of them were completely different from their own majority. Maybe she was overthinking it a little bit. She felt like a documentarist thinking about how to classify the species she saw on the run.

The truck in question took them all the way to Las Esbirras downtown, which Nico made Carmen know by touching her shoulder with his left index finger. "We should get off here," he said while waiting for the next red light. Carmen looked at him perplexed, telling him with her eyes that she didn't know what to do. If she stayed behind, she would hardly get off the vehicle on her own, given the state of her body. This option would eventually get her to the driver's final destination where he would either report her and get the police, or where he'd take advantage of her. Thus, following the youngster seemed like a better choice, even if it could potentially end in a similar fashion. She nodded her head to accept her captor's choice, still unable to speak. Indeed, once the truck stopped, both of them got off as silently as possible as they didn't want the driver chasing them, too, thinking of them as possible thieves.

The city of Las Esbirras was quite different at that hour of the night. At one in the morning, it felt like an inhospitable place full of possible attackers, criminals, and murderers.

Carmen even felt that the sidewalk might bite her legs off if she walked slow enough. The environment itself overwhelmed her senses as Nico guided her by holding her right hand down the street. Eventually, they made it to a bridge overlooking a badly polluted river.

"This is where we'll pass the night. It's not as *cómodo* as other places, but it could be worse," said Nico once they were under said bridge. He brought some brown cardboard, he got from tearing boxes he had found lying around, and placed it as an archaic bed on the floor. Carmen would've never imagined that her first day as a free woman was to be her first day as a 'bum', as Jason used to call them. If her father could see her now, his disappointment would've hit the roof for sure. Such a thought gave her sadness and relief at the same time since criminals usually didn't sleep under bridges, or at least that much she had assumed. They were committing their felonies in order not to sleep in such a place to begin with.

The place, in general, looked like one of those they used in horror movies with low budgets. The smell of piss mixed with alcohol and putrefaction, accompanied by graffiti everywhere, and the lack of overall cleaning told Carmen that she was definitely in one of the city's red zones. She remembered that part of the city: The Drift Row district. She remembered perfectly the few times she had been there: she once witnessed the theft of a woman's purse, live, when she stopped at a red light and no one raised an eyebrow at the deed. Carmen knew by that point that there were other signs of high criminal activity in the area. This district had had the highest homeless population in Las Esbirras since the 1970s. This very realization made Carmen want to scream, but she was too weak to do even that. Besides, it was pointless as no one would help her, even if she did manage to scream. She could only watch Nico's every move, who despite the situation, seemed quite confident and calm. A behavior from which some things started to attract her attention. For instance, he was always moving some part of his body regardless of him being seated or lying down. There was also the fact that he was wearing earbuds the entire time.

Normally this would make a regular person have a hard time listening to people, or anything else for that matter, and yet there he was, picking up every single sound around him. Sounds not even she could fathom were surrounding them. For example, if someone had closed a bottle nearby, he put himself into a defensive stance and waited for a few seconds. Then, he would relax and explain, after seeing Carmen's worried gaze on him, that he thought someone was about to throw a bomb at them, but that in reality, it was someone putting a cap back into a soda bottle. Of course, Carmen didn't say anything in reply.

Nico also avoided touching any surface for a long time, including his cardboard, flipping it around and holding it at different parts when he carried it. What if he was like her? An escapee from an asylum with weird customs? He was quite the mystery.

As Carmen was deep in thought trying to figure him out, he went to a trash can nearby and produced a backpack. Afterwards, he approached Carmen slowly as he started taking something out of it. She raised her arms to cover her face preparing for the worse when she felt the surface of soft plastic close to her arm. "Take this. I think it'll help."

Carmen opened her eyes and realized he was handing a bottle of water to her. Without question, she snatched the bottle off his hands and drank it all in one shot. She had forgotten she hadn't eaten or drunk anything after the escape. As she gulped it down, he smirked sweetly at her. While that was the only thing she could drink right then and there, she couldn't avoid feeling that the taste of said water was different. It felt pure. It even reminded her of her old days back in Estú and her days before the asylum. The water they had served her at Sanatorium was pretty sour compared to this one.

"*Desgraciadamente* this is all I can offer you for now. I'm turning in, and you should, too," he gently said as he covered himself with his cardboard. "If you need help, just wake me up. This place is dangerous." Then, he fell deeply asleep. Notwithstanding, unlike him, Carmen couldn't sleep as she could only look at him, waiting for something to happen.

Maybe he would reveal his true face and his true intentions once she was dormant. However, all she saw were his feet performing some sporadic movements from time to time, as if he was tripping over something in his dreams. Did he ever stop moving? As she watched over him, she remembered that it was the middle of Quintillus, or the beginning of summer. This notion was further reinforced after judging the temperature. Given that she had lost track of dates and seasons, she couldn't even begin to fathom how long she had been locked up in Sanatorium. While her thoughts ran around her head in circles, as well as plans to escape this newfound savior out of pure fear, her eyes slowly closed, and she joined Nico in dreamland. As she slept, she could just watch the murder of her son once again in the depths of her mind, unable to stop it. Jason watching her perform it with empty eyes.

Jason...

Where was he? Was he aware of her escape? Had she only confirmed her guilt by doing so? It didn't matter. The judge had decided her guilt a long time ago, however, it wasn't clear for Carmen if she was guilty before his eyes. This also made her wonder about how the world saw her at this point. Maybe she would eventually be able to get a hold of newspapers or something that would tell her of the actual situation, but, before that, she had to flee this Mizelas youngster. Something about him terrified her, albeit she couldn't tell what it was. Indeed, she didn't know him, and still had many questions about him. Nonetheless, the only most important question wandering around her mind was regarding his attitude: the way he reached out to her at Sanatorium, and in the basement, his firm grip when he helped her up. The determination he portrayed all over his face. Perhaps he wasn't all that bad, but until his true intentions and past would reveal to her, she would remain cautious of him. *Better safe than sorry*, she thought, that much she could promise herself.

Good luck with that...

The sun hit her face in the morning, waking her up abruptly. Carmen slapped her face softly to verify if she was truly awakened, or alive. She was fearful of checking her body for possible intrusions made by Nico, yet none were to be found. Subsequently, she quickly looked around and found him next to her, exercising and practicing what looked like martial arts. He seemed extremely focused on his endeavor, ignoring her completely, breathing deeply and avoiding the sun she hadn't seen in so long. Even though gray clouds covered it instantly afterwards, it was nice for a change.

This spectacle prompted new questions to arise in her mind: Where to go afterwards? How to survive? As much as her fear of Nico acted like a strong deterrent from escaping, it was that same fear that allowed her mind to ignore these kinds of future predicaments. Thus, she concluded that if she got away at least she would be alive to worry about those issues later. Therefore, on the fifth morning, after receiving junk food from Nico--regardless of where he had gotten hold of it--she felt well enough to finally make her move.

So, Sanatorium's food was nutritious, all in all, she thought after only eating a chocolate bar for an entire day and feeling weakness go through her body like an electric current.

The first task to do was to get away from Nico without him noticing and then out of Drift Row. Besides the countless stories she had heard about this district, she was also aware that not even the police dared venture to this forsaken place which was, on its own merit, good and bad for her current situation: if the police were to enter the district and find her, they would take her right back to Sanatorium while, on the other end, criminals would just... she'd rather not think about it. She still remembered the statistics she found once online and how much danger the Drift Row meant, prompting her to recall how her 'assigned nurses' had called Nico 'filthy wetfeet'. She couldn't say she hadn't heard the term before, but she was aware of what it meant. No wonder Nico would live here out of all places. Even if he looked like a fine young man at first glance, Carmen didn't want anything to do with any of it. His crime was quite evident.

Later that night, she covered herself with her cardboard

and pretended to fall deeply asleep. As she did so, the breeze of the night reminded her of those times that seemed so distant now. The vineyard, her father, her servants. She cried soundlessly at this mere thought. Why were these thoughts in her head at a moment like this? After touching her shaved head, she remembered once more what her reality was now. How even *that* had been taken away from her. However, time was of the essence. Nico was in deep sleep when she packed the little food they had in a paper bag and left the place. Nevertheless, before leaving the 'den', she couldn't avoid looking back at her savior one last time. Whatever his intentions might have been, he had still done something nobody else had. Thus, before leaving, she thanked Nico in a low whisper before stepping out of her new 'comfort zone'.

Wandering down the dark alleys of Drift Row at night suddenly didn't feel like a good idea. She could feel eyes everywhere, prying on her. Waiting. Noises in the dark that frightened her. She could only remember she had already been to Hell itself, trying to scare these fears away. *This is nothing compared to those days…* Or so she thought.

While walking at a hurried pace, and looking at every direction, she stumbled upon a bearded man. She couldn't tell how this had happened as she hadn't seen him coming. She couldn't make out his features right away either due to the poor city lighting. Without talking, she quickly distanced herself from the man and tried to keep going her way, but he grabbed her by the arm and pulled her against his chest.

"This one's a looka! Havin' fun wi' somethin' so tasty… I can' wait!" he said. To Carmen's horror, there were two more men lurking in the dark. She tried to fight back just to get a punch to the face, so hard, that made her fall flat on the floor. She hadn't noticed, but she had now a black eye. As she tried to get back on her feet, one of these men took her paper bag and tossed it away while the one whom she had stumbled upon held her wrists down. All of them were licking their lips eager in anticipation. They seemed to have never seen a woman before as their lusty gaze quickly gave away their intentions.

She remembered then why this had been a bad idea. The most likely reason why Nico had chosen that place as their hideout... so that she couldn't escape. These men, or savages, as Carmen was thinking of them, were quick to speak out their minds. As they did so, memories of Tom and Joe came to her mind. She had escaped one Hell just to get into another. If she was lucky, they would kill her right after their deed. The feeling of regret started to fill her mind given that, even if Nico happened to be a terrorist, or a psychopath, or whatever he could be, he had never lifted a finger on her. It was then that she realized that she needed him more than ever. The uncertainty of the situation she was in left no room for any other sort of hope. However, she knew deep inside her hope was beyond realistic. She knew this would be her last mistake. Thus, she just closed her eyes to prepare for what was to come when she heard a foot hitting the face of the man on top of her, who in turn fell to the floor, releasing her, and covering his face with both hands. She was afraid of opening her eyes, but she could feel clearly how these men were being hit as their groans of pain entered her ears. Once she fell a third body hit the floor, she opened her eyes. As she was breathing heavily, the sensation of hands holding her wrists still in her mind, she saw Nico there. His face showed slight anger. *I guess this is the last nail in my coffin*, she thought as the possibility of begging for mercy appeared as an unlikely option to succeed. But, why bother? It was over anyways. She just sat there in silence, with her eyes closed, waiting for the final blow.

"¡¿*Estás loca?!* What's the matter with you?" said Nico in a burst of rage as he approached her. Carmen only stayed still, with her eyes closed, waiting for her punishment and termination. Nevertheless, he continued his reprimand in a calm voice this time to her surprise. "Look, I know you don't want to be near me. But let me help you, at least for now. I was once in a similar situation. If you wanna leave, that's fine, I won't stop you. But, let's just stick together for now. I won't harm you; I promise." The youngster extended his right hand to her again, just like in the asylum, just like in the basement.

Carmen looked up at him perplexed as he didn't seem bothered at all by her betrayal, and his burst of anger had been quenched as quickly as it had started. What was his deal?

Carmen didn't reach back to him. Instead, she remained seated on the street in silence, looking down and trying to assimilate what had just happened. Lifting her eyes just to see around her, realizing the men who had attacked her were just unconscious and breathing. He hadn't killed them. Why?

As she pondered on such matters, she heard his steps going away from her, further and further. These sounds made her heart ache, making her cover her chest with both of her hands. She looked up at Nico. *My only chance... I can't let it go...* she thought as she extended her left hand towards him. This realization changed something in her chest as she now felt as if something had started to blossom within it. A sort of rage. A motivation. Her family appeared before her very eyes within the shadows trailing after Nico. Juan Fernando smiled at her as a knife came from a wall shadow and shattered his image. A crime she'd allow to remain unpunished.

"Wait!" Nico stopped short as soon as Carmen finished uttering this word. "I'm sorry... I just don't know who to trust in anymore... I'm too scared... I swear! Please help me! Please! I beg of you!"

He turned around and looked into her eyes. He showed her a gentle smile and said in a soft voice. "Like I said, we're in the same boat." He walked back to her and extended his right hand towards her, once again. This time, however, she took it without a doubt. This time, she wouldn't let it go.

"Carmen... my name is Carmen..." she finally said once Nico had helped her up.

"*Bonito nombre,*" replied Nico, still smiling. Once Carmen was back on her feet, he picked up the paper bag and its contents splattered on the floor. "It seems we got food until tomorrow. We'll be fine. *No te preocupes.*"

Carmen couldn't hold it any longer. If she was to trust him, she had to know. "W-why are you... you know... being chased?"

He looked into the sky for a few seconds. Then, he replied, his voice showered in sorrow. "I'm sorry, but I don't want you getting involved in all this mess, so… I can't tell you." He looked into her eyes and continued. "Let's go home. This place gives me the creeps." He took her hand and guided her back to the bridge.

Carmen, however, couldn't stop thinking about it, especially since, whatever his deal was, she was already involved in it. Besides, there was what his gaze had given away. Those eyes, glassy, noticeable even under poor lighting, told her there was a sad story going on, apart from hers, that was, as that question alone had seemed to break him apart. She then realized that she was crying, unconsciously, when thinking about her past, too, on their way 'home'. Once they made it back, Nico lied on his cardboards and started sleeping right away. He had an expression of peace on his face which somehow awoke envy in Carmen. How could he sleep so peacefully in a place like that? Most importantly, how did he know she had fled and where? Those questions floated in her mind but flew away when she saw that, as usual, he was moving his feet as he slept. Carmen didn't understand it, but it was terrifying and secure at the same time as she felt safe, ironically, within the most dangerous district of the city. Even if this meant that she wouldn't be able to escape him for the time being…

The following days were pretty much the same routine. Nico would go to the streets to beg for money after performing acrobatics, or juggling, near traffic lights. Carmen's eyes delighted at his performances at first, until they became quite monotone. She would usually wait for him around a nearby corner for fear of being alone or attacked under the bridge. Still, she knew that under all that newfound peace, she was yet his prisoner, even if he wouldn't watch her every move nor seemed to care at all. It was as if he was always in control, even when he wasn't nearby. This feeling became ever-present when she saw how he could feel even when others would try to sneak under the bridge in order to sleep, or other things, during the middle of the night, and how he would kick them out by word, or by force. After seeing such actions around her as a part of her day-to-day life, she realized she was learning about a world hidden to her, as well as her hidden self.

Even though they would initially speak in a mixture of Estúan and Stonian, this came to pass as Carmen's nostalgia dominated the environment in that regard, so they spoke in Estuan. Nico didn't mind, as he claimed that one could only be truly oneself if speaking in their mother tongue, something onto which, over time, Carmen came to agree with as well. Nico explained it in a simple fashion. "When someone says 'I love you' to you, what do you feel?" he asked one day out of the blue. Carmen wasn't sure what he was talking about at first when he made it clear right after, giving her no time to answer. "And when someone says 'te amo' to you, what do you feel?" Carmen felt like dismissing the subject altogether as some bullshit a teenager with too much free time had just made up. However, she soon realized that there was indeed a difference. While the first one felt alright, the second one really struck her to her core. She guessed that was because their language was a part of themselves as they grew up, fusioning their minds to it. Curiously enough, their accents were radically different to the point where even someone who didn't speak Estúan would be able to tell that they weren't from the same country. Nico's neutral accent somehow fascinated Carmen, although he didn't see anything special about it himself. Sometimes he would propose phrases that made sense in Estúan into Stonian, like "I'll be your shoe," for "I'll accompany you." Carmen found it awkward at first, but that was the only entertainment she could have as reality often hit her hard. She would often despair and cry incessantly out of nowhere, rendering Nico powerless and unable to tell what to do to calm her down. Nonetheless, this would change a month later as Carmen was having another one of her usual breakdowns.

She looked into emptiness, with tears flooding her face when Nico approached her and seated next to her. "Carmen… I wanted you to know that you have beautiful hair…" he said shyly. Carmen looked at him perplexed as she touched her head unconsciously and remembered its existence. She had been living in Sanatorium without it for so long, and without any mirrors available under the bridge, that she had hardly even noticed it was back. Even though it was still quite short, at least the police would have a harder time looking for her. "And also, I wanted to know what happened… you know… to you?" Nico put his hands in his pockets as he tried to avoid Carmen's gaze. She smiled softly, and after breathing deeply, she started her tale. Something she needed to take out of her chest for a long time. As she spoke, her cheeks moistened even further with a river of tears. Nico didn't know whether to approach her or not, or if this had been a good idea to begin with. Eventually, Carmen finished her tale but kept on crying regardless of any words of consolation the youngster could come up with. Nico's eyes glistened over time as she groaned in pain; without any other solution in his head for this situation, he simply hugged her. As nobody had done that in ages, Carmen answered in kind.

"Thank you…" she said after wiping her tears away with her left arm.

"You know…? I thought you were truly insane at first," Nico continued while chuckling slightly. "I'm glad that's not the case. I had to deal with a lot of tension being on guard the whole time down here…"

Carmen understood that was why he was acting in such a wary fashion towards her. Nonetheless, he was always acting in that fashion, even when not around her, also at the traffic lights doing his acrobatics. "And… what about you? I opened myself to you… so…" she said, realizing she was using one of those made-up expressions translated from her mother language. She meant she had told her past and her secrets to him. Needless to say, Nico understood it. He opened his mouth, hesitant, with words about to leave his tongue when his face grew grim. "I don't wanna get you involved in this. I only wanted to help you out," he said while strolling to and fro. "But, since that wouldn't be fair, I'll let you know some things… like… hmmm…"

"Like… why are you helping me?" completed Carmen. Her greatest question came along with her greatest curiosity. "You said we were in the same boat," she remembered back then in the dark alley where she had been saved by him. "What did you mean?"

Nico's eyes once more evaded hers. He turned around showing his back to her. "We're both being chased around by *certain* people. That's what I meant. Nothing else, nothing more." His sudden shyness contrasted greatly with his overall general attitude. He had never shown fear, even against bigger guys than him. Whether they were older, younger, or had better arguments. For the first time in a lifetime, she felt her age to be a factor here. She was older than him, and it pleased her to possess at least some sort of power over him, even if it was insignificant. She remembered when her body used to be in the same position as Nico's slouched posture, while the tone in his voice shivered in weakness. Thus, she pressed on.

"Why would you do all of this for me?" said Carmen now firmly as Nico's words refused to come out. She could tell he was trying to come up with an answer, though.

"I know how it feels," he finally answered, his back still turned to her. "I don't want anyone to have to pass through the same thing." Nico turned around and looked into her eyes. "I can promise you that much… that… I'll do everything in my power to help you out."

"Look, you didn't know my past just until now. How do you expect me to believe that you're doing this out of the goodness of your heart? Don't I deserve an explanation at least?" she said, standing her ground.

Nico's face showed a certain amount of guilt. "What happened was… I was running away from those men when I stumbled upon you… and-nd… and… I saw what those bastards were about to do to you… and… I just… couldn't allow it… Let's just say that my heart couldn't take it." He was looking down now. Somehow, his words sounded sincere. He was a teenager, after all.

"What's your true name?" she pressed on. "I gave you mine." She was enjoying this, especially being able to take his power away to the point of making him stutter. His almighty captor now seemed a small child trying to avoid getting hurt by simple words.

"I'm… Nicolás… Marqués…" he continued, still shyly. "That's why… you may call me Nico…"

"Why did you rescue me? You could've just knocked out the guards, released me and left the place without any further thought." She continued while sitting straight with her arms crossed. She was so close, and so far at the same time…

"I-I… couldn't avoid it… I-I knew those bastards would've tried again… I-I've seen plenty of people like them…" explained Nico, having a hard time speaking. "Those people… never change…" he continued bitterly, clenching his fists. This latter reaction took Carmen's recently gained power down a notch. "You were in a disastrous state… I couldn't leave you there… and… well… I felt alone… and-"

"That's the true reason after all this heroism of yours? You needed a woman?" Carmen answered, also bitterly. "That's despicable!" she reprimanded in anger.

"If that's what you think, leave. You're free to do so. I told you that from the beginning," he answered furiously to Carmen's surprise. His reaction finished the last bit of power Carmen had gained. He knew that she was at his mercy, that she couldn't leave him. Not like this, with half the police force looking for her. She was dancing on the palm of his hand, and she hated him for it. Thus, she fell silent.

Later that night, after a long day of work, he picked up his cardboard and slept further away from her. Even though he had never tried anything, his overall attitude made Carmen feel guilty this time. She understood that he could've had his way with her if he had wanted to a long time ago. *Maybe this is good,* she thought as this gave her some breathing room. At least the illusion of having gained more freedom from her captor, most notably since she didn't know if his attitude served him to avoid the question of telling her about his past, or if it was a power move. And yet, contrary to what she felt as soon as she turned in, with him further away from her, she didn't feel as safe anymore.

In the following days, Carmen evaluated his behavior towards her and the rest of the world instead of just watching over his habits and thinking about escaping. Like most scientists did to catch a specimen off guard, she had to study her prey in all contexts. Whether he wanted a woman or not, it didn't matter. He had never touched her against her will, so far, and he had shared the little food he could get with her without asking for anything in return. She had seen such tactics in other men to get into her pants, even more so back when she ran the company. Yet, he didn't seem all that interested in that aspect of life. Something more important occupied his mind, and she had to know what that was. Thus, even if he was still pissed off at her, she decided to press on one more time.

"You said that... you would never allow me to go through the same experience as you did..." she started the talk when he was cooking instant soup with boiled water. He seemed to try to ignore her, but she placed herself in front of him. "What's your end goal, Nico? What do you want to do?"

He seemed reluctant at first, focused on his food. So, she approached her face to his and looked into his eyes, carrying on with her attack. "I have to save my parents. That's all I'm telling you," he uttered casually in return. Carmen could feel those words hid some anger in them, as well as guilt and regret.

"I'm sorry about what I said before... when I said you were... despicable. I guess no one likes to be alone," she said condescendingly. "You know what? I'm feeling better now. I think I'll be on my way so that you may continue this mission of yours."

Nico's anger turned into surprise and worry. "What are you gonna do? No one will help you out... at least according to what you told me. You got nowhere to go. Are you sure you're okay?"

"I have a friend... I think she might be able to help me..."

she said trying to sound convincing, probably more to convince herself than to convince him. Hopefully, Kelvin had lied about Eliana all those months ago, or at least, that's what Carmen wanted to believe. "So, don't worry about me, I got this covered."

"I'll go with you then," he said after finishing his soup in one sip, almost burning his tongue in the process, hardly containing the pain. "I'll be your shoe until you meet your friend."

Carmen couldn't avoid showing her surprise. "Why are you doing this? You don't have to."

"I... just donno... I guess this is part of my promise," he explained with a slight smirk. Whatever his explanation might be, deep inside, Carmen was glad he wanted to come along. For some reason, she had predicted he would do it. Without realizing it, it seemed she had learned what buttons to press to get what she wanted out of this seemingly innocent teenager.

"Wouldn't that deviate you from the saving of your parents?" Carmen insisted in a preoccupied voice. The horns of the cars around them and the polluted river beside them orchestrated her words.

Nico took a deep breath and continued. "If there's anything my dad told me, it was to always keep my word," he explained. "Let's just say... it makes me feel better." He had kept some animosity in his voice, and yet, there was unmistakably some truth to his claims. He would help her out of selfishness, or was he showing selfishness as a way to avoid showing weakness to her? Even if she already knew him more or less, it was hard to tell. They had been together under that damn bridge for one month and a half now. At this point, she even knew their 'neighbors', and far from feeling a prisoner or a foreigner, she felt like one of them. Indeed, they were quite a big family. They treated them as such, and it wasn't for free. Carmen could tell ever since she had witnessed, on more than one occasion, how Nico had defended some of these 'tenants' near the bridge against gangsters and such folk.

There was an old man called Old Joe, or one of the nearby

bums in other words, who had grown very fond of Nico. When asked about it, he told Carmen that Nico had saved his bacon from some kids who were beating him up a few weeks ago. As this event had happened twice, he decided to 'move' near Nico's 'home'. It seemed the Mizelas youngster was quite popular among these people who saw in him some sort of protector. These hobos came from all sorts of walks of life and origins. As word spread around the neighborhood like wildfire, more and more of them started to concur near the bridge. Over time, they started to call Nico under one nickname, and one alone, with a sense of respect.

"Hey Immigrant!" said Old Joe in a manner of greeting as Nico walked back home, only when he was sober. "How's it going?!" This had become a common occurrence, mostly when they learned Nico wasn't a Panthean, but a sub-Panthean. In other words, from one of the kingdoms to the north of the U.K.P.

"Doesn't it bother you when *those* men call you names?" Carmen asked one day when they were boiling water.

"Well… I can't say I dislike it. It's the truth after all. Besides, so far all I've learned is that not everyone can be an immigrant. Even though I wish I wasn't, I cannot avoid but to feel some pride in it," he answered with a sincere smile. "Someday, I won't be an immigrant anymore, but until then I think I'll just stick with it."

"So… you planning to go home?" Carmen added out of curiosity. She had thought about that at some point in her life, too. Going back to Estú was still a possibility.

Nico took the boiling water and poured it into two glass bottles he had managed to find. The best way they had to disinfect them was that method, unfortunately. "I must confess that my parents had planned for an eventual lawful residence here, like many others. It was either that or to stay home and face an uncertain future." He shook the bottles and emptied the dirty water on the river. Nico's crime had been quite evident ever since that day at Sanatorium. It didn't take Carmen long to confirm what his crime was, but she had never had the nerve to ask him directly about it, especially due to their recent dispute.

"By home, you mean?"

"I'm from Peruvia," he continued with a nostalgic voice. "I assume you're from Estú," he said without any doubt in his voice. Carmen's accent was way too evident, so there was little surprise there. In the case of Nico, his neutral accent was hard to place. Something that still fascinated Carmen after all this time, even if she now knew the answer.

"And… you want to go back?" pursued Carmen. Nico closed the bottles after washing them, adjusting the bottle caps back to their respective places.

"Who doeshn't wanna go backsh…?" said a voice approaching them. It was Old Joe stumbling on his way there. He seemed to have drunk quite the usual, or in other words, eight bottles of watered-down beer. "I'm from the northsh ofsh thish countrysh… I…" he stopped as if something else had come up in his mind. "I needsh helpsh, man…"

Nico wasn't surprised. This happened from time to time. "The same guys?" he asked after placing the empty bottles near his cardboard bed.

"N-no… big sharksh… I owesh money… to 'em…" the old man continued without being able to prevent signs of shame showing on his face. "They'll killsh me… helpsh me… pleashe…"

Nico stood up after taking a deep breath. "Alright, let's go. I hope I can do it properly this time," said the Immigrant, as he liked to be called, and followed Joe out of his 'base of operations', as Nico liked to call his home under the bridge. At such a sight, Carmen couldn't avoid criticizing Old Joe and the other bums for taking advantage of Nico's good nature. At the same time, she couldn't avoid feeling some guilt as she was doing exactly the same thing. In the case of the hobos, they had clearly moved near him to use him as protection, which ironically was something she was about to do as well in order to go to Eliana's house. *Those shameless assholes… they aren't being chased by the entire country like me… I need Nico more than them…* she often thought.

In truth, Nico enjoyed helping others. Maybe there was some selfishness to it for him. Maybe not. The lines between selfishness and generosity had become blurry when applied to Nico long ago. Fortunately for Carmen, the protection Nico was granting Old Joe and his fellow hobos would be short-lived as, contrary to what she thought, Nico explained one afternoon, the week before, that he had stayed under the bridge for so long just because. In the end, there wasn't a need for him to move out, unless necessary. In reality, he'd be leaving soon. Carmen knew that, in truth, he had done so only for her sake. If his parents were his main objective, why would he stay there for no apparent reason?

He eventually confirmed Carmen's thoughts one week later, mostly due to her undying insistence on the subject. "Look, my initial plan was to investigate this city and find clues as to where my parents could be. But... let's just say that I've been spotted by *some* people... and the idea was to leave this place in a week, not two months," said Nico while hanging up their clothes so that they dried. "So, hopefully, we find this friend of yours. I fulfill my promise to you and we part ways."

Carmen frowned upon hearing that last sentence. *That's exactly what I wanted, right?* she thought. Then, she simply shrugged it off as, along with Nico, they reviewed their current progress regarding her plan to see Eliana. For the past two weeks, they had been observing the police patrol schedules and patterns. Old Joe and the others had been quite useful for this task as the information they had was a shared encyclopedia about the underworld of Las Esbirras. Carmen would've never guessed that the most primitive means of communication, the word of mouth, was so efficient in that environment as the homeless men of the city were now their intelligence network. Nico had his doubts about it, though. As incredibly sweet as he could be towards others, he could also be considerably cold when stating his honest opinion. For him, according to what Carmen had told him, Eliana was dead, and he said it without mincing words. Carmen's sensitivity to the matter came out as soon as it happened, the reason why Nico had to hug her after noticing his mistake, every time. At any rate, Carmen's logic also pointed to Nico's conclusion, even if her heart wouldn't agree to it.

At the same, something started to change inside of her. As she never left any favors unreturned, a lesson she learned the hard way through her father, she felt compelled to give something to Nico in return for all his help. She could remember how she had learned this lesson as if it was yesterday, back in the days of her childhood. Of course, she wouldn't tell anyone that, when she turned seven-years-old, she had received a gift from her closest friend--and the one she was looking for now--Eliana. It wasn't long for that gift to become one of Carmen's favorites. A doll she had never seen before; the shape of her face was so strange that it deeply fascinated her, triggering her fascination for things she couldn't understand for the rest of her life. However, young Carmen thought too highly of herself. Thus, when the time came for her to give a present to Eliana, she decided to give her something of lower quality, that was, an old book she had found in the attic. When she showed it to her father and was about to wrap it up, he angrily forced her to give her the most expensive doll she had in her room, instead. Ever since then, Carmen learned that she wasn't in a higher position regarding other people and that every favor had to be repaid at some point.

Are you sure that's all? That's quite... anticlimactic...

I guess I should start by treating him better... she thought as memories of the relationship between him and her came to her mind. So far, he had been the only breadwinner of the two. If it wasn't for him, she would've starved to death a long time ago as she didn't do anything to help him. She quickly assumed it was because she had been used to being treated like some sort of queen her entire life. Despite herself feeling that she was the same as her employees, she had always been served, and without realizing it, she was acting the same way with Nico. He, of course, didn't seem to realize, or care, even if, unconsciously, he was a servant for her. Was the fact that he was a man an excuse to turn him into some sort of scapegoat for her recent horrible experiences with his sex? Did she, for a second, think that he had to bear with the responsibility of those who had hurt her? Was he responsible for her well-being as a result? Carmen knew her mind would say no to all those questions, but her heart would beg to differ. She had never had the chance to let off some steam regarding her anger. The cold way in which she treated Nico would have prompted anyone else to think she was mad at him for some reason. It wouldn't be easy, but this had to change. She wouldn't be just another hobo, like Old Joe, asking for protection for free. *My payback will happen before you know it brat!* she often thought.

Then, before she knew it, Nico had come back home. Unscathed, again, which never ceased to amaze her. How did he do that? She was aware he trained every day for at least an hour in a form of martial arts she couldn't identify, but that didn't mean he was supposed to be invincible or untouchable. At first, she assumed it was due to his fighting skills, but the more she saw him fight, the more she thought there was something else about him. Something extraordinary. Nevertheless, that was his secret, and his alone, no matter how hard she'd try to pry into it.

"Thanksh… you're the Immigrantsh!" said Old Joe before drinking another sip of beer. "How… can Ish pay yoush?"

"Don't worry, it was nothing," replied Nico as he folded his cardboards for the night.

"C'mon man! You shouldsh comesh with ush one of theshe daysh…" said the old man before leaving the place stumbling around, bottle in hand. It was as if he had completely forgotten what he had been doing a second ago. His erratic behavior worried Carmen beyond belief at first, until she got used to him and his seemingly unharmful visits. His smell of piss and alcohol often bothered her, but not to the same level as Nico as he would usually plug a piece of cardboard up his nose whenever Old Joe came too close to him. She laughed when she realized he always kept that plug around just for the old hobo's visits. However, there was something else about Nico's senses Carmen couldn't really understand. Whatever his nose was, it could detect several things, and the same went for his eyes. On certain occasions, he even knew how much alcohol percentage Old Joe had drunk just by smelling him before he had even arrived at their home with phrases like "again with the 40% one." Carmen thought he was joking at first, but it all changed when Old Joe emptied one of his bottles and forgot it there. The percentage matched.

"What?" asked Nico, looking at her. Without knowing it, she had been staring at him since he had arrived. In response to her intent gaze, he quickly observed his own body. "Did I get some sort of injury?" he asked in a calm fashion while looking at his body. She knew he knew there was no injury at all.

"It's just that… I will pay you back," she finally asserted. "I swear I will help you find your parents and get you back on track. Also…" Carmen continued, having a hard time pronouncing what she was about to. "I… I… I will help you out from now on. I don't like to be a freeloader."

Nico looked at her, perplexed, and yet, he smiled. "Thank you, but like I mentioned before, I can't get you *involucrada* in this. I'm helping you because I don't want to see you end up like me." He was looking down now as if remembering something. "I appreciate it, nonetheless. It's time to go back to sl-"

"No!" Carmen pressed on. "I swore I'd help you and I will! Whether you like it or not!"

If it weren't for the serious moment there, Carmen would've burst in laughter at Nico's poker face. "Eh?" he managed to reply, looking directly into her eyes this time. She felt as if a tiger was looking into her mind, imposing his presence before her very core. "Look, I don't know what you think this is, but this isn't a *juego*. This is MY mess. I'll solve it as I see fit. Clear?"

Nico returned to his cardboard when Carmen interrupted him midway.

"No!"

"What do you mean 'no'? What do you plan to do? Get killed just to help me out?" he said in a skeptical voice. At least a part of him was listening and considering this alliance, even if it sounded like a joke.

"Once I get my life back… I will use all my money and influence to help you. That much I can do!"

"You know it's very *difícil* for you to ever get your life back, right?" he fired back. His cold honesty, kicking in once more. "Next to impossible. Don't get pills you can't swallow."

"If I can't get my life back… then I'll help you out with whatever else I can do… I'll stick with you until you make it, then. Deal?"

"Could we talk about this later? I'm really tired…" yawned the Immigrant, clearly wanting out already. Hard as the truth might be, she knew what he meant. She was next to useless compared to him. Albeit the same couldn't be said about her knowledge after years of reading and writing, she had never experienced reality as such a hit to the face, rendering her wisdom useless either way. Still, similarly to the reason why she had struggled so much to make Juan Fernando's cake on his birthday, even if it didn't help much, she knew there was something she could still do. The same thing she had done during all those years in what felt like a lifetime ago.

"Would you… teach me how to fight?" she finally demanded, shyly.

"Why?" Nico replied after a moment of silence, moving his body around to find the most comfortable position. "You'll see your friend soon enough, won't ya?"

"Well… because… I don't think we'll see her… at all…"

Nico sighed. "You weren't as hopeless as I thought. You knew it all along?" he replied, cold as usual.

"As long as there's hope, I won't be certain of it. She's my only card out of this mess," Carmen explained, feeling tears about to come out. This time, however, Carmen withheld them. "If she's gone… then there's nothing else for me to do…"

"There's always a way," affirmed Nico. "Now, please shut up…"

With that said, the Immigrant closed his eyes, moving his

feet ceaselessly, as usual. Carmen obliged. *I guess you might be right,* she thought. As she covered herself with her cardboard sheets, she couldn't stop looking at him. How could his face be so peaceful while moving his limbs around like a madman while sleeping? She couldn't prevent her fascination from controlling her neck into keeping the same position, allowing her to look at Nico directly. At the same time, her mind had several questions regarding the campaign she would soon begin. Something deep inside told her the end result beforehand. It seemed she would need Nico's lessons on martial arts, after all. It was evident by now that Eliana would most likely be dead. Sure enough, she had struggled to visit her unpleasant memories back at Sanatorium to see if everything matched: Definitely, Eliana's visits had stopped in a snap of a finger and she never did any effort to contact her again. For Carmen, such an attitude was unthinkable and had never happened before, not even when Eliana had been angry at her for any reason. Besides, if she were alive, Carmen would've known through any means by now. Something felt terribly wrong.

The next day, they departed. Eliana should live near Las Esbirras downtown, as Carmen remembered at least. They had been told by their 'wandering' allies that there was some law enforcement around the area, so much, that not even they got close enough to the desired address because of it. Thanks to Old Joe, who had managed to give them his spare clothes as disguises, quite dirty by the way, they looked just like him. Your regular Joes, like Nico liked to put it. Even though the heat of summer was bothersome with this attire, it wasn't like they had a choice. The stink of alcohol was also part of this improvised disguise with which Nico seemed to be greatly troubled. "I hate this pungent smell!" he complained as they kept walking in plain daylight. Carmen simply laughed and realized how wrong she had been as she had always assumed boys had a greater resistance to bad odors. It seemed she was completely wrong.

"It's just around the corner," said Carmen in a seemingly

encouraged voice and a smile upon her face. It was as if the pain and bad times had never happened to her. Nico couldn't avoid getting her happiness to rub off on him, prompting him to smirk slightly. As they approached Eliana's home under the gaze of several officers around them, who didn't seem to worry about their presence, nor to expect them, Carmen could hardly contain her excitement. "Once we see her, I'll help you out Nico, you just wa-" Carmen stopped talking and stood there, frozen. Speechless.

The apartment her best friend had once pridefully showed her was now completely burned. The outer walls were charcoal black when they had been white before, its insides in full display in the same color. It was easy to tell no one was living there. However, the rest of the building seemed to be perfectly normal. How was that possible? "The fire didn't spread at all… this isn't possible…" she muttered, unable to look away. "No… they really did it…" She grasped her head with both hands trying to assess the situation. It didn't take long for her memory to kick in some words into her mind.

"… and the little rabbit burned…" she repeated unconsciously out loud, looking into the emptiness of the black walls in display. Nico looked at her, feeling her pain. "He… he said it… then… he wasn't messing around… no… no…" Carmen's broken voice crawled its way into the Immigrant who approached her to support her with his arms when she was, seemingly, about to collapse. Nevertheless, as he came to her aid, a man in a suit bumped into him. "Oh, I'm sorry," he said and kept going.

"It's okay," Nico replied humbly, covering his face with his right hand. Nonetheless, his eyes intently stared at a symbol on his arm.

"We gotta get outta here. The *tombos* are getting suspicious," he explained as he dragged Carmen out of view, back into the safety of the corner they had just turned around. Carmen couldn't take away her hands from her head while falling to her knees. "It seems *they* are also here. C'mon Carmen, we got no time to lose. Let's move," Nico whispered in a soothing voice, trying to pull her back to her feet. It was useless.

Such a pity... not!

"I'm sorry for what I'm about to do," said the Immigrant regrettingly to then slap Carmen across the face. This, indeed, made her react, still confused, but back to Earth. Nico took her hand and pulled her back on her feet, this time successfully. "*They* are onto us. We gotta go, now!"

"Why... why her? She hadn't done anything wrong... *¿por qué?*" Carmen mumbled to herself as she was guided out of sight by Nico. The crowds moving around at rush hour helped quite a bit in this regard. Once in a safe spot, a deserted terrain in the middle of the city, namely the 'Wasteland', or so Old Joe called it because of the abundance of junk it possessed, Nico helped Carmen sit down on top of some old tires. Her expression was still the same, frozen in time.

"This is worse than I thought..." said the Immigrant while looking around. "I guess I might have to help you all the way, after all." Nico let a deep sigh take hold before continuing. "It seems... you're already involved."

Carmen wasn't even listening to him, still trying to process how her last hope of regaining her life was now gone. It had actually been gone before she had even realized. If at least she knew where Eliana's body was, or where she had been buried. The fact that she didn't even know where her son was buried, either, added to Eliana's death, hit Carmen's very core. *I don't deserve to breathe... I don't deserve to be alive... It's all my fault...* she thought as she looked at Nico looking for an answer he couldn't provide. Thus, without realizing it, she took a piece of glass lying near her feet and prepared herself to slice her throat with it.

"What in the world are you doing?!" Nico's firm grip wouldn't budge from her wrist. Her blood now covered his hand as the glass had cut into her palm.

"Leave me alone!" she answered trying to commit to her purpose, in vain. Nico tightened his grip on her wrist until she dropped the piece of glass out of pain.

"I thought you wanted to fight. I thought you wanted to clear your name and get your life back... I guess I was wrong." The regret in the Immigrant was too evident. "I've always seen the easy way as the wrong choice. Nothing is easy, but that should never stop you. Living is for the brave, dying is for cowards."

"How would a kid like you know? You have no idea how I feel right now!"

Nico's tiger eyes set on Carmen's. It was all he needed to calm her down. *He knows...* thought Carmen, unable to look away. His eyes always reminded her that sometimes he would be a shy, weak teenager, and sometimes he was the strongest man she had ever known.

"I guess it's time for me to explain all of this..."

Carmen's eyes widened in surprise. "W-what do you mean?"

Nico looked at her as he produced a bottle of cheap vodka from one of the improvised pockets included in his hobo disguise and poured some of it on Carmen's wounded palm. "The question you asked last time. What's my end goal and why... let's just say that I have no right to be in this country... but there's more to it." Nico's words burned with bitterness, almost as much as the vodka disinfecting her wound. "Not the wisest choice for anyone to do. Guess we were too desperate at that moment in time."

Carmen's body stiffened with fear. She felt as if she was his prisoner, once more. His strength was intimidating, making her feel powerless, and she hated it. However, she calmed herself down. She had often watched Nico perform some sort of meditation of his own, always at 3 p.m. in which he wouldn't talk, or even hear, anything for around fifteen minutes. Then, when he wasn't around, Carmen would imitate him. She didn't want to be seen by him as she felt it was embarrassing, so she always stopped doing it whenever she heard steps approaching their 'home'. She assumed it'd be pretty easy to keep one's mind blank, but it was harder than it looked. She wished she could use it in case of depression and despair as well. Maybe over time…

"Once we crossed the border with a *zorro* we had hired, into the Silencia Desert. There, he took out a gun and pointed it at us," Nico continued as he tore a piece of clothing from his t-shirt and bandaged Carmen. The wound burned more and more as the alcohol did its job. "There we wandered for about two days, looking for water. I'm not gonna play the victim, though. We knew what we were doing was wrong," said Nico hardening his face. "I just think we didn't deserve what would happen to us next."

Maybe his meditation is his secret to be so strong in moments like these, Carmen thought.

"A border patrol saw us and came for us," Nico stopped short for a few seconds, as if trying to dig out a treasure six feet under. "We were happy to be deported. Of course, that… that never happened."

Maybe over time I can use it for myself as well effectively, wondered Carmen.

"We were taken to their office, I think. That's when they separated us. They never explained a reason whatsoever. All I know is that they kept calling us "wethands." After crossing the border, through the river, I'm not surprised they call almost every Mizelas they see with that insult." Nico tightened the improvised bandage on Carmen's hand, a bit too tight, causing Carmen to moan in complaint, and sat down in front of her onto what looked like an old cardboard box. "They took me into what looked like a big white dome in the middle of the desert. There, there were many others like me, captured at the border. They wore gowns similar to the ones used by patients in a hospital. Of course, they made me wear one after taking away all of my belongings."

Carmen looked at him skeptically. Was he joking? That sounded like the Great Massacre that happened in Fiutic over 60 years ago. She couldn't avoid making a comparison between that and the U.K.P.'s history. For instance, drugs had been tested onto the poorest communities of the largest cities without them aware of it, as well as forced sterilizations that apparently everyone had forgotten about. Thus, conspiracies regarding the fall of the Twin Castles as an inside job didn't seem too far-fetched for Carmen as they had fallen at near free-fall speed, something completely absurd. Subsequently, if they had been using unlawful immigrants for illicit purposes, that was, people who had no way of defending themselves in a trial of law, as they had no documentation, was certainly possible. She limited herself to listen to his story, though.

"The thing is, once they put me into a cell, I was scared to no end," he paused, as if trying not to agitate himself. "Not because I was in that situation, but because of the people around me. They had been mutilated. Some lacked an arm, a leg, or their eyes. Or all their limbs altogether. And they were wearing the damn gown. I was wearing the damn gown. It wasn't hard to deduce who was next... if at least there would've been some sort of obstruction or obstacle to our foolishness..."

Carmen saw the terror in his eyes, as if he were reliving the exact same moment to the utmost precision. "Yo-you don't have to continue. It's okay," Carmen said in a soothing voice as she quickly realized it was the first time she was trying to comfort Nico. It had always been the opposite way for that month and a half under the bridge. "I think I get it. They were sick bastards." This latter declaration of her own also surprised her. Was Nico's way of talking rubbing off on her? She would have never even dreamed of using the word 'bastard' under any other circumstances. Nico simply ignored it, or most likely he didn't notice her doing it. He wasn't that keen to details after all, or at least *this* kind of details.

"I'm okay," he continued. "Thanks for worrying about me." Carmen didn't know what to say. This response had been quite sudden and unexpected. Was she worried about this kid? She simply looked down as he resumed his tale. "The thing is, it didn't take long for them to grab me out of my cell and strap me to a mobile bed. I simply... didn't wanna look. Later, they just injected me with a substance. My Stonian wasn't as good back then, but I understood that they intended to saw off my left foot. For some reason, they desisted, though." He took a deep breath in order to continue. "Instead, they threw me into a different cell with walls made of transparent plastic. There, day and night, they would test several things on me. They made small incisions while wiring electrodes on my head, or they shone the brightest light ever near my eyes to the point of leaving me near blindness. My ears didn't escape, either. After three days, I realized what they had done to me... and there was no going back."

He stopped. His face changed from relative easiness to sudden fear. In the blink of an eye, he took out a small piece of metal out of his hobo disguise, around his left shoulder. He then threw it on top of the nearby roof. "Quickly, we must go now!"

He took her unharmed hand and raced through the junkyard, pulling her with all his might.

"*They* are onto us! I thought we had gotten away! Damn it!" he said as he guided her throughout the city, looking right and left, up and down. She had never seen him like this, so vulnerable. It wasn't like last time when his shyness and lack of self-confidence rendered him vulnerable. This time, he was truly scared.

As they approached the bridge, Nico took an unexpected turn and took her into a dark alley. There, he broke a window and got into a building. Carmen couldn't believe her eyes. What in the world was going on? Before she could ponder about the answer, Nico pulled her violently inside a room.

"Nico, what's going on?" Carmen said as she looked at him in a serious gesture. Even though her depression had virtually disappeared thanks to the current situation, it still lingered within her head as her legs started to ache after running for so long. Nico was quite agitated himself, and that alone was starting to get on her nerves. Still, he wouldn't answer. Instead, he took her hand again and pulled her through the building. Ignoring her complaints, Nico guided her to the building's elevator, surprising everyone inside it, and rode it to the rooftop. Then, without notice, Nico took her near the edge of the edifice and pushed her onto the closest rooftop, right beside the one they were on. As both buildings were next to each other, he jumped onto it as well. Carmen felt as if she was in an action movie.

Nico pulled her behind some wooden boxes supporting what looked like a rooftop minigarden, hiding from the view anyone could get from the rooftop they had just been on. "Nico, what-" Carmen's protest was interrupted by Nico's index finger on her mouth. "*They* are coming," he said in a barely audible voice. "*They* are two floors away. *They* should be surfacing... right about... now."

Carmen was perplexed. How did he know that? Could he read minds or something? By the time she decided to ask him, she could hear them, too. They kicked open the door leading to the rooftop Nico and she had just been on. She stayed behind the box, not daring to take a peek due to the fear of getting spotted. Nico wasn't doing so either. "They are armed to the teeth. Don't move a muscle or it's over," he whispered in the lowest voice she had ever heard. Hearing him like this was too weird... reason more than enough to be truly scared.

"Fuck my life..." one of *them* said. "They got away..." he continued as his voice seemed more distant over time. Carmen was about to check on *them*, but Nico stopped her from standing up by grabbing her shoulder. She looked at him and found the terror in his eyes was quite visible. Nevertheless, that wasn't the reason why he was stopping her from looking. "*They* are still around... *they* know we're here," he whispered. Carmen could hardly believe him. She had clearly heard their voices and steps go away. He had to be insane or something. And yet, she could hardly blame him. By now, she knew better than to doubt the Immigrant.

"I'll take *them* out. Wait here," he said reassuringly. Then, silently, he left. She lost sight of him as soon as he turned around the corner of their 'hideout'. She could hardly hear his steps, but he was still there. How would he do it? He was completely exposed upon that rooftop. There was hardly any cover. What was his plan? It was amid her wondering that she heard a small tilting sound on the rooftop those men were supposedly on. Right afterwards, she heard *their* cries of pain as their bodies fell limp on the floor. She wanted to see, she wanted to witness the spectacle with all her might, and yet, she wouldn't dare disobey the Immigrant.

He should be done by now, she thought, eager to peek over the boxes. Unable to resist, she started to raise her head slowly when a hand touched her left shoulder from behind. She jumped out, scared, almost crying out loud, just to realize it was Nico. He seemed agitated. "Let's get outta here, now!" he commanded. He took her hand and guided her back to their former rooftop. There, she saw *them*. The men dressed in black suits, lying on the ground, their handguns still in their hands.

"Shouldn't we grab one of those?" asked Carmen before they headed downstairs, pointing at their guns. "They might be useful in the future," she continued. Nevertheless, Nico simply ignored her. Refusing to accept his indifference, and against all odds, she released her hand from his. "We must get at least one!" she said as she approached one of them and crouched to do it when Nico stopped her. When she turned around, she felt something pulling her skirt down.

"Fuck you... trash..." said the man in the black suit lying on the floor. "We'll get you for this..."

Nico didn't wait too long to knock him out by punching him across the jaw. His lack of hesitation to do so impressed Carmen as it was the first time she was witnessing it properly. "I thought I had hit him hard enough... whatever, let's go now!" Carmen tried to take one of the guns again, Nico stopped her once more by grabbing her by the left shoulder, though. He looked at her, serene as a summer night. "Sorry, but using those *armas* might kill someone," he explained. "Even if they're my enemies, I don't kill."

Carmen looked at him perplexed, once again, being unable to avoid admiring his attitude. Those men were onto him and wanted him dead. And for the looks of it, this chase of his had been going on for a long while. She wondered how he had not snapped yet. His assertive steps guiding her downstairs provided a quick answer to that question. *I guessed he's used to this by now*, she concluded.

Once back on the street, they continued their way home in a hurried pace as the night loomed on the horizon. After a few minutes in the city bus, they quickly made their way back to the Drift Row. Carmen couldn't prevent herself from pouting as, although she still resented Nico for not taking any gun with them, she respected it. However, she still couldn't understand it. Better safe than sorry, was it? Or… did Nico think of himself as some sort of hero? Maybe this whole 'Immigrant' thing was getting to his head. Heroes didn't exist in the real world, especially not in hers. What was he then? She simply erased these questions from her mind as they arrived at 'home'. Tired as they were, she just turned in without asking questions.

And once again, she couldn't sleep as she couldn't stop looking at him. Why had he been scared there out of all places? Those men were armed and all, but they didn't seem that terrifying. Maybe they didn't feel so threatening for her just because of Nico being there. Perhaps Nico had another motive to be scared she'd never know. Any theory she could come up with would be meaningless. And yet, she couldn't stop her brain from going in all sorts of directions. Thus, as his breathing accompanied his erratic movements while asleep, Carmen started to analyze how she felt back there at the rooftop, and right there down the bridge. Somehow Nico had managed to fascinate her even more as she could only draw a single conclusion after a million hypotheses: he was the strongest man, or teenager, she had ever met.

He made her feel protected and safe. Even back at the rooftop, she could hardly believe the lack of anxiety or stress she had felt during that situation. Nico had always been managing these aspects of their lives ever since they were there together. She realized how soundly she slept every night, even though she was right in the middle of the reddest zone of the city, alongside its most dangerous criminals. That mere thought invited other memories as she kept her eyes fixed on him…

She remembered how, once, Nico had caught a *sicario* at 3 a.m., sent by those loan sharks he would sometimes beat up. She found out when she saw blood on the floor and Nico explained it had come out of the attacker's nose. As she kept on looking at him, she couldn't avoid wondering if she had ever looked at Jason with the same fascination. Besides, she couldn't recall any similar experience, and Jason wasn't a man like Nico. Actually, she realized she had never known what Jason would've done in a situation like that one. Given her current situation, keeping in mind that he had simply abandoned her and betrayed the trust he, in theory, had for her, it wasn't that hard to figure out. Where was he? She couldn't care less at this point, but she couldn't avoid making comparisons. "I guess those fighting lessons won't be useless after all," she whispered to herself with a smirk on her face. As she was about to be defeated by her closing eyes into the oneiric realm, one question still pounded inside her head like the bell of a church at noon.

Why would having a weapon be so dangerous? They weren't the ones that killed, it was the people who used them, even though some cases could be the exception. Nico could be wise in several subjects, but he was still too naive and idealistic. He was still a teenager after all.

Carmen limited herself to smile at his foolishness as the land of the dreams claimed her thoughts… how could she ever kill another human being? It was ridiculous… How in the world could that ever happen? She wondered…

III

AND SMILE SHE DID... as she saw Hoover's brain splattered on the ground.

O'Connell couldn't believe his eyes as his entire force laid dead before him. The powerlessness started to build up inside of him as things like this were the kind he wished he wouldn't see again. The demon calmly turned around and started walking back towards the neighborhood, stepping over the dismembered corpses as if they were part of her everyday life. The only ones feeling the rain of anguish and anger were the occupants of the helicopter who could only watch. Thus, clenching his fists, O'Connell had only one more move left.

"You will fall today Black Cross!" yelled the War Hero with a megaphone. "Get ready the M134!" he commanded. Ryan Asprey was perplexed after hearing that choice. That was a military-grade weapon. What was it doing in a police chopper? He had seen it before departure but had turned a blind eye to it. He knew how regulations were regarding using such a weapon on civilians or criminals, even if these criminals happened to be monsters without empathy, but fear had gotten the better of him. So, slightly hesitant, Ryan quickly arranged the setup as the helicopter placed itself in position for a good aim. "I know we can do this, son," said O'Connell in a calm fashion, even though the young officer knew O'Connell was barely containing himself. If this gun couldn't shred this demon down to pieces, nothing else would. Of course, there was always *that* other last resort...

"Fire!"

The rain of lead didn't take long to reach the Dire One. Indeed, O'Connell kept firing furiously. Nonetheless, the demon wasn't taking any damage as, similarly to her recent fight, she covered herself with one of her crosses, rendering the projectiles useless. O'Connell smirked at such a sight along with Ryan: simple marble wouldn't hold out much longer. As the fired lead kept bathing the cross, both men's faces started to change as their confidence in success waned. It was as if the cross was made from some indestructible material, making the bullets bound onto it and falling on the ground.

"Ridiculous!" said O'Connell in a renewed rage. "What the fuck is that woman?!"

Ryan had never heard him swear before. He was losing it. "Get closer!" commanded the War Hero. The pilot looked at Ryan, confused. "But sir... we're hitting the target. There's no need to-"

"I said GET THE FUCK CLOSER TO HER! NOW!" O'Connell insisted. "I'll deal with her myself! She won't be able to deal with fire on two fronts! I'll get her from behind while you keep shooting from here! Just let me down on a rooftop and it will be finally over!" The pilot was still doubtful about the idea, that was, until O'Connell pointed his gun at his head.

The young officer couldn't believe his eyes. The hero he had always aspired to be had given in to despair. The pilot had no choice but to approach the closest rooftop as Ryan kept on shooting the massive machine gun. As the chopper rotated around the monster, she rotated her 'cross-cover' accordingly, avoiding getting hit by such firepower. The fact that her damn cross had not even a dent on it from all the shooting baffled Ryan. *Something smells fishy about this... fuck!* he thought when he realized they had just walked into her trap. Now, they were too close.

Indeed, the Dire One threw her remaining cross towards

them, aiming at the tail of the chopper. The confidence Ryan had had up to that moment vanished when he saw the cross almost amputate the vehicle in question. What the hell was going on? His shots went everywhere as the chopper fell down, turning around like the blades of a blender, its beeping sound indicating emergency orchestrating the tragedy. In less than five seconds, they had crashed onto the street. Fortunately for the young officer, his memory, fresh regarding emergency training, allowed him to keep his head cool, jumping out of the helicopter just before it crashed. Unfortunately, the same couldn't be said about O'Connell who, alongside the pilot, had remained in the cabin. Ryan, having landed nearby, ran back to the chopper and quickly opened the door, trying to get the pilot, now unconscious, but the security belt wouldn't budge. As fire had started engulfing the chopper from the tail, Ryan considered that, since that wretched woman had hit the gas tank, probably a spark had been created from the marble destroying steel… nothing made any sense.

"Help me…" said the War Hero, crawling towards him. "I can't feel my legs…"

Ryan's questions vanished as his anger flourished at the sight. Then, taking advantage of this surge of energy, he placed O'Connell's right arm over his shoulders and walked forward. Then, he felt it. The fear, death itself approaching. Insanity made laughter. Ryan felt like dumping the old man and running for it, but he couldn't. He could only look over his shoulder to check if the demon was already making her move, that was, throwing her weapons to kill them. Nonetheless, he only caught a glimpse of the fire consuming the entire vehicle, burning the pilot as he came back to his senses, trying to release his security belt, in vain. His screams of agony only reinforced the utter hell they had been exposed to. As the pilot died in flames, Ryan heard an object being pulled out of the metal of the bird.

He quickened his pace. Whatever it was, it forbade Ryan from slowing down. However, as he got further away, so did her laughter, dimming in the distance. He looked over his shoulder once again just to find no one there. "She… she has ignored us?" said Ryan in disbelief. "She's going straight towards Kelvin's house."

O'Connell could only look down as he was dragged away. He finally understood why he had failed. Even with his impeccable strategies from the past, even after sacrificing men that trusted their very lives in his hands, nothing had changed. The Black Cross was a monster that no man would be able to stop. No normal man. Not men like him. *I have failed to see that and now I have paid the price*, he thought while looking at the gray pavement.

Ryan kicked open a door belonging to a house nearby and got inside. Fortunately, as the whole neighborhood's population, apart from Kelvin's family, had been evacuated, there was no resistance to their intrusion. Ryan quickly placed O'Connell on a leather sofa in the living room as he took out his radio.

"I'll contact help… maybe we can still-" he started to dial on his cellphone when O'Connell grabbed his wrist.

"Enough people have died today," said the War Hero. "It's enough…"

Ryan was both surprised and relieved that his chief had finally regained his senses. The old man didn't even try to move, that was, until he started to slowly punch the sofa with his right fist. His pace quickened in a matter of seconds. It didn't take long for tears of desperation to flood his face. He looked up at the ceiling and cursed destiny. He cursed the Black Cross, crying like a kid who had just lost his mother. Ryan started to share his tears soon afterwards. He wanted to touch his mentor, yet he restrained himself. How she had turned his hero into a sad loser. He couldn't bear to watch O'Connell like this.

"Sir… we must get out of here and fast!" Ryan raged as he approached his elder in the dark room, "we must survive to send that fucking bitch to hell! We must live to avenge our brothers!"

O'Connell squeezed his eyes shut, and then stopped his

crying short. He then looked into Ryan's eyes and saw the determination that flooded them. "You're right, son. I'm sorry. I won't make the same mistake again," he said, trying to hide his sudden embarrassment. "This is far from over. But, one life is not worth so many... something I learned long ago is to know when to throw the towel... I had just happened to forget it."

Ryan smirked. "We did all we could. We are the only survivors of the entire department. Nothing more can be expected from us," he encouraged the old man. "At least for now..."

For sure, Ryan had never said such pessimistic words before from the War Hero. Notwithstanding, it was from him from whom he had learned them. Those words took him back to a time when his brother had just died out there, serving the country. His brother had been the main reason for him to be in the police force to begin with. "Don't worry man! Everything comes around eventually!" his brother Marcus would usually say whenever things went downhill, like when his father was diagnosed with pancreatic cancer. When it happened, besides hitting him like a truck, Ryan was already in police school.

"What's wrong Asprey?" instructor Newell asked when Ryan couldn't hit the intended target during shooting practice, not even once.

"I-I'm sorry. I just suffered a big loss and-"

"Don't worry about that. Go take the day off," Newell said with a comprehensive voice. Ryan accepted his advice and went home, which just ended up making everything worse. Just by looking at his backyard, memories of happier times would invade his mind. Playing cowboys with Marcus that always ended in fistfights. Serious back then, sad right there. Ryan sat down on the grass and looked up at the stars. The full moon and its craters did little to provide company. As he stared into the sublime, his phone rang. "Asprey here," he answered in a cold and nostalgic voice.

"A shooting threat has been received. It seems someone plans to do a mass shooting at a school near your district tomorrow morning. You'll be assigned with Chief O'Connell for this patrol. We must ensure that nothing happens," explained Newell calmly. "Lives are at stake. Failure is not allowed. Do I make myself clear, Asprey?"

"Clear like clean water, sir!"

"You're graduating in a week anyways, so you might as well go for a real task," continued Newell. "Besides, you're one of the few in this academy who knows that neighborhood like the palm of his hand. It might come in handy if the attacker plans to run away… oh, and by the way… unfortunately, we have a shortage of officers. Vacation time and such… so you'll have to manage on your own along with the chief."

"Very well, sir, it shall be done," answered Ryan with determination, and hung up. "Marcus, I won't allow this to happen, you have my word," he swore to the night sky. "Nobody else needs to die. Nobody."

He went to the school in question the next day, at 5 a.m., and waited for further instructions in the parking lot. "So much for a threat nowadays, heh," said a voice behind him, startling him to the point of making him draw his gun out. However, as he was in the process of doing so, the man behind him grabbed him by the wrist and took him down, Ryan's back now lying on the ground. "Don't pull those stunts around here, son. Children come around these parts," he warned while helping him up. "I'm O'Connell, by the way."

Asprey wished coffee would wake him up for once as he couldn't believe what had just happened. Back at the academy, he had heard of the famous War Hero, Augustus O'Connell. A legend and a role model for any aspirant willing to serve the country. As the young officer would learn that very day, O'Connell was on his usual brainstorming process: scribbling something on his little notebook.

"Reporting in, sir!" Ryan stated with certain emotion in his voice once it dawned on him. He could hardly believe his luck. Somehow, for him, O'Connell was what his brother would have become had he survived the war. "Private Ryan Asprey!"

"Very well, son, we have the future of our great nation in

our hands," O'Connell greeted. "I know this isn't an easy time for you, but it never is, especially in this job. The security of every Panthean citizen is up to us. Always remember that."

His short speech would've sounded like standard police bullshit for any other recruit, except for Ryan, even more so at that moment. Somehow, his words revitalized the pedestal where his brother was inside his heart. "We'll be on patrol watch from now until the end of classes. Any questions, son?" the war veteran continued assertively.

"No, sir!"

"Very well, son. Let's do that which has been ordered to us, then," said the War Hero imposingly. Thus, in the blink of an eye, the kids started arriving at the school. They seemed quite unaware of the danger they were in. Probably everyone was pretty oblivious in their youth, or at least Ryan thought so as he couldn't remember if he had ever had to go through something like this. It didn't surprise him, though, as mass shootings had been on the rise when the twenty-first century hit their calendars. Many didn't know what, or who, to blame. Other nations had managed just fine by banning firearms, even though this process did not always work. Guns would be obtained illegally there in the end. On the other hand, applying that in the U.K.P. would go against the freedom of every citizen, as stated by the Second Panthean Royal Decree. Ryan often considered that some people were too far away from the forces of order not to have a weapon for self-defence, while others were too close to them and didn't need firearms at all. At any rate, Ryan never thought too much of it. He loved guns.

"Sir, I wanted to know…" Ryan asked, showing eager curiosity as O'Connell continued scribbling on his little notebook, and only nodding as an acknowledgment of having heard his words. "You see… My brother died in Vayaq. He died during an enemy attack. So… I was wondering… how do you cope with pain like this?"

O'Connell stopped his scribbling and looked at him. "It's simple, son. You don't." As Asprey wouldn't say anything before such an answer, the War Hero resumed scribbling in his notebook. Upon a closer look, Ryan noticed he had drawn a map of the school and was analyzing every possible exit for evacuation. His focus was quite unique in this regard as nothing seemed to break him out of it. Even when they checked within the backpacks of each student at the entrance, O'Connell would usually write something in his notebook if something piqued his interest, like a metal fork that he deemed dangerous and a possible weapon. Nevertheless, as no weapons of any sort were found, they stayed nearby as promised, stationed outside the school. For some reason, O'Connell seemed anxious about something Asprey couldn't predict. Indeed, something didn't feel right. It never did.

Acute screams of terror came out of the building.

"He's shooting everyone! Help us!" said a little girl running and crying from the main gate. Nonetheless, as she stepped outside, she fell dead with a bullet in her head. O'Connell and Ryan took out their reglementary weapons and proceeded to advance slowly towards the entrance. "This is the police! You're surrounded! Come out with your hands above your head, now!" O'Connell ordered in a seemingly calm fashion. His order was answered by a barrage of bullets, due to which both law enforcers had to take cover behind a nearby car. It seemed the shooter had done what he had intended from the beginning and was getting ready to escape. He was just creating a cover, probably something he had seen in the movies. "He's just a damn kid. If he had thought this through, he wouldn't be trying to escape using the front door. Somehow, we're lucky just because of that," analyzed O'Connell.

Ryan was paralyzed behind his cover with his hands shaking. It was the first time he had been shot at. The first time he had seen someone getting killed in front of his eyes. He quickly glanced at the War Hero who looked as if he was having a walk in the park. Seeing the hesitation in Asprey prompted the War Hero to touch the private's shoulders. "Now you see why not everyone can do this. We signed up for this, son. We got a job to do. C'mon."

The officer's apparent fear had made the kid in question more confident, which provoked him into coming out of the building. "No one understands me! No one!" he ranted as he sprayed over the car the officers were taking cover with, with a rifle.

"Drop your weapons now!" O'Connell ordered with determination. "Surrender!"

"Fuck you cop! You have absolutely no idea! NO IDEA!"

O'Connell lied onto his stomach, having a full view of the kid's feet through the bottom of the car, and without thinking too much, he opened fire. The kid fell to the floor, unable to stand up with bleeding ankles. The policemen quickly approached him and kicked his weapon away. "You're under arrest! Anything you say can and will be used against you!" declared the War Hero as Ryan kept aiming at the kid's head, trembling. Notwithstanding, once the kid was handcuffed and secured, O'Connell opened up his cellphone. "I need an ambulance! Immediately!"

"Crap! The kids inside the school!" Ryan claimed with his eyes widened. He then rushed inside the school. The image was horrifying. There were corpses everywhere, making the young officer puke. And as he did so, he felt a pat on his back which prompted him to turn around.

"Don't worry son, man up to it. This is just the first out of many..." he said while continuing his walk down the blood-stained corridors of the school. Asprey couldn't believe it when he had already counted twenty-nine victims in the building later that night, twenty-five of them confirmed dead. It seemed that the shooter had brought the rifle piece by piece into his locker and had assembled it that very day. Ryan couldn't avoid feeling guilty as he saw the parents in tears and unable to quell their pain. He could've done more. If he had just...

Before his face full of regret, O'Connell uttered those same words that would be engraved within his mind with fire. "Son, we did all we could. Nothing more can be expected of us. Nothing less." These words soothed his aching heart, knowing that, had he been besides his brother, he would've died anyways, right there, instead of in a foreign country at the hands of a kid. The fact that the War Hero was no hero, just a man among many others, slowly started to sink in.

The next day, the Lord of the country, representing Her Majesty, as he had been elected out of two houses of parliament, offered his thoughts and prayers for the massacre. Thoughts and prayers that had become quite common as these kinds of events had started to reproduce faster than rabbits. Had he known what a true massacre was back then…

As the breeze of the night got through an open window of the house they were hiding in, carrying the awful smell of death emanating from the numerous corpses on the road, and making O'Connell remember he was still alive, the Creature was still laughing out loud just enough not to be heard by the Dire One herself. The limbs and blood spread everywhere made a perfect setting for his revenge. However, he wouldn't make a move just yet as he suspected she knew of his presence there. He could feel it in his guts.

He simply watched from afar how she danced among the chopper's flames, using the screams of the burning pilot as music.

Still watching from the forest, the Creature couldn't understand why she had let the old cop and rookie go. She simply picked up her cross, stuck on the chopper's tail, turned around and strolled towards a certain house painted in white. Why was she there in the first place? What was she looking for? The Creature would've loved to see it, but he knew it wasn't the right time. She was at her full might, and he had no new plans to stop her or to kill her. At least not for now…

Once she reached the intended house, she crushed the door open with one of her wretched weapons and entered the building. Even though she was far away, her malicious grin still made the Creature tremble. Every time he saw it, regardless of when or how, it always had the same effect on him. Even when he fought her, he had a hard time looking at her face. Even if he happened to be on the winning side, her smile would haunt him all the way into his dreams. Whatever the man she was looking for had done to her had to be quite important. He wished he could talk to said man, disclose the secrets of the monster and finally rescue his family.

His family…

What were they doing? How were they doing? For the first time in his life, he started to fear what might happen in that very moment to any children that might be inside the buildings. Of course, he knew of the evacuation that had been carried out by the police prior to the engagement, thanks to the stolen police radio still in his stolen car, but the possibility was always there, mostly because he didn't know who else was still at Kelvin's house, besides its owner. According to police reports, the bastard had decided to bunker himself inside his house. If there were kids in there, they would definitely die smashed by those damn crosses.

Not even I got that far… the Creature reminded himself with certain regret.

When he had to deal with kids, back in the days when he was the big boss, he'd always allow them to live as he had always deemed unfair the common practice of eliminating the whole family of those who opposed him. That was the only time when his empathy would kick in. He even facilitated any paperwork necessary for the new orphans to be accepted into an orphanage, or to be adopted directly by a random family. "To think that at one point I was so *potente* like to decide over people's lives," he whispered to himself while watching the scene playing before his eyes. Now, beings out of his understanding were doing just that. Maybe that demon was doing everything she wanted just because of her power, just like him in the past. Perhaps, and hopefully, her power would run out eventually and she would become a weakling like him. If he remembered something from his former boss and mentor was that everything that goes up must also go down. If that demon was a human, which the Creature quite considered a fact, she would follow suit. He was still deep in thought when a loud voice caught his attention coming from inside the house. A woman's voice.

"What do you want from my husband, you monster?! Why do you chase him?! He didn't do anything to you! Leave us alone!" said the woman in question holding a shotgun. The woman's gaze showed clearly that, whether she was scared or not, she would fire without hesitation, even though it was clear that she was trembling in fear as much as the Creature back in the forest. The image before her was dark on its own: a woman with yellowish skin, malicious grin, dry destroyed hair, ragged bloodied dress, and blood-dripping crosses. A usual portrait for the Creature by now. If this woman hadn't seen the demon with her very eyes, she would have taken the dreaded Black Cross as a myth to make children go to bed at night. "Get the fuck out of here! Now! I'll shoot you! I mean it!"

"Eyes that don't see... a heart that doesn't break..." said the demon without any emotion as she continued her advance without a drop of remorse.

What does that even mean? the woman holding the gun thought, standing her ground. "How can someone be such a horrible monster?! What are you?! Why do you want to harm my family?!" the woman continued to reprimand the Black Cross, although she had been told by her husband not to interfere. She knew this was a very bold move as death itself rarely forgave such nuisances on its path. Last time she checked her tarot, the cards had told her that this night would be a success. They had never failed her ever since her grandmother taught her to read them, thus, there was no way this would be a failure. This demon was just a fucking woman, nothing more, nothing less. And yet, trembling in horror as she was, the woman steeled herself and aimed her gun to the demon's body. *My cards have never failed me!* the woman thought, *they predicted I would find a Rolve man with whom I would marry and have a family... They can't be wrong! Today, I'll save the day!*

"Back off monster! I'll kill where you stand! I swear!" she yelled as she defied the demon without a shred of a doubt. "This is your last warning!"

The Black Cross directed her sight towards the stairs

instead, and proceeded to walk towards them, ignoring the woman completely.

"You asked for it!" declared the woman, shooting the demon in the stomach. The demon turned her head to her and looked into her eyes in response. The utter lack of empathy and insanity these displayed made the woman in question step backwards. "Not yet!" she cried regaining confidence and shot again. This shot went for the demon's heart, missing it by a few millimeters. The holes, the pellets were ripping into the body of the monster, started to bleed and to show her insides to the defending woman.

"What the hell are you doing down there, Jennifer?! Come up now!" ordered a male voice from upstairs. "I told you she won't die!"

"I think I got her! I got this! Trust me!" the woman answered with renewed confidence. "That's right! I'm not alone! You're not getting past me! You bleed just like everybody else!"

The demon smiled widely after hearing Kelvin's voice, in response to the woman's surprise.

"So… There you are…"

"Die! Die! Die!" screamed the woman shooting all her bucks into the Dire One, pushing the latter all the way outside the building, more and more with each shot. The confidence in the woman grew as well as she started to step forward with every shotgun pump. A slight smirk started to draw on her face as she kept on gaining ground. Sure enough, the demon had been driven outside the building. This smirk quickly transformed into a hopeful and victorious smile when she saw that the Dire One was now lying on the grass of her front garden, in a pool of her own blood and her body full of holes. "Almost there! Just a few more! I'll defeat you!"

However, her relentless attack was then interrupted by a click coming from her gun.

"Shit!" she cursed as she reloaded her gun as fast as she could. However, her hands trembled when she realized all her pellets were being ejected out of the Black Cross' body. The demon reincorporated as if nothing had happened and smiled at her, mockingly. The bucks in the woman's hands dropped as if she were holding sand between her fingers. "No! No! No!"

"Love… the greatest misfit…"

By the time the woman pulled back the weapon's forearm to shoot at the monster once again, she received one of the crosses to the chest. The sounds produced by the lethal weapon against her body told her that her ribcage had just been pulverized. She fell flat on the ground as breathing became harder and harder, feeling her own blood flooding her lungs, her mouth spitting blood like a fountain. She realized it was too late. She looked up just to see the demon looking down on her, mocking her defeat with a broad smile.

"Peter… Tim... I'm… sorry…" said the woman as her eyes closed to the darkness of death. "I should've…"

The Dire One didn't bother to listen to the agonizing woman. The demon proceeded, instead, to leap over her corpse, picking her weapon up while doing so, and continued upstairs in a calm fashion as the woman's breath slowly vanished from the world. It seemed Kelvin was definitely up there, waiting. The demon could feel his breathing, agitated. Nevertheless, there was another breathing there, too. Maybe it belonged to a policeman, or maybe to one of *them*. Both breathing patterns shared a common trait, though: they showed fear to some degree, even if one of them wasn't as deep as the other. Besides, from the two heartbeats, one was not as loud as the other one.

Something felt wrong...

IV

IT WAS DEFINITELY WRONG.

"C'mon Carmen! It's not that hard!" the instructor said, demandingly. Pablo would usually look at her painful struggle while hiding behind the entrance door. After a few torturous minutes, stretching her legs all she could, Carmen finally gave in and fell to the ground.

"Very good! You made it!" congratulated the instructor. "The class is over!"

The instructor, a former ballet champion, then took his trench coat and left the mansion. He would usually come twice a week, always showing no consideration, nor compassion, for anything, or in other words, no room for mistakes. And yet, somehow, Carmen loved his merciless discipline, even if she suffered with it, especially since puberty had hit her doors a year ago. She felt more confident whenever she got his approval after what felt like a century of efforts and failures. Indeed, many of the servants loved to see her struggling performances at home and showed so by offering her their loudest applause. Her father would simply smile at the sight probably because, unlike how her mother had once been, she wasn't of the rebellious kind. Verbatim, she followed her father's favorite phrase: "No pain, no gain." So far, it seemed to be working just fine.

Her father would then enter the large ballet room within the mansion, or so he liked to call it, and congratulated Carmen every time she succeeded. When she didn't, he would simply tell her that she would make it next time, or that she had to make a greater effort.

As she reincorporated, she looked towards the door, waiting for her dad to come to her. Nevertheless, there was someone else by the door frame. Soon enough, she looked around and realized she was actually all alone in the giant room.

"Wh-where is everyone? Hello?! *¡¿Papá?!*" she asked with increasing despair. She started to feel nauseous as the room started to spin around her. In order to prevent her head from losing her balance, she tried to keep up with the rotating room, in vain. She was about to pass out when a female right hand grabbed her right shoulder.

Our reunion is coming soon... I can't wait...

Carmen opened her eyes. She sat down as she looked around in despair, showered in her own sweat. She saw Nico, quietly snoring where he always slept. She knew by now that he was aware of her awakening but pretended not to realize.

What kind of dream had that been? She touched her forehead to check if she had a fever and if that dream had been possible hallucinations from it. She sighed in relief when she realized that wasn't the case. She hadn't been sick ever since she had left Sanatorium, and she preferred to keep it that way. Thus, she lay down again and closed her eyes. Eventually, through a lot of effort, mainly due to fear, she struggled to fall asleep again. However, after what felt like one second, she could feel a foreign hand pushing her on the back, slightly. "Wake up! Wake up!"

It was Old Joe. Carmen looked around as the sunlight showered her body, confused. Nico was right there, sitting down, in what looked like a deep concentration. How long had it been? "What's going on?" Carmen finally asked.

"*They* found us. It seemed we were followed. The sweet time *they* took was probably because not even they would dare come to Drift Row unprepared," Nico answered in a low tempered voice, his eyes still closed. "We must move, now. We will be surrounded quite soon."

"But how-"

"Don't worry, we spotted them a while ago. One of the boys and I managed to divert their attention a little bit, but it won't be long until they find out the information we gave them is wrong. You must go now," Old Joe replied with his face full of worry. For the first time in forever, he didn't seem to be drunk.

Carmen stood up and got together all the things she considered necessary for their journey. At this point, just a couple of blouses, one t-shirt, a pair of pants, a pair of shoes, and the underwear she had managed to buy at the flea market. She put everything together in a small bag and strapped it on her back. It surprised her how free she was with the little she had. Before, she would always feel anchored to her country, or to Friornia, just because of all the real state she had to manage. "Joe, you guys must get out of here, too. Those guys don-" Carmen uttered when Old Joe held his left hand up signaling her to stop.

"No can do," he declared. "Our Immigrant here has already told me what those bastards are capable of doing. Whatever *they* think they are, I cannot simply stand by and watch. Here in Drift Row, you pay for the favors you receive. I wish we could do more than just stall them, but I guess this is it."

Carmen couldn't believe his words. As she wondered about her assumptions about the old Frisk man, and how different was sober Old Joe from regular Old Joe, he explained, "I already lost my wife and son to gambling. I lost them for not doing the right thing on time." Guessing Carmen was still confused at such a statement from the look of her eyes, he continued. "I always wanted to feel useful and reliable for people. At least once. Please go now, and good luck!"

She turned to Nico, asking for an explanation from him with her eyes, to which Nico simply looked back and nodded.

Then, without any response, Carmen looked back at Old Joe who happily smiled at her. Thus, unable to decide what to do next, she unconsciously kissed the old man on the cheek and followed the Immigrant. "We will get out of the city. That's the safest bet for now. Otherwise... *they* will hunt us easily," said Nico calmly and confidently. Carmen felt as if she was trapped inside some summer blockbuster. Just who the hell were *they*?

As Carmen and Nico got further and further away, to the point where their beloved bridge was no longer within their range of sight, several men dressed in black arrived at their former home. "The readings indicate the specimen was here. Unfortunately, the trail vanishes as soon as we step outside under the bridge," said one of *them* as *they* positioned themselves around the place. *They* seemed to be using some sort of device which beeped constantly when *they* were close to where Nico used to sleep. As ten of *them* inspected the place, two of them dragged Old Joe over there rudely. "We were able to capture this man. We think he might hold some clues as to his whereabouts," the same man continued. "He's the one who gave us false information on the specimen whereabouts on the highway. What do you think of it, doctor?"

A blond man in rounded shaded glasses, lab coat, and a tall black hat appeared from behind *them*, all of *them* letting him pass to the scene without delay. Said man walked up to Old Joe who had been beaten up before being tied up and placed onto a chair. It seemed *they* had barely contained themselves from breaking his jaw for the sole purpose of allowing him to talk.

"Oh my, my! What do we have here?" said the man in round glasses. "It seems our little rodent left some leftovers..."

Old Joe could hardly look at him. His left eye had been punched into oblivion, while he could hardly see with the one he had left as its inflammation was quite severe. "Whatsh the fucksh do you wansh...?" Old Joe mumbled. It was harder to speak with the teeth he had left. His fate didn't seem pretty at that rate.

"Oh, poor you! The boys didn't treat you well it seems!"

the man in round glasses continued in a patronizing voice. "Alright boys! Who did this damage to this poor man?!"

This last question surprised Old Joe. Did this man actually care about his well-being? Was he like the Immigrant? A little ray of hope appeared in his mind. Then, one of the men in black suits came to the man in round glasses and introduced himself. "I-I was the one who did it, sir. He wasn't spitting anything out and I thought that-"

He hadn't finished his answer when the man in round glasses slapped him across the face with the back of his hand. Not happy with that, he punched him in the stomach and kicked him in the chest causing him to fall on his back. He tried to get up but the man in round glasses stepped firmly on his torso. "You know this man is a fellow Frisk, right?! What in the world was going on in your tiny skull?!" he reprimanded. "We don't do that to our own! That's a reserved action for non-Frisks! If I see this bullshit again, you know what the consequences are. Understood?!"

"I-I'm sorry... Won't happen again..." the man on the floor said, trembling as the man in round glasses stepped away. Slowly, the injured agent reincorporated holding his chest with his left hand and panting. Afterwards, he quickly went back to his original position among the rest of the men. Was the man in round glasses some sort of protector? Maybe he was reliable after all... Maybe...

As Joe pondered on this possibility, the man in round glasses turned to him. "So, now that that's over, would you be a dear and tell us where this youngster went to? It's quite important that we capture him... a matter of national security in fact..." he said in a sweet voice, as if talking to a child, along with a gentle smile, crouching close to him. Old Joe didn't know how to react, and yet, the answer was obvious.

"I'm sorrysh... he didn't mention wheresh he was goingsh... I'd tell yash if I couldsh..." the old man answered calmly. "I thinksh he might be goingsh souths... or somethingsh..."

The man in round glasses stood up and started to walk

away while fixing his glasses back into place. "My, my! You have been very useful! Alright, guys... go ahead... we're heading south." The eccentric man kept going towards a van into which he got in. A silenced gunshot could be heard not far away. "I hate poor Frisks... it goes against every logic... Frisks can't be poor," he muttered to himself to then talk to the driver. "Let's go... at least the others won't be a problem, either." Right after him, the rest of *them* followed suit, leaving behind the corpses of Old Joe and his friends on the floor, right under the bridge.

Far from there, Carmen and Nico were on board an old pickup truck. Sitting next to each other, with Carmen at the steering wheel, she turned to her right and looked at Nico intensely every time she could, as she didn't understand why Nico had covered his ears with cotton when they got in. Remembering back when she had been rescued, he had covered his ears with his fingers when boarding the van after fleeing Sanatorium. She guessed he must have had very irritable ears back then. Now she knew that wasn't the case, but then, why? As she couldn't answer that question and hadn't really had the courage to ask him directly, she could only ponder on how the weirder he was, the more fascinated she became with him.

"Nice ears..." Carmen whispered to herself in a very low voice. Nevertheless, Nico looked at her perplexed. "What happened?" she asked surprised, her eyebrows raised thinking of imminent danger.

"Nothing," Nico replied. "It's good that you know how to drive. I'm not feeling good about... you know... this car theft thing."

Indeed, it was a first for Carmen, too. Old Joe knew the owner of that old van, one of those *sharks* Nico had to protect him from. Thus, he snatched the key out of this shark's pocket and gave it to Carmen without any regrets. "I'm sorry," she said while looking at the car's ceiling before turning it on. It wouldn't be long for the police to show up after Old Joe and his friends. Carmen couldn't avoid wishing them a good result out of this. Nico had told Old Joe they would go north. Nevertheless, he knew that Old Joe might not be very trustworthy in the secrets department, mostly because of his near-permanent drunken state, so, although he had said that, he was actually going eastwards. His apparent lack of trust in Old Joe baffled Carmen a little. Maybe he wasn't so naive as she had thought all this time. Even in the worst-case scenario, this false information would buy them some precious time. Besides, and contrary to what Carmen had thought, Nico had no intention of leaving Las Esbirras just yet. The information he was looking for was still in the city. Despite having discussed with Nico about a decision that seemed like a no-brainer for Carmen, that was, leaving the city at once, she still didn't understand one thing…

"Nico… back on that rooftop… you were scared of those guys… are you *seguro* that you want to stay in the city?" asked Carmen out of the blue as she kept driving peacefully not to raise any suspicions. Nico looked back at her, blushing slightly.

"I-I wasn't *asustado*, alright?" he said in a slightly shaky voice Carmen thought of as cute. But again, he was just a teenager. Somehow, this thought unsettled her as well. "It's just that… well…"

"Is the almighty Immigrant embarrassed?" Carmen teased with a smile.

Nico looked back at her, took a deep breath, and answered. "It was… because of you."

Carmen wasn't expecting that. She was speechless for a few seconds, trying to think about what had just been said while keeping her eyes on the road. "I thought that you might get hurt if they found us… that's why…" he continued, red like a tomato. Then, he looked out the window trying to evade her sight. Carmen smiled to herself as she kept on driving. It had been a long time since someone else had been worried about her like that, or maybe he simply felt some sort of responsibility he had entitled to himself as her protector. Or, in the worst-case scenario, he might be falling for her. She had heard stories of the sort on the internet: mature women and young men. Not as young as Nico, though. If that was the case, it was absolutely wrong. It had to be stopped.

"Look Nico, I'm a married woman and-" she started talking when she met his eyes.

"So?" he replied without a hint of a doubt. However, and after seeing Carmen's shocked expression on her face, he immediately understood her concern and laughed it off. "Oh no, no, don't get me wrong. I'm not interested in you in that way. I thought that was already obvious," he continued in a calm voice to her surprise, without a hint of irony. "There's someone I gotta return to. *Alguien especial…* is waiting for me..." He looked up to the sky as he uttered these words, again with his cold honesty. As for Carmen, she felt a slight discomfort within her chest.

"That's... nice!" she replied with a forced smile.

Disappointed? Oh well, it had to happen sooner or later...

They stopped by the peripheries of the city, in a district called Concrete Table. Unlike Drift Row, it wasn't considered a red zone. Ironically enough, not being a red zone was actually more dangerous for them as any of their pursuers would be able to find them quickly, not worrying about the zone itself. They left the car in an empty lot and walked around the city. Where would their new 'home' be? Nico had thought of it on their way there.

"Follow me," Nico said. With a small stone he had found in the river near their former home, kept inside his pocket during the entire trip, he approached the back of a building and knocked the safety lock off its emergency stairs. These fell to the floor and allowed them to climb them all the way to the rooftop. "It's not the best hiding place, but it'll do for now..." the Immigrant declared, putting his little bag of goodies down once they were standing there. Fortunately, summer was still a long way from over, and sleeping outside wasn't as bad. Just, how long would they be there until someone decided to cook some barbecue there and spot them? At least Nico had considered that already, to which he declared he had an emergency plan. Carmen knew he would simply make it up as the problem happened, so she wasn't really worried about it. The only nostalgia she was feeling was because of how she had grown fond of their old home. The peace she had felt during that month and a half, albeit false, had helped her quite a lot. She wished she could get those days back, even if they had been quite horrible, nasty, and recent. Both of them extended the cardboard they had managed to salvage on their way there, ready to turn in. Carmen laid on her back, with her hands behind her head and looked at the stars.

"Nico… please don't forget your promise…" she uttered.

"What promise?" Nico replied with a slight surprise.

"You said you'd teach how to fight!" Carmen refreshed his memory. "I'll need to learn. I don't want to be an *estorbo*!"

"Sure, sure," he dismissed her as he tried to make himself comfortable onto his cardboard.

Carmen simply gave it up for the moment and kept looking at the stars, wishing they could grant her her life back. The stars were so far away, and yet so close, that she felt just like one. Few knew that the image they were observing was the current state of that celestial object millions of light-years ago. She was just the same. The life she had lived had been lost and imprinted into her memory a million light-years ago, or at least it felt like a million light-years ago. As she looked at each star, she thought of the people she had met prior to her current predicament. People like Pablo, Eliana, her father… her son. Each one of them being a star she could see far away, in her mind, in the past, unable to reach or help her. As she kept looking around, finding more stars, she started to think of more people. People like her former family, her servants, her dog Spunky, the people that had helped her… Then, it hit her.

She stood up and ran to Nico abruptly. She tapped onto his shoulder desperately without overdoing it, since she knew Nico was pretty much always half asleep. He answered her call in a sleepy voice, nonetheless. "What's going on now? Nobody's here. Let me-" Nico could hardly finish his sentence when Carmen pulled him by the arms and forced him to stand up. Nico could only look at her with eyes wide as plates. She was smiling, the happiest smile Nico had seen upon her face. Her eyes were shining like the morning sun. As Nico came back to his senses, she took him in her arms and started to spin around in place, alongside him, as if dancing with him.

"What is going on?! I'm feeling dizzy!" complained the Immigrant as Carmen kept going just to hug him tightly once they stopped.

"I think I can get my life back Nico! I think I know how!" Carmen exploded in ecstasy.

"So, you're hopeless... again?" Nico said in resignation.

"No! Listen to me!" she insisted. "There was a doctor who helped me out when I was being judged! He faked my papers so that I wouldn't be executed! He knew Eliana quite well! Maybe he can help me!"

Nico opened his eyes in surprise. "That's... actually a good idea!" he said, infected with her joy. "Alright then! Let's find him tomorrow!"

Carmen held his face near hers with both hands and looked into his eyes. "Thank you... for being there for me," she declared, slowly approaching her face even more to his. "I will help you, too. Remember that."

Nico didn't budge, nor did he approach her. His body was stiff as a brick. "Don't thank me, yet... if he can't help you, we'll be back to stage one," he said. Once more, his honesty threatened to make Carmen's hope fall from the delicate string it was holding onto. Carmen released him and went straight back to bed.

"Good night, Nico," she said. Although she didn't receive any solid reply on his behalf, she knew he had heard it for sure. Once again, she looked at the stars. "This fight isn't over yet."

What happened to me just now? she thought.

She closed her eyes and slept soundly until she felt a gentle push on her left shoulder. She quickly opened her eyes, having gotten used to being in perpetual awareness while sleeping by now. It was Nico. "It's time... let's train!"

Carmen rubbed her eyes as she sat down on her cardboard. "What's going on? Usually, we never wake up this early..." she complained. The Immigrant was looking into the horizon, watching the sun come into view as the city slowly gained its usual life.

"We're no longer at our former home... we should always be one step ahead of the enemy from now on..." explained Nico. "That's exactly why I decided to go serious with your training. It wasn't *fácil* when I trained, either, but this is the best way."

Carmen stood up as she yawned ceaselessly. "Alright 'master', how do we start this?"

"We'll start with grabbings," Nico said. However, Carmen's perplexed expression prompted him to explain. "The first thing you need to learn is what to do if the enemy gets to grab you, which is most of the time the case."

Carmen wasn't really all there. She would wake up completely soon enough, but for the moment she was half-listening to the Immigrant, nodding at every question he threw at her. "Very well, we'll start then..." said Nico. Carmen wasn't ready by the time he grabbed her into a lockdown where she stood. The pain in her arms woke her up right away. "Ouch! That hurts! Stop it!" Carmen cried. Nico didn't stop. Contrary to her pleas, he squeezed her arms with more strength. "Please stop! Stop! I beg of you!"

Finally, after a cascade of pleas, the Immigrant let her go. Carmen remained on the floor, breathing heavily and checking on her arm, on which, incredibly enough, there was no sign of the recent attack. For the first time in an eternity, she felt terrified again. Did he enjoy causing her pain? Was he the same as those two nurses at Sanatorium after all? Her fears and the recent pain combined into a time bomb that wouldn't wait to explode. Nico approached her, but she crawled away while covering her face with her left arm.

"G-get away from me... I'll scream! I swear!" she threatened, her eyes about to get out of orbit. Nico simply looked at her with curiosity. Then, he understood what he had done.

"Sorry if I overdid it. I wanted you to feel what the true

danger ahead will be like," he explained, looking down. "I see that you're not ready, yet. And I don't blame you for it. Men are physically stronger than women after all."

He stepped away slowly and started to fold his cardboard. As for Carmen, she dared not budge from the spot she considered safe as she cautiously watched the Immigrant's every move. A few minutes later, as she calmed down, the voice of reason didn't wait to come back into her mind. He could've had his way with her just now, and he could've also killed her if he had wanted to. It was obvious at this point that he could always have, but there she was, breathing in fear, still alive and in one piece. Her evident fragility made her realize she was quite weak... and that maybe, just maybe, Nico was right in his earlier assessment. Once it dawned upon her, she slowly stood up and approached him as he had his back turned to her. She then gently touched his right shoulder. "I'm sorry... Let's continue."

Nico looked back at her. The fear that had left her eyes had been replaced by anguish. "No can do. You're not ready, yet. I don't wan-"

She could see how his words showed genuine care for her, which encouraged her to stop him halfway in his arguments. "I want to be able to watch your back. I-I-I... said it before, and I say it again now. Please, let's train again."

Nico simply walked back to the middle of the rooftop in response and gave her instructions, again, but this time he made sure she was aware of what was going on, especially since it didn't take a high IQ to understand she had been dozing off during her first training just a minute ago.

Carmen placed herself on guard, or what she thought meant to be on guard, and waited for the Immigrant to initiate his attack. This time, she promised herself to focus on something else in order to prevent fear from taking over her mind. Thus, as Nico grabbed her again to perform another lockdown, she couldn't avoid feeling his powerful muscles against her body alongside a gentle touch, as if he was watching his body strength, being careful to use just enough of his might to not break her. Nevertheless, and unlike the previous and painful exercise, being at his mercy didn't seem to be... unpleasant...

"Are you ready?" Nico warned. "I'm about to start the lockdown. It'll be painful. So, as a real enemy, I won't stop, even if you implore me. Just do what I tell you when we start, and you should be fine. Clear?"

"Clear."

Subsequently, Nico started the lockdown, and like before, he also explained what to do step by step. Carmen lifted a foot and stepped with all her might upon one of his feet. He evaded this attack. However, he also loosened his grip which prompted Carmen to proceed with his instructions by scratching and attacking his face by attacking behind her head, him being behind her. As she did so, he once again evaded her attacks and loosened his grip even more. After a few hours of practice, Nico decided to stop the training. He was about to go get money at the nearest traffic lights and to buy food on his way back.

"May I go?" asked Carmen with a smile just to collapse on her cardboard a second later due to tiredness. Once there, she simply passed out.

"Not bad for the first day... I'm impressed she was even thinking about coming..." said Nico with a small laughter accompanying his statement. This training had actually lasted two hours, which he was sure Carmen hadn't even noticed. And so, they continued this routine every day. Over time, and as she improved, she realized she had started to enjoy it. Without realizing it, though, she had grown accustomed to the touch of a man once more. Her fear of being betrayed was gone, as well as her fear of pain. She realized she now trusted Nico with her life.

Carmen, don't tell me... are you...?

As her body gained strength and long-lost shape, she continued to think about her plan to contact Doctor Gupta. She would discuss it with Nico from time to time after their practices, to which he would usually verify the information she conveyed to him when he went out for money. Nonetheless, there was always *that* problem.

Gupta seemed to be surrounded by guards without his knowledge, or, probably, his consent. So, both of them continued their training keeping this problem in mind, studying several strategies to avoid said guards. Fortunately, as Carmen no longer collapsed onto her cardboard after training, she was now able to help Nico in the scouting. Then, one day, once she turned around quickly to avoid being spotted by a police officer during one of her 'missions', her long hair hit her on the face. It had grown almost to the same length she had had it before entering Sanatorium. She quickly realized how quickly two months had just passed by since their exodus from the bridge. At least by now, the preparations were over...

It took longer to make a plan this time because it proved to be way harder without their former allies. As they continued their strategy and their studying of the area, they soon learned of the fate of Old Joe and the others. Several bodies had been discovered under the bridge, their former home, according to a local newspaper. Once back at the rooftop, she cried at her powerlessness and the surge of guilt that hit her. Once again, dead men were on her conscience. She wished they hadn't helped her.

"Keep it together. This is far from over," Nico said with determination, trying to encourage her. By now, Carmen had simply learned to deal with his lack of tact, since, as painful as it was, he was still right. "I won't allow their sacrifice to be in vain. The last thing we can do is to regret it. C'mon, we have a psychiatrist to visit."

Having learned all the patrol paths and schedules these mysterious men had, including some policemen, the pair sneaked into Gupta's backyard during one chosen night. His numerous garden ornaments allowed them an easier time getting past some of these men's surveillance by hiding behind said decorations. Doctor Gupta, indeed, had been escorted to his office downtown. It seemed that he wasn't aware of his escorts at his tail this entire time. The fact that he never got aware of it reminded Carmen of herself, and how sucked up by work she was. Back then, it was little to no surprise if these men had been secretly stalking her, too, as she would've never realized. Maybe that was what had actually happened…

"*Vamos*," Nico whispered. As they had done previously to escape Sanatorium, they opened a hatch leading to the basement and got inside. Once there, the long waiting started. Doctor Gupta would arrive around six o'clock, as he usually did on Verdays, the fifth day of the week. As the hours passed, they couldn't avoid wandering around the place. Carmen bumped into many things in the process, unable to see in that deep darkness. Of course, turning on the lights was out of the question for fear of alerting those men outside. Her numerous stumbles made her realize that Nico was walking just fine, as if he had infrared vision. "How do you do it?" she asked in a low voice, unable to quench her curiosity.

"It's not that hard to see in the dark…" he simply answered. Carmen frowned at his explanation remembering she still didn't know much about her savior, at least regarding these skills of his. As her eyes got more used to the darkness, she noticed that Nico was approaching some shelves from which he produced two boxes full of clothes.

"What on Earth are you doing?!" Carmen reprimanded in a low voice.

"Here this guy's got old clothes, for a woman and for a child. That's weird, I don't remember seeing anyone living here besides him…"

"Put that down!"

"Alright, alright… follow me," said Nico while grabbing her left hand. Fortunately, the door to the basement was unlocked. Nico guided Carmen upstairs and peeked over before venturing into the living room. As they couldn't turn on the lights in the living room, either, Carmen would stumble here and there with the sofas. She was still impressed as to how Nico was moving, as if he was showered in plain daylight in such darkness.

"It's weird… there is a smell I haven't felt before," said the Immigrant as he inspected the living room. "It's like there was some heavy cleaning done in this house. But why?"

Carmen had already accepted the fact that Nico had watched too many movies, and that perhaps that had turned him into a somewhat paranoid individual. "Maybe he just wants his house to be deep-cleaned every time he hires cleaning services. I've met people like-" Carmen was explaining when they heard a click from the front door. Quickly, they went back to the basement as Gupta entered his home.

"He threw his suitcase onto the sofa and sat down. I think he's gonna watch TV…" Nico described to a perplexed Carmen. How in the world did he know that when all she could hear were his footsteps? The more he hid from her, the more he fascinated her. She often thought that, even if she learned the answer, that fascination would take hold deep inside forever. By this point, she had also realized he liked to impress her. *Teenagers*, she guessed.

"Now, let's go as we planned," Nico indicated. "Whenever you're ready."

Carmen took a deep breath and approached the man in question as quietly as she could. Thanks to him being so focused on the TV, the lights had not been a problem for the couple in their nearing of their prey. Nico knew that he was to reduce Gupta as soon as he saw them given that he might scream out of panic, or surprise. Thus, he approached him slowly and silently from the back of the sofa and grabbed his head in a headlock while covering his mouth. Carmen placed herself in front of Gupta who widened his eyes at what he was watching.

"Shh… calm down. It's just me," she started. "We won't hurt you. I promise. We just need your help." With that said, Nico slowly released his mouth, but not his head, just in case. However, to the Immigrant's surprise, Gupta wasn't even trying to escape his lock. "We need to talk about a lot of things…" continued Carmen.

"Mistress Wright... I never expected to see you again," he initiated, awfully calmed. Carmen assumed he was using a harmless voice to get out of such a dangerous situation. *Psychiatrist stuff*, she thought. "I had heard of your escape. However, if I daresay, we can still help you and-"

"No. Unfortunately, the system cannot help me," Carmen interrupted him. "You see, I've been framed by someone. You helped me back during the judgment. I know it's selfish on my behalf to ask for this, but I have no other options. You're the only one left I can trust with this."

Gupta seemed to be in a trance trying to remember when, or how, he had helped her. His extreme tranquility gave Nico enough confidence to completely release him, staying close behind him, nonetheless. One could never be too careful those days...

"Alright, how do you think I can help you?" he asked after his quick moment of silence. "I'm telling you already that I absolutely won't risk my career, reputation, or life for you," he warned harshly. "I've got a family. A daughter to take care of."

"I see..." replied Carmen in slight resignation while Nico frowned at his last statement.

"I know that you might kill me if I don't help you... I'll let you know that, if that's the case, I don't care," he continued his warning. "You may do as you wish. My family will always come first."

His last words tore a hole in Carmen's steeled determination. Nevertheless, she had learned to contain herself thanks to Nico's training. Still, she couldn't avoid a small tear coming out of her left eye. "I... I understand," she nodded. "We just need information on my husband. Doctor Jason Wright."

Gupta looked at her, perplexed. "You're not serious? You don't think he will help you out with all this, do you?" he said incredulously. "I saw his face at the trial. He was devastated. He absolutely won't-"

"I know that," Carmen cut him off, again. "We believe he might be the one behind all of this."

Nico looked at her with a smirk. It had been his very own logic which had brought about that conclusion. Carmen would've never even considered suspecting her husband otherwise. Nonetheless, the Immigrant and his cold honesty had hit hard once more back at the rooftop they were living in. For him, it made perfect sense. Nothing else could be possible for the youngster.

"What do you expect to get from Gupta once we get him?" the Immigrant asked her two months ago, the morning after that little spin Carmen had given him that last night, after her realization by looking at the stars, while he was playing with a little rubber ball he had found in a dumpster, bouncing it back and forth against a wall. "He's already helped you once, risking his career according to what you've told me. I don't think he'll help you again."

Carmen couldn't look at him directly as even she knew what she was about to say would be reprimanded by the Mizelas boy. "I… I-I… I want information…" Carmen barely managed to say.

Nico stopped his game and looked at her, waiting for an explanation. As her silence continued, he was about to ask her, but she said it first. "He might help us find my husband. And my husband will help me for sure. Once he does, we will-"

Nico exploded at the notion. "Are you insane?! He abandoned you right there! That nonsense alone tells me a lot of things!"

"Like what?!" Carmen rebutted, seemingly hurt at his lack of tact.

"If he truly loved you, he would've been there for you, or at least he would've doubt what he was seeing. He just forgot about you when you were in that shithole," he continued furiously. "For all I know, he's the killer!"

Carmen stood up and approached him. She raised her hand and was about to slap him across the face, yet, she stopped. Nico simply looked at her, seemingly not scared at all her recent reaction. He would've evaded it anyways, but that wasn't the reason for her to stop. "I've never thought of that…"

she uttered as she lowered her arm. She was mostly lying to herself just there. After all, she had thought of it before, back at Sanatorium. She had simply 'forcefully forgotten' about it. Because of this remembrance, her eyes indicated she was about to break again.

Nico took a deep breath and spoke in a passive voice. "Look, I'm sorry. I tend to say things straight ahead without thinking and-"

"You might be right, *pequeño*," she said as she kept looking at the dawn appearing in front of them. It was the first time out of many where Carmen would call Nico *pequeño*, meaning 'short man' in Estúan. "Although... although there's a chance that might be true... I can't simply accept it. We need evidence, even if it breaks my heart forever..."

"Look," Nico continued. "I know it hurts, but it's the most likely possibility. So far, I can tell you're not insane 'cause, if you were, none of this would hurt you," he explained as he approached her. "Besides that, I've been watching you all this time. You might be moody, but you would never kill another human being, of that much I'm sure. You don't have another hidden personality either, despite having had a rough time in *that* hellhole. So, this has to have been an inside job. As much as any of your servants could've been the culprit, that husband of yours is involved somehow... of that much I'm sure!"

His logic was far from flawless, but he had a point. He had watched her, and over her, way more than the psychos at Sanatorium ever had. She suspected he had watched her even while sleeping. Nevertheless, there was *that* little detail...

"By the way, regarding that video you mentioned... it could've been made up," Nico continued, as if reading her mind. "Black-haired Frisk women aren't hard to come by."

"B-but how do you know that? How can you be so sure that I'm not a criminal of the sort?" Carmen retorted. Her eyes showed the Immigrant she felt far from innocent.

"I just... know it," said Nico. "I can tell you have a good heart."

Probably the sweetest thing she had heard in a long while.

It didn't matter how corny or stupid it could sound; it was enough to give her new hope. Even if she had to temporarily stop trying to figure out how he was able to tell such a thing.

She couldn't avoid having a smile on her face at the memory when Gupta continued, sounding surprised at her past statements and snapping her back to the present. "That's a bold claim to make Mrs. Wright. I can assure you that if your treatment is finished, you'll be-" Gupta muttered again, but Carmen interrupted him, again.

"It seems you have no idea what's really going on," she patronized him. "Just tell us what we need to know, and we'll be out of your hair before you know it."

"Very well... but first, let me ask you a question. Why me? You could've found good information online, Mrs. Wright. I don't think I can pinpoint you to your husband's exact location, either way," Gupta explained.

"Even a computer-savvy like Carmen couldn't crack it down," Nico said, prompting Gupta to turn around and to look at him. "All his information is obviously hidden. We need any bone you can throw at us."

I'm not a computer-savvy, far from it... I guess he says that because he has a hard time when using them, thought Carmen, blushing slightly at the remark.

"I'm your only hope, aren't I?" Gupta said after taking a deep breath. "Well... what really happened was that, since I was the psychiatrist who signed your papers, I wanted to be informed on the matter of your recovery, so I called Doctor Wright to make him go to Sanatorium to pay you a visit. He was supposed to do so on a daily basis around five months ago," Gupta explained looking at both in the eyes. "I thought that-"

"He never appeared. So, please tell us where he is," completed Carmen.

Gupta joined his hands together and looked down. "I see... last I heard, he was going to Danan for a season and that he would come back in around three months."

"Where will he be staying when he returns?" Nico asked,

running out of patience.

"I know where," Carmen said firmly. "Thank you for your cooperation, Doctor Gupta. We'll be on our way now."

Both of them went through the basement door and disappeared from Gupta's view. He slowly got up and followed their trail. By the time he descended into his basement, they were nowhere to be found. Although they looked like improvised fugitives, they had timed their exit to match the lack of stalking guards outside. Gupta could hardly believe his eyes when he went to his backyard, where his hatch leading to the basement had been opened, and didn't find them there, either. Scratching his head in mere confusion, the doctor returned home. As per the pair, they were walking fast down the street with their new hobo disguises. At least these latter didn't stink like the past ones, they only seemed to do so.

"It looks like we made it," said Carmen in relief with a wide smile. "I thought for a second that we were wasting our time there."

"I donno," Nico answered while looking all around him. "There's something fishy about that guy…"

"What do you mean?" Carmen asked in surprise. "He was the same bald man that interviewed me all those months ago. I don't think there was anything off…"

"You see… he smelled like… a girl," Nico said. Carmen couldn't contain a burst of laughter to the point where Nico had to cover her mouth and force her to keep walking in silence.

"That's hilarious *pequeño*!" she said, laughing at her heart's content the second Nico removed his hand off her face. "How would you even know that?"

Nico blushed before answering. *Now that's something I haven't seen in awhile*, thought Carmen while looking intently at him.

"Women have a different odor than men. Of that much I'm sure."

"Maybe you haven't seen anything of the sort before, but he was divorced. It's obvious that he'll spend his nights with other women. I mean, maybe that's the reason why he got divorced in the first place," Carmen said, full of herself. "Besides, he's clearly a man. That's what we saw, right?"

Nico placed his hand on his chin. Carmen knew by now that he was focused on it. Nonetheless, as she had realized he had somewhat of a sixth sense, or whatever it was, that allowed him to 'see' things with the utmost precision, this confusion of his seemed quite out of place. After a few seconds, Nico simply shrugged. "Alright, maybe I'm just imagining things. Let's go, we got training to do."

Once back home, they decided to cancel their training session due to it being too late as night-time, and the lack of lighting, made it way harder than it should be. Either way, they had a lot of time to spare until *that* day arrived. Jason would be back in Friornia in three months according to Gupta, and Carmen knew exactly where he would stay. What she didn't know was if she would be able to bear the pain of going back to that place.

Nevertheless, there was yet another problem bothering Carmen as both of them unfolded their cardboards.

"Nico..." she whispered in the middle of the night. "I'm sorry. I know this is still far from what you want, and that I'm dragging you down. I'm sorry about it and-"

"Carmen, I'm trying to sleep here," he complained. Carmen tried to continue her rhetoric when Nico continued his. "I promised you to help you out until the end, and so will I. Is that so hard to understand?" He moved around in his cardboard, accommodating himself. "Sleep now or we'll be too *cansados* tomorrow. This trip is far from over..."

Carmen was unable to reply. So, after all this time he was just keeping his word? When was the last time people stuck to their word? To be fair, Eliana had done so, the main difference being that she didn't know what was coming to her. Indeed, there was no one else she could count on. Not even Jason.

By now, Carmen knew that the world of adults, or the real world, was quite harsh. No matter how hard she'd try to trust in others, she'd never be able to. Thus, by seeing Nico being his naive self was sweet, and convenient. Had not Jason promised, actually sworn, to be by her side until death drifted them apart? Had not the system promised her to bring her justice? If she were hanging by a thread with an abyss below, Nico would be the one holding that thread. At the same time, if he were to back down now, she wouldn't blame him either way. This hope of hers swung in just one direction.

Downhill.

I just hope Gupta doesn't leak any information about us, she thought as she closed her eyes. *What would he gain from this either way?*

Whatever you want to believe will be fine… since it won't change anything.

The next morning, Carmen woke up holding onto her piece of cardboard with both of her hands, to Nico's mild amusement. The way she held it reminded her of Derzú, her teddy bear. She had completely forgotten about it. That stuffed animal had been the first gift she considered of importance received from Jason, besides the tons of love letters he had sent her as a stalking bandit. At least that's what she had liked to call him back then.

Those letters…

Thinking about all what Jason and she had gone through together started to crack doubts into Carmen's determination. Whether Nico's logic could be hardly argued with or not, her heart wouldn't believe it. Even with the evidence presented, she might probably not accept it.

"You okay there?" Nico asked. "You've been holding onto that piece of cardboard and looking at it with so much concentration that I almost envy your focus," he continued as he changed his t-shirt. Now he had managed to have three of them: grey, black, and green. "Or… are you looking for a gold mine?!"

"W-what?" Carmen answered out of her stupor. Knowing Nico, it was probably one of the jokes he liked to make from time to time. Sometimes, he would even show her definitions she had never heard of before. For instance, when asked what he thought about her, he would blatantly declare that he viewed her as a *cheesy* woman. Carmen wouldn't understand at first as Nico wouldn't explain it to her, so it became a custom for her to try to guess what it actually meant. After one month of trials and failures, she finally managed to understand it. "Are you referring to actual cheese?" she asked as they walked towards a traffic light one morning. Nico would still do his acrobatics, albeit wearing sunglasses, along with a white baseball cap he happened to find in a dumpster.

Nico looked at her and frowned. "Again with this?"

"You mean it in a melted state, right?" she continued with increasing confidence and excitement. "The way I am when talking about specific themes! I like to cover everything regarding any topic we come across! Like melted cheese on potatoes! That's why you call me cheesy, right *pequeño*?!"

Nico widened his eyes like plates of soup. "It seems you ARE a genius, after all," he answered without a hint of irony in his voice, "why on potatoes, though?" Indeed, this trait of his was something Carmen had just discovered. He was probably also keeping in mind her constant stares and pieces of advice. From suggesting him with slight improvements for his job as an acrobatic performer to money spending, budgeting, and general knowledge, Carmen had hardly realized she liked to study everything she saw around her and change it, for better or for worse, at least most of the time.

I think I'd be something more of a bookworm, she thought after hearing this remark as she had never even dreamed about being a genius. She could've done everything so much better if she would've been one. Maybe he also said that because sometimes she would talk for hours on end on a specific subject, whether it was political, economic, or scientific, to Nico's ever-increasing boredom. Once she got started, it was hard to put a stop to her mouth. The only thing she hadn't managed to know was just that *cheesiness* of hers given by Nico, until then, that is.

"I just remembered something, that's all," dismissed Carmen as she stood up, after placing the piece of cardboard she had had in her hands on the ground, and prepared for the morning training exercises.

"You said you know where your husband will be at when he comes back," Nico said as he did some push-ups. "Can I know where?"

"He always goes to only one place," she answered as she jumped on both feet as a matter of warm-up. "Our- I mean, my mansion."

"Do you think Gupta will betray us?"

"The possibility… is always… there…" Carmen said as she became more and more agitated. "The worst-case... scenario... would be for him... to avoid us. I haven't... been home... in a long... while…"

Nico had his doubts about that. The worst-case scenario could, in reality, be way worse than just that. The fact that *they* were all over the place like flies around trash had him quite concerned. *Those* people would stop at nothing if they wanted to get Carmen or him. Having seen *them* so many times close to the places they were supposed to visit raised many red flags on its own. It wouldn't be a surprise for the Immigrant if this 'Jason' was involved with *them*, some way or another. Nevertheless, there was a slight ray of hope that that wasn't the case as, by judging Carmen's pure heart, her husband couldn't have been that bad. Hopefully.

His father once told him that good people tended to attract one another when he was five years old. Something he had believed all throughout his short life. Something that had allowed him to believe in that special girl waiting for him back home. Since he couldn't communicate with her under any means, he could only look at the stars, the same ones she gazed upon at night, and hope she could somehow know what he was thinking. *Luna…*

He wasn't cheesy like Carmen, but he knew he was definitely cornier than her. *I wonder if I really abandoned everything for a better life*, thought Nico as he balanced out the outcome of his actions within his mind. His home country, Peruvia, was a complete mess on so many levels that he was usually unable to know where to start describing them when talking to Carmen. As a friend of his had put it once at school during lunchtime, priorities in this sub-Panthean nation were upside down. Nico had analyzed how to fix the country as soon as he saw one limbless man playing five musical instruments with his mouth and shoulders at the same time in a market, and getting probably three Suns--the currency of Peruvia--as payment from the people hearing his music after one entire day. As three Suns were equivalent to one wollar--the currency of the UKP--he would be able to buy one sandwich, probably.

Nico would also emphasize that, in Peruvia, important problems that needed urgent solving were usually put aside for ridiculous reasons. His favorite example was when the country got into an international competition in the most popular sport on Earth, wristball. Ironically enough, the players of this sport hardly ever used their hands or wrists. When the competition started, people would stop working, studying, or producing. The entire nation was paralyzed until the competition ended, which also gave a lot of leeway to politicians and monarchs to do as they wished with anything or anyone. Thus, as problems remained always unattended, some people survived earning barely three wollars a month in the north of Peruvia, while others would simply freeze to death in the coldest parts of the country. A problem that had been going on for at least forty years. Others would simply stab each other to steal the fallen's stuff. The problems in Peruvia were several, however, his parents had chosen to leave for different reasons. As hard to believe as it was for Carmen when Nico told her, said reason were the university fees in Peruvia which were at least twice as expensive compared to the ones in the U.K.P.

His parents couldn't afford it, which prompted them to design a 'master plan' to establish themselves in the country Nico was in now. It was hard to let go of the world he had known for so long, along with the people and the girl he loved, but that had been his final choice. It was no longer a matter of self-benefit that had driven him to go there, but that of accomplishment. The second he stepped onto the plane that would carry him to the Kingdoms, he vowed to become the new king, or at least the new prime minister, of Peruvia and finish the mass emigration they were having by fixing the country. He wanted to see his country flourish in power it had never had before. Even Luna laughed at the idea at first, a laughter that would usually move cords inside his chest he never knew existed.

Had he known all of this was bound to happen, he would've simply listened to *her* and ran away with her into the jungle to the east side of Peruvia. A plan *she* proposed to him during the last minute before his departure. Sometimes he wondered if he should've... but then, the same conclusion would always loom over his mind, reminding him that his dream would never come true. That Peruvia was destined to its self-destruction under corruption and the general selfishness of its population. Laws existed, yet they didn't. History had taught him that his plan to change Peruvia would never work, that it was a little too late. It was hard for him to understand the cold truth as his dream broke like a cheap glass hitting the floor. Now, instead, he had a new mission: saving his parents. Now, there was also Carmen...

He looked at Carmen as sweat started rolling down her neck as she exercised. *She has definitely changed*, thought Nico as he compared her to her past self. She had gone through a worse fate than him. That much he understood. What he didn't know was how truly well she was. He could only think that Carmen had once been like his dear Luna, innocent and radiant like the rest of his high school classmates, as well as himself.

As Carmen kept focused on her warm-up, Nico produced an old piece of paper out of his left pocket and looked at it intently, remembering how, before entering the Kingdoms, he had received Luna's last message. She claimed she'd light small white candles on her window as a form of guiding lights that would guide Nico towards victory in any endeavor he might get into. At the same time, said lights would also guide him back to her. Nico smiled when he remembered, to her parents' displeasure, that Luna would actually light them up every night, and that it wasn't *floro*. Bullshit, in the slang of Peruvia. After all, her parents didn't like him very much either due to different reasons. So, since there was no way to communicate back to her, he could only look at the stars thinking they were the candles she was lighting for him.

Young love! How amazing!

"Alright *pequeño*, let's do this!" claimed Carmen full of confidence and standing on guard. Sure enough, she had improved quite a lot regarding her fighting skills. Now she was no longer easy prey, whether it was to Nico or to an agent, something the Immigrant discovered when practicing surprise attacks on her. She preferred to use judo-like techniques that would favor her by using the attacker's own strength, something Nico had encouraged her to do since she would be fighting people physically superior to her most of the time. At the same time, through practice, it was that she discovered another one of *those* Immigrant secrets.

"Ready?" Nico asked about to jump on Carmen on a practice morning.

"Whenever you're ready *pequeño*!" she answered with a smile on her face, confidence in her body.

The Immigrant did as expected and she evaded him. Nevertheless, she also did something unexpected by punching him on the stomach. To her surprise, Nico's reaction was extremely different from what she had predicted in her mind: he didn't evade it, for some reason, and rolled on the floor while holding onto his punched belly screaming in agony.

"Are you okay?" she asked, crouching to see him closer. Seeing that he was on the verge of crying, she could only show a perplexed face. Was he messing with her? She was about to kick him to find out, but then she saw true suffering in his eyes. After a few minutes, he got up and walked away from her, with his head down.

"I'm sorry, I didn't know..." apologized Carmen as Nico simply got himself into his cardboard. Far from what Carmen thought, he wasn't angry but deeply embarrassed.

"It's my fault, *no te preocupes*," he said without looking at her. "The thing is... I can't receive hits. Just one could be the end of me," he explained in a deep saddened tone to his voice.

Carmen looked at him, puzzled. "What did they do to you?" she asked in a slightly angry voice. "Will you die if you get punched again?" she continued, this time with her voice showing deep concern. Deep inside, she thought of this concern as a by-product of her need for him to get her life back. Deeper inside, she wasn't sure why she was this concerned, or angry to begin with.

"No," he said, calmly. "It's just that I'll be left at the mercy of my attacker for a while. I guess I underestimated you just now, and now I'm paying the price..." He sat down and lifted his shirt, which showed Carmen that there was no mark whatsoever from her punch, only his hardened muscles. Even though they weren't the first athletic abs she had ever seen, these always had the same effect on her: a weird sensation she had never felt before. One that would traverse her spine and would get her lost in thought until Nico said something and snapped her back to reality. This time, however, she didn't lose herself and was rather relieved to see him well.

"Alright *pequeño*, get up and let's continue!" she said while pulling Nico upwards.

Over the next weeks, as they prepared themselves for their 'Jason' visit, they decided to take a day off. One of those Carmen's cheesy ideas, as Nico would put it. As he had no objections to it, he simply followed along and, while using their disguises, they went around the city. Unlike the Drift Row district, this part of town felt like being worth a visit. The clean air, the green leaves starting to fall dry on the ground, the lack of people. Maybe that was all Carmen needed.

She was wrong.

"An... ice-cream store!" she said with excitement as Nico was no longer sure whether she was an adult or not. "Let's go in! *¡Por favor!*" she begged. Given that she had done nothing wrong so far, he accepted. Albeit he wouldn't eat ice-cream under the excuse of not liking it, he still accompanied her inside, just in case. As their outfits, or hobo disguise, didn't invite precisely to optimism, most people would simply kick them out of places due to their poor appearance, thus, they simply took their outfits off and entered. They had no choice.

As they ordered their ice-cream and sat down on a table, Carmen couldn't avoid feeling weird. It felt like centuries since she had eaten something publicly. Surveilling the area around them like *locos*, both of them ordered different things when the waitress approached them. Carmen asked for a vanilla-chocolate ice-cream, while Nico just asked for a glass of water without ice. His refusal to have ice-cream, once again, fascinated Carmen beyond measure. "What are you looking at?" asked Nico, blushing slightly at her intent gaze.

Her order arrived and looked quite generous. Nico paid and Carmen held the receipt in her hand, looking at it as if she had just found a piece of gold. "Are you okay?" asked Nico at the display, in response to which Carmen put it inside a pocket she had sewn into a second-hand dress she had managed to buy. Then, as she ate the ice-cream as fast as she could, and felt a little brain-freeze, she realized what was going on... finally...

"You're... sensitive!" she said out of nowhere before a perplexed Immigrant. "That's your big secret! I've figured it ou-hmmmm!!" she had continued until Nico covered her mouth with his hand. Carmen soon realized everyone around them was looking at her. "Sorry," she said while looking down. "I just got excited about that... so... is it... you know... true?"

Nico seemed resigned as he shrugged. "Once again cheesy girl, you nailed it. What gave me away?"

"There's the fact that you could hear those guys in the building, despite seeming like they had left. There's also the fact that you had to cover your nose for simple bad smells. There's also the fact that you received one soft punch and you were crying on the ground like a little girl. There's also the fact that-"

"Alright, I get it," interrupted Nico. "What will you do now? It's hard enough as it is."

"Well… I just wanted to know one thing…" she continued while licking her ice-cream happily. "How dare you fight then? You'd be knocked down in one punch. I think it's too risky for you to fight just about anybody. How do you do it, and why?"

Nico closed his eyes this time, as if he was in deep concentration. He usually did this as a meditation practice every day, which meant that, whatever he was about to say, had to be of the utmost importance. Carmen accommodated into her chair to receive such vital information, her eyes glistening in expectation, and waited eagerly.

"I don't know," he said in the end.

"Eh?" Carmen replied with her expectations shattered.

"That was just a joke," said the Immigrant to later giggle at Carmen's look of temporary disappointment. "'Cause I can hear pretty well, I can also feel and hear the air current around a person. When they attack me, I know where their punches or kicks will come from. It's hard to explain, really."

"But… Why do you take such a risk? You could simply use a gun and… oh…" she stopped, realizing the obvious. A gunshot would blow his ears apart given his sensitivity. "I guess you don't have a choice then…"

"One more time, you nailed it, cheesy girl," he said as he started to drink his glass of water. "Who we're against doesn't care for *inválidos* like me. They already know what you just figured out. So, I guess they weren't prepared for- WATCH OUT!"

Nico took Carmen's head and plunged it downwards. Right after that, a bullet passed through impacting the wall nearby, prompting everyone in the store to panic. "*They* are here! We gotta move now!"

To her surprise, she was scared. Too scared. As throughout all their experiences together, she had never faced direct gunfire. This brand-new situation was terrifying and exciting at the same time. Her body wouldn't answer her calls to flee.

"We don't have time for this! Move!" Nico insisted to no avail. "Tch! Whatever. If I get away, they'll prioritize me," he said while shaking Carmen's shoulders trying to force her to react, in vain. "Just stay here until the coast is clear. Don't stay here any longer than you need to or you'll be a sitting duck! See ya soon!"

He knew that *they* were closing in, so he did the best he could think of: he threw a chair at the nearest window, prompting *them* to shoot at the chair instead. Using this little time he had gained, he ran into the kitchen making sure to be spotted by *them*. The men after him didn't waste any time and started their pursuit. It was clear to Carmen by now how Nico was calm in such a predicament; however, it was the first time she was aware that she was being shot at. At least the first time it counted. Back at Sanatorium she was too weak to care, and, besides, she also wanted to die. For some reason, she was scared of dying this time. With *their* steps going towards Nico, and away from her, new questions arose in her mind: Where were they to meet once out of there? What was she going to do now? How would she even get out of here? The police would come sooner or later, and them finding her was just as bad as *those* guys, if not worse.

To her surprise, the gunshots started to disappear in the distance after a few minutes. Nico was definitely leading *them* away. Thus, she carefully peeked over the table. No one was around. Even then, *they* could be hiding, readying *their* next shot at her head. "What do I do now?!" she muttered to herself in despair. It wasn't long when the sound of sirens started to loom on the horizon. Her legs started shaking as the consequences of her possible capture started to appear in her head, especially the likes of Kelvin looking down on her, again.

She quickly crawled around the now empty ice-cream store, cutting her palms with the broken glass in the process. She was too scared to care, indeed, but she also felt ashamed to see people with no training having no problem prioritizing their own lives more than her as everyone had already escaped the place. She slowly looked out the door and, after seeing no one was around, she made a run for it. She ran, and ran, and ran down the streets as a big crowd had started to assemble nearby. By the time she was two blocks away, she saw the police arrive, guns in hand. So, as Carmen looked at them, she overheard someone nearby.

"Look! It's her! Freeze Carmen de la Cruz!"

"My costume!" Carmen exclaimed, realizing she had left her disguise back at the store as two men started running towards her. Fortunately, and contrary to what had happened last time, her legs didn't resist her will. She dashed out of there, zigzagging her way in order to lose them, street after street, alley after alley, with her strength starting to run out after half an hour. She hated to remember that she hadn't done the cardio exercises Nico had assigned her before. After what felt like an eternity, almost out of breath, she hid inside a big dumpster in one of said alleys.

"Damn it!" said one of the officers with apparent physical weariness. "We lost her again, but she couldn't 've run far! On the move! Now!" Then, the men ran out of the alley.

After a few seconds, their steps had completely gone silent, and yet, Carmen didn't dare show her face. What if these men were using the same tactics as the ones Nico had taken out before? As she kept wondering about these possible threats, another worse possibility came to her mind. What if Nico had been captured? What if... he was now dead? What was she going to do without him?

Being forced to keep her doubts locked in a compartment of her mind, and contrary to her best choice, she opened the lid and looked outside, one inch at a time. The silent and empty alley gave her the answer she wanted. So, as quietly as she could, she slipped out of the dumpster and advanced towards the main street by taking cover behind all the things she could find, even though she saw no sign of the men chasing her. *I gotta find some sort of disguise*, she thought as she walked around in a hurried pace, covering her face with a newspaper she had found on the floor as if she was reading it. Realizing no improvised costumes were available nearby, she felt the temptation of stealing clothes. She remembered what Nico had said about the last time they had stolen clothes from that basement, just outside Sanatorium.

"We're doing this only because we absolutely need to."

Wasn't this one of those situations? Why was it so hard? The officers were still around, and they could be following her right there. They could even be…

She looked over her shoulder out of paranoia as many times as she could, only to find there was no one there. And so, without realizing it, she eventually arrived at 'home'. As soon as she recognized the building, she quickly climbed upwards. However, and unlike the other times, she couldn't avoid watching all around her as she made her way up. A smile grew upon her face as she approached the rooftop. Nico should be there, waiting for her.

"Nico! You won't believe what-" she had started to say when she realized there was no one there. The place looked empty of life as it was. Nico's cardboard laid there under a rock, untouched. As night was coming soon, along with some rain, they had already decided that they would open the door leading downstairs for these sorts of days. Besides, the sound of the rain, which rarely happened, helped disguise the sound they had made when forcing the door open. Thus, she opened said door and sat on the stairs, watching the staircases disappearing into the darkness of the building, holding her head with her hands supported on her knees, feeling as if that darkness was trying to claim her very core. Everything was different with Nico around, and she had just realized it. Nico would usually tell her about his adventures, laughing at her from time to time. Was this the famous Stockholm syndrome? She kept thinking about what had happened as her eyes slowly closed, her head now falling in her arms.

When she opened her eyes, the sun was about to make its morning presentation. It wasn't her first time sleeping on those stairs, but it was the first time she wasn't using Nico's shoulders or chest to sleep there. As she got up, she quickly looked around, searching for the Immigrant. No one had come. Cold sweat started to roll down Carmen's face at the realization. Where was he? He should have arrived a long time ago… unless…

No! He will come back before nightfall for sure, she thought. He had to come back, as always. No matter how long he might take, deep inside she knew he would be back. Thus, she waited. And waited. Nevertheless, by that day's evening, despair started to invade her head as there was still no sign of the Immigrant. It was obvious by now what had happened...

"Oh no... Nico... no, no, no!" Carmen started ranting on her own. "What am I going to do? Please don't get captured! Please!" she continued looking at the sky, begging at the nothingness. "I... I'm nothing without-"

"Who are you talking to?" a voice declared behind her. She turned around and saw him, leaning onto the wall with his arms crossed. "It was hard to make it, but those guys are miles away from beat-"

Nico couldn't finish his sentence as Carmen jumped on him and kissed his lips. The Immigrant couldn't react to this surprise attack as she was holding him hard, as if she would never let go. After a minute or so, Carmen released the teenager as he looked at her in astonishment.

"I... I don't know what came over me... I'm sorry..." she claimed, unable to meet his eyes.

Nico approached her and held her chin with his right hand, delicately. "I understand, we're both in a difficult spot here. If this is a mere confusion, I guess-"

Nico was interrupted once again by another kiss, after which he could no longer restrain himself. Although his body was doubtful to obey his will at first, it eventually did. And so, Luna, the rest of his world, and his memories were gone for that night. The same happened to Carmen as her bad experiences, the death of her son, and her entire life in ruins also disappeared from her mind. Both had never felt like this in ages: two human beings under the starred mantle of the night, even if Nico's condition wouldn't allow him to last as long as he would've wished.

You'll be normal again, I swear it, thought Carmen with a sweet smile on her face.

Either way, once the deed was done, she felt how a

hangover of regret showered her being. Had she just committed a crime? With a minor? What was the minimum legal age of consent in the kingdom of Friornia? Did it even matter at this point? He was six years younger than her. What on Earth was she even thinking?

"So, you regret it, too. Huh?" Nico said while looking at the stars as Carmen looked back at him in surprise. His face wasn't that different from hers in the regret department. "I guess we both lost control of ourselves just now…"

His voice had gone shy, again. He was shaking as if he had done one of the worst things he could've ever imagined. Of course! He felt bad for that girl in Peruvia he talked so much about! But, how long had it been since he last saw her? Why was Carmen even thinking about this?

"It's normal, Nico," she explained in an understanding voice. "Everyone goes on with their lives over time. How long has it been since you saw this… girl of yours?"

Nico's expression changed dramatically. "What are you implying?" he said nervously. This time, he was the one unable to look directly at her eyes. "Yo-you mean to say that…"

Carmen felt this was also a good time for payback in cold honesty. "Everyone goes on with their lives," she repeated. "She has probably found someone new in her life, and that's normal. No one waits forever, especially for a silent guy who never replies."

Nico's face had gone truly sad for the first time since she had met him. Was this girl of his one of his the source of his enviable hope? She was enjoying the reaction he was putting off, shattering his illusions and destroying what was, most likely, his first love. And yet, she couldn't avoid the feeling of guilt that was starting to overcome her being.

Evil can come in several disguises… evil doesn't exist, though.

She hugged her arms around his neck and kissed his cheek. "Don't worry about it, *pequeño*. You were bound to learn this… sooner or later…"

"I-I kinda thought about it before… but never took it as a fact…" he replied in a guilty voice. "I… I just don't think she would do that... We've known each other since we were ten and..."

"I guess you need to hear my story again, don't you?" she answered gaining more momentum and confidence. "Look, I'm as appalled as you are, but I think we do deserve a second chance. Besides... right now at least... you're all I have..." she said as she held his chin up with her right hand, this time. "I think that we should try it out..."

Nico still couldn't look back at her as Carmen felt very happy, and pathetic, at the same time. This was the first time she was asking for a relationship, a fact that she didn't seem to realize at the moment. Nico just went silent and lay down on his cardboard as his face would stay hidden from Carmen. *Is he crying?* Carmen wondered. By the looks of it, he was. What she couldn't guess was if he was crying at his broken heart, or at his betrayal to that girl. Feeling a mixture of pity and guilt, she couldn't avoid hugging him from behind.

"You've been through a lot, *pequeño*," she continued. "You were right after all... we indeed are on the same boat. *Pero*, there's a difference this time..." She proceeded to whisper in his ear, "I realized that... as long as you're by my side, I can do anything." Nico turned his head slightly towards her, still hiding his face. "Don't worry, everything will be alright," Carmen continued. "You're not obliged to accept this, *¿está bien?*"

Nico remained silent. Regardless of his discomfort, Carmen felt that she had to hug him even tighter. He must have probably mentalized himself to beat any obstacle in front of him, hoping to see this girl again. In the end, and despite his incredible deeds and decision-making skills, he was still just that: a simple teenager.

Said and done, the next couple of months went by fast. As Nico had come to terms with Carmen's feelings and his need for her caresses and kisses, both of them enjoyed the company of each other as time flew by. Without realizing it, the time when Jason was supposed to be back in Friornia had arrived. Thus, in order to keep watch, they made a new 'home' near

Carmen's former residence and surveilled the mansion and its surroundings every day. At least training and cuddling had become a good distraction against monotony, among *other* activities. Nevertheless, this monotony ended as abruptly as it had started.

"Look!" Nico said pointing at the main entrance. "A car with tinted windows is entering the mansion. My guess is…"

"It's him," Carmen asserted in a doubtful voice. "I don't know if I'm ready for this, *pequeño*…"

"Whatever the case may be, that car got in all alone. Nothing will be more perfect than this, trust me. We'll pay him a visit tonight," he continued confidently. "It's time we got your life back, Carmen."

Once night fell upon them, they climbed over the wall protecting the manor's enormous garden and closed in on the main door. Even though it was her home, Carmen felt like a sneaky thief about to break into a snobby house. The mansion seemed to be in a state of utter disarray, which prompted Carmen to remember several unwanted memories that weren't welcome, especially at that moment. All of those moments in the past, added to her current situation, felt as if the mansion in disrepair was laughing at her, showing her that she wasn't necessary for the world to keep spinning; as if it had prepared a nice concoction ready to blow up on her face once she triggered the trap. She looked at the doors and the doors looked back at her. The knockers hanging on them and their fading paint made them look like living beings with a perverse grin. She placed her hand on the knob and prepared herself to open it. The sensation of the knob brought her back several years ago… familiar days of happiness.

She wished she had known what lay beyond that door beforehand, though.

V

THAT'S WHEN I felt her smashing the door open.

She looked exactly like papa said: a monster covered in blood. Her eyes alone made me tremble. Her grin was something I've seen not even in my worst nightmares. Dad's shivering wasn't helping. What was going on? I've never seen him like that before. That was scary on its own, but this was different. Why was this monster in my room? I was too afraid to even look up. I covered my face with my hands, but they were also trembling. She even brought an awful smell into my room. I hated it! Why did this monster have to do all this? My birthday is going to be ruined! Worse than that, my dad's grip was tight and was hurting my body. He was hugging me with all his strength. His heart pounded like crazy. I still wondered how he managed to put me behind him.

"It seems you finally caught up to me! But I don't fear you! You hear me?!" Dad said while still trembling.

The monster-woman wasn't listening to him. She maintained that same horrible grin that was driving me nuts. Wait a second… that awful smell… where have I smelled it before?

"Eyes that don't see… heart that doesn't feel…" she said. "Fear will covet the darkness of the solitary stone…"

What did that even mean? She was insane for sure! I've

seen crazy people before on TV but never thought I'd see one for real. Her awful stench started to bother me. But where have I smelled that thing?! Why can't I remember?!

"I did nothing wrong! I'm the victim here! Get out of here, now!" My father didn't sound scared at all, although his heartbeat said something else. The weird woman limited herself to smile again and lifted one of her big black things, that looked like crosses, above her head. I just expected the end when my father pulled me in front of him with both arms as a shield between him and her weapon. What the heck was he doing?! I just closed my eyes, waiting for what I've seen in horror films when my parents weren't home. At that moment I didn't care what my father had just done. How he was using me or not. I squeezed my eyes with all my strength and clenched my fists and felt like screaming. What else could I do? After a few seconds, I slowly opened my eyes only to realize that nothing happened.

The weird woman had stopped there as if frozen by some invisible force. Her arm looked as if it was shaking, still over her head, as if trying to hit my head but unable to do it. I looked at her and sighed in relief at her powerlessness to strike. I turned to my dad who was laughing now... What the heck?

"I knew it! Hahahahahahahahaha!" he laughed out loud. "The direst monster on Earth cannot harm a child! Hahahahahahahahahaha!" I would've rolled my eyes, but I couldn't. He approached me to his chest as the weird woman remained there. She seemed petrified. She looked surprised. "In that case, let me be off! We'll see each other... soon enough!"

Dad carried me like luggage... now that was something I've never seen before... Who was the man holding me? I wasn't sure what was going on anymore. Scratching my hair, trying to understand, I finally remembered that smell. Dad took me once to my uncle's farm where he had a slaughterhouse. A horrible stench was all over the place. Dad told me *that* was the smell of death. The smell of rotten flesh and blood. This weird woman smelled just like it... oh... I think I get it now.

Now I was even more scared, even worse when my father jumped out the window holding me in his arms. Not even in my favorite TV shows have I seen one of my heroes do something like that with a kid in arms. I didn't know whether to consider my father a total badass or a total idiot. By the time I opened my eyes, we were already outside. Dad was running quite fast across our garden like some sort of Olympic champion. I thought he had been shot in the leg when he came home, but I guess it was just my imagination. I looked behind him, up to our window. We were getting further away from home, and the weird woman still didn't seem to move. She just stood there inside the room. It was as if she had realized something we hadn't. Whatever it was that had frozen her in place had saved our bacon, that was for sure. For some reason, I heard a click coming from my Dad's hands and looked at them.

"Night night!" he said. When I saw a remote control in his hands with a big red button, I assumed he had just pressed. As soon as he did it, I heard an explosion coming from home. I turned around just to witness how my house had been blown up to pieces and how it was falling apart from the inside like a pyramid collapsing. But, what about mom? What in the world was going on?! No matter how many times I tapped on his shoulder asking for an explanation, Dad wasn't giving me one. Instead, he quickly approached our car and dumped me inside onto the backseat. He got into the driver's seat and dashed away.

"Why are you doing this?! Where is mom?!" I asked impatiently. After one minute, he stopped near what looked like a grey armored vehicle by the side of the road. He descended, ignoring my questions, as if I didn't exist, and not happy with that, he also locked the doors just in time before I could get out of our car. Wait... where the heck were the handles?!

"Wait... this is not our car!" I yelled, hitting on the window trying to get my Dad to get me out, or to stop this stupid prank. I looked up to him for an explanation when I saw it… He wasn't Dad.

I couldn't believe my eyes. My Dad had suddenly transformed into a Frisk black-haired young woman with some sort of metallic parts around her whole body. In the middle of the road, there was also a blond man with round glasses and a white lab coat smiling at her. That smile of his was disturbing… even more than that of that weird woman back at my house. I kept observing them, but I couldn't really listen to what they were saying. She, my former dad, lit a cigarette and approached this man in glasses.

I didn't know what to think anymore.

"What we do with the brat?" she said. "I hope your willingness to save him wasn't for some noble cause… nah, you wouldn't do that."

"Oh my, my! Let's just say I was running out of young'uns! You know the rest…" he answered, smiling and looking at me. His mere sight gave me the chills. "I wish our new holographic prototype was already finished. I know the current one you use weighs quite a bit."

"You don't say," she answered while looking at the metallic pieces attached to her wrists. "It's already hard enough to walk with these extendable limbs, but whatever…"

"You're our best agent in disguise, after all… you still want to be called the Make-up Artist?" the man continued, always smiling in a gentle and disturbing way. "I think it's kinda lame."

"Yeh. Don't judge, old man," she continued after using her cigarette. "I just wish my recent jobs were less… eccentric, you know?"

"For the record, I'm only 33! Anyways, don't worry, my dear. The rest of the operation is on our hands. Good job!" he congratulated her by trying to pat her on her shoulder. She pushed his hand away before he got to touch her. I also realized several men had surrounded the vehicle I was in, pointing at me with laser sight rifles. "I was running out of guinea pigs…"

I started to tremble after hearing that. "This job wasn't *that* bad," my former dad continued. "It has no comparison with that Gupta job," she chuckled a little bit. "I only accepted it because I would get to kill that bitch later." She lit a new cigarette after tossing out the one she had been smoking once she got to its half. "You'll never imagine my disgust after having that filthy immigrant so close to me. It still gives me shivers to this day. Brrr…"

Immigrant? My nanny was one of them, and she was a good person. She went home today, so I missed her voice when she tried to cheer me up. All the opposite happened to me when I listened to this woman in metal thingies. Her voice had started to piss me off.

"But, you know what?" she continued to my discomfort. "At least I got away with it. That trash sonuvabitch will be gone while we breathe. He'll probably miss his old partner in crime, though." She started to move away into the distance. "Since, you know… that bitch is finally dead…"

"Oh my, my! I'm sorry my dear, but I beg to differ…"

"What?!" she looked back at him with a funny face. "She can't be alive after having the entire house falling onto her. Especially after that explosion and all those C4s! I've seen supernaturals before and even I know an ambush like this it's an end game for any of them!"

The man in glasses chuckled. "I guess you still have much to learn, my dear. This isn't just any supernatural we're talking about here. No, no!" he continued while using weird gestures. "I came specifically to capture her alive… I made sure she would not die after this… she's still vital for our research."

The woman tossed her cigarette to the floor. "What the fuck?! This goes against my contract! You know perfectly well that I don't accept any job where I'm not guaranteed to kill at least someone! You know that perfectly well!" she complained, raising her voice. "You know what? Fuck you and fuck this! I'm out!"

"So… I guess you don't want to go against the runaway immigrants?"

She stopped for a second. "Alright, alright, let me think about it... geez... dealing with you guys is always such a pain..." she continued in a complaining voice. "You know what? Let's do that. As much as I hate this woman's guts more than anything, it was *that* mofo that touched me back at Gupta's house that I hate the most. I'm in." She took out a brown folder from a bike and burned it with her cigarette. "That mofo Kelvin was trying to blackmail me with this info on us. He even stayed in that asylum until he found it. He sure had his priorities straight, and bam! He got a deal after all... a free execution! Haha! Whatever. Nothing to see here..."

"What I'm still curious about is..." the man in glasses cut her off looking like he didn't hear her while walking around in circles. "How did she learn of Kelvin's address? I'm sure we had made it secure enough so as not to kill him unnecessarily for this project," he said holding his chin. "I'm sure she wasn't aware of his address, and bam! She appears out of nowhere. She must have some sort of intelligence aiding her out... but who?"

"You know what?" my former dad replied. "If you asked me, I'd say it's her damn instincts." She lit up a new cigarette. "It isn't like I care or anything, anyways..."

The man raised an eyebrow. "How so?"

The woman looked at the man with glasses pitifully. "I hid Kelvin's body on the second floor, in his own room..."

"What?" I said out of the blue... I wanted to cry. Now I knew where dad was... I tried to open the door again thinking I'd be able to help him, but I couldn't. I was still trapped inside that stupid car. I could only cry when she continued her tale. I also started to wonder who the real monster was...

"That bitch came upstairs without even looking around on the first floor," she continued while making big puffs of smoke. "The boys outside had told me so... she came straight to us."

"Interesting... maybe there are some things to her that we still don't know," the man answered. "We're in for a long night!"

"Just send me the pics of her butchered body once you get her," she said while walking away. "I want to see that bitch suffer..."

"Absolutely!"

"Now, if you don't mind, I have better things to do... especially if I'm to kill that immigrant pest... See ya around, boy!" She approached a purple motorcycle behind another vehicle with bright lights and took off.

"You never cease to amaze me, agent Carter..." murmured the man in glasses. "Now... please, take care of our guest inside- I mean, under the house, would ya boys?" he continued while a group of men with rifles made their way to my house.

He turned around and fixed his gaze on me with a big smile on his face. "Where was I? ... oh my! What project can I use you for? Would you be a dear to provide me with any suggestions?"

I looked back at him. I was so confused like to utter any words at all. "We better get you outta here, young'un... the main show is about to start..." he sneered at me.

"We're gonna have so much fun..."

VI

"I KNOW IT'S NO FUN, but we have to do it," said Nico, trying to comfort Carmen as she used his shoulder to get back on her feet. "This is our best shot at getting your life back, c'mon. You can't turn back now."

It had been quite a difficult decision as to where to go first. In the end, the obvious became their best bet: the front door. Since Carmen wasn't able to get to touch the doorknob, Nico suggested something else. "Is there any other place you might want to visit first? It's not like Jason knows where we're at..."

Thus, retreating her hand from the doorknob, Carmen walked to her right towards a small building in the garden. "I'd like to see my parents first, *pequeño, sígueme...*"

Nico promptly followed her and together they entered the small chapel. Carmen sighed in relief as she saw her parents still in the same place, each one of them with their respective black marble cross on top of their graves. Long ago, Carmen had decided to be the first to disrupt such a weird tradition, at least when she first learned of it. Now, however, she'd be glad to have the same honor done to her. *So much has changed*, she thought while caressing said crosses.

If at least Juan Fernando's grave were here... she thought. Amidst the deep darkness, hardly being able to see anything else, other than what was engraved in her memory, she couldn't avoid remembering what had happened there mere months ago. Where was he? Was this a final punch to her face on Jason's behalf? Those memories only accelerated Carmen's agony, making her burst into tears.

Nico wouldn't intervene this time. This whole scene had brought up thoughts of his own, like the big possibility of him being in Carmen's shoes, watching over his parents' graves in the near future. The sole hint of it becoming reality had shaken him a little bit. *If everything's already lost, I don't want to know, at least not just yet,* he thought. Instead, he would distract himself by looking at Carmen's beauty, thinking of the days that lay ahead. She was wearing the white dress he had given her on her birthday. He still remembered how hard it had been to save the money for it. Whether Carmen had understood it or not, it was his way of congratulating her for having improved in all regards he considered useful. There was also the fact that she had started to occupy his mind in different ways. Somehow, the fascination she felt for him had rubbed off onto him towards her. She was so different compared to Luna that-

"Whatever happens… I swear I'll get our heritage back! I'll do justice on your behalf and find Juan Fernando's real killer!" she claimed out loud in front of her parent's tombs, drawing Nico out of his thoughts. "I-I think we should go now…" said Carmen after cleaning her tears with her hands. "We'll come back here once everything is clear. We'll have plenty of time for crying later…"

Nico smiled at her newfound confidence. Nevertheless, he couldn't avoid feeling as if he wasn't being cautious enough. Given that the mansion seemed empty of life, it was way too easy. Something had to be definitely wrong; experience told him that much. As black clouds started to gather above their heads, they walked at a slow, but secure, pace back towards the main doors, Carmen's hands shaking more and more as the distance to the entrance closed in. Once they were one meter away, Carmen fell to her knees and started to puke.

The Immigrant crouched to her level and placed his right hand over her back. *She's been puking quite often lately, probably 'cause this day coming got into her*, he thought. He could feel her fear. What he couldn't see were the memories going on in her mind. Memories of hands and brute force submitting her to the will of her fate, bindings on her limbs, restricting her freedom. A razor stripping away her happiness. Somehow, being in front of her former home felt the same way.

"Are you okay?" Nico asked, trying to comfort her. "The longer we wait, the longer you'll take to get your life back, remember?" At least Nico's coldness was useful for once. Whether it was due to her having gotten used to it, or to the fact that he was absolutely right at that very moment, she shed no more tears. Nico helped her up.

"Carmen… you're no longer alone. We can do this together," said Nico approaching her and kissing her lips. Carmen forgot she had just puked and closed her eyes. She later remembered that Nico could feel any taste three times more which made her regret accepting his affection, wondering how could he not puke as well? Nevertheless, those words of his made all the difference. Slim tears of joy rolled down her face as she got back into balance.

Should I roll my eyes yet?

"*Pequeño*… thank you… thank you so much…" answered Carmen, wiping away her tears, with a soft and broken voice. Such a sight alone broke Nico's heart, again. Nonetheless, sights like this one only steeled his eyes, trying to show strength; showing any weakness was forbidden, even more so at this very moment. After rubbing her eyes with her left hand, her face had changed completely. Her eyes were now full of hope and her smile came into existence, irradiating happiness into Nico. For once, he started to smile at the sight. After all this time, was her joy sipping into his core? He wished so…

He remembered then. *Wait… that dress…* he thought. Indeed, she had promised him to use it for a special occasion, that was, after trying it on for the first time and looking at herself with a broken mirror they had managed to scavenge. There was no other occasion more special than that one. That day… her life would start anew by Nico's side, of that much she was sure.

Could you just get into the mansion already?

They stood in front of the main doors as they looked at the tall oak-made doors, Nico struck by what Carmen had always hinted at: the life she wanted to get back. He felt quite small at such a sight as he had never visited a mansion such as that one, or any other for that matter. The darkness of the night and the limited light provided by the, not so well maintained, outer electric lights only strengthened the contrast with the days of old. Nico wondered if, besides her own hesitation, Carmen was having a hard time trying to open them just because of them being in disrepair, or in other words, for fear of getting hurt with rusted metal. Then, he remembered that she couldn't see as well as him in the dark.

Carmen extended her left hand, shaking at every second, trying to reach the right knob, but stopping midway also at every second. "Don't worry, we've been through so much worse," said Nico, taking her hand and placing it on the left knob in a comforting fashion. Right after, he placed his right hand on the other knob. "Let's do this!"

Both of them turned both knobs around and pushed open both doors in unison. As these moved inwards, with their hinges screeching, the darkness of the main hall greeted them with pleasure. Carmen instinctively went inside the building, as if some sort of mystical force had taken hold of her body all of a sudden. She walked forward, looking around everywhere, in a trance Nico couldn't explain.

What was she seeing there? Or there? And there? Whatever it was, he could only follow her, not daring to break her focus. At the same time, he couldn't prevent himself from moving his ears back and forth. The fact that he could move his ears had startled Carmen the first time he did it in front of her. At this point in time, this feature of his would only be added to the already long list of things that already fascinated her about him. She still couldn't believe that he had learned to do it just from trying to imitate a dog he had when he was a kid. Whether the Immigrant moved them or not wouldn't make any difference regarding his sensitive hearing, though. He wished it would. On another note, the mansion didn't help his sense of smell as the amount of dust and humidity forced him to cover his nose.

"There's someone in a room nearby, burning something..." Nico said in a low voice, breaking Carmen's trance without realizing it.

"There's only one room where things can be burned... the hunting hall..." she also replied in a low voice. "He must be there..."

Nico found the whole situation more and more threatening. Jason Wright couldn't possibly be alone. No way. Where were the other people? No servants? No helpers? No bodyguards? It was way too easy. The silence of the mansion only increased his fears, as it was perfect for an ambush for either side: Jason's or his. Whatever had happened to Nico that had made him become a freak of nature, he didn't wish for that to happen to Carmen as well. If this wasn't her mission to accomplish, her reason to exist in other words, he would've gotten inside the mansion on his own, completely alone. And precisely because this was her mission, and hers alone, he would watch from the sidelines, or at least he would try to remain neutral. After all, even if Carmen had learned quite a bunch to defend herself, she was still a normal woman who had seen Hell itself. She had seen enough. He could suffer more in her stead. However, he wouldn't speak his mind on this issue as assertions like these often got him looks of disappointment from Carmen when he said them out loud. "You don't trust me, is that it?" she would usually claim. Thus, Nico simply stopped saying them altogether, although his innate coldness would betray him sometimes. He tried his best to explain that that wasn't the reason why he had said that, but she would have none of it. "This is my suffering to experience, not yours," she would usually retort in these cases.

As they continued their advance, getting deeper and deeper into the mansion, Nico followed Carmen into what looked like the main hall. There was a piano covered in a thick layer of dust. She approached it and gently caressed it. Nico touched her shoulder. "Let's go," he said, this time in a pressing manner.

"I'm sorry… let's go," Carmen replied, leaving the piano alone and approaching Nico. She took his right hand and together they continued their way into the mansion. No way Jason, or whoever was there, hadn't heard the sound of the hinges screeching, or their steps, for that matter. They were way too loud and, yet, Nico couldn't feel anyone around or approaching them. Surrounded by darkness as they were, as well as by silence, the whole situation only deepened Nico's fears of a possible ambush.

As they made their way to the room where the burning sounds were coming from, they passed through the kitchen, which offered a view of the garden. This mere sight made Carmen almost knock over some dishes on top of a big round table. She felt like fainting, again. Notwithstanding, Nico caught her in his arms on time alongside two dishes that happened to fall. "Are you okay?" he said, starting to regret his decision of choosing that day to do the 'mission'.

Carmen stood up while looking at the garden in question, shivering. "Let's go… I just… happened to remember something… I'm sorry…" She slowly stopped shaking as she took his hand. Once composed, she led him to the hunting hall at a slower pace. Nevertheless, the restlessness that Nico had started to feel had only begun to increase. Why were there no other lights on? As far as the Immigrant knew, he was the only one he had known so far to escape unscathed from *them*. But, what if this Jason had gone through a similar treatment? That would be an entirely different story. Hopefully, he hadn't, and he was just a normal man.

Knock, knock, Captain Obvious…

Nico simply walked faster, leading Carmen this time across the darkness towards the hunting hall through sound alone, following the wood burned by the fire. Carmen looked at him confused, not knowing what to do but to let him guide her. After a minute, they had arrived at the room in question.

Albeit she couldn't catch a proper glimpse of it, she could tell the mansion's halls and rooms had remained the same since the day of her arrest, except for the ever-present decay affecting the whole building. Once they stepped inside said room, Nico stared in awe as he could tell it had been a place full of life once. Its walls displayed paintings that spoke of a glorious past, as if it had been conceived during the times of the Renaissance, if he remembered correctly that time period.

As the fire cracked some sparks at the wall opposite to them, providing a warm light to the whole place, several animal heads hanging on the walls looked down upon them in disgust. A single red leather sofa at the end of the room turned around to greet them. Within it, a blonde man smoking a brown pipe smiled at them, his legs crossed, his arms resting on the sofa. The fire behind him produced a giant shadow towards Carmen and Nico, big enough to cover them both. He was in a red and white bathrobe alongside a condescending expression on his face. In his arms, he was holding Carmen's old companion, Derzú.

"I've been... expecting you..." Jason said.

Torment of the Black Cross

I

"DEATH wasn't expecting that," said the Black Cross, erratically. "Unlike the waters of the abyss..."

The explosion had done its homework as the monster had a hard time getting up, hardly being able to get off the debris on top of her. Good riddance. *They* weren't trying to kill her, of that much she was sure, judging from the force of the explosion, and past attempts, it seemed like *they* never were.

Her fingers had been crushed and twisted in different ways, as well as her left leg which now had a new articulation near her knee. It didn't take long until the sounds of her bones readjusting back to their places started crackling and echoing throughout the dead building. She had learned to listen to them like an orchestra of death, failing yet again. An orchestra destined to never stop.

Once she was able to stand up, greatly struggling with the weight of a few bricks on top of her chest, she looked around. The whole place was a mess, now just a huge and empty structure like a giant disemboweled corpse. She could still see some glimpses of the room divisions among the upper floors, on the wall, as some of the wooden structures were now on fire. If the rooftop had collapsed as well, she would've had a difficult time waking up as nearby fumes would take their toll on her, trapped and swirling around her lungs. Maybe luck?

She didn't think so. As she realized the main door--she had previously smashed--was right above her head, it was obvious she was now in some sort of basement. Her nose soon detected several and weird smells surrounding her, like the ones flies felt when they were near garbage. Even with the debris blocking most of her sight, something was clear about the place she had fallen into: it was some sort of fetish dungeon. Chains, plugs, cuffs, leather straps and contraptions of all sorts and sizes had been splashed everywhere on the floor, on the debris, or under it. She knew Kelvin had some sort of perversion, but this level was way off her expectations. Nonetheless, the time she had to admire this hobby of his was running short as she could hear running steps outside the dying building. *They* were taking position as *their* unique patterns in movement gave *them* away. Even though she had faced them before successfully, it was the first time in a while since her last direct encounter with *them*. She simply looked at the chains hanging on the wall and grinned maliciously…

On the outside, near huge speakers that topped the whole terrain like robotic giants, there was the man in the white lab coat and round dark glasses. Besides him, three agents had their hands on top of some sort of laptops placed upon large plastic tables. He grinned from ear to ear while walking in circles, stumbling upon his own feet. "Is everything ready boys?" he asked in a subtle voice. "It's been a while since I've been this excited! Oh my! Oh my! I can't wait to see her in action! Although Kelvin's brat's face was also a sight to behold, it's nothing compared to this!" he continued with increasing excitement as he approached a device that looked like a walkie-talkie to his smiling face. "Are you ready to get in boys?! She's not going anywhere!"

"Yes, sir! We're on it!" answered an intimidated voice from said device. "We're entering in G-minus 10!"

"Very well boys! Let the melody of death begin!" ordered the man in the lab coat while extending his arms to both sides and looking into the sky, seemingly feeling great inner peace. He had brought only forty conscripts, recently trained ones at that. *They should be enough to put up a fight against this gorgeous demon*, he thought while admiring the landscape before him. Out of them, only ten would go and venture inside the blown-up former Kelvin residence. Ten brave ones, as this man liked to point out. As a matter of fact, the gender or age of these brave ones didn't matter, which was a plus in this case. Death didn't discriminate, either.

"We're going in!" they claimed through the walkie-talkie and stormed inside, or at least they tried to.

As the first of them stepped near the door frame, a big black cross appeared from the depths of darkness, from inside the building, and crushed his head, severing it from his body. The rest of them stopped short as the cross went back into obscurity as fast as it had come out, soaked in blood. As the body of the first victim among them fell limp to the ground, the rest of them surrounded the entrance in a circle, keeping their distance from it, while aiming their guns at it, their laser sights looking desperately for their target. She was nowhere to be found.

As sweat ran down their cheeks and necks, and their ears hunted for the minimum sign of danger, their laser sights trembled in the shadows behind the door frame. "Order cannot stand chaos..." said a motherly and sensual voice, accompanied by a yellowish face grinning devilishly, emerging from the darkness and covered in visible black and gray veins. Her messed up hair, along with her ragged dress, which had probably been white at some point, embedded with blood clots all over it, sprung the agents into action. There was no need for orders to fire.

The demon in front of them laughed out loud to then launch her deadly weapons against them. This time, and unlike herself, her crosses emerged from behind her, still showered by the darkness, granting the agents no time to evade the cursed objects, or to even expect them. The selected ten dropped like flies as, after a few seconds, they were all lying on the floor on the verge of death, if not dead. From the distance, the man in the lab coat smiled in excitement while watching the spectacle.

"The one who is supposed to be alive... isn't..." mumbled the Black Cross as her face seemed to show a certain amount of anger.

"It seems she has finally realized... oh my! This is so awesome!" screamed the man in the lab coat while jogging in place and spinning like a rabbit on acid. "Go my brave ones! I will help you, this time! Play that funky music!" At his signal, the giant speakers started to play some sort of Classical music, the kind that was hardly ever heard in Panthea, albeit quite common in Danan as most of the composers were from there. Not to mention that it was in Danan where these masterpieces had been created several hundred years ago. None of them were from Estú, though.

Once out of the shock, and contrary to what had been instructed prior to the mission, the surviving agents nearby retreated further to keep more distance with the demon, then, they restarted the circle around the entrance of the building, remaining static like statues. "What in the world are you waiting for?!" criticized the man in the lab coat. "Kill or be killed, you idiots! Don't you see that she has attached chains to her damn crosses?!" Those chains made it seem as if the relative distance between the monster and the agents was significant, which in turn had given them a false sense of security, added to the fact that the chains were rolled around her forearms, making them hard to spot without proper lighting. Either way, they had no choice as the Black Cross was approaching them at a quick pace, charging once again.

"Fire! Fire now!" commanded one of them.

The bullets coming from their weapons rained upon the monster as she exited the building, like a massive ocean wave about to hit the coast announcing its presence with drops. Nevertheless, as they hit and penetrated the demon's skin, her rampage remained undisturbed, this time taking advantage of the new additions to her crosses as they allowed her to reach them from several distances without losing control of her weapons.

"Interesting... ten meters..." mumbled the man in the lab

coat while holding his chin with his right hand. "She had nothing of the sort when she got blown up... just how did she attach them' chains to her things? Interesting test subject... quite, quite interesting..." The man then walked a few steps forward, still stumbling with his feet, as if to get a better look at what was going on. "On second thought, I wished I had trained these idiots in bullfighting... like that they would've been able to provoke her without dying so much. Good riddance..." Afterwards, he performed a short jump and raised his right arm to the sky. "Come to think of it... some of them just might know how to... how silly of me! My agents aren't from Panthea...! Hahaha!"

Meanwhile, as he watched in comfort, the Black Cross had started to dismember the remaining agents at will. Despite watching their comrades being slaughtered, with blood streaks running down the pavement, they didn't stop firing. Some of them, unable to shoot, had their legs shaking, but they dared not retreat.

"Everything is going according to plan... she's slowing down her movements... This is a resounding success! Keep at it guys!" commented the man in the lab coat with a smile from ear to ear. After a few minutes, there remained only nine agents who kept on firing. To their surprise, the monster initiated her retreat back into the hollow building she had come out of.

"Oh my! She realized *that*, too!" screamed the man in the lab coat in excitement. "Oh well... I guess it's time to get inside again!" The agents near this man simply looked at him and smiled at each other as he approached his walkie-talkie to his face. "All of you there! Get ready to enter! She's finally ours!"

"Sir... we need more ammunition. The sleeping darts and bullets are in short supply. Even if they seem to work on the subject, we need these supplies as an emergen-" said a voice from the walkie-talkie just to be cut short by the man in the lab coat. "Do you need a reminder of what's going to happen if you don't comply with my orders?" he replied with a gentle voice, smiling. "Our strategy is working so far... don't make me grumble…" he continued in a calmer voice. Then, he placed some binoculars over his eyes when a hand touched his right shoulder.

"What is this madness?!" said a voice behind him, which the man simply ignored. "What the fuck do you think you doing?!" continued the same voice. Due to its insistence, as well as the constant tapping on his shoulder, he turned calmly around and looked towards its source. The man grabbing his shoulder was an old man, probably in his fifties, accompanied by a younger man. The first dressed in a trenchcoat while the young one in a police officer uniform. They looked battered, defeated, and furious. The old man was bleeding from his head. It didn't take long for the man in the coat to realize who they were.

"Oh my! I thought there were no survivors from the police department…" he said with a fading smile.

"What… what the hell did you just say?!" replied the old man in anger.

"Oh my! Oh my! I apologize for my rudeness to my fellow man! How may I be of service?" replied the man in the lab coat as he extended his right hand to shake the old man's in a delicate fashion. Nonetheless, his kind gesture was vastly ignored. *You will regret this*, the man in the lab coat thought as certain disgust started to imprint onto his brain.

"Who the hell are you people and what are you doing in my jurisdiction?!" complained the old man slightly less angry this time, trying to control his rage as much as he could. The young one simply looked at their interaction as he, contrary to the old one, seemed angry and disturbed at the same time.

"Don't you see you're tangling with a demon from hell itself?! You're either too brave or too stupid!" continued the old man in his rant.

The man in the lab coat chuckled a little bit. "How rude of me! I'm sorry! My name is Pietros Tatakolis and we belong to an important governmental branch! Do not worry about that woman. This situation is completely under our control," he replied, showing them an identification card. *Fortunately, the experiment is going according to plan*, he thought, *these fake IDs are really something though...*

The old man sifted through the strange man's ID. "I see... I'm Augustus O'Connell, chief of the police department of this jurisdiction. The young man beside me is officer Ryan Asprey. With this 'unique' situation, even with your credentials we must demand explanations," said the old man in a forgiving voice, this time.

"Well... as you may have witnessed, we're applying the latest technologies in order to solve this problem as soon as possible..." continued the man in the lab coat, smiling gently, albeit begrudgingly. "Currently, we have her cornered inside that building... that woman has nowhere to flee now."

Ryan walked towards him and looked directly into his eyes in apparent rage. "Are you insane?! How dare you even consider that monster a woman?!" he stormed, pointing to the plethora of corpses all over the ground, "just look around you! Look at how many of your men lie dead before your eyes! Are you blind or just plain stupid?!"

The man in the lab coat chuckled blatantly. "They knew what they had signed for. Now, I don't mean to be rude, but we're in the middle of a grand scale... ehmmm... operation... this predicament is no longer of your concern, so I'll ask you kindly to please leave... at once," he continued, "if you refuse to comply, we'll be forced to report you to our superiors and you'll be subjected to the penalties that that entails..."

"Look pal!" stormed Ryan once again, "that bitch has killed all of the police department! All our friends and comrades! Husbands, brothers, and sons slaughtered like cattle! I will see the end of this whether you like it or not! I don't care who the fuck you are! Are we clear?!" Ryan looked right into his eyes, his anger seeping through the crack of his trembling fists. Although O'Connell shared his sentiment and wanted to join him in this affront, he couldn't avoid keeping caution before this situation. Experience had told him so.

"Oh my! What an attitude! Actually... I don't mind you being here and all... as long as you don't interfere with us, you're free to stay…" replied the man in the lab coat with a benign smile, "just sit back and relax my friends! Night's young! You'll be entertained, I promise!"

O'Connell grabbed Ryan by his shoulder and moved him aside. Ryan wanted to resist at first, but the old man's hand had a calming effect on him, like so many times before when anxiety and fury had taken over his head and mind. "Sir, I apologize on behalf of my apprentice," O'Connell humbly said while trying to regain some sanity for himself as well, given the effect the mangled corpses lying on the ground had on him, too. "But I must protest about your methods. Your agents are being slaughtered as we speak, and you don't seem in the least disturbed by it, or worried. What is your game, sir? If you don't mind my asking." Ryan was amazed at how the chief was controlling himself. He could easily tell the War Hero wanted to punch that man in the face as much as he did, if not more.

The man in the lab coat simply rolled his eyes and turned his attention back to the operation in question. His nine remaining agents were about to enter the dying building. "Unfortunately, this operation is classified. Its details will be disclosed upon a given time that I'm not at liberty to say… nonetheless, you can rest assured that… we'll subject this person to her merited punishment."

"I can deduce that you're a royal agent and all, but all this music and equipment… you know more about this monster than what you're letting on, I presume?" asked O'Connell, his eyes widened with fear and anger of what the answer might be, "I don't mean to jump to conclusions, but… are you the ones responsible for her… existence?"

"I'll hunt you down myself if that's the case, I can promise you that much!" sworn Ryan with evident anger in his eyes, with his clenched teeth. His fists were bleeding due to the pressure his nails were doing onto his palms. His overall posture said it all.

"As I've mentioned, I'm not allowed to disclose information to the likes of you… however, I can tell you this.

We're... how could I put it... partially responsible," replied the man in the lab coat, this time with a calm expression, "let's just say... it's a long story... in short... I love life..."

"And you think that's enough of an explanation?! I've had enough of your bullshit!" yelled Ryan as he went towards the man in the coat, his fists ready to punch his face. However, as his steps raced towards him, O'Connell appeared in front of him and stopped his fist with his right hand in mid-air. The man in the lab coat didn't seem concerned in the least by any of this as his back kept turned towards them. Ryan struggled with his superior until he finally calmed down.

"Calm yourself down, son," O'Connell said in a soothing and pretty low voice. "We must resist! I understand your anger, I wanna kill him, too! But this isn't the time. He might be our only chance back at that demon. Do I make myself clear?"

Ryan nodded, begrudgingly.

The man in the lab coat looked at them out of the corner of his eye. "You know... what you just tried to do there... that's high treason..." he said patronizingly. O'Connell couldn't see his face, but he could tell he was smiling again, "you could get executed for that... take it as a, let's call it, a 'friendly warning'." The War Hero could tell this man was enjoying this moment. He could also tell he couldn't resist his rising anger anymore at this pace.

O'Connell walked towards the man in the lab coat and placed himself in front of him, interrupting his view of the operation and annoying him in the process. "I know you might not be the one directly involved in this mess, but this is a mess that can't be taken lightly. Many lives have been lost and many more are at stake. If we, as Panthean citizens, don't get a disclosed report of what's going on, I just want you to know that we'll be suing your ass for this. I'll turn your existence into a living hell! You hear me?!"

"Go ahead," calmly said the man in the lab coat as he kept focused on his entertainment, "you can do as you wish... there won't be any difference. I love life way too much to care for that..."

"And one more thing," continued O'Connell, "that bitch you're messing with right now... IS MINE... AND MINE ALONE!"

"Oh my! You should calm down, officer... you never know what might happen to you if you don't know who you're messing with..."

O'Connell was hit by those words. It wasn't hard for him to relate these words to what had happened that very night with his, now dead, comrades. If they had known who they were messing with from the get-go, all of them would have been alive. Thus, the War Hero finally stood down.

"Note to self... bring at least twenty additional agents next time..." murmured the man in the lab coat, lost in thought. "Now... it's just a matter of time before the test subject comes for me... she must have realized the purpose of these speakers by now..."

O'Connell and Ryan looked at each other, perplexed. "What is this all about?" finally O'Connell asked out of curiosity.

The man in the lab coat simply ignored him. "It seems our time is up! Here she comes! This might be... more enthralling than I thought..." he said while turning towards them with a malicious grin drawn on his face. "I can barely wait!" They heard gunshots anew as the Classical music kept on playing at an all-time high volume. The Black Cross had emerged from the building back into the field. In turn, thanks to the moon offering enough light, reinforced by the enormous light projectors brought in by the agents, the three men were able to see her terrifying red eyes, once again, with perfect clarity.

"Wretched bitch..." said Ryan unconsciously, both in fear and anger after seeing her again. O'Connell simply looked down, unable to watch what was about to happen.

"Such bloodlust! Such cruelty! Such unparalleled beauty!" said the man in the lab coat, with a genuine smile of happiness across his face, while the Dire One commenced her slaughter against his remaining nine agents, one by one. "How many times have your hands regenerated by now woman?! Five?! Seven?! Twenty?! Just fantastic! Show me death itself, Black Cross! Show the bounds of your power to the lover of life! To me! The Biologist!"

II

"IS THAT ALL YOU HAVE TO SAY?!" Carmen exploded, "after all this time?! All these months?! Where were you when I needed you?! Where?! Tell me!"

Jason slowly stood up and walked a few steps towards Carmen, whose angry fists, brow, and arched spine gave Nico all he needed to know. In contrast, Jason seemed calm with Derzú in his left hand.

Carmen hated him, and at the same time, she didn't.

Could you make up your damn mind already?

Nico suddenly felt like a third wheel in this conversation as, still nervous about letting Carmen go on her own, he had to struggle not to intervene. The Immigrant felt his feet about to disobey him at any time, a sensation that had increased in his mind as he was the one carrying the voice recorder to catch Jason red-handed. By looking at his face, the young Mizelas could tell there was something disturbing about his persona. His condescending expression, almost seeming to be mocking Carmen's pain, made Nico sick. He didn't need further proof: it was him. He was the real killer. How could a man go to such extents as to kill his own son was beyond him. Nonetheless, the youngster knew that, even though he had never killed anyone himself, this was entirely different. For some reason, he wouldn't hesitate to kill this man. Said emotion was further reinforced when Jason finally replied to Carmen after lighting a small brown pipe, full of luster.

"You're deeply mistaken, my love... I have always expected you to come back home..." Jason's gentle and soothing voice seemed to have taken hold of Carmen's heart, mind, and core. Nico could only watch in astonishment as her resolve weakened while she remembered the days of old. The days she had been longing forever since they had met at Sanatorium. She stopped midway and looked down...

Nico was about to step forward at the sight, however, Carmen resumed walking slowly towards Jason just to stop short when her husband approached her and held her in his arms. Hopelessness and betrayal started to flood the Immigrant's heart, something he hadn't felt in a long time. Why had he done all of this for? What had been the point?

Nevertheless, and unbeknownst to him, in Carmen's head all that which she had experienced for the past eight months had become nothing more than a horrible nightmare. A nightmare about to end. Her one and only dream was right there, before her eyes, waiting for her to take it back. She looked straight into Jason's eyes, still undecided whether to hug him back or not. Then, as Nico couldn't believe his eyes, slowly and steadily, her arms wrapped around Jason's back.

Nico couldn't take it anymore. "Didn't you want your life back?! Didn't you want to avenge your son?! What the hell are you doing Carmen?!"

His voice felt like a dim light in a sea of darkness inside her mind. Nonetheless, this small dot of light started to increase in size as the memories of her recent past started to take over. As Carmen raised her head, Jason looked at her face. Contrary to what he was expecting, her eyes had transformed: They were now full of rage. She released herself from his grip by pushing him away and stepped backwards. "Tell me... why did you do it Jason? Just... why?"

Jason didn't stop smiling as he continued with his gentle voice. "What's wrong my love? Come back into my arms and let bygones be bygones... I'm sorry about my attitude after all this time... had I known that-" continued Jason but was abruptly interrupted by the Immigrant.

"Why don't you confess already? You piece of trash!" barked Nico with notable anger in his voice. He had seen right through him while, at the same time, breaking Carmen's immersion of undoubtable hope. Despite having recovered her conviction, she was still unsure as to who to choose. The tension in the air had become so thick that, had it been something solid, it would've been able to block their breathing. Jason didn't wait for her to decide.

He approached Carmen, getting ahead of Nico in that regard. Notwithstanding, his face had changed completely into that of pure hatred. He simply moved his right arm back and forth towards Carmen, and in a split second, he had stabbed her.

Carmen immediately felt the pain and placed her left hand on her belly, just to confirm the wound by looking at her palm bathed in her blood. All the doubts or fears Nico could've harnessed had transformed into bestial fury. His rage was so visible that even Carmen could feel it. She had never seen him in that state, not even in his most stressful days. Still, he ran to Carmen to hold her as she felt her legs giving way to this last betrayal on Jason's behalf. The wound had been made on her liver. She wouldn't die immediately, but that didn't change the fact that she had little time left.

This will be so much fun!... So close, and so far at the same time... of being complete!

"You're fucking trash!" yelled Nico in plain anger. "This shall not stand!" Nico quickly and carefully placed Carmen on the floor, sitting her down and applying pressure to her wound with her right hand just to go for Jason at an accelerated pace. However, Jason threw his pipe away and produced a gun from his back pocket, with his right arm, and aimed directly at Carmen making the Immigrant stop short in his tracks.

"How can a fucking and filthy ricer call me trash?! A rapist and a thief who shouldn't even be considered within the declaration of Human Rights! Get the fuck out of my house you fucking wethands! I won't tolerate any insults from beings that are BENEATH ME!"

"So, now you show your true colors!" said Nico with a forced, yet confident smile. "This means I can punish you properly after all! I'm happy I didn't come all the way here without having some action at least!"

In reality, there was little the Immigrant could do other than playing with Jason's strings while he studied the room to find a path to run away. Thus, he needed to buy all the time he could muster and make him confess at the same time. Once they had what they wanted, running away wouldn't be a problem. However, a retreat where he could kick Jason's face into the ground was a more appealing idea.

The youngster could barely resist the temptation of going all out; however, Jason's firm grip on what seemed to be a magnum revolver told him that he wouldn't hesitate if push came to shove. "Get out of my house worm! You don't deserve to be in this great country! This is a matter of husband and wife! You have no place here in this mansion, or in this country. GET THE FUCK OUT, YOU FUCKING RICER!" continued Jason in a major display of rage. A display of who was truly the owner of the situation.

"It's MY mansion, Jason," interrupted Carmen in a weak voice to Jason's surprise. She simply looked up to him, still sitting on the floor. "What has happened to you? You were not like this..."

"Oh Carmen... How can I put this gently...? I regret to tell you that... I've ALWAYS been like this," replied Jason with a smile from ear to ear. "It's been a tiresome endeavor, you know? Pretending to be someone I wasn't... You never truly understood me... Well... you never could've... at least I found comprehension in wonderful people... people that helped me out in so many things... and today, I can finally be myself!"

"What on Earth are you talking about?" Carmen answered, trying to unhear his words, forgetting the pain burning her insides even if it seemed impossible. "Please tell me!"

Jason laughed softly. "It's been hell itself to cope with you, with your damn father and your damn people," he continued with a cold gaze. "It's been unbearable… but not anymore! This game will finally be over! I will finally be free!"

"No… Jason… not you… please tell me what's wrong! I can help you!" said Carmen with a trembling voice while tears of sadness and regret flooded her face.

"You wanna know the truth, sweetie? I've always hated your guts! There! I've said it! I've always despised your fucking existence! Yours and that of your fucking father! Your fucking perfect princess life!" he replied happily without ever taking the sight of his gun off her. "Fortunately, I found a way to turn you into a being that'd be beneath me…" he continued with a broad grin, "I turned you into… get this… a criminal!" Jason laughed wildly while shaking Derzú, still in his hand along with the knife, violently in all directions and splattering Carmen's blood over the floor. "You should be happy… that means killing your father actually paid off!"

"You, sick bastard!" yelled Nico as he ran towards him to punch him but was stopped by the sudden change in aim of the gun in Jason's hand, this time aiming at him.

"That's right! I don't need perfect aim to kill a fucker like you this close! Hahaha!" continued Jason. Whether it was Nico's life or Carmen's, there was no recovering from this. If the Immigrant were to fall there, Carmen would simply follow him shot by Jason. If he were to shoot Carmen first… there was pretty much no difference in the desperation the Mizelas boy would feel. In both scenarios, he was fucked.

"You… you killed… my… my father? Why…?" said Carmen. She was now completely shaken. Her heart felt as if a screwdriver was penetrating it and twisting in its place, replacing the burning pain flooding her stabbed torso.

"Isn't that obvious? I had to destroy you… so, the first step was… what was it again? Oh yeah! Giving cyanide to your damn father in little bits. Injection by injection. Just enough not to kill him right away. It's funny, you know? You idiots trusting your awesome Doctor Wright to heal him when in reality... it was all the opposite!" Jason's triumphant look was unbearable. Nico could hardly refrain himself. "Once dead, conquering the pathetic daughter and last of the La Cruz lineage was a piece of cake! Who could ever love someone like you? Someone so pathetic? So stupid? Each time I kissed you made me wanna throw up! Just remembering it right now makes me want to puke out of disgust..." he took a deep breath and cleared his throat before going on. "Anyways, let's not remember those horrible times... I have a favor to deliver for those people who were able to understand my pain... "

"And what is that? To skin us alive like the fucking psycho you are?" said Nico challengingly, looking into Jason's eyes like a tiger about to kill his prey.

Jason simply ignored Nico turning back to Carmen. "*They* are here right now. *They* told me you would come looking for me. Quite nice guys if I say so myself. I'm sure you've had the pleasure and honor of meeting *them* already, my love," he said confidently as he snapped his left fingers right after. "*They* haven't been looking for you my love, but for that piece of shit that came along with you."

How could I have been so stupid?! They've been here the entire time! thought Nico when he finally felt them. Six men armed to the teeth rappelled down on the spot, surrounding them, their assault rifles with laser sights pointing at their heads. The logo on their armbands was easy to tell apart.

The Block. They've made it... they've finally captured us... he concluded.

Now Nico knew he had no chance. He would have to submit to them like a dog if he wanted at least for Carmen to survive, or to give her a chance to do so. Still, he knew this chance was next to zero.

"Oh Carmen, Carmen, Carmen... if you would've just remained a fugitive... if you would've FUCKING KILLED YOURSELF IN THAT ASYLUM LIKE I HAD PUT SO MUCH EFFORT TO PLAN...! nothing like this would be happening now... it's your fucking damn fault!" continued Jason, sounding frustrated out of the blue. "If you would've been executed by the court, it would've been even better...! Whatever… I guess one can't have everything..."

Carmen's eyes widened while looking back at him, unable to assimilate the situation. "That means… that means…"

"That I killed our son? Pfff! Of course, I did! I couldn't stand looking at that fucking brat! Just to think that my genes were mixed with yours was nasty beyond belief! I couldn't bear for him to exist! That motherfucker got what he deserved! You should've seen his face when he was gasping for air! Hahahahahahahaha!" Jason laughed in the cruelest fashion Carmen and Nico had ever heard. The Block agents didn't seem to bother as they simply smiled at their predicament.

Carmen couldn't take it anymore. "Please, stop..."

"And do you know what's even funnier? How that bitch resisted! What was her name again...?" continued Jason in a mocking manner, snapping his fingers while trying to remember.

"Oh no… you… you… killed… Eliana..." Carmen said in an almost inaudible voice, feeling her heart about to blow up. She covered her ears in despair. "Please stop! I DON'T WANT TO HEAR IT ANYMORE!"

"Oh yeah! That was her name! That stupid bitch thought she could escape my wrath! And I always thought that sawing limbs off was a pain in the ass! It was actually quite enjoyable, if I say so myself! You should try it sometime!"

"SHUT UP! SHUT UP! SHUT UP!" Carmen screamed on the border of madness, rocking her head back and forth.

"As the saying goes, if you want it done well, you gotta do it yourself! That fucking Kelvin had ONE job! ONE FUCKING JOB! AND HE FUCKING MESSED IT UP!" Jason's face transitioned from momentary rage to relative peace. "I guess it doesn't matter anymore… I got you now..."

Carmen couldn't speak anymore. She simply kept her ears covered and her eyes to the floor. Her wound was still there, yet she could no longer feel it. The agents approached their prey slowly and handcuffed the couple with no resistance. They knew it wasn't like Carmen could offer any and Nico couldn't risk it. Carmen only observed everything in silence, gone inside her mind, unable to bear that her happiness, the treasure of her whole life, had been nothing more than a mere lie. All those years of her youth wasted in a hatred she couldn't even begin to understand. She felt sadness, regret, and defeat. The thought of vengeance was not even a suggestion in her mind. As the floor beneath her, now wet from her own tears, reflected her face, she saw herself in this improvised mirror after what felt like ages. Her face showed premature wrinkles from the lack of care. She looked like an old woman.

Who cares?

Now she would simply go back to Sanatorium, or worse. She looked up to see the ceiling of her beloved home one last time as the agents finished restraining her. The bitterness within her heart was hard to contain at the realization that she was branded by society and the law, condemned forever to ruin by the man she had sworn to love and protect above all things. She couldn't help it but scream out loud in pain... in silence.

Nevertheless, there would be no rest for her as her life withered away with her uncovered wound, now releasing her blood all over the floor. Thus, Jason pointed at both mockingly with his left index. "Wait a second... don't tell me?! Are you and him... together?!"

Carmen wasn't even listening to him at this point.

"ARE YOU IGNORING ME BITCH?! I'M FUCKING TALKING TO YOU!" screamed Jason, this time next to her ears. Carmen couldn't cover her ears this time as her hands had been cuffed behind her back. Her lack of response only made Jason angrier, ending up in him slapping her face.

"Aaaaaaahhhhhhhh!!!!!" Carmen screamed back in desperation. Jason simply slapped her again, and again.

"Just shut up already! You fucking criminal! You whore! You were fucking a minor, didn't you?! DIDN'T YOU!" said Jason, enjoying all the possible guilt he could extract from Carmen. "Don't you know that is a fucking crime?! You're nasty! You make me sick!"

The Block agents pushed Nico violently into the ground as he was struggling to set himself free. He had never felt such an emotion before... the genuine will to kill someone.

"Jason... please... kill me..." begged Carmen in a weak voice, to Nico's surprise. "I can't live on this Earth anymore... you've destroyed my life beyond repair... you stole all of my hope away... you killed my son... so... kill me... please... just kill me... I beg of you... or I'll never leave you alone..."

"Are you out of your mind?!" complained Nico just to receive a punch on the back of his head on behalf of the closest agent, stunning him slightly. Still, he continued his useless struggle. The position he was in, his right cheek sticking to the floor while one of the agents had his left arm pressing his head down, allowed him to use only half of his mouth. "I wash wrong... you there... the blondie motherfucker... you're worshe than trash... there'sh not a definition for shit... like you in exishtence..." the Immigrant dared say, just to receive another smack on the head.

Jason looked at him with a killing intent just to explode with rage. "SHUT THE FUCK UP YOU FUCKING INFERIOR MIZELAS TRASH! YOU HAVE NO RIGHT TO EVEN BREATHE THE SAME AIR WE REAL PEOPLE DO! CAN'T YOUR LOWER IQ UNDERSTAND SOMETHING SO BASIC?! HAH?! HAH?! JUST SHUT THE FUCK UP ONCE AND FOR ALL!!!!"

By the time he was finished, he was next to Nico's ear, filling it with spit.

"Why don't you release me and make me then?" taunted Nico, raising his head just to look into his eyes, never losing his cool. *If I get myself killed, then, maybe, just maybe, there's a chance they'll let Carmen go... or if they lose sight of her while focused on me, she might escape somehow... I would've never thought of betting on luck or hope before... but, aquí estoy... thought the Immigrant. These imbéciles don't like to kill Frisks if possible... That's my only shot... I'll take any chance I can get... no matter how slim or small... my promise must stand... I can't fail.*

Indeed, the Block's motto was to serve and protect the true

owners of Panthea. The ones who had defeated the Sarks, its original inhabitants, and that had confined them to the *encirclements* they lived in in that country. Still, Nico knew better. Even by his standards, his plan based on hope sounded completely insane, but that was the best idea he could come up with. Not that the blows to his head and the handcuffs were helping much.

Jason took Derzú and threw it to the floor, using all his might, right next to Nico's face. Then, he stepped on it, with such fury, that the interior of the stuffed animal simply popped into existence. The teddy-bear ended up beheaded by Jason's heel.

"Insolent worm! You're fucking lucky you're required alive..." concluded Jason, just to turn his attention back to Carmen. "Unlike my dear wife..."

Nico looked at him, his eyeballs about to leave their orbits, having realized his mistake too late: that man would have Carmen killed, either way. Now, more than ever, he needed to buy some time to make up a new plan. A good one, this time. "I guess... you didn't have the balls to kill me yourself... *cobarde*... No wonder you joined a pathetic organization like the Block... A bunch of sad little losers with a superiority complex... It seems the one who's pathetic... is you... hahahahahahahaha!" taunted Nico, once more, raising his head as much as he could, rebelling against the hand that pressed him down.

Jason roared, "YOU PIECE OF SHIT! HOW DARE YOU?! YOU DO WANT TO DIE, DON'T YOU?! DON'T Y-" and stopped short for apparently no reason to then continue calmly, to Nico's surprise, after clearing his throat. "Ehem... You're... extremely lucky..." Jason pressed his fingers repeatedly against his nose while taking deep breaths. "Besides, I do owe you some credit for the success of your own capture... and that of my wife..." the youngster couldn't believe his eyes at the way Jason had managed to calm himself down. It was incredibly effective, to the point of even impressing the Block's agents. "It was the conversation you idiots had with Rasheed that told us exactly what you were planning… quite ironic, isn't it?"

"What?" Nico couldn't believe what he was hearing. It had been him who had accepted to contact Gupta with the truth, after all. *It's my fault*, he thought as his eyes couldn't avoid looking down. Carmen wasn't even looking at him, or anyone else for that matter. She was still trapped deep inside her mind, trying to assimilate all the information she had just received. Thinking over and over: the past, the present. While doing so, she remembered something crucial, something so important that it gave her an unknown strength she had never felt before. Something that was none other than what she had still to tell Nico. At last, she looked up, straight into Jason's eyes, begging no more, her ebon black eyes full of a determination made her husband respond by taking a stance.

"Oh, Carmen… if you just had come into my arms, at least I would've killed you in the same fashion I killed your damn daddy… and not in the way I'm thinking of right now," he continued in a saddened voice as he looked at the gun in his right hand in a lovely fashion. "You know how much I hate firing this gun and putting bloodstains upon my brand-new rug… not that I visit this property often nowadays, but I like to keep it neat and clean, as you may remember…"

Nico realized his new plan was also a failure. If at least he had another one, just another one, regardless of how bad it could be. No matter how much he taunted that man, he wouldn't turn his attention solely on him. And Carmen, being the King he had to prevent from falling into a checkmate, wouldn't budge in her current mental state. Maybe if that man would've been just following his emotions, there might've been another chance. Nevertheless, Jason was following orders, preventing him from making foolish mistakes of that kind, and nothing Nico could say would change those orders. However, that made him realize something else…

Jason had said it earlier: they wanted *him* alive. Thus, if they couldn't kill him just yet, he could try to attack them and buy time for Carmen to escape, this time without restraining himself. Given that the last thing he wanted was to see someone else he loved die at the hands of the Block, it wasn't hard for him to arrive at the conclusion that his life didn't matter anymore. Fortunately for him, he had learned to control his anger a long time ago, although this situation was proving too much for him, either way. *Now!* he thought as he, taking advantage of one of the agents' tired arms to spring back to his feet, charged towards Jason.

"Like I'll let you! Carmen run! Run now!" Nico yelled as he tried to headbutt Jason, but he was stopped short by a bullet to his left leg, falling flat on his face. The sound of the shot had disturbed Nico greatly, in addition to the pain of the injury, prompting him into lying on the floor while screaming in pain. He had never received a bullet wound before and he had never imagined the first time he got one would be three times as painful. Jason approached him and stepped on his wound without too much force, making the Immigrant scream his lungs out in pain.

Is there anything else in store? This is getting boring...

"As I said before... you're quite lucky, scum..." Jason said as he lessened the pressure from his foot on Nico's wound. "Even I know, being a doctor and all, that extreme pain could kill you. Otherwise... I would open up that gift I just gave you even more under my foot." Jason changed his target. "Aaaand as for you, my dear Carmen, what should I do with you...? Let's see... You keep looking at me like that and I might just think you still love me... how sweet..."

Sure enough, Carmen was now looking intently at her husband as anger sparked in her eyes. Nico's screams were resounding inside her head. "Leave him alone! Now!" screamed Carmen. "I'll kill you myself if you don't!" However, Jason's mocking smile, added to his constant change in pressure against Nico's wound, made her realize the obvious. "Please..." she changed her voice to beg for mercy. "Kill me if that's what you want... but leave him alone..."

"And I thought you had forgotten what position you're in right now... oh well, whatever. I'm tired of your fucking voice, of your fucking sight, and of your fucking EXISTENCE," Jason cocked the hammer on his revolver in his right hand and aimed at Carmen. "If that's your deal, I'll gladly take it! Any last words my dear? Because... you know how this ends... just... just don't hold it against me, okay?" His words sounded compassionate, and yet sarcastic.

Her newfound awareness made her realize this was it. She wished she had told Nico her secret sooner... maybe everything would've been different. She wished she had known him earlier, in another time, in another place.... She wished she had regained her hope way earlier. Now, it was too late. She was about to motion her lips to Nico, to make him read her mouth and tell her secret to him in silence, but decided to keep it as she knew it would only increase the Immigrant's pain by the time Jason shot her. She could taste blood coming out of her mouth, probably a product of her wound messing around her internal organs. At least, Nico still had a chance to escape. He was young and skillful--that was all she had now. She'd have to go down with that hope in her mind.

Carmen looked at Nico, who was having a hard time assimilating what was about to happen. "*Pequeño*... Thank you for everything... you taught me many things... but especially that... I could be loved again..." Carmen started talking in a shaken voice as tears streamed down her face. "I wished we had had a different life... a different world... thank you for helping me get back on my feet when I had lost all hope... at least I know... I know that... you still have the chance to escape all this... my heart will always be with you... the last person I was able to trust on this Earth... *te amo mi pequeño*..."

"What are you talking about?! We'll get out of this one alive and well! Don't say that!" said Nico, forgetting his pain for a few seconds, trying to get up only to get kicked back down by one of the agents. The pain from the kick to his face proved too much for the Immigrant who could no longer stand.

"I'm so moved... Whatever... Are you done yet? I got

things to do, you know? This is very inconsiderate of you!" said Jason casually aiming at Carmen's forehead. "Guys, would you please move that slut closer to me? I want a clean and nice shot!" Two men took Carmen by her arms, dragged her and placed her a mere two feet before Jason. He smiled broadly as he checked his magnum ammunition in the drum. Thus, with the hammer already cocked, he proceeded to aim with both hands, completely focused on the task at hand.

"NO! DON'T DO IT! PLEASE! I'LL DO ANYTHING! PLEASE! I BEG OF YOU! DON'T!" Nico yelled with all the air he could gather as Jason turned his face towards him just to show him his triumphant grin.

"Fuck you ricer! and… good-bye, my love!"

"NOOOOO!!!"

Carmen smiled at Nico, nodding at him with affection as Jason pulled the trigger. The sound shook Nico's core as Carmen fell limp to the floor. As shadows began clouding her eyes and the broad hole that traversed her head from forehead to back filled her black raven hair with blood, Carmen kept her sight locked onto Nico. She couldn't listen to him anymore as darkness took over her. She could only remember that Nico had tears coming out of his eyes.

Thank you so much for giving me a reason to go on… pequeño… she thought as she let death take care of the rest.

Demons and darkness aren't always mutually inclusive, right?

III

AND FROM DARKNESS, the demon emerged.

Killing left and right, the men and women attacking the Black Cross were no longer able to regret their foolishness. Nonetheless, and contrary to their given instructions, the last one of them threw his weapons away and begged for his life on his knees. As he looked down, embracing himself, the demon walked calmly towards him, wearing her iconic devil-like smile, and, to his surprise, she simply went past him.

"*Por favor*… don't kill me…" he kept on saying, with his eyes closed. Upon opening his eyes and realizing he was safe to flee, the kneeling man immediately got up and started running away as fast as his legs could carry him. Such a reaction surprised the spectators, especially the Biologist. This latter had always wondered about a lot of things about this woman, like why was she wearing that dress if it was destroyed beyond recognition, or why was she always smiling… or why had she become a psychopath in the first place. All he knew was that her creation was partly thanks to the Block. Even though guilt was an unknown concept for him and his organization, he did feel guilty… only because he wasn't supposed to be having a hard time capturing a wild beast.

"I guess it'll require more than just bullets and sedatives to bring her down…" said the Biologist in a confident fashion, ignoring his fleeing agent. "I guess we'll have to stick to the same plan... now that I think of it... she's already figured out our entire plan... it seems..."

"What plan are you talking about?! Getting killed is what you call a plan?!" O'Connell exploded while the Biologist put both of his hands behind his back, undisturbed. There were five agents left near him manning the stereo equipment...

"What are your orders, sir?" asked one of the remaining agents in a shaking voice through his walkie-talkie, "may we retreat?"

"No..." said the scientist, dryly, visibly happy at the situation "She's already onto you, anyway."

The men looked at the looming menace running towards them and despair soon ensued. "We need to retreat sir! Please! We have to-"

"Shush... shush..." replied the Biologist with a mockingly calmed voice, "you know what will happen if you fail to obey your superior's orders, right?" he continued as he calmly held his hands behind his back, "you knew this outcome was within the possibilities... actually, you knew it was almost certain... most simulations ended like this..."

Tired of the cruelty and indifference of the Biologist, Ryan snatched away the scientist's walkie-talkie and put it near his mouth. "You're free to go! I repeat! You're free to go! Go now!"

The Biologist looked at him from the corner of his eye as he shrugged and raised both hands to shoulder level. "Oh my! My! Quite impatient you are... let's see... no elements present here... it should still be fine..." the scientist mumbled to himself.

"Fuck off asshole!" raged Ryan in response. "What the fuck is going on?!" he yelled at the realization that no one had moved out of their posts. "Leave now! For fuck sake! You're about to die!" he pressed on to no avail. The last five agents standing were unwilling to move, and yet, their eyes showed how fear had invaded their very core. Nonetheless, as they kept fixed onto their posts, they continued to plead the Biologist. "Wait! Please help us! Please allow us to escape this monster! Sir! We're begging you!" continued the same agent, now in deeper despair.

O'Connell, who had tried to stop Ryan as soon as he caught a glimpse of his intentions, wouldn't stop him anymore. Nevertheless, his expression, along with that of Ryan's, changed completely when he realized the Biologist was laughing his lungs off. "What is the matter with you?!" screamed the War Hero, unable to believe his eyes.

The Biologist had tears in his eyes as his increasingly insane mockery displayed in his voice, "I must admit... that was... cute!... but they're done for... they always were!"

Both police officers looked at the scene in horror as the expected was about to happen. There was little the remaining agents could do as they shot the demon with their weapons just to end up slaughtered all the same, some of them in the most unthinkable ways. One of them had his arms amputated and his head crushed as the remaining four agents stood their ground, contrary to the orders Ryan had issued them and to their own desires of survival, keeping on the fight against the Black Cross. The result was unavoidable. At least their pain didn't last long as the demon would slay them in one hit. By the time there was one remaining, opposite to what duty ordered, he begged for mercy similarly to the agent who had managed to escape before him.

"*P-por favor*... don't kill me..." he cried in an almost inaudible voice with both his palms together over his head, as if praying to Kothat, and kneeling while looking down. "*Eu imploro*... don't do it... please..."

The Black Cross looked at him intensely, and yet, she was reluctant to strike him down. Her eyes seemed to have seen something of the sort before. To O'Connell and Asprey's surprise, she simply lowered the arm that was about to hit this last agent with and kept walking past him. The man didn't look up until he heard her steps behind him. Once he realized he had been spared, he made a run for it without a second thought.

"Tch! Not like this is a first, but whatever..." ranted the

Biologist in a low voice, completely ignored by the two policemen beside him.

"She… she spared him… why?!" exploded Ryan, unable to believe his eyes. However, as this spared agent was dashing away, a blood hole appeared at the back of his head, which also appeared in the middle of his forehead. Then, he fell limp to the floor. Both officers turned around and saw the Biologist with a smoking pistol in his hand.

"Oh my! Oh my! What an unfortunate event! It seems no one survived the assault!" said mockingly the Biologist along with a small chuckle. It didn't take long for the officers to realize that the agent who had escaped prior also lay dead. His skin was covered in black veins, probably poisoned. They looked at the Biologist who had his gaze fixed on the Black Cross, "it seems it's just the two of us my darling!"

"Are you out of your fucking mind?!" reprimanded the War Hero, his veins about to pop. Ryan was unable to move, shaken to the core. He had never seen anything of the sort in human nature or comradery among brothers in arms. For a moment there, he felt more hatred towards the Biologist than to the Dire One. And yet, it didn't make any difference for the monster before them as she started to quicken her pace towards them. In the blink of an eye, she was already running at full speed, charging against the Biologist.

"Death always goes well with those who seek immortality…" said calmly the Black Cross. "No empire lasts forever…" Without any hesitation, she threw one of her crosses at them, now chained and wrapped around her wrist, vertically so that it'd fall on top of the Biologist. It was as if a small flyswatter was about to hit an oversized rat.

"Stay behind me!" said the Biologist to both men near him with great worry drawn on his face. An order they promptly obeyed. "We must stay clear of her weapons at all costs! She's too fast!" The Biologist placed himself in front of them in a protective fashion. *You deserve what's coming to you… your intelligence is not worthy of a Frisk*, he thought.

As the monster approached, and the airborne cross fell

onto them, the Biologist pushed the two officers further back while he jumped out of the way of the lethal weapon just in the nick of time. The cross in question buried itself into the ground, so deep, that they could barely see its lower stipes. The Biologist looked up and saw the demon using that buried cross as an anchor, in other words, the center of a centrifugal force with which she had enhanced her jump by pulling from the chain onto her wrist, accelerating downwards with the other cross in her right hand. After one second, she was merely ten meters above them. Her wide grin made her seem oblivious to the death of the man she had just spared; probably more oblivious than the Biologist.

The Biologist's eyes shone in delight. *She will get one of us for sure… and it's not gonna be me,* he thought as he planned his move. *Whether I move out of the way on time, or whether I put these idiots behind, she could throw her other cross at a selected location… if I time this… just right...*

"I still remember how it felt to shoot that old man!" taunted the Biologist. "What was his name again?! Oh yeah… Old Joe!"

The taunt, whether unnecessary or not, provoked the expected effect as the falling demon pulled the chain with more eagerness in order to accelerate further her descent upon him. And as planned, the Biologist grinned mockingly and moved aside, letting one of the officers behind him take the fatal blow in his place: the younger one. As this latter's body wouldn't obey him, remaining in the same place, like a statue, the War Hero pushed him away while taking his place in the process. The old man looked at Ryan with a small smirk right before he received a direct hit to the head, vertically, to the point where it was buried between his shoulders. Then, his body hit the floor like a brick from a falling building, splashing blood all over the ground.

"NOOO!!!" yelled Ryan in despair.

"Another… supernatural..." murmured the Black Cross, looking at the Biologist while pulling the buried cross back to herself just to step aside and resume her swings at the scientist.

Even though she seemed slightly surprised at the discovery, anyone else would've thought she had just killed an ant. The Biologist once again evaded her attack by jumping upwards and getting near the stereo equipment, still playing Classical music. Without relenting her attacks, moving away from Ryan, the monster got her crosses close to her once more and resumed her charge. "You look for... that... beyond the sky..."

"Oh my! That's rude!" replied the Biologist in fake irritation. "Are you implying I lied?! Not cool, not cool at all!" he continued as he got beside a box near the stereo. "You should've told me about that before! You got no manners?!"

Ryan could only watch what was happening before him, lying down on the ground, unable, and uninterested, to understand what they were talking about. His legs still refused to budge as his watery eyes refused to look anywhere else, fixed on the corpse of the War Hero. Meanwhile, the Black Cross closed in on the Biologist who jumped behind a table with a million buttons on it.

"Oh my, my! I get it now! Let me just tell you that... as long as we have the power... we'll do what we want... the future's not ours, but the present is! My dear!" stated the Biologist out of nowhere to then produce a strange looking gun from under said table at an incredible speed and aimed it at the Dire One. As the demon was in mid-air, she tried to evade it to no avail. "I've been waiting an eternity to test this! Eat this!" The weapon in question shot an electric ray hitting her upfront. She fell to the ground like a dead fly, unable to move, feeling paralysis taking over her body as she struggled to move. "Oh my! How unfortunate! It's never good to receive a discharge for free! You should know better!" he continued triumphantly with a grin that was as wide as the sky was dark. "By the way, how are you feeling, darling?"

The electric current was constantly being pumped into her body and didn't allow the Black Cross to even speak. Ryan, seeing this and, now wrapped in rage, took out his statutory handgun and shot the demon in the head several times. His face said it all. After thirteen rounds, the constant clicks from his handgun, as he kept on pulling the trigger, suggested that he had run out of bullets... and that he wouldn't mind shooting air at her for at least a hundred more times.

"Well..." continued the Biologist, looking at the Dire One, "I do owe you an explanation! You'll see... the syringes that we shot at you contained a special substance... which, combined with electricity, should prevent your skills from triggering... so it means that... it's over for you, darling! Quite a pity, actually! I had great plans for you! I guess one can't have everything..."

Where had she heard that before?

Her body was going number and number as her sight was going darker and darker. Her lack of self-awareness had been her own undoing. Perhaps her willingness to die was really the one to blame. *Death can't be ended*, she thought as the electric ray kept battering her body constantly with no signs of letting up. No matter how hard she tried, she wasn't getting up. She couldn't fight back. It felt painful to be in the same situation she had been a year before. For the first time in months, she wished she had Nico by her side. Maybe then, just maybe, she would've had an actual motivation to get back on her feet.

"What the-" said the Biologist as the electricity from his ray started to decrease, its lights dimming to the point of no return, its power slowly disappearing into nothingness. The speakers had stopped working, too. The same could be said of all the other computers around them.

The Biologist tried desperately to restart the weapon, but it was no use. The Black Cross soon reincorporated, and, in a few seconds, she had pulled her crosses back to herself thanks to her new added chains. She prepared to charge again.

"I think it's time to go..." said the scientist to Ryan.

"No! I won't leave until she's fucking dead! You hear me?!" the latter said menacingly, blinded by rage. His fists tightly closed in anger. As his only weapon was out of ammo, it became clear that he no longer cared about his likely death.

"This is exciting!" said the Biologist as he took a remote control out of his pocket and pressed a big red button on it. In turn, it summoned a strange-looking car from far away which, upon a closer look, looked more like a downsized grey tank, dashing towards them. The vehicle in question stopped right before hitting Biologist. Soon enough, he grabbed the young officer effortlessly by his shoulders and threw him inside it, despite his protests and struggle to release himself from his grip. Since it was proving too hard to do so, and the Black Cross was likely to attack at any moment, the scientist knocked Ryan out with a punch to the back of the head and proceeded with their escape. The door closed tightly behind them as the vehicle accelerated away from the Dire One. *Even I know who I should mess with when it comes to close-quarters combat...* the scientist thought, watching the Black Cross standing where he had left her, grinning at him as the distance between them grew larger.

That O'Connell... he had seen too much... too bad I had to kill him... a waste for a Frisk... thought the Biologist as the car drove itself away. Ryan lay there on the car floor, still unconscious. *At least the experiment was a success...*

Then, the Biologist pressed a button within the car panel just to make a small screen pop out of the ceiling. As soon as it appeared, it automatically dialed a number and made a call, or so it seemed. "How did the experiment go? I hope you will provide a... favorable report," said a deep and confident voice from the device in question. The Biologist grinned satisfactorily as a face turned up on the monitor before him.

"It went *almost* as planned... it seems there was foreign interference during the final phase... at least it wasn't a complete waste... it confirmed my suspicions... she's aging faster than a normal human... I calculate her body will be that of a seventy-year-old by the time she's fifty... maybe even older..." reported the scientist without letting his smile rest. Then, he sighed. "That's the problem with prototypes... so, I advise following close surveillance on the subject at hand... and, as for the deployed agents... all of them perished at the hands of the subject... *unfortunately.*"

"Very well," answered the man in a voice that seemed pleased, "your excellent performance has earned you full authority on this project, Chief in command Pietros. Do not disappoint my trust in you."

"I wouldn't even dream of doing such a thing, Herr Smith," said the Biologist while holding a vial filled with blood in front of the camera. "On another note, has the media been dealt with? We're on the critical phase of research right now and-"

"Who do you take me for?" retorted the man, displeased, to then finish the call.

"I guess I doubted his capabilities unnecessarily... well, whatever..." muttered the Biologist to himself while looking at the prize he had obtained, now between his fingers. The blood he had captured that very night from the Dire One was now his most valuable possession. How he had done it wasn't really that hard to figure out. Small robots with the shape of flies had collected the samples as his agents died and the Dire One's blood was spilled everywhere due to the excessive wounds on her body. *There's nothing like using expendable resources on the task at hand*, he thought as he placed the small tube inside a metallic briefcase. *I only hate that those robots are so expensive to replace*. Although he never truly knew why he liked spending in general, he kept himself in check regarding these fly-like robots. Besides, without the music playing during the operation, the buzzing produced by these robots wouldn't have been so easily disguised. The real bullets and silent injections had also been made hardly distinguishable thanks to the same strategy. *She never knew what really hit her... no, scratch that, she did*, concluded the scientist as the young man beside him started to wake up from his sudden 'fainting'. The Biologist approached him with a visible expression of preoccupation on his face.

"Where... where am I?" said the young man, completely confused, looking around. "What happened to Major O'Connell?! Where's he?!"

It seems the head trauma did its work perfectly, thought the Biologist, smiling to himself. "You'll see... he was killed by the Black Cross. It was a horrible sight to bear... I regret it wholefully, but there's still hope... and... because I want to finish this hell... and since I want to make the world a better place... I joined a peaceful organization... an organization that wants to see the end of innocent lives being taken by such a monster... Therefore, I have... an offer for you, private Asprey," said the Biologist with a sad and determined expression on his face. *Get them young, keep them forever.*

Ryan looked into the emptiness, ignoring his speech. "No... he was like... my father... no... this can't be happening..."

The Biologist touched his right shoulder gently with his right index, to which Ryan turned around and looked at him. "What do you say, son? Would you like to join me and destroy that demon?"

The private's face slowly changed into that of new determination. "Whatever it is you say... I'll take it... I'll avenge him! No matter the cost! I have to avenge all the lives she has taken! Even if it's the last thing I do on this Earth!" yelled Ryan without a hint of hesitation.

"Very well... I'm glad to hear that... you'll see... my organization thinks you'd be perfect for a new project of my own... I call it... Project Tourniquet," said the Biologist with obvious greed in his voice. "We need brave men just like you to fight the evils of this world... evils such as the Black Cross," he continued as he extended his right hand towards Ryan, "do you accept, then?"

The young officer first grabbed his hand and then went all the way to his elbow, his eyes lost into nothingness. "Hell yeah! It's payback time!" the young officer claimed, smiling at such an opportunity as hope had been brought back to his core. That was, until his face darkened out of the blue. "Wait a second! She'll go for Kelvin! We must stop her! He's in danger!"

"Oh my! Don't worry! My organization got it covered!" said dismissively the scientist while patting Ryan softly on the back, "Kelvin should know by now we're his best hope anyways..." *If he was still alive...*

Ryan's eyes glistened in the dark as his surge of energy

started to die down. Then, he simply fell onto his stomach and fell asleep. As the young officer lay on the mini-tank's floor once more, other screens popped out of the vehicle's inner walls and showed a car driving behind them, closing in at a high speed. The Biologist saw it with widened and sunny eyes. "It's her, isn't it?! Nothing that can't be solved with the touch of a button!" he added as he pressed another button near the vehicle's back door. Outside, the armored vehicle released missiles that hit the car behind them, setting it on fire and stopping it for good. "You see?" he said patronizingly to a fainted Ryan. "Nothing to worry about!"

Nevertheless, the Black Cross was still near Kelvin's house, still recovering from the past attack. It had definitely affected her in more ways than one as her muscles had a hard time being themselves once again. She was lucky the Biologist had jumped to the conclusion that she was back on track just from watching her getting ready to charge. More so, for him to have run out of juice the moment he had her where he wanted. *No, it couldn't be mere luck.*

If there was something the Black Cross had learned over the time ever since she had started her new mission, it was that luck didn't exist. Something or, most probably, someone must have intervened. Perhaps a competitor of *them*, if there was any. Hopefully, an ally. She didn't give it much thought as she started to walk again, knowing she was being observed by somebody from the nearby forest. She couldn't tell what, or who, was it that observed her every move, yet, it dared not come forward from the shadows. No matter how hard she looked for it, she couldn't find said stalker, or stalkers. Fortunately, it didn't matter, not as long as it didn't interfere with her quest.

She went back to Kelvin's house and found the body of the doctor again, this time, with an irritated expression drawn on her face. At the sight, she proceeded to smash his head with enough force to make it explode like a water balloon. Then, she growled in anger. Had she known that expression of hers would have been treasured by the Biologist, she would've had an easier time drawing him closer to her to finish him off in one swing. Once done leaving her 'mark' on Kelvin's body, she exited the hollow building and looked for the cleanest car she could find and entered it. As she closed its door on the driver's seat, she couldn't avoid looking back at the dismembered corpses lying on the floor outside the building. People who were truly innocent of such a fate. Innocent because they didn't fight her on the grounds of defending an ideology, but that of sheer fear of death.

"*Lo siento*," said Carmen as she took off. Her heart, still feeling no regret, nor remorse.

IV

"I'LL NEVER FORGIVE YOU FOR THIS!" burst out Nico in uncontrollable rage. "I'll fucking kill you! You hear me bastard?! I swear you WILL die! I SWEAR IT!"

Jason yawned mockingly at the display. "Spare me your bullshit, trash. Barking like a dog is the only thing you're good at. Instead of having deliriums like the piece of shit you are, you should get ready for what's coming to you," said Jason as he couldn't stop showing a confident and radiant smile.

Nico couldn't take it anymore. Using his head, he hit the man pinning his right shoulder on the chin while using this very impulse to release himself from the one on the left. Nonetheless, a third agent appeared in front of him and, by kicking him in the face, he knocked Nico down to the floor. Then, said agent let his body fall on top of the Immigrant, with such force, that Nico coughed drops of blood. And yet, his eyes were still fixed in Jason who returned his furious gaze with a condescending one. As the Immigrant kept struggling, ignoring the pain as much as he could, the agent who had been hit on the chin, now irate, produced a metal cord out of his operations belt and placed himself behind Nico. In a matter of seconds, he wrapped said cord around Nico's neck and started to pull. As air became harder and harder to grasp for the teenager, he received a blow on the back of his head with a pistol grip. "Good night, worm," said the agent in question.

These three agents readily took Nico outside the mansion while the remaining three stayed inside to follow any last instructions Jason could issue to them. They watched the whole scene with cold eyes as they had seen way worse than that. Of course, they had done way, way, worse than that.

Jason quietly approached Carmen's corpse with visible disgust on his face. "Say something now! FUCKING SAY SOMETHING, YOU WHORE!" he yelled as he kicked her lifeless body repeatedly in a fit of rage. After kicking her around twenty times without receiving any answers, he crouched near her and using his index he checked on her jugular. The absence of pulse made him sad. His sadness was so evident that even the agents felt sorry for him.

"I had hoped…" he muttered to himself, "you had felt more pain with my kicks… it's so unfair." Then, he stood up as his face changed to that of extreme happiness. "Well, whatever. My friends, I have yet another favor to ask of you."

"Yes, Mister Wright?" answered one of the agents in a voice of slight grief. They felt sad as they didn't like their show to be over so soon, either. At the same time, the gentle way the agents spoke to Jason carried him back to the past when he was contacted by the Block for the first time…

"We're granting scholarships for those willing to enter an additional program within our corporation," said the man on the other side of the phone line back then. "We have been… observing you, Mister Wright. I strongly believe you'd be an excellent candidate for our student scholarship program. What do you say?"

As this offer meant his dream was just at his fingertips, he accepted eagerly. Once he was admitted into said program, Jason realized he was but one piece in the giant puzzle this corporation was playing. Sometimes they would call themselves an organization, though. Thanks to them, he graduated from the renowned University of Juswusf, which also granted him the chance to visit the country he had idealized so much, the U.K.P. During these years, his plan started to take form, and the Block was there to help him all the steps of the way. If successful, he would escalate within the Block's ranks in no time, and his reasons for doing so were as mysterious as his methods from his peers' perspective. Nonetheless, everything didn't go according to plan as the wretched whore had managed to survive the farce he had had so much trouble to make and complete. She was supposed to be executed, not sent to an asylum by the judge. Although the judge was dealt with by the Block after that sentence, back then he could only wonder what else he could do to finally get rid of her. Now, that question no longer revolved around his mind. *If you could see me now, mom,* he thought with a smirk of true happiness drawn on his face.

"Sir?" said one of the agents, waiting for his orders while breaking him out of memory lane.

"I need you to bury this bitch. I know we have good influences in the justice department and all to get rid of her in the legal way... but I'd rather reserve those resources for something more... useful," declared Jason. "I wouldn't want to have to use them to explain this unfortunate event to the authorities and be in their debt... at least not yet. So, I got the perfect place for her final rest! If you'd please follow me outside, and while you're at it, take that nasty and bloody rug with you, too. I'd have to use tons of disinfectants if I ever wanted to clean away her vulgar blood."

"As you wish, Mister Wright."

The three men wrapped the corpse with said rug and carried it outside, led by Jason whistling his 'pain' away with a joyful melody. The casual way they walked would've made anyone else think they were going for a picnic. After throwing the rug and corpse onto the grass without any care, they proceeded to dig a small and shallow grave. Besides the tomb they were making, there was another one present and visible onto which the name "Spunky" had been engraved. *I'm sorry for doing this to you my dear pup,* thought Jason at the sight. As these three agents were busy digging, the other three could be seen at a distance carrying an unconscious Immigrant into their van. It had been parked among the trees, covered in bushes to cloak it, behind the small chapel the whole time.

Taking advantage of their short break, the diggers took off their sound-inhibiting gear. Said gear was most evident on their helmets, feet, and vests. It had been thanks to this equipment that they hadn't been detected by the Immigrant from the start, also allowing them to jump onto the youngster and Carmen without any problems. *Nothing like having the best technology at our disposal*, thought Jason, his chest filled to the brim with pride. As he admired the digging, he could see, at a distance, how the Mizelas had been put into lockup and how the agents who had carried him had jumped into the van's seats and were now reading their PAD's.

The digging agents finished the grave after five minutes. *No surprise there, I've heard their training includes solutions for all sorts of situations. They seemed relaxed... Oh, I see why...* thought Jason realizing that the pouring rain was quite refreshing in that heavy gear, and that that, mixed with the cold of fall, helped them loosen up a bit. "The grave is ready, sir," informed one of them. Jason nodded and they carried the body into it.

"Wait!" ordered Jason when they were about to throw the body into the hole. "Even though that rug is beyond recovery, burying her with it would be way too much for what she really deserves. She'll go out of my life without taking anything else that belongs to me... even if it's trash..."

The agents shrugged and obeyed. They rolled Carmen out of the rug with deep disgust, trying not to tarnish their combat gloves with her blood, and threw the rug away. Then, by kicking her around, they finally got the corpse into the hole and proceeded to bury it. Jason looked at the scene with certain impatience. At the same time, he felt so happy to have people who could understand him. He wasn't alone. He would never be alone again.

"Good-bye, my love!" said Jason with a wide smile looking down at Carmen's blood-soaked corpse inside the hole as she had fallen face up. Her dead eyes were still looking straight, now into the grim sky.

"Please, leave her face for last," asked Jason kindly, and so they did. Thus, Jason spat on her forehead before placing the last 'shovel' of dirt on her. "Finally… it's over…" Jason sobbed in silence. His inner suffering seemed like a rollercoaster that had finally stopped. Of course, this suffering didn't produce any reaction with the involved agents present in the scene. Not that Jason expected any sympathy from them as they weren't supposed to have any for him. They had already done a lot by helping him in such a manner, after all. Subsequently, the agents collected their equipment and presented their salutations to Jason.

"Thank you so much, my friends! My contribution to the Block will be greatly increased thanks to you! Don't doubt it for a single moment!" Jason claimed, hope and pride reflecting in his eyes. "We'll finish all those damn invaders! This is just the beginning!"

"*Munditiae et Superioritas!*" replied the agents in unison while showing their index and middle fingers together to Jason, in a way that he could see their thumbs, pinky and ring fingers touching each other's tips. Jason answered in kind, showing absolute respect for the bunch. Right afterwards, they went their separate ways. The agents joined their partners in the van as Carmen's husband happily waved them good-bye as they disappeared into the darkness of the night. Whether they waved back at him no longer mattered. What mattered was that he would fulfill his end of the bargain: The La Cruz state now belonged to them. With such an accomplishment bursting in his chest, Jason didn't feel like sleeping, so he returned to the main hall. "Even if they'll get most of it, there's also a piece for me," he muttered as he got his pipe out and prepared it to smoke. Now, all there was to do was to take a hot bath and relax. The hardest part had been done: his greatest torture, the biggest weight on his shoulders, had finally been lifted. His dream had finally come true, and nothing would change that. And yet, unbeknownst to him, a mysterious figure in the shadows had observed the whole event in silence from the rooftop. Once Jason got inside the mansion, almost dancing every step on his way, the figure in question descended upon the backyard and looked at the recently made grave with great concern on his face.

"*An!* I got here too late!" the figure said with utter rage in Asrepian. "*Mn ma khwahm!*" the figure continued his rambling while walking to and fro, anxiously. Asrepian, being the language of the country of Narin, in Calintia, on the other side of the world, as some often put it. Looking down at the fresh earth on top of Carmen, given that rain had been pouring furiously upon the ground, and him as well, he kept his seemingly aimless pacing. As lightning braced the skies, bringing light alongside them, the man in question seemed easier to discern. He wore square glasses, a white t-shirt wrapped in an open green and large hoodie sweater, and khaki cargo pants. He seemed to be in his mid-twenties. He kept walking back and forth relentlessly, his right hand holding his chin and his left behind his back. Thinking.

"What do I do? What do I do? I can't fail this! I just can't! There's so much at stake..." he kept mumbling to himself in what seemed to be increasing despair. The rain had soaked his clothes entirely, reminding him of his past failures, and now of his soon imminent failure. He hated to walk under the rain for that very reason. Thus, after mumbling a continuous flow of different words in Asrepian, he stopped short.

"Wait!" he shouted, bumping his right fist on top of his left palm, now with his eyes full of hope. "Maybe... there's still a chance!" He readily lifted his right wrist, where he had some sort of machine-like bracelet, and approached it to his face. "Perfect! I still have some left...! She's been dead for less than one hour... so... hmmm... if I use that..." he concluded. As he approached the grave with this newfound hope, his face turned pale with an expression of utter disgust. "It might be nasty, but I guess I got no choice... I hope I don't regret it... too much."

He quickly dug Carmen's face up and looked at her with even more disgust as coagulated blood had invaded almost all her countenance. Her hair was now crimson red from the dried blood resting on its surface. Indeed, the caliber of the bullet that had drilled through her head had opened a big hole that bathed her head with the vital substance. The resignation in Carmen's face, alongside her pain, was also engraved in her now static expression. The figure had a hard time beholding such a sight. Somehow, it pained him greatly.

"Pardon me… auntie Carmen…" he continued. "But it's the only way. I'm not a necrophile… for the record," he said to then kiss Carmen's lips. A minute had passed when he let go. "It should be enough with that alone… this was so gross…" He quickly stood up while trying not to vomit, placing his hand on top of his mouth. Once his struggle was over, he approached his left wrist to his mouth. "Start disinfection and suturing," he commanded in a neutral voice, "proceed to discharge the adequate voltage and fluid-forced pumping…" He lowered said wrist and looked back at Carmen, her sight now unobstructed from watching into emptiness, still dead. "It may not keep you alive forever. Probably just for another six or eight hours… but it's the best I could do… if that idiot would've told me who to save from the get-go! Damn him!"

As he spoke these words, Carmen's face began changing. It looked more and more alive as it started to recover color. The man in question sighed in relief. It brought a smirk on his face as well realizing he had somehow completed his mission. The hole in Carmen's head, which permitted an uninterrupted sight to the soil behind her skull, like a gory telescope, bled no more. It took awhile for the man to verify this as it was hard to tell with precision since her face and hair were filled to the brim with blood. Slowly, her breathing came back and her heart started beating again. This was further confirmed by the device mounted on his left wrist.

"I'm sorry to bring back your pain. A pain I wouldn't be able to bear, but I had to. I have someone that needs saving… I hope you will understand it one day," he continued as his being started fading out of existence. He looked at his hands, realizing what was about to happen. "It seems I barely made it… hehe… I made it! I did it! *Bale!*" he celebrated by punching the air upwards and jumping all over the place, unable to believe his good luck when his eyes caught onto something he had never seen before.

"Wait a minute… is that what I think it is?" he said as he stared at the event before him in wonder: a shadow had appeared in the blackened sky, only visible to the man thanks to the occasional lightning. He looked at Carmen one last time as he could barely see his own hands, becoming more transparent with every second. "So… that's how it happened… it was because of me…" he muttered in surprise. Then, he vanished completely.

The shadow in question swam up in the sky, snaking smoothly among the black clouds until it was exactly above Carmen's grave. Once it was above it, the shadow plunged downwards at great and increasing speed, as if it were competing with something else, something invisible, even to itself. After a few seconds, it had entered Carmen's body…

*   *   *

Carmen woke up and looked around. She found herself in a place she had never been to before, while at the same time, she felt she knew every inch of it. She was somehow surrounded by a reddish aqueous environment that blurred her vision. She felt bound and free at the same time. Before her, she could behold her memories lining up one after the other. From her first steps to her first words, to her first joy, to her first disappointment. People in her life also strolled in front of her in a parade of memories. Her mom's picture, her first friend, Eliana, and her first son. It felt wonderful.

However, this feeling radically changed when the memory of her first sight of Jason Wright appeared. She felt utterly sad as she saw herself smiling at that moment in complete happiness, and ignorance. She couldn't believe the irony.

Unwillingly, she kept going through the events of her short life, focusing on all the important moments, or at least the ones she considered as such. Nevertheless, she felt sadder, and sadder as the parade continued, seeing how her life became more and more miserable as time went on. Like a wounded jugular slowly draining her life away. Nothing would ever be the same. She also saw the best moments she had had with her dad. Nonetheless, her smile when she was a child now contrasted with her knowledge that *papá* had been killed. There were also the best moments she had with Juan Fernando. Nevertheless, her motherly smile now contrasted with the knowledge of how her son had really met his end. Then, there were the best moments she had with Jason. All those nights and days that she had wished were eternal back then. Notwithstanding, her smile in love now contrasted with the knowledge that his apparent happiness and smiles were just a cruel disguise to hide his sheer disgust towards her.

She felt like weeping, but she couldn't. No matter how hard she tried, not even all the moments that amounted to her demise couldn't do it. Then, she saw it once again. Her death at the hands of Jason, feeling an acute pain within herself at seeing her husband's true self. The most arduous moment of a life of torture. It felt like a rollercoaster of agony. Did it matter at all? She knew she was dead. Was this how the dead saw the world? Was it the way she would stay forever? Was that her core? Still, she wondered where the light at the end of the tunnel was if there was any. Thus, looking for said light, no matter how hard she swam, the exit appeared to be nowhere. As her memories kept streaming all around her without end, she started to feel despair. Swimming with all her might in vain, she simply stopped her struggle. Was there still something she had left undone? Something worth fighting for?

What was it?

She closed her eyes and felt her surroundings, letting herself be dragged by the flow around that weird place. Realizing she didn't feel tired, she decided to open her eyes to resume her swimming when she saw it. She would've screamed in fear if she had been able to feel it. Right in front of her, she had stumbled upon two big glowing red eyes, looking intensely at her within a dark strand of this vacuous place.

Contrary to what she, or any normal person, would have done, she kept looking into them. The being in question became more and more visible as she was able to discern it from the overall redness dominating the place. It was a humanoid being. It had petrol-like skin, wearing a crooked disturbing smile with ivory-like fangs. Its eyes became more and more vicious as its form came into full view, looking down on her with great intensity. Its pointed ears made him look like a creature out of a fantasy world. He had no genitalia and no clothing.

What was this supposed to be? She had long ago arrived at her own conclusion regarding gods and the supernatural, and yet, maybe the answer of her only remaining, and eternal, doubt was right in front of her. Was this the Devil himself coming to claim her core? He could be. After all, his appearance fit somewhat to what the church of Pillarism had always preached, or maybe he was an older god. Whatever the case may be, she started to consider that perhaps this process was just part of a routine that happened to all dead people. A routine this being before her had done for millennia. As it didn't look exactly like the devil she had always thought of, and given that the only and true devilish thing he had was his smile and gaze, her assumed conclusion started to turn into confusion. Unable to feel anything towards it, and having nothing to lose at this point, she approached it. Nonetheless, there was something bothering her…

She had known of his existence all along. But how? She guessed there was one way to find out. So, reluctantly, she broke the ice.

"Who are you? Have you come to claim my core? Are you the Devil?"

Carmen de la Cruz, the strange being said in a voice that sounded as if it had a million more attached to it, colder than ice, echoing strongly across the watery surroundings, *you, human woman who lost everything… I came to you with an offer,* he continued, his face unchanging, *for I am Sadness, the sylph spirit of pain and regret.*

"A sylph spirit… my knowledge about your kind is quite

small, unfortunately."

Since humanity's conception, sylph spirits were thought into existence. Mankind's constant search for answers not available to them allowed our creation, replied the being, its voice still unchanging.

"That's not an answer... I don't understand anything..."

And you don't have to... for that's not your place as a human... absolute knowledge is not allowed for your kind for you would never fully comprehend it...

"How do you even know that...?"

I have been observing you throughout your entire life... I never understood why I have done so, for you are nothing special among your kind... I guess this is similar to what humans define as love... beings such as myself rarely experience these types of feelings, for when we do experience them... we forget... I guess you possessed great potential for suffering... I guess that's what drew me to you... whether you're a man or woman... it would've been the same result...

"You are in love... with me?"

I guess I have always been... I've watched from the shadows as your life provided with suffering enough to make you worthy of a pact...

"So those eyes following me everywhere... it was you all along... I need to know who you are... Are you anything I've heard of before? Are you a demon or an angel or something of the sort?"

I find it amusing... those inventions humans in the past and the present have. Beliefs, as you call them... Inventions that have your species as the center of it all... Pathetic... For us, beings out of your reach, have better things to do than tend only to you, humans...

"Then, where do you come from? Why do you exist? And why do you tend to me?"

By misfortune, I am unable to pinpoint an answer for my birthplace... I know, nonetheless, as well as my brothers, that we came to 'life' due to a certain individual... As for my existence, I exist as a force of unending hunger for sadness, pain, and regret. It's what I feed on, said the being, now looking directly into Carmen's core, *and you have plenty of that…*

"Have you done this pact you talk so much about before?"

Humans are a great source of sadness… the last time I forged a pact of a similar kind with a human happened in 1453… using your human time measurements, of course… As a result of our pact, he lacked the empathy to impale his enemies as decor in front of his citadel, if I remember correctly… for you see… he couldn't feel any remorse or sadness after doing such deeds…

Carmen realized who he was talking about. "You mean…"

Whether he was what you humans call 'legends', or not, it's an entirely separate story on its own, it continued with the same stiffness in his voice, *for it doesn't concern me…*

"Then… the only thing that I would gain from that pact would be… cruelty?"

Cruelty… empathy… those are purely human concepts… since there is no more knowledge I can provide to you about myself… and taking into account you don't possess much time left… regarding the pact I'm offering you… will you accept it?

"I should feel despair… I should want to disappear… but I can't feel anything… still… I don't think I care at this point whether you're a demon or not… I don't think I care whatever you're offering…"

As mentioned before… your silly beliefs are amusing. There's nothing else beyond this moment. There's nothing beyond the choice you will make now. My offer is your last chance of redemption before you pass away, its voice escalated in confidence, even though it felt all the same to Carmen, *a last chance at getting revenge… and saving the one you love the most.*

"I don't want revenge… I don't care about anything anymore… I sincerely don't know who you're talking about…"

Oh yes, you do… you're just too afraid of facing it… of going back and facing the pain that holds you down… the pain that might appear in front of you if you fail to protect him, as you failed the others… You father… Your son… The responsibility and regret of not being able to save them from a danger that was right in front of you the whole time… The fear of feeling the same once again if you fail him, too. Even in this state...

Carmen realized the sylph was right. There was still a reason worth fighting for. A youngster who had been able to make her smile again and who had accepted her despite her horrendous past. The only person left on the planet she had been able to trust, and the one who had protected her all along...

Carmen looked back at the creature in question, full of doubt. The eyes of the being looked pleased at Carmen's reaction.

His current fate is quite... gruesome, continued the sylph, *for I can see far and wide... I can tell he will have his limbs amputated soon enough... He will be bled to death on a clinical table... like cattle. His captors are quite extraordinary at their mission if you ask me... Empty of regret regarding their actions... The least attractive humans for me to feed on...*

"Then... how am I supposed to defeat them? Even if it's the last thing I do, I know I stand no chance against those men. You're asking for the impossible. You want me to suffer once more and feel more pain for you to feed on... the pain I'll feel when I fail and see another man I love die at the hands of those demons."

The sylph extended his right hand towards Carmen and touched her, *then... look for yourself...*

Carmen saw an influx of different images as her memories disappeared to make way for others completely different from her own. The sylph's uncountable hosts and their memories came into view: Human beings from ancient civilizations to human beings from modern times. There was no shortage of sadness within them. And yet, all of them had the same element in common: the same level of regret as hers. The sylph stopped touching Carmen.

So, are you willing to accept my offer?

"What do I gain in return? How would I be able to save him with that pact of yours? Why should I trust you? Besides... I am dead. You could simply take what you want from me. You may claim my core if you wish... it wouldn't make a damn difference… there is nothing else I can do now…"

Carmen looked down into emptiness having realized her defeat. Resignation was a hard pill to swallow, especially when feeling powerless to save those she loved. Feeling despair again, that very same feeling she had felt already twice, wasn't in her plans. Death seemed a way better and painless option to go with.

Sometimes, I wish I was human to do as you say… for you see… taking advantage of others… is quite a human thing. It's easy to realize this when you look at the deities you have created on your own… and their attitudes towards their own creations, continued the sylph, *beings unable to relate to you, humans, because of them being the very knowledge you lack… while we, the sylphs, have been conceived from your very search for knowledge…*

Carmen still looked down in disappointment. "What difference does it make? The dead are beings who no longer exist. There is nothing I can do anymore…"

There, you are mistaken, for if you truly were dead, I wouldn't be here, the being approached Carmen as he pronounced these words, *let me mention that, unbeknownst to you, you have a few hours left to live… meaning this is your last chance. This applies to me as well… for I can't let go of all that pain… All the sadness you hold inside… it's just too alluring for a sylph like me to let go to waste… it has always been…*

Carmen tried to look surprised if she had known how to, as those emotions were somehow nullified in that place. "I can't be alive… I died… I was shot in the head… I may not be a doctor… but even I know that death came for me right there…"

Alright, I'll drop the act, said the sylph, changing his voice to a casual one, *there is this guy who revived you somehow. Does that answer your question?*

"What?" Carmen asked, confused.

You heard me, dear. I think I may have gone overboard with this… oh well… the sylph continued to then change back to his monotone way of talking, *an unknown entity came to help you… albeit too late… for you were already gone… he used some sort of technology to grant you life… I don't know his motivations or what this technology entails… All I know is that you are still alive for sylphs like myself cannot interact with dead entities…*

"Even if I were still alive, or whatever, either way… My life has been destroyed beyond any conceivable hope… even if there is someone worth fighting for…"

If I could take your body, I would gladly do so for we're wasting precious time. However, as I mentioned before, I can't… for sylph spirits are not humans… We cannot do whatever we wish. We need to be attached to a 'host' to consume, or increase, said host's emotions, said the being, keeping its unchanging voice, *we need to make a contract with the intended human…*

Although Carmen wouldn't admit it outright, she had started to feel a bit lighter. As if all the heaviness had been lifted from her shoulders. As if there was… hope.

"What have you done to me?"

This is but a taste of what my pact will grant you… When an individual accepts this pact, he or she will obtain a related attribute to the sylph in question. Were you to accept it, I will feed on your sadness and regret for as long as you live… You will lose your natural empathy for others for you won't regret any of your actions, good or evil… which also means you will be unstoppable for guilt will never drag you down… You will also be able to choose the necessary companions you consider useful for your last journey, continued Sadness, accentuating his crooked smile, *you will never feel sad or guilty again…*

"How am I supposed to live like that…? How will I be able to tell friend from foe?"

It's simple… you will use other emotions, or logic, rather than empathy to do so… In turn, I will reside within the companions you happen to choose, connecting your body to them for they will become part of you… They will be your artifacts… your weapons of vengeance.

It didn't matter how Carmen thought about it, thoroughly or not, she couldn't come to a solid conclusion. Was she willing to sacrifice the last moments of her life and her natural emotions to make one final attempt at the inevitable? Could she at least get revenge upon those who had wronged her? Was the sylph telling the truth about the inexistence of the afterlife?

So many questions… so little time…

As she kept deliberating with herself, the feeling of lightness from before started to become a feeling of happiness that flooded her heart. The memories of Nico, still present in said place, surrounded her as her mind started to consider the offer. Upon watching those memories from afar, it didn't take long for her to realize the obvious. Besides… there was the secret she hadn't been able to tell him. The secret she knew had died with her the moment Jason had destroyed her brain and, in turn, had shut down her entire body. A secret that effectively awoke deep hatred within her heart. That secret being her last chance at a normal life.

As she thought of it, she could also see Jason killing Juan Fernando with a big smile on his face, strangling him by the neck. Jason killing her father, with an even bigger smile on his face, poisoning him. Jason killing Eliana, with his biggest smile ever, setting her on fire. And finally, Jason killing Nico in a burst of laughter, with the same revolver he had shot her with.

Hatred awakened inside her, quickly becoming a snowball, growing and growing as memories went on. She wouldn't let this go away. She couldn't anymore. The shame of ever thinking of giving up started to loom in the horizon, the same as the regret of ever thinking of abandoning Nico, which grew and grew until it became overwhelming. By the time her heart was about to blow up, her mind was made up. "I accept your offer, Sadness," said Carmen, extending her right arm towards the sylph, "I accept to be your host. In exchange, lend me your strength to avenge my father, my son, my secret… and to save Nico."

Be warned… for if you ever fail to feed me, I will take over your body and will… if you are still alive, of course… From now on, all the regret and pain you would usually feel from any action or event that would normally provoke said feelings will be fed directly to me… for I am, from now on, part of you, Carmen de la Cruz… I'll accompany you on your journey until it's over... You may rise once more, said Sadness as it grabbed Carmen's hand.

Immediately, she felt how the mysterious being was absorbed within her essence, making its way to her very core. Then, she closed her eyes.

*   *   *

Carmen opened her eyes. She couldn't avoid coughing as she gasped for air and pushed the mud away from her body, looking at the black sky and feeling the pouring rain. She touched her forehead, trying to use the last bit of denial she had left, trying to think that it had all been just a terrible nightmare. However, as she touched the hole through her head, she realized it wasn't. After confirming that her nightmares had indeed come true, she saw her thighs. They were covered in blood.

"I guess this was to be expected... I'm sorry I couldn't bring you to life..." she murmured in a neutral voice as her want for revenge and hatred increased tenfold. She tried to get up, but fell instantly since her brain, still severely damaged, seemed to give her troubles in the locomotion department. As she could barely stand on her own two feet, she started walking carefully, and clumsily, having a hard time on each step, tripping over and over on the grass and falling flat on her face. Eventually, she managed to walk successfully by supporting herself on the nearest mansion wall. Her brain felt heavy and numb, the same as her body. Nevertheless, she felt there was an unknown force moving her body, aiding her, helping her to keep herself close to the mansion's wall. Thus, moving slowly like a snail, her body was the one leading her to the small chapel within the mansion grounds.

"I guess... I now know why I'm going there..." she mumbled.

Looking at the La Cruz chapel, tetric and filled to the brim with Estúan designs, Carmen realized she would've simply stood there admiring it if she had more time to live. Despite the one in front of her being a mere replica of the one back home, she could only think about what it represented. Her parents, true to what the church of Pillarism preached, had built it for the occasional prayer originally. After her mother's death, the chapel was often used by her father, who stayed there praying for two hours every day while visiting his deceased wife. At that memory, Carmen wished she had paid attention to him when he did. When she was a child, sometimes her father would even take her inside the chapel to teach her the prayers. Given that she never put the effort to learn them, and that she was unaware of the reason why he uttered them, she preferred to keep wondering if that praying of his was useful or not. Still, he never forced her to imitate him as he claimed he only wanted her to observe him and hear his words.

The chapel's white walls, porous as the ones from the one in Estú, reminded her of happier times when Spunky used to hide in there when playing and she'd spend around three hours looking for him. Sometimes, Eliana would choose it as a hiding spot, too. As her eyes traversed the building, half sunk in the shadows, she hoped the chapel would only bring her good memories, but her recent visits had been of the mourning kind. Her parents were supposed to be still buried inside, or at least they should be. Even she knew that Jason wouldn't move them around if there was no need to do so, more so knowing that moving them on its own was quite expensive. She could only wonder if his hatred for her family could overcome that fact. She also wondered if someone else had visited the chapel recently as, compared to the mansion, its decay was next to none…

Unlike during her recent visit, the darkness inside the chapel didn't seem to be a big problem for her as the occasional lightning served as a natural flashlight. This source of light, in turn, also answered a question that had been going on inside her head since her imprisonment in Sanatorium. Indeed, as lightning kept flashing, she found a name she hadn't noticed when she had visited the chapel before: Juan Fernando.

There he was, between the tombs of her parents. Carmen

simply looked at it in shock, and yet, no tears would come out of her eyes. *I guess Sadness was telling the truth*, she concluded as she felt no nostalgia or sadness at the sight. Thus, she simply kept walking past it until she reached the wall at the end of the building.

Similarly to the La Cruz family seal, standing there for generations, a fifty-kilogram black marble cross stood on top of each of her parents' graves. Carmen placed her hands upon both of them, touching and feeling the cold stone-made coffins, barely able to keep standing by supporting herself on them. Eventually, she finally placed herself between her parents' tomb heads and placed each hand on top of their respective crosses. Her right hand on her father's and her left one on her mother's.

"*Papá… mamá…* please accompany me on this journey… my last journey… to avenge my son… to protect the last person I will ever love…" said Carmen as she closed her eyes and the cold black marble under her hands took her back to the past…

"Ewww!!! This is so nasty!!!" claimed Carmen as she spit out the wine she had just drunk while her father laughed at his heart's content.

"*Carmencita*, we, the La Cruz, are the best wine caterers there are! Someday all of this will be yours!" said her father nonchalantly.

"But I'm only eleven!" protested Carmen.

This had become a common occurrence once she had turned ten, for her disgust. Each day she had to learn how to differentiate and analyze the quality of good wine. Although she quite hated it at first, she started to take a liking to it over time. Nevertheless, her father would never allow her more than a small sip until she turned sixteen. Afterwards, once the wine torture was over, Carmen would usually go speak with her mother where she always was, on top of a white altar in the hall of the mansion. A portrait of her.

"*Hola mamá*, how are you doing today?" said Carmen with both of her hands together, looking directly into her eyes. "If… if you could tell me who's that that watches me all the time…

maybe I would sleep better at night… You know, *papá* isn't exactly my role model to follow, but he's always good and caring. I guess he doesn't know what I'm talking about because he always says that someday I will understand… that the weight of being a La Cruz is related to the blackness of marble. You know… I just wished I could meet you one day…" As she was completely focused on her task at hand, she got startled and stopped when she heard Margarita, one of her servants, calling her over. "*Señorita* Carmen, your friend Eliana has arrived. She's waiting for you in the main hall."

Eliana had arrived late, as usual. This never changed, not even by the time she was studying at university and had agreed to see Carmen on a specific time. Once she arrived, she would usually tell the same story: how she had to copy notes from her classmates as she hadn't gotten to see them on the blackboard, due to her inherent lateness. Every time she came, Carmen would come running to see her knowing she often brought her favorite dolls, among other toys. However, this wasn't the main reason why she rushed to see her friend as she never knew why Eliana brought them in the first place. They would hardly even touch them. Carmen often thought of her visits as a break from her confinement, but she wasn't sure. Instead, games like Hide 'n' Seek were what they mostly spent their time on, and encouragement for Carmen to play more physically active games wasn't lacking, especially since Carmen's father would participate whenever he could in their games. Out of these outdoor games, their favorite one was "*el cuenta uvas*" which consisted of harvesting as many grapes as they could. Eliana almost always won at it which wasn't always well-received by Carmen. Nonetheless, this fascinated Carmen as she couldn't understand why she lost, nor could she get mad at her friend, probably due to Eliana's huge optimism being quite contagious, prompting Carmen to feel like a winner despite losing. This never changed, not even when Juan Fernando was born…

"*Perdona tía…*" said Eliana, panting and covered in sweat. Indeed, it had been a hot day in Friornia. "I swear I thought

Juan's baptism was at noon! I swear!"

Carmen smiled in response to her with her son cuddling in her arms. "Don't worry, I know you…"

"Anyways…" said Eliana, gasping for air. "I brought you this!"

Eliana then proceeded to give her an iron ring, wide enough for Carmen to fit both of her hands inside it. Carmen looked at it surprised as she didn't know what to make of it. "Thanks?"

"C'mon girl! Don't give me that look! This represents the future bond you'll have with your son!" said Eliana enthusiastically. "Trust me on this one!"

Carmen never truly understood why Eliana gave her that iron ring, but she kept it in Juan Fernando's room. She always assumed that she had picked it up on her way to her son's baptism in an improvised attempt at a gift. Either way, there it was, looking back at her on top of Juan Fernando's grave. It reflected a small glint of light thanks, again, to another occasional lightning raging on the outside. But who had placed it there?

She assumed it had been possibly Eliana when she visited the tomb while Carmen was about to be judged. Carmen would never know. She smiled slightly at the sight. Then, by grabbing firmly the top tip of the black marble crosses, she pushed them both down. Extraordinarily, both crosses fell down easily, even though they had been part of her parent tombs' structure all along and had been carved as part of the coffin itself. Both crosses fell to the pristine ceramic floor, causing some cracks to it while suffering no damage themselves. Carmen would've been amused by this if her brain had the energy to do so. Marble wasn't the strongest material, after all. Once both crosses had stabilized themselves onto the ground, with their bases bare to her sight, she went to her son's tomb.

"Eliana… my best friend… my son… the one I loved the most… please come with me to avenge your deaths… lend me your strength in this final battle… I need you…" continued

Carmen as she grabbed the iron ring with both of her hands. Then, by using little strength on it, she snapped it in half. She turned around and placed each half at each base of the black crosses. "Thank you so much… I love you with all my heart…" Once in position, she pushed the iron ring halves into the marble. Surprisingly, it took next to no effort to press these 'handles' and tear into the rock with them. The marble felt like butter as the steel made its way into it.

"*From now on, I will inhabit these objects when you touch them. They will be a part of you. From now on, it will be where all your pain and regret will go to. Good luck, Carmen de la Cruz,*" said a voice within her chest. Sadness then proceeded to make its way into the crosses through Carmen's hands as she lifted them up. Despite them weighing around fifty kilograms each, she felt them as if they were lighter than a feather. At the same time, she could feel all her sadness and regret go away through her hands. As said feelings abandoned her body, the expression on her face was forever replaced.

A small grin appeared on her face…

"I'm the final laughter… eternal sadness… I'm… the Black Cross."

V

THE BLACK CROSS had never experienced anything of the sort before.

Her body had taken quite a long time to recover. That was, way more than usual. Way, way more. She couldn't stop shaking for around fifteen minutes as the Biologist's car lost itself in the distance. As her spasms continued, she tried to remember if she had felt anything similar to it before, but she couldn't. Her memory blurred easily when it came to feeling pain as she had stopped caring about feeling it a long time ago. She couldn't remember when she had started to enjoy it, either…

As she stretched her body, trying to get rid of the shivering sensation, the cool breeze of the night reminded her of that certain someone watching her every move. It wasn't the man who called himself the Creature, of that much she was certain. That smell didn't match his. Who it was didn't matter at this point. Given that he would show himself sooner or later, which experience told her was likely to happen, she simply ignored him.

Kelvin was now dead, but why had she failed to kill him? Obviously, someone had been one step ahead of her. Why would they kill him? He might have failed in his mission for the Block, but that didn't necessarily award the capital punishment, or at least of that much she was sure. Was he even a part of them? It had never crossed her mind that he wasn't. Not that her mind had been doing wonderfully for the past six months. Either way, this deserved further investigation.

Thus, as she kept on wondering about the reason for Kelvin's assassination, she changed her mind and stopped the car to later walk back to Kelvin's house to, possibly, find more clues about this whole ordeal. On her way there, she stumbled upon one of the dead agents lying on the floor. It was that last man she had spared before, now looking into nothingness with a wound in the forehead. Such wounds were usually hard to forget.

She lifted his wrist and looked at the clock he had attached to it. By now, she knew these were no ordinary watches as Nico had once told her how they kept their agents in check. She could only remember half of his half-made explanation. Another man she wished she had paid more attention to in the past. The watch in question had more information than just the time as it showed the heartbeat and GPS location of the subject. At the same time, it was deeply embedded onto the agent's skin, almost welded onto his bone. In the past, the Dire One tried to separate a watch from a wrist, but she ended up pulling out the entire bone from the corpse, laughing at her surprise at that time. She simply wanted to study it in the hope of finding more clues about *their* whereabouts, or Nico's current situation. Mostly to see how close *they* were to him. She didn't really need information about a random agent.

As for the Immigrant, she hadn't seen him in a long while. That was, she didn't know for certain how long it had been since *that* day in the cave. At least she knew he was still alive, hopefully also doing well. That was good enough, for now at least. Despite her wishing to see him again, she couldn't do that due to several… reasons. Mostly when the same question popped back into her mind: Would he ever forgive her?

Then, the same answer appeared: Probably not.

Given that it was pointless to ponder about that any further, her thoughts would often wander into an analysis of what had always made her victorious in her encounters with the Block, and other enemies: the factor of her unpredictability. Notwithstanding, in spite of her enemies being always taken by surprise by her random actions, they knew, better than anyone, that she would eventually go and meet the Immigrant. It was just a matter of time. Until that happened, however, the way her brain worked had helped her achieve victory as *they* tended to be very methodical and stuck to whatever plan *they* had made up. At this point, she had also learned to predict *their* ways. Thus, her encounters usually went the same way: her triumph. She remembered how once they had her cornered in a dead-end in the city of San Justiniano, to the north of Friornia. They expected her to do the obvious: Massacre the agents in front of her and run out of there the way she had come from, ending back in the street. If she had done so, she would've been finally captured with ease. At the same time, *their* policy regarding *their* agents was the same: not caring at all for them, probably for the same reasons displayed not long ago. Indeed, they were ready for her to come out, waiting, and waiting...

She never came out.

By the time *they* decided to check what had transpired, *they* discovered that she had, effectively, killed all the agents that had gone in and that she had smashed open the wall impeding her escape. And just like that, she was gone through the tall building that had blocked her access initially. Thanks to cameras in the city, *they* discovered that she had escaped by jumping onto a truck that never noticed her being there. Whenever something seemed impossible to achieve, she remembered that she was an impossible occurrence herself. It worked like a charm. She only wished she could talk properly for once...

As she took a deep breath of air, she relaxed her shoulders and started to shake her limbs. The wind that blew on her face from the path she was about to take indicated that there were no enemies approaching, at least not from that direction. However, she knew additional agents would soon swarm the place if given enough time. Since risking another fight against *them*, especially if *they* had the same weapons *they* had just used on her recently, would put her in a delicate situation, she finished her stretching quickly and started her way back to the vehicle she had chosen prior. She had to get out of there and fast.

Once again inside the car, she realized that the automobile belonged to one of the police officers who had a high rank among the others. Probably the ones who didn't engage immediately because they had to issue orders and all those important reasons. She would usually kill them for last as cowards deserved to feel most of the horror she could produce in their hearts. Sometimes, nonetheless, she would come to respect the ones who went into the fray alongside their men. They died all the same, but Carmen had the gallantry to remember their faces.

"Even before Death comes around… calamity prepares a welcome…" she murmured, admiring how the neighborhood, on its own, had become a perfect battlefield. Empty of all its residents and filled to the brim with destruction and fire. It looked as if they truly thought they could stop her for good. Sometimes, she wished they could…

As she had done previously, she placed her deadly weapons on the passenger seat and started the engine. Seeing the steering wheel always prompted her to remember the first time she had driven one. Given that she didn't want to draw any attention, she stuck to the usual controls. Any other button, or computer, in the car that she didn't have knowledge of was off-limits. This attitude, albeit wise from her perspective, sometimes betrayed her intent of keeping herself hidden as the patrol lights, red and blue, were almost always still on when she drove these cars. No sirens would come from them, but a spectacle of lights would draw more attention than a luminous Pillimas tree in the middle of summer, and this was no different.

"Death may exclusively pursue its core…"

She would find Kelvin's killer and all the answers she needed sooner or later as said killer hadn't gotten too far, yet.

Thus, the Black Cross accelerated to the East. *I know exactly where you're hiding…* she thought, *just keep thinking of how safe you are… and you'll be in for a rude awakening.* As she kept going down the road, she felt some comfort in the cold breeze of the night that showered her face through her open window. Destroyed window, to be precise. It felt quite refreshing and colder than usual. She just wished she was just as cold, if not colder. This mere fact reminded her all too well of how cold her actions were supposed to be when killing Kelvin, or when killing that kid in the room. Her contract with Sadness was supposed to have her gotten rid of that lame weakness, so she shouldn't have hesitated with so much at stake. She should've had no guilt in killing the damn brat. No regret. And yet, she hadn't been able to. She tried, with all her might, to strike the kid down along with 'Kelvin', but her body wouldn't obey her commands. She hated herself for staying like a statue right there. If at least that wasn't the worst part…

Now *they* knew she had a weakness, and any weakness *they* could easily exploit was bad news. If she at least had an answer as to why. It was the first time she wished she could talk to Sadness again and ask him what the problem was. Was it her fault? It was because of these kinds of situations that she was glad she couldn't feel any regret. Any remorse would've only been a waste of time at this point. Wasn't she supposed to be a full-fledged monster already? It seemed she would have to find the answer to that herself as the Sylph had stopped talking to her ever since that fateful night. She had tried many times to communicate with it, whether by hitting the crosses against her ear, just hard enough so that she wouldn't rip her head off or by tapping, or rubbing, her fingers onto them, just in case he worked similar to a genie from a lamp. At the lack of response, she also cleaned them off with water and soap, taking off some blood stains in the process, with no success. She often talked to her weapons, thinking of her parents, but that didn't cause the sylph to show up, either. Its prolonged absence made her wonder if that was the nature of all sylphs, or of Sadness alone. Maybe that was the very reason why no one knew about them.

At any rate, since looking for an answer from Sadness was a dead-end, there was another question in her mind that maybe could be answered. Was there any other person she wouldn't be able to harm? Nico immediately came to her mind. Although this wasn't the first time she wondered about this, this was the first time she was *truly* wondering about this. It wasn't hard to imagine a million different situations within her head harming, or killing, the Immigrant while weighing her reactions to each. Notwithstanding, it mattered little as the result was always the same in her head: she understood that even if he were to attack her, or betray her, she wouldn't oblige. She knew perfectly well that she would rather die than attacking Nico.

She could only assume that she hadn't lost the notion of love. Her feelings for him were one of the engines that kept her life having at least some kind of sense, besides revenge. Her life might've been doomed forever if it weren't for Nico. Additionally, he didn't deserve what had happened to him and his family, of that much she was still aware. Even if he had always assumed full responsibility for his wrongdoings, including his unlawfulness, he had never claimed to deserve such a massive punishment, and he wasn't wrong. However, he had rarely mentioned it, or complained about it. Perhaps that was the reason why he was usually in a good mood. Maybe he had become way too accepting of his awful reality for his own good, unlike her. It was this very self-inflicting curse of his that had taught her how to smile again. A debt she felt she would never truly be able to repay. If she ever wanted to repay him, that was. Regardless of how many times she could save his life now, as the Black Cross, it wouldn't matter as it was a debt she wanted to keep having. Why? She wasn't sure.

As she looked up into the stars, her patrol going at eighty kilometers per hour, she figured it out. By now she knew that killing the Immigrant, whether by accident or not, would cause no remorse or guilt in her core. Nonetheless, as love hadn't left her heart, Nico was still like a star to her, frozen in time to her eyes when immersed in the dark sky, and, at the same time, she'd be indifferent if he were to disappear in that vast darkness the next night. She often wondered if maybe that was the reason why she wanted to keep that debt alive as his demise was, realistically, just a matter of time. Perchance she'd rather keep this debt as a way to keep him alive in her world while denying his future undoing, or to keep her purpose to live also alive. There was also the possibility that she knew she wouldn't attack him because, to her heart, it wasn't fair as part of that debt. The fact that he had done so much for her rendered her unable to pay him back that way, fortunately. As she remembered how she had spared O'Connell and his companion, as well as those Block agents back there, she realized the obvious once again… It had been in front of her face the whole time.

She felt quite stupid for a moment as the engine roared down the road. Even if those men had attacked her, she knew they were no longer a threat, nor did they try to get in her way. Perhaps, likely to what she felt for the Immigrant, this phenomenon was due to her sense of justice. Probably Kelvin's kid had the same 'property', or maybe the reason for her inability to kill him came from her past. Even before Juan Fernando was born, in her eyes, every child in existence was completely innocent from that putrid world she inhabited, thus, she felt children were no threat and didn't need to be killed. There was also the possibility that, maybe, just maybe, the memories of her dead son Juan Fernando were preventing her from killing infants in general. Perhaps they were the only ones able to override her contract with Sadness regarding her feelings of guilt. She didn't know for sure, and, for the moment, there was no way to know for certain, either. As she kept on unwrapping her thoughts, her eyes started to close…

She hadn't slept in ages…

When she opened her eyes, Nico presented himself to her inside the La Cruz mansion, surrounded by agents, tied up and kneeling, gagged and looking directly into her with glistening eyes.

"Prepare!" commanded one of the men as the others got their weapons ready, assault rifles to be precise, checking if their weapons were loaded. All of them surrounding the Immigrant like the petals of a sunflower.

"I won't allow it! *Pequeño!*" yelled Carmen as she started to maul the agents with her partners while *they* didn't seem to notice her, still focused on preparing their weapons. All of them moving further and further away while the same man continued with his commands. "Take aim!"

"*¡Malditos!* Stop this!" threatened Carmen as she continued killing them in massive numbers. As *they* kept dying in several forms, and the Black Cross massacred *them* out of her way, the men near Nico aimed at his head.

"No! No! No!" raged the Black Cross as Nico kept moving away, along with his captors, further inside the mansion. Carmen was now bathed in blood as more agents kept swarming on her like ants, preventing her from ever getting closer.

"Fire!"

"Noooooo!!!!"

Nico's head was blasted away by several guns shooting it in unison, blowing it up to pieces. Carmen could only watch in astonishment while the same men kept on shooting him until their clips emptied. The Black Cross grinned in madness to *them* as her visible rage burned away the little confidence *they* still had in themselves.

"Death is too sweet a reward for scum like you…" she said as she charged towards *them*, wrapped in bloodlust…

Then, she opened her eyes again, just in time before her car hit a tree. By turning to the right, she managed to steer away from it, mostly for the car's sake. This turned her vehicle into a drifting spin on the pavement that eventually stopped in the middle of screeching sounds. Carmen got out of the patrol to check for possible damages. Fortunately, there was nothing major other than the wear on the tires reflected on the road as dark lines. Relieved, she returned to get inside; however, as she had opened the door to get back in, she stopped short. The same presence that had been watching her back at Kelvin's was there, and unlike last time, it was getting closer. As the wind carried his scent to her, she looked towards the direction the smell was coming from. Effectively, it didn't take long for her eyes to catch onto something moving among the trees. Two bright fire-like figures within the forest on her left had now come into existence. Her pursuer was letting himself be seen on purpose, clearly as an invitation on his behalf. Now she could understand Nico as he had been right all along back at Gupta's apartment: she knew from the smell alone that this stalker was indeed male. On top of that, despite the darkness of the night all around her, and almost no moonlight, she could make out the shape of a man amidst the shadows. He stopped by the side of the road, not having abandoned the cover of the forest completely, watching. Waiting. He was no occasional traveller, that was for sure. He was there for her, and, even at that distance, she could tell he was no ordinary human through the same method. His smell was… amusing…

She had smelled a similar odor before, although she couldn't remember exactly where. However, after a few seconds of forced reminiscence, she remembered. When she fought the Creature, his smell had become stronger when she crushed his bones and ripped his guts open. It was different than that of a normal man, keeping in mind the countless agents she had slaughtered. Even then, the Creature's smell was nothing out of the ordinary compared to the Biologist's, and in turn, the Biologist's smell was nothing out of the ordinary compared to this peculiar fellow. He was clearly a supernatural. That alone explained how he had easily been able to keep up with her car. A speed of that calibre was no usual feat.

Whatever he wants will have to wait, she thought as she continued to walk calmly towards him with her crosses in hand, ready to hit. She had learned from past mistakes that, even if her opponent didn't emit any want for killing or that he might just want to intimidate her in the form of a subtle warning, she could never lower her guard. She looked into his eyes as her pace remained steady. They were penetrating. They described a life of pain and disappointment. Seeing the Black Cross make her move, he responded by jumping out of the trees onto the middle of the road, landing a few meters in front of her. By showing a part of his power, she understood the underlying message. Indeed, his bluff worked perfectly as she knew she couldn't risk him destroying her only means of transportation and her only way to catch up to Kelvin's murderer fast enough. Thus, she stopped right in her tracks, both of them *en garde*.

"Beautiful night we're having, eh *laska*?" he said in a really thick Unskevian accent. The expression on his face didn't show any amiability, nor anger of any sort. A neutral face, as the Dire One would usually call it. He also displayed a big scar across his face along with a powerful and muscular body.

"Is War looking for Peace?" answered coldly the Black Cross, "or the mockingbird looking for the sky?"

"Oh no, no. This *stary druhu* just wants to chat with ya," he answered, fixed like an oak tree, his hands in front of him and his short blond hair glistening with the moonlight. "If you got the time, *laska*..."

The Black Cross lowered her hands, which had been tensed up to that moment, just enough so that she couldn't be taken by surprise. She quickly took a look at her hands, checking how the blisters and injuries caused by the rusted iron ring on her palms would be gone in thousands of a second. They always appeared every time she grabbed her partners, constantly reminding her of the path she had chosen. And she always enjoyed seeing them disappear.

"Death does not see the implication in your words," she said, as if she was walking on clouds. "Timber does go along with rain..." Having said that, she turned around and started to walk back to the patrol. She knew that if he were to attack, he would've done so already. He knew perfectly well what she was capable of, if he had been an avid observer, that was. Besides, as the possibility of him being a decoy for Block agents to come to his aid was increasing exponentially, she couldn't stay there any longer than she should.

"I might say that I have information you might be interested in," he said confidently. "What if I told you that there is a certain someone that's still alive, eh *laska*?"

Carmen stopped short midway and looked at him over her shoulder.

"Since you seem interested in the subject, allow me to introduce myself…"

VI

"JASON…" Carmen whispered to herself as her trembling steps made their way towards the mansion entrance. Thus, as her feet presented the issue of bad coordination, along with her entire body, she used her most recent weightless companions as improvised crutches by placing them in front of her every step of the way, sometimes tripping with them in the process. As her continuous falls were starting to take its toll on her body, she stuck close to the outer walls and followed their surface towards her objective, instead.

"Why… did it have… to be… so hard…?" she mumbled as her life was being drained away with every step she made. She had to hurry and make the most of it before the inevitable came since, as far as she was concerned, she didn't know exactly how much longer she would be alive for. The pressure of death waiting for her just around the corner was heartfelt as her body felt heavier with every breath she took, and her lungs felt more pain with her every gasp.

"Jason… Jason… Jason…" Carmen kept repeating, in an almost inaudible voice, over and over as she approached the doors she had known for so long. Fortunately for her, the doors had been left open. Had she had to open them, she would've probably been way too weak to push them, especially since using her new weapons to smash them open didn't even cross her mind at that moment. Not that thinking with a hole through her head made it any easier. "Sadness never… mentioned that he would… take away that kind of pain," she murmured as she kept going on her way, feeling how physical pain had started a slow, but effective, invasion of her entire body.

"Jason… Jason…" she kept whispering as she slowly walked inside the mansion's hall, unable to realize, or care, where she was in that very moment, her heart guiding her every step to her objective. Her eyes, barely working in the darkness of the mansion, weren't her main means of direction as she trusted in the map of the building imprinted in her brain, or what was left of it. Turning left, and then turning right, and there it was: "the Great Hall." As soon as she entered it, her feet touched a cold puddle on the floor, not realizing it was her own blood. It seemed her dear husband hadn't cleaned up, yet. Fortunately for her, it was dry enough for her not to slip on it. So, she kept going, eventually feeling the warmth coming from the fire within.

Indeed, there he was: Jason, smoking his trusty brown pipe. She could tell as a small smoke tower coming off his red leather sofa gave him away, his back was facing Carmen. She could feel how relaxed and comfortable he was. Maybe that was why the main doors were still open, a phase of his she had never seen before. They say that excessive happiness makes everyone careless, and Jason seemed to be no exception. He wanted to enjoy his newfound freedom all he could. That was, freedom from his deeds and freedom from her… A freedom she was determined to end.

Carmen stood there for a second, trying to catch her breath, dazzled by the towering smoke. *Time is running low*, she thought as she initiated her approach. Shoeless as she was, since the Block agents had taken her shoes away, her steps were barely noticeable. Besides, Jason was way too happy to notice her, too full of himself. Carmen could tell as she could literally feel his happy heart as if it was beating inside her own body. She didn't remember Sadness granting her that skill, still, it, whatever it was, was surprisingly pleasant. If her suppositions were correct, it seemed that she could now feel what any human heart was feeling, but most importantly, that human being's location as well. As she came to this realization, the pressure of her imminent death harassed her mind to no end. In order to escape said harassment, she dared to say his name out loud once she was a few meters away from him.

"JASON!"

Jason jumped to his feet and turned around as fast as he could. He couldn't believe what he was seeing. Unable to utter a word and paralyzed by the unknown. The expression on his face said it all. Complete disbelief was a more fitting description. His mouth opened up, and yet no sound would come out, seeming to spell "impossible" over and over, in silence.

As he remained in this state of shock, Carmen continued her march towards him as fast as she could, which wasn't much, dragging her feet at this point while keeping her eyes fixed onto what he might do next. She knew that, despite the darkness of the mansion helping her conceal herself and her new partners, being slightly lit only by the fire near Jason, her husband would eventually be able to spot her weapons and dash away. A result Carmen wasn't prepared at all to take.

"You... you... you killed him... you killed him..." continued Carmen with increasing rage in her voice. "You just... did it... you... did it..."

Slowly, Jason started to regain control over his body as he started to step backwards, away from Carmen. He almost tripped over the sofa he had just gotten out of as he tried to gather his thoughts. What was he seeing? It was impossible. The sound of that voice... It couldn't be...

"Who the fuck are you?! If this is some kind of sick joke?! It ain't going well!" he finally yelled with a sudden surge of anger, his body tensed in fear.

"It seems..." said Carmen, as she stepped closer into the light, "you have forgotten... about me... my love..."

Jason saw, horrified, the being before him, especially the

hole in her forehead alongside the dried blood on her hair. Her skin was paler than white marble and her black eyes empty of any will to live. Even from all the experiences he could've mustered as a doctor, he could've never thought of something like that as possible. Her shaking steps and her horrible aspect made him shiver, cold sweat running down his face. What was going on? What should he do? Whatever choice he could think of was quickly overshadowed by his inability to understand the situation he was in. All of this was impossible… it was as if he had suddenly been dumped into a horror movie…

Wait… horror movie… that's it! Jason thought. As his wife strolled in his direction like a walking corpse, a point of clarity lightened up in his mind. He had seen something of the sort before. When studying cadavers, mostly provided by the city morgue, he had developed a keen interest regarding bullet wounds and their effects on the human body. Thus, it was evident that she didn't have much left to live as her locomotion was compromised and the brain damage had been massive. Based on this diagnosis, it was obvious that she was harmless. Additionally, it was apparent that this walking corpse couldn't be Carmen.

"Oh well… I might've forgotten just a little tiny bit and-" he said, relieved and about to smile when his gaze caught up onto something else: she was carrying two giant black marble crosses that seemed extremely heavy. He had seen them before, somewhere. He couldn't recall where exactly, though. But, how could she lift them? Was this the Block's doing and their thrilled experiments he had heard so much about? Or maybe… were they testing his resolve through one of said experiments? That was it! That had to be it! They had made a Carmen-like clone or robot and wanted to study his reaction! That explained everything! Even how a thin-bodied woman like Carmen in such a state of disrepair was able to lift those damn things! Those sneaky bastards!

Soon enough, Jason cleared his throat, and, albeit hesitant at first, continued. "H-hello there!" he said joyfully, waving at her energetically with his right hand.

If they're going through all this just to test me, it means they're taking me seriously, he thought, *if I pass this test, I'll be part of the family for sure! I won't disappoint them, not in my life! They'll get my best performance ever!*

"I don't know what you're thinking of, darling," Jason confidently continued as he placed his hands on his hips, looking straight into Carmen's eyes, as she continued her increasingly slower march. His voice and face showed slight mockery at the sight. His body was now straight and his legs solid like a rock, standing his ground. He lifted his face a little bit, just enough, to look down on Carmen with well-deserved superiority. Then, he turned his back to Carmen and walked casually towards his desk, at the far end of the great hall near the fire, without a worry in the world. *It's time to show how serious I'm in my commitment to my new family*, he thought, *it's time to put the final nail to the walking coffin standing in front of me.*

"But I gotta admit it… you got me there for a second," continued Jason as he kept walking calmly. "You may drop the act now… I know exactly what you want… and what you are."

Carmen kept walking, almost empty of life, without stopping her erratic pace. To Jason, it looked as if she was impaling her feet with invisible and sharp nails on the floor.

"Like I said before… before, you know… before you ended up like this. We could've been happy again. It's your own fault things escalated this quickly, but… I'm a reasonable man. I may still forgive you."

Jason looked back at Carmen as he received no answer. Perchance the integrated artificial intelligence on that thing couldn't process something so advanced. So, he guessed the act had to keep going until everything had reached the conclusion expected from him. "Now, as a token of forgiveness, let me get a new gift for you, my love. A gift you'll carry for eternity, this time."

"Who says… I'm acting… my love…?" said Carmen in response to Jason's surprise. "This time… you're the one… getting a gift…" she continued as she lifted her right cross to the height of her head. "Your death…"

Jason looked over his shoulder. The anger in her voice was way too vivid to be a mere act. Whether she was a doll or not, something smelled fishy about it. Her reactions were too realistic to be mimicked. Even though he had to acknowledge the great advancements in technology made by the Block, he knew all too well they were not at *that* stage yet, even more so in the cloning and robotics departments. Otherwise, they wouldn't need so many damn 'wethands' for all those dumb experiments. Something was off, yet he couldn't tell what it was. As the possibility of him being the target of a trial by the Block started to vanish, his mind started to slowly realize the obvious. Her want to kill felt all too personal, irradiating like the rays of the sun. With his nerves on the edge, he quickly examined her appearance over and over with quick stares until he realized a small detail he had ignored altogether due to the darkness that bathed her. He remembered now. Those crosses… he had definitely seen them somewhere before!

"They… they came from the chapel…! then you are the real one…" concluded Jason, nervously, as his brain slowly made the connections. "The real Carmen…"

Had Carmen become one of those the Block tagged as "supernatural"? If so, how? Anyone who was a part of the Block knew perfectly well that a supernatural didn't have to be created in a lab, necessarily. He knew all too well his wife hadn't gone through any procedure of the sort, so this made no sense. Her movements, even though clumsy and erratic, added to the way she spoke, gave her away. *I gotta finish this and fast,* he thought. *If she was an experiment of the Block to study my reactions, I know I've already provided his best acting and an ideal response to this threat, I got nothing to lose.*

Even though his mind was made up, he kept looking at her over his shoulder, trying to find another characteristic that might refute his most recent conclusion. As blood had invaded her, now ragged, white dress in the crotch area, Jason realized her thighs were bleeding without any wound done on them. Indeed, he didn't remember shooting her there. Was it due to his repeated kicks? Did it matter? Jason wondered so many questions as he unconsciously dashed towards his desk with all his might. However, when his hand was about to touch the desk's refined oak wood, he fell flat on his face. He tried to get up and continue, and yet, he couldn't.

It was then that he felt it.

An acute pain coming from his left leg. He gave a quick glance at it and opened his mouth in utter horror. His eyes widened like soup plates as he witnessed his limb, pinned and crushed into the ground, under one of Carmen's crosses. Had she thrown such a heavy object across the room at *that* speed?

No way… She's about to die! She can't possibly have the energy or the strength to do something like this! What the hell is going on?! he thought as he quickly tried his best to ignore the burning pain. He placed his hands onto the wretched object and pulled, and pulled, in vain. The only sensation he managed to increase was his misery. As it became harder to ignore, as well as the sound of Carmen's encroaching footsteps, Jason pulled the cross even more desperately without any results. That damn cross was incredibly heavy.

Why did I have to dispatch the agents?! Why is this happening to me?! he regretted. *Why did I have to leave my fucking revolver in my desk?! Damn everything!*

Sure enough, no matter how he tried to do it, the cross wouldn't budge. Not even pushing it to the side seemed to work. Although the cross was holding him mostly by the skin alone, since his muscles and bone below had been pulverized, he couldn't get away from it. It was like a massive bear trap refusing to let go of his victim.

As Carmen's steps drew closer, Jason simply retreated his hands from the cross. *I'm done for, aren't I?* he thought. He was at her mercy whether he liked it or not. Probably that was why she strolled towards him as if the rest of the world didn't exist. Perhaps he had become the center of her world once again, albeit in a different manner. The recipient of her enormous rage, the vessel of her pain, the fuel of her vengeance… any equivalent would do. Whatever the case would be, he knew she wasn't the Carmen he had met and married in the past. As she continued her path, she stepped over Derzú, now torn in half. For some reason, though, he couldn't avoid feeling a sense of self-identification with it. And yet, her indifference towards the teddy-bear, while her eyes were still fixed on him, led Jason to believe that she still cared for him. Of course, she cared about the suffering he was experiencing.

As for Carmen, she realized she had gotten used to her 'new body'. as it had become easier to control the more steps she advanced, and the eager she had become to get closer to her husband. Feeling like fainting at any moment, getting some spasms in her neck which made her turn her head around for no reason, she kept her advance steady. Jason wasn't going anywhere, after all.

"The judgment of the righteous is always done by monsters…" she said. "I'm no one to judge you… I'm nothing more than a shadow upon this world… and as such, I'll grant you your true wish… my love…"

By the time she had uttered those words, she was a mere meter away from him. Consequently, she raised her left cross over her head, looking down on Jason as he raised his hands to his face in a vain attempt to protect himself from the upcoming punishment.

"Wait! Wait! I was wrong! I can change! I swear! I can see now the error of my ways! I can see how mistaken I have been! Spare me Carmen! For the love we once held for each other! For the past we have in common! For the life we once shared! Don't let vengeance consume you! I've always loved you! I'll make it up to you! I swear it for what I hold sacred the most!"

Jason begging sounded pathetic. Carmen had stopped short, though. She stayed still, listening to his words of supplication. Realizing she wasn't attacking, Jason slowly opened his eyes and uncovered his face. Relieved, he smiled sweetly at Carmen. "I knew you were reasonable darling! This is so not like you! Carmen de la Cruz always showed mercy and understanding to those who needed it! That's how a hero of justice should be! Everyone will look up to you in the future once the world knows how you forgave a man like me!" continued Jason, now brimming with confidence despite the intense pain he was feeling. "We'll be together again! Like it should've always been! Like we were always meant to be!"

Jason looked into her eyes, hopeful. Nevertheless, Carmen's eyes described no emotions. No reactions. Nothing Jason could aspire to place his hopes on. Instead, she kept staring at Jason with an empty gaze, so cold, it made Jason shiver. Was there any hope for him to begin with? "I'm sorry, my love... so sorry..." said Carmen with apparent preoccupation after a short while. His plan had worked! He had been saved by his superior intellect! He had done it!

"But... you're deeply mistaken..."

Jason's smile vanished from his face as his minuscule hope and confidence had melted like snow in spring. Thus, realizing the inevitable, he went back to trying to remove the cross and set himself free.

"Damn it! Listen to me, Carmen! I didn't kill our son! I swear!" Jason continued his begging as he wouldn't accept that fate. All his effort, all his pain... Had they been for nothing? He wouldn't allow something of the sort. Never!

"You transformed me... into this..."

As Jason kept on making his futile attempts to save himself, Carmen placed her remaining cross right above her husband. Upon such a sight, he moved his torso away, as far as he could in reflex. "No! No! Please!" he begged as his wife dropped her lethal weapon onto his crotch, smashing his genitals and coccyx in one go. The sound of his bones breaking, and the subsequent pain, almost made him pass out, barely hanging onto his conscience. "Aaarrrggghhh!!!" he managed to scream, hardly keeping control while avoiding death from said pain alone. His eyes, now glassy with the tears of defeat, looked at Carmen once again.

"Why...?! Why won't you die...?! why won't you leave me the fuck alone...?! I just wanted to be happy! Is that a crime?! IS THAT A FUCKING CRIME?! You have no right to take that away from me!" complained Jason in a mixture of pain and rage, his face red like a tomato. "I DESERVED TO BE HAPPY! I DESERVED TO BE FREE! I AIN'T GUILTY OF ANYTHING! WHY IS THIS HAPPENING TO ME?!"

"Tch, tch, tch," dismissed Carmen gently, as if trying to calm down a child. She crouched clumsily to his level, almost falling to the floor, and whispered to his ear in a sweet and motherly voice. "You'll find happiness... I assure you... once your pain is gone... once death comes..."

"YOU'RE INSANE! WHO THE FUCK DO YOU THINK YOU ARE?! YOU'RE A FUCKING MONSTER! LEAVE ME ALONE! YOU'RE AN ABORTION OF NATURE THAT SHOULD HAVE NEVER BEEN BORN!" retaliated Jason, gaining hope and strength with each word he said, his voice more and more demanding with each breath he drew. "GET AWAY FROM ME!!!!"

Carmen stood up, almost falling on her back in the process. "Shhh... it'll be over soon..."

She then raised her right cross above her head, releasing Jason's destroyed crotch and causing him to grit his teeth at the pain and the sound of his broken bones moving around. Readily, she also lifted her left cross, revealing Jason's smashed leg, also above her head.

"Until death do us apart... my love..."

"FUCKING BITCH! FUCK YOU! YOU'LL PAY FOR THIS YOU PIECE OF SHIT! YOU WILL PAY! I SWEAR IT FOR THE MOTHERLAND THAT GAVE ME LIFE!" Jason barked as loud as he could, despair being a clear part of the contents of his voice without a glimpse of fear or guilt. He looked at her with fiery eyes, waiting, prompting his chest outward all he could as if he was about to be executed with honors.

Carmen simply remained there, with her cross above her and looked at his defiance. Then, after what felt like a lifetime, Carmen smiled widely at him. She grinned in an unexpected and crooked manner he had never seen before. A grin that had something to it that made Jason stop his act of bravery and tremble. *So... this is what true defeat feels like...* he thought.

"Good-bye... my love..."

The dying woman proceeded to crush Jason onto the floor with both crosses, repeatedly, and with full blunt force. No holding back, not in the slightest, as if a flicker of life had reignited her being. She crushed his body, flesh, and bone in a vicious manner she didn't know she could as Jason's screams of agony flooded the hall and his body got mutilated more and more. His entrails exploding and spilling everywhere, his guts staining her dress all over. She felt the hot substance touching her skin, relishing in taking a bath of blood, as well as a bath of his screams and his terror. As she crushed his ribcage in its entirety, Jason's screams finally fell silent. Nevertheless, she didn't stop, and even if she tried, she couldn't. Eventually, however, her movements became slower until she completely ceased. She had left his head for last. The rest of his body could now be considered a rug. A carpet that served as a souvenir for what had happened there. Carmen looked at him proudly as she relented.

"*Hasta luego*… my love…" she said as she gave her final touch by smashing only the right side of his head with her right cross. Then, she lifted it and admired her work once more.

It was disturbing to see Jason's insides.

It was annoying.

It was… interesting.

In her past life, she would've felt the uttermost repulsion before such a sight. Now, it was completely different. She smiled, she grinned, and for the first time in ages, she laughed and laughed at her heart's contempt, so hard that she couldn't breathe anymore. Notwithstanding, as her decaying body forced her to stop her mockery, she looked down on Jason's corpse one last time to later turn around and walk towards the door and exit the building.

Jason simply lay there, unrecognizable, as his body wasn't even human-looking anymore. Even so, his remaining eye was now looking into the emptiness. And yet, his remaining pupil rolled towards Carmen as she limped away…

Torment of Love

I

THUS, the man in question rose from the floor, evading a direct attack from the Black Cross.

Hit after hit, he had no apparent problems to evade the dreaded woman and her lethal partners. Not that it was due to his skill or powers, unknown to her, but something else entirely. The ground started to gain a moon-like surface as her crosses smashed into it with medium force after missing her attacks. Besides the fact that the man in question didn't seem impressed in the least at the display, the Dire One noted that the more he evaded her attacks, the more annoying the whole situation had become for him, judging from the irritation drawn on his face. Maybe it was her attitude that bothered him, unlike his smell which was what bothered her in ways she had never felt before.

Added to his fantastic maneuvers, his speed helped him even more as, no matter how much she increased her attack speed, he was able to keep up and evade accordingly. At the same time, she wouldn't let him get the first blow, keeping him at a distance. Due to his lack of offensive moves, he was probably trying to wear her down, waiting for the time she would be extremely tired to keep her attacks going and then to counterattack and finish her with ease. Whatever it was, it seemed to be working. Indeed, his success was just a matter of time as she could notice how her movements had become steadily slower and clumsier. Who would've thought that the Black Cross could actually get tired?

Thus, she had to figure out first what was preventing her victory. How could she beat him? For now, the only thing she could do was to prevent his strategy from working. Therefore, she ceased her attacks altogether and stood in guard, resting.

"May I continue now?" he barked, also stopping in place. Then, he cleared his throat, "as I was saying before being rudely interrupted, my name is Rikkard Kaplan. You may call me the *Rozbiórka*, or the Eradicator." He paused for a moment, as if waiting for a reaction from her. As the wind blew past him and into the Black Cross, he could see that something else was going on in her mind. *Maybe this laska wasn't even listening to me this entire time*, he thought. Given that the demon remained silent, looking at him, and still on guard, he continued in a friendly voice, "I'm not here to fight you. I'm here to warn you."

The Dire One gave him a puzzled look in return without letting her guard down. In response, the Eradicator, as Carmen would have laughed at his nickname if she would've been able to remember how humor worked, placed his hands in his pockets and kept going. "As much as it pains me to admit it, I work for the Block. However-"

The man had to pause again as the Black Cross swung one of her weapons towards him aiming at his feet. He jumped and rotated in midair as another cross aiming at his head passed by. The Dire One had tried the element of surprise a little too late. Subsequently, the man in question landed on his feet as the dreaded woman retrieved her partners, thanks to her new chains, and returned to a defensive stance. He cleared his throat while wearing an expression of disappointment. "As I was saying..." he sighed and continued. "I can't say I truly like what they do..."

The Black Cross dropped her guard for half a second. The Eradicator didn't seem to notice it, or maybe he had ignored it altogether.

"In simple terms, I'll help you out."

She positioned herself back onto her attack stance in response while looking at him intently. What was he trying to accomplish? Still, she had to admit this was the first time seeing a Block agent talking about treason to the organization. All the ones she had faced before preferred death before unveiling any sort of information, or of regret for that matter. This situation was always unchanging, regardless of how much she mutilated or tortured them. This was the main reason why she killed them without any hesitation nowadays, that was, besides feeling ecstasy.

Thus, Carmen decided to play along, as she had yet to figure out how to strike him properly if she were to defeat him at some point down the line. "How will downfall recognize your legitimacy...? Even if that were the case... Death may abide before faith is achieved..." the Black Cross said, grinning maliciously at him, as her words echoed in his head. "Those who play with fire never learn..."

This time, however, he was the one who looked at her intently. Then, he sighed and turned his back towards her. She was about to strike again at this opportunity, but she stopped short once new words came out of his mouth.

"Those you think as dead... are not."

The Black Cross was puzzled once more, unsure as to how to answer or how to react.

"My job's done now, *laska*," he continued as he started to walk away. "By the way, just so you know, I was the one who took out the power supply that immobilized you back there. And also, just so you know, I can, and for sure will, bring you down if needed... of that much, you can be sure."

The Dire One lowered her guard once he was far away enough to be out of her reach, and her out of his. And yet, he continued in the distance with a voice showered in authority. "We share a common origin, if I'm correct, *laska*... I've been watching you, and I'll continue to do so..."

The Black Cross looked at him in disgust as he kept on his way back into the forest. "Labor for the dark beast is enough for Death to commit..." she said in a low neutral voice.

The Eradicator simply ignored her and bolted away. Upon observing him running, properly under the moonlight and without trees obstructing her vision, she was able to assess that his speed was quite impressive. He seemed to be able to run as fast as a sports car. This also reminded her of a news article she had once read... some man who had been seen doing the same in Fiutic. Was that this very same man or someone else?

As the mysterious man vanished in the distance, she went back to the car in a calm fashion. She turned it on and investigated the car's ceiling. Her partners now rested, as usual, on the passenger seat next to her. Regardless of the amount of dried blood and the smell it brought all the time, that man's smell still felt close, as if he was sitting right next to her. His stench had probably filtered through the air ventilation system thanks to the air blowing in her direction. She gritted her teeth slightly at the realization.

"Death may be infinite... but time it does not possess..." she concluded, as she looked back to the road and accelerated to the maximum, scraping the road in the process. As she heard the mini explosions of the engine, while feeling the small vibrations of the vehicle, a moment of her life passed right through her mind. Strangely, she couldn't tell which. Unable to decipher what her memories wanted to show her, she looked far into the stars as the engine roared its way into the night. *So far, and yet... so obvious!* she thought.

She braked immediately, marking the pavement with her tires, while her eyes widened as her memories finally showed her the way. That smell, that damn smell right by her side... it was similar to someone she had come to admire once... someone beloved to her.

Prior to meeting this man, she had assumed supernaturals, in general, had a particular smell to them. Keeping this man's smell in mind, she could say she had faced up to three supernaturals, including him: the other two being the Biologist, and the man who chased her constantly who called himself the Creature. They both had a plastic-like stench to them. When the Creature was split open by her crosses, she felt as if she was inhaling bleach. Maybe the Biologist shared a similar feature to the Creature if opened in half. Nonetheless, the Eradicator defied all of this notion in one go. His smell felt like having dust blown up into her nose. She had nobody else to compare that smell to, besides herself. And that would have worked perfectly... had she not been covered in the blood of her victims almost all the time, and her nose not gotten used to her present smell. Still, that dusty sensation was something she had felt before, albeit in a weaker fashion. This smell... it was...

The Eradicator's words echoed in her mind: *'Those you think as dead... are not'*.

She held her head on one hand as her deduction had finally come to fruition, sweat running down her face for the first time in ages. Had *he* survived her rage on that fateful night? If *he* was a supernatural, that would be the case. Regardless of whether it was true or not, thinking back on it, it was quite plausible. She was pretty much a walking corpse *that* night. Her brain felt numb, as well as her body, during those moments of agony. By remembering those same struggling steps, another memory came to her mind.

She remembered how many times she had defeated and butchered the Creature, and yet, there he was, chasing after her every time he could with his body fully restored as if nothing had happened to him. Something didn't add up, though. If *he* was truly alive and well, would he not be chasing her down like the Creature did? Wouldn't *he* be consumed by revenge, too? Even if *he* were, it didn't matter. If the Eradicator were to be right, then it would just mean she would have to kill her *dear* husband... again.

To think that her old self would have felt too guilty to go for it... Back then, she would've thought that he might have learned from it and that dying once was worth her mercy and forgiveness. Indeed, despite all the damage he had done to her, her old self would have eventually forgiven him. Something the Immigrant had taught her back in the day through his own actions. Needless to say, that wasn't the case anymore.

Notwithstanding, going after him meant that she'd have to give up her current mission, especially since he would probably be far away. Such a detour was unneeded as he didn't seem to be willing to appear anytime soon or to become an obstacle on her way. In the end, the one she was chasing now worked for *them*, as did Jason. *I'll run into him… eventually*, she thought.

Recovered from her revelation, she continued her pursuit by accelerating at full throttle once again. Her only track to follow was that damn kid, the one she hadn't been able to kill. She wouldn't hesitate this time, or at least she kept telling herself that.

Company… again? she thought as, with the car raging down Route 13, she noted that the ambience was far away from being quiet. Although it wasn't weird for her at this point to see another car hot on her heels, she knew no one was supposed to know her current position, at least not yet. So, she checked her rear-view mirrors. As expected, it was the pursuer she had just 'killed' two hours ago. Their eyes met thanks to said mirrors: The Black Cross' mocking gaze matched by the Creature's furious one. His hands, keeping a tight grip on the steering wheel, along with his gritting teeth, was truly an interesting sight to behold. The Dire One had never seen him this angry. Knowing by now that he grew madder with each defeat, she enjoyed feeling his fury all the way from his car.

In the Creature's eyes, the humiliation of being defeated by her, three times in a row now, had been enough to make him forget momentarily why he was after her in the first place. Thus, when he spotted the blond man in the lab coat fighting her, and running away back near Kelvin's, the former king of New Zesl changed his course and chose him instead. However, little did he know that a bunch of missiles would strike him down, forcing him to go back to the destroyed neighborhood to get a new car.

I still haven't lost all my pride, cagna maledetta! he thought as his car approached that of the Black Cross. The plan was simple: he would throw her off balance by hitting her rear at full speed when approaching a steep curve. Both of them would lose their vehicles which would, in turn, stall her long enough for reinforcements to come to his position once he had made enough noise. It didn't matter if said reinforcements came from the Block or the county authorities. He would be able to easily defeat her then. Even so, he wouldn't wait for *them* whether he succeeded or not. Unfortunately for his plan, the curves he was hoping for were way too far ahead which only thinned out his already near-zero patience. By now, he had forgotten that it had been this very characteristic of his that had allowed him to rule with an iron fist. For instance, whenever any of his men failed a single task he commanded, no matter how small or insignificant, they knew they were dead for sure. What they didn't know was that this was a lesson from his mentor, and one that he'd follow verbatim: Ruling with an iron fist was never enough to rule the city's underworld, however, making quick and correct decisions was. Quick being the key word. Something his impatience was quite suitable with. Thanks to this trait, one he always made sure to thank for every dinner to the almighty, he had always had an edge over his competitors and had remained the King of New Zesl for so long. At the same time, it was precisely this trait he loved the most, the one that had betrayed him the hardest. Had he taken his time to decide whether to betray the agreement with his former, and current, 'associates', he wouldn't be in this fiasco in the first place. When that fateful day happened, and his life as a free man was essentially over, he prayed to good and evil in an effort to get it all back, promising all he could think of. Of course, it didn't work. Yet, that had never stopped him from trying his luck at praying again, always telling himself that if it didn't work the last time, that didn't mean it wouldn't work the next time.

"*Madonna mia…* allow me to kill this wretched demon!"

And just like that, as he accelerated down the road, he started to feel it in his chest… that feeling he had felt so many times before… that everything would be alright… It was there… it had to be it!

His luck was back! It was payback time! At last! The time

of the Black Cross had finally come!

"For Viellentus!" he screamed in enlightenment, as he charged in full throttle.

II

SHE COULD FEEL HIM. The beating of his heart indicated he was feeling rage and sadness.

Remember, what doesn't kill you only makes you stronger, he used to tell her all the time, and it wasn't truer than that very moment. As weak as she was, she was glad one emotion wasn't taking over her core: Fear. Instead, another one entirely different had rolled over her conscience. Fortunately, it wasn't regret. Subsequently, Carmen walked as fast as she could, which still wasn't much, falling and causing ever-increasing pain to her near-dead body. Feeling heavier every time she got up as the wounds all over her body reminded her of their presence, scorching her body, in turn, informing her that she was still alive.

I can't give up… yet.

She was running out of time, not because of her imminent death, but because the Immigrant wouldn't be alive for much longer. By the time she fell for the sixth time, she had realized how powerless she truly was. Regardless of the promises made by Sadness, she was far from being anything close to unstoppable. Her own body, in its numbness, was trying to force her to lay down her will and rest… forever.

Barely able to get back on her feet, supporting herself on her new blood-stained companions, she realized how much of a coward she had been all this time. She had accepted death thinking, not to say just hoping, that Nico would be able to escape on his own and continue on with his life, somehow. Her despair before getting shot in the head had made her overestimate Nico's capabilities beyond that of a normal human, which he hardly was. Maybe it was the fact that he was a sort of hero before her eyes that had driven her mind in that direction. Ironically, it had been this very admiration towards him the reason why she had abandoned him during her last moments.

Pequeño…

As she did her best to keep her legs from collapsing while walking towards the main entrance, her mind could only fathom about the disgrace that was about to befall the Immigrant. She couldn't forgive herself for it, even if such an emotion no longer held any meaning in her heart. Loving such a man, despite having no guilt or regret, somehow made sense. Of course, Sadness hadn't said anything about love. Carmen smirked a little at the discovery as she deduced her fuel to keep going was still intact. Thus, using her weapons as crutches once again, feeling her trembling and cold body on the verge of collapse, she kept struggling to advance, noting that her vision had started to blur increasingly while her breathing had become arhythmic. Even her burning wounds started to feel as if they weren't there, her body becoming ever number.

I'll save you… even if my decaying life reduces to nothing… this is… my final mission… Success is my only option… no other result will suffice for my heart.

"Nico… wait… I'll be… there…" muttered Carmen faintly as the rain gradually came to stop. She felt some relief when she was able to feel every small pool of water with her bare feet, contrasting with her being unable to understand why her body was moving towards the East for no apparent reason.

As she stepped on the asphalt near the main entrance, she spotted Jason's sports car. Afterwards, she walked towards it while asking for mercy to the skies for the keys to be inside. Unable to pull open the door, she smashed it open in two weak swings, each with a different cross. Then, after the door fell off and her weakness prompted her to fall face down, she managed to get her hands and head onto the driver's seat. Crawling slowly inside the vehicle, she positioned herself and her companions to her side on the front seats. Next, she closed her eyes...

...

...

...

"Ah..." she gasped upon waking up. She couldn't tell how long it had been, however, judging from the amount of blood dripping from her crosses onto the leather seat, she could say about an hour. With both of her hands, she managed to distance herself from the steering wheel, ending slouched on the seat's back. She was in luck--the keys were in the ignition. Jason had probably thought of leaving that same night once his job, and relaxation, were done. It wasn't a first, though. Living in a mansion had allowed him to keep such habits. *That man... always driving his Corvetta,* thought Carmen at the reminiscence. She could remember how he would always mention that this car had never let him down, and she could attest to it as this vehicle reminded her of the countless trips they had done together as a family, along with Juan Fernando. To think that that memory alone would've been enough to break her down to tears two hours ago...

With great effort, she managed to turn the engine on, feeling as if her fingers were about to break apart from the struggle alone. The grumblings of the vehicle made her feel as if there had been ages since she had driven a car. Additionally, feeling the comfort of the leather seats and their smell brought her happy memories of old--trips and adventures that would now remain buried in the past. She would have smiled had she not Nico and his fate constantly in her mind.

I have to make it... I have to... please... please... allow me to make it... please...

Feeling she could faint any moment again, she stepped on

the gas and increased her speed as much as she could control, that was, in a straight line. Thus, she ventured into the city below after running over the main entrance doors. Fortunately for her, there were hardly any curves on her way downtown. Additionally, the current hour allowed her to keep her way through the city without running over potential pedestrians, among other living things. Nothing like driving at 4 a.m. on a Marday, the second day of the week.

Looking at the empty city, which still had some life in it, some bars here and there, she realized the very few times she had gotten out of home back then. Still, the city lights started to vanish as her eyes started to show her an invading creeping darkness, her breathing harder and harder to draw. Since her speed was quite unusual for that time in the morning, eventually, an idle police patrol caught sight of the shameful display.

"It seems we got one, Josh," said one of the officers as they saw her pass by. "Let's go get'er!"

The pair had been stationed there for a while without anything to do, especially since that day of the week wasn't popular for going out at night. Since most people tended to work until late, and most pubs and discos weren't prone to give any sort of discounts or specials that day, there was hardly anyone driving drunk. Thus, catching imprudent drivers was harder than usual, and made patrolling boring, in general.

"I donno Mark, I'm feelin' indulgent today…" said the other officer while drinking a strawberry smoothie through a straw. "She might be learnin' how to drive. It wouldn' be the first one to think of driving at this time for practice."

"Whatever, Josh! She's stil' drivin' in a dangerous fashion. You know what? I'm gonna follow her just in case!" answered Mark, turning on the engine.

"I didn' get to see her clearly. I think she wasn' using her seat belt. Apart from that, she IS drivin' at an insane speed now that I see'er closely… alright Mark, you win. Let's follow her. As a last resort, let's just pull her off." However, their relaxed attitude turned into unbelievability when they saw how

Carmen had almost run over a hobo while turning around a corner, taking a mailbox along with her. "Let's get her!"

As they made themselves noticeable to Carmen through her outside mirrors and the screams of their sirens, accompanied by red and blue lights, they noticed that she wasn't showing any sign of stopping or reducing her speed. With more casualties over time, given that people couldn't get out of her way on time, the officers kept chasing her increasing their speed to the point of almost touching her vehicle. Even if that meant they had to run over some of the victims in the process, their priority was clear.

"STOP RIGHT NOW!" ordered Josh through the megaphone, prompting some light bulbs to be turned on inside the buildings they happen to pass by. "STOP RIGHT NOW OR YOU WILL BE FORCED TO DO SO!"

"Where this road goes to? Where the heck's this gal going?" said Mark as he kept focused on tailing the fugitive. Josh, who had thrown his smoothie out the window in order to reach the megaphone, simply ignored him.

"She isn' slowin' down! She's gonna crash into the Alboeida Infection Care Center! This is insane!" screamed Josh, prompting Mark to slow down their car.

"What about the guards at the entrance?! Let's warn them!" demanded Mark as he stopped the car close enough for the people there to hear them. "Use the damn megaphone now!"

"GET OUTTA THE WAY! SHE'S GOING TO HIT YOU!"

Only one of the guards realized this in time and jumped away. The other one got his body crushed against the barred entrance doors as the car crashed them open, unhinging them in the process. At the same time, these doors served as an improvised brake, screeching against the pavement and stopping the car right before it went through the main glass doors that were on the building itself. The corpse of the guard was launched by inertia into said doors, breaking them into pieces. Given the time, the majority of the active staff wasn't in the facility. However, there was a contingent of guards encircling the place as fast as they could. Little did they know that Carmen and her crosses had also been launched into the building through the windshield, landing on top of the guard's corpse. As she got up, her body on the brink of giving up, feeling the pain of glass impaling her skin and the soles of her feet, the alarms started to sound and a message was spewed by the edifice's speakers: "All remaining personnel and specimens are to be evacuated from the facility! Warning! Warning! All remaining personnel and specimens are to be evacuated from the facility...!"

Nico... is being taken away... I can feel it... I won't be able to make it... I can hardly breathe...

"Stop right there! Lay down your weapons at once!" commanded one of the guards from within the building, aiming at her with his pistol alongside two more who did the same. Nonetheless, their confidence dropped as soon as they saw the hole in her head. This, in turn, petrified them as they didn't know what to think of it. It seemed these hadn't been trained for this.

Carmen felt projectiles penetrate her body in the leg and torso, as a bullet seemed to have lodged itself in her stomach. They were screaming more things at her as they shot her, but she could no longer tell, nor understand, their words. As the last of her vision gave way, she managed to swing her crosses and to decapitate two of them, mostly following the sound of their voices. She could tell the remaining guard ran away as his voice in despair got farther and farther away. Her ears could only give her so much information as her eyes were now next to useless. Because of this, it was simple voices talking and dim lights coming from a room that caught her attention. Losing even more blood from her recent wounds to a great degree, and on the border of falling to unconsciousness, she simply followed these signs.

With every step she made, she could tell Nico was getting farther and farther away from the building. What else could she do? Had she revived for nothing? Her life was almost gone, and she had managed to fail yet again.

I wish I could feel regret...

Her only hope was to repeat the same mistake as before, since, as much as it irritated her, she had no choice. Maybe if she could create some sort of distraction in that place, which was definitely part of *their* facilities, they might loosen *their* watch on Nico and maybe... just maybe...

Still, even if her senses were pretty much dead, there was the remote possibility of more personnel still in the facility. Perchance she could hold said personnel hostage for a while until death came to claim her.

"*Esas luces*... guide me... please... I beg of you..." said Carmen, approaching the only room with lights on in the pavilion.

A star in a sea of darkness.

III

AS EXPECTED, his headlights had become more visible to her.

The Creature should have known by now that that was a bad idea. Even though his past life would've made anyone else assume he was very good at driving, it was quite the opposite. His short temper usually got the best of him, like when he passed another car with a dangerous maneuver, against the traffic, simply because he had wanted to be in front of said car and the driver hadn't let him two streets prior. *Sciocco*, he thought with a smug smile, feeling like he had won a million wollars once he heard that man honking at him as he continued on his way to the bank. What he had never been able to realize was that he had managed to do these dangerous maneuvers of his, successfully, due to the other drivers being pushovers, and not his own skill.

Questa diavolessa è mia! he thought as he approached Carmen's car, unable to contain his excitement. As he kept on his chase, the Black Cross changed lanes, driving on the wrong side of the road, and then she changed back, and so on. *You can't escape me cagna! You'll die today!*

He could see her smirking through her rear-view mirror. Perhaps his longing for blood had become so overwhelmingly obvious that she was having fun feeling it, or maybe she was simply mocking him by making him remember his past failures. In either case, he rushed in and finally bumped into her rear, grinning at his achievement, touching the monster as if his car had become an extension of his body.

Nevertheless, the Dire One changed back to the right side of the road. As the Creature started to change back as well, he noticed two big and blinding lights. *Maledetta puttana*, he thought right before being run over by a huge truck.

The Black Cross grinned at the scene as she accelerated away from the place. The Creature had effectively destroyed his car, his body, and the front of the truck. His vehicle was now unrecognizable, and so was he. Only a pile of steel beams entangled with each other remained, with his body, now mostly a pulp of flesh impaled among them.

"... oh... my head... what the hell was that...?" whispered the truck driver as he emerged from his vehicle with a broken arm, crawling out of the cabin through his window. Indeed, the truck had turned over due to breaking at such a high speed. He couldn't believe his good luck as he had never seen someone surviving a hundred-kilometers-per-hour crash before. He produced a cell phone out of his left pocket and called the police while he checked his merchandise in the container. As his potato cargo had also survived the debacle, he smiled slightly. *Thanks Kothat...* he thought. Nonetheless, as he prayed his words away, he saw with horror the fate of the other driver. The man in question couldn't help himself but puke all over the place at the sight.

"Oh my God... what have I done?" he regretted out loud, looking into the night sky about to pop tears out of his eyes. Nonetheless, he took deep breaths and calmed himself down. "Maybe he holds some ID or somethin'," he continued as he approached the disemboweled man. "I must... contact his family... that's the least... I can do..." Notwithstanding, he stopped short when he heard the sound of bones creaking within the mutilated car.

Meanwhile, as the Black Cross lost sight of them, she happily hummed a lullaby. *Would you have done the same, pequeño?* she wondered. A question that always popped up in her mind every time she did something rash, which was almost always. Then, the answer would come up right away, and it was always the same: a resounding no.

Regardless of what she could conclude, she was glad to know that at least *he* wasn't in any danger he couldn't handle, as far as she could tell, or feel. To think that, back then, they used to talk and laugh together all the time. Now, he wouldn't even dare give her a smile as a gift as he no longer understood her, or so she thought. Sure enough, a smile, so sweet that it alone could cause diabetes, appeared on Carmen's face whenever she remembered him. Her memories concerning him were several, but it always had the same effect on her... that of irremediable hope.

"Wherever the light might be... Death wants it to be safe..." murmured Carmen as she continued her march. "Whatever the path might be... Death wants it to be painful," she continued as soon as she spotted that, ahead of her, the road forked into three paths. Grinning devilishly at the sight, she couldn't stop herself from braking violently to the point of almost turning the car over and going out of the road.

That damn kid is on the right one... but...

Her heartbeat had suddenly become agitated, as if she had just run the marathon. It emanated despair with each beat... as if it was in grave danger. She touched her chest, reminiscing about the other times she had felt a similar sensation... that of anxiety taking over her mind. Indeed, she had felt this particular heartbeat on numerous occasions ever since she became the Black Cross. However, this beat was unique as it contained utter fear.

Should I take the left path?

Her hands grabbed the steering wheel in evident uneasiness as her eyes lost themselves on the horizon in front of her. Her hands tried to turn to the left, and yet they couldn't. No matter how long it had been, she still froze at the mere thought...

Has he forgiven me?

She would usually tremble just by suggesting the idea to

herself, and this was no exception. Sure enough, as her heartbeat subsided, her smug smile vanished from her face. She gritted her teeth and drove the car back to the right path. When she was about to step on the gas, her heartbeat rose to a speed she had never felt before, way faster than the unique beat she had felt a few minutes ago. Then, it dropped completely, to a point of being almost quiet. She quickly glanced to the left path.

That awful place… if I let that kid escape, the Block will forever hold an edge over me with this stupid weakness… but if I don't take the other path… my existence will lose its meaning…

As she thought about it, memories of her past appeared in front of her, along with her lifelong held promise that would someday come true, or rather might… the left path would have to wait…

However, when she stepped on the accelerator and the car advanced on the right road, her discomfort grew even further. Something she had never felt before which kept growing as the distance between the bifurcation and herself increased. *What is going on?* she thought as her annoyance became strong enough to make her stop the vehicle again. As she noticed a couple of cars behind her, which didn't show any sign of being pursuers or Block agents, she simply parked the car on the safe lane further to the right. The other cars, thinking she was a hidden officer on duty checking their speed limits, drove carefully and passed by at the exact limit allowed. One of them seemed to be drunk but still managed to clear the line without too much suspicion. As for the Black Cross went, she preferred to keep up her guard just in case until the dizzy vehicle had vanished in the distance. After checking if there were any more unwanted sightseers, she closed her eyes and focused on this newfound feeling. With the world around her vanishing into nothingness, she was able to clearly see what her heart was pointing at. And so, after a few seconds, there it was…

Will he be able to make it…?

It was the first time she had wondered about such a question. How could she have been so blind? She kept struggling for a while with her current decision as different outcomes flooded her mind. Among them, as she was unable to choose the most probable one, a phrase came up from within her memory.

'You know, you can always use your heart'

Whether I fear you hating me… I fear more you getting killed… she thought. Thus, ranting against the steering wheel, she went backwards all the way to the fork and took the left road instead. *Besides, even if I manage to destroy that weakness, they will eventually find another one… that damn kid may live… for now.*

As she accelerated down said road, she started to feel some reminiscence about that path in particular. It seemed more and more familiar the longer she went through it. Of course, it had to be. The night was still young… like *that* night. The trees, the signs… all led to the same conclusion…

After a long time, she was coming home.

Back in the day, nothing would've made her happier. Now, it produced chills down her spine. *Why are you there out of all places? There are way better hideouts… unless…* she thought as she pressed even more on the gas to go faster. *I guess this is just like that time… seven months ago…*

"We won't make it *pequeño*! Let's surrender!" said Carmen when they were surprised by the Block agents on all sides, back then. They were inside a five-story abandoned building, and with nowhere to run, they had no other choice than to defeat the agents if they wanted to get out. Of course, even Nico knew that was not possible, at least not facing all of them at once.

"*Tranquila*, you remember the three-man rule?" Nico said as he kept running upstairs, holding Carmen's hand. He was incredibly calm, even smiling at the situation.

"What does that have to do with anything right now?!" replied Carmen, fright in her voice. "We're done for! Running is useless!"

"If the only option we have left is to run, let's do it intelligently!" said Nico, still smiling. Then, out of nowhere, he pushed Carmen into an empty dark room, closed the door, and kept running down the building's aisle. Carmen fell on her back, unable to assimilate what had just happened, so she quickly got up and went straight to the door to follow Nico but stopped short when she heard the herd of agents running behind it.

"Oh no…" whispered Carmen as she realized what had just happened. Nico had explained his so-called "three-man rule" to her before. If he were to defeat anyone, it would be best if the opponent was alone and unarmed, which pretty much never happened. If he were to defeat two opponents, that was still feasible if he possessed the element of surprise. Back at their rooftop home, Nico had explained that the element of surprise against the nurses at Sanatorium was them underestimating him based on his appearance, as they were bigger and stronger than him, not taking into account that the teenager was a martial artist. If he were to defeat three opponents, though, he would rather run and find a way to separate them. Thus, unless he absolutely had to, he wouldn't engage with three agents at once as the odds of winning were next to none, not to mention that a fourth agent could jump into the mix at any given moment. However, Nico would have a hard time applying his rule right there as the agents after him were all running in a straight line. Being in constant visual contact with one another also complicated things for the Immigrant.

Knowing Nico, he would hide in one of the floors and produce noises in several areas, by throwing objects, to confuse *them* and force *them* to separate. He had explained this strategy on his way to the building. Nonetheless, even Carmen knew that wasn't enough this time. There were way too many agents. After hearing their stampede, Carmen could tell there were at least ten agents, if not twelve. *I'll help you pequeño*, she thought as she opened the door, slowly, right after she had heard the last of their steps vanish into silence. She looked around and, after making sure there was nobody around, she ran upstairs in the most silent fashion she could afford. *I know what's on your mind pequeño… I know you pushed me into that room to protect me… I know you're desperate against these odds… by mentioning your rule you meant to override it... and I know there's just no way you can pull this off... but you're not alone!*

Normally, the Immigrant would be extremely careful, but now it looked as if he was another person altogether. Even if he somehow managed to separate the agents, all of *them* would be looking for him on the same floor, preventing him from escaping to an upper or lower floor while being in close proximity to each other. Not even the low lighting inside the building would save him this time. There was just no way this could work by any stretch of the imagination.

As she placed her foot on the first staircase going up, Carmen stopped, shaking to the core. *This isn't what he wanted me to do... but, then, what the hell do I do? If I make a mistake, his sacrifice will have been for nothing... but I'm tired of always being the damsel in distress...* she thought while looking around when she saw a bucket lying below the staircase. *I got an idea!*

...

"What is that?" said one of the agents. "Where is that noise coming from? Wasn't that bastard on this floor?"

"There is noise on this floor, too! Maybe there are more people in this damn place! It might be an ambush!" said another agent.

"Calm your horses. It's probably that damn woman accompanying him! Not to worry, she isn't dangerous! Just two of us should suffice to get her!" said another agent to then point his fingers at two of his partners. "You two, go downstairs now!"

As requested, those two agents went downstairs and started looking for Carmen. In order to cover more terrain, they separated once they arrived at said floor, walking extremely carefully, almost in silence. As Carmen had never dealt with them directly, watching always from afar, or not watching at all, she could only refer to the practice afternoons she had had with the Immigrant back at the rooftop.

"Always go for the weak spots," Nico would always say

while showing Carmen to aim at the throat, eyes, and groin of her opponents. "Most people expect fair fights, even if they are trained agents. It's always good to have at least one element of surprise, no matter how small." Carmen never knew if he was serious whenever he said that, given that he sounded like an action movie star to her. In turn, she would hold her laughter not to make him mad. Now, trapped in the decaying building, she had to hold her breath not to be discovered by her pursuers. Even though she could tell that these agents were aware of Nico's tactics, they weren't aware of hers.

Hearing their incoming steps, Carmen prepared herself. Thus, as silently as she could, she got on top of a couple of wooden boxes inside another empty room, right next to the door frame, rendering her out of sight from the aisle. Still, the little noise she had made by doing so would soon attract at least one of her pursuers towards her, which was part of the plan. Meanwhile, she had also placed a bunch of bricks in a delicate state of equilibrium, one on top of the other inside another room. It was a trick she had practiced before when she spent her days inside the wine cellar, checking how much vibration they would be able to withstand without falling over. Indeed, the agents' mere steps were enough to make *them* fall and, soon enough, the trap worked as intended causing each of them to go their separate ways: one towards Carmen and the other one towards the empty room with the fallen bricks. Just as planned. So, she waited, and waited… and then, before she knew it, there he was.

The agent in question entered the room, holding his gun with both hands, aiming everywhere at a hundred-eighty-degree angle, horizontally, around him. In order to keep his eyes stuck downwards, Carmen had thrown a small piece of wood onto the floor within that very room, prompting him to aim towards the far corner. Once he was in position, Carmen dropped a brick onto his head. He was knocked out instantly.

"Phew… he's not dead," she whispered to herself when she descended to the ground and touched his jugular. "Nothing to feel bad for." Nevertheless, the other agent didn't take long to catch wind of the predicament and made his way to that room. As his steps grew closer, Carmen picked up the fainted agent's gun and fired towards her attacker without aiming. Given that she had never fired before, the gun almost escaped her hand, making her think she had broken her fingers for a second. Fortunately for her, the agent hadn't shot her back before taking cover while she had stood there like a statue, dealing with the pain.

"Wh-what did I just do?" she wondered just to feel a bullet passing near her head. She quickly realized what was about to happen next and took cover inside the room.

"She's armed! I repeat! She's armed!" said the agent into a walkie-talkie. "I need reinforcements!"

Three more agents descended to her floor and surrounded the entrance to the room she was in. Then, slowly, they started their approach. Knowing their tactics, she made a warning shot through the door and made them stop short. *They aren't asking for me to surrender... guess they aren't interested in taking me prisoner... but if they do take me prisoner, that'd be the end of it all,* she thought, shooting two more warning shots as soon as she heard their steps advancing again. She quickly looked around, hopelessly looking for an exit, knowing this was a storage room without windows or additional exits. Thus, there were two possible outcomes: she would either run out of bullets before they entered the room and get her, or they would enter it regardless of the risk and get her. It was just a matter of time...

Sure enough, as her shots had become less frequent, their steps sounded closer. Eager. The gun had a counter on top of it that had been going down from twelve every time she shot. Her hands had started shaking once she realized she had one bullet left. She looked at it intently as she cried in silence...

"Thanks for everything *pequeño... lo siento tanto...*" she lamented as she placed the gun in her mouth. She prepared herself as she heard a couple of steps rushing to the room. She closed her eyes and was about to pull the trigger when a strong hand grabbed her hands and took the gun away. Carmen stood there in silence, unable to look up in fear of who she might see.

"*¡¿Estás loca?!*" reprimanded Nico, clear fury in his voice. "What the fuck were you thinking?!"

Carmen couldn't believe her eyes. It was Nico's face, red like a tomato due to him bleeding from his head. "H-how?" Carmen managed to utter in shock.

"Well... I had to-" Nico couldn't finish his sentence when Carmen hugged him with all her might, producing Nico to moan in complaint. "We have to go... now..." he said after pushing her away and taking her by the hand once more to then guide her downstairs.

Once they were back to the relative safety of their beloved rooftop, Nico explained that, after hearing the sounds downstairs, he had come to two conclusions: the first being that Carmen had produced these sounds accidentally; the second being that Carmen had produced them on purpose to draw the agents away from him. In both cases, she would be done for. Notwithstanding, the Mizelas employed a similar tactic thanks to her idea, producing noises in several rooms by throwing objects inside them while running upstairs, taking advantage of having fewer agents on his floor. Then, as he continued his improvised concert, this had the intended effect and the agents spread like ants in a colony. And like ants alone, they were easier to deal with.

Still, he got hit on the head by one of them with the blunt of his gun. Nico had barely managed to keep the pain to a minimum and had blocked a kick to his stomach. He then threw the man to the ground into a lock and asphyxiated him with his arm around his neck until he was unconscious. By the end of it, the Immigrant had managed to defeat fifteen of them, a new personal record for him. As for the ones shooting at Carmen, *they* were too focused on her to notice him approaching *them* from behind, allowing him to lock their necks as well, and repeating the same technique. Once they had been dealt with, he ran towards the room to find Carmen and stopped her just in the nick of time.

"Crazy problems require crazy solutions," he said

confidently as Carmen bandaged his head with a piece of cloth they had managed to 'borrow' from a neighbor's hanging clothes to dry. "Still… what were you thinking?"

"I-I don't know…" replied Carmen shyly. Not even the thought of getting captured had crossed her mind at that moment. *Why?* As she wondered about it, she saw a punch coming to her face which stopped millimeters away from it. She had kept her eyes open, not even blinking once. Indeed, that had been part of her training under the Immigrant: to assume that she would be hit sooner or later.

Nico retreated his fist. "It seems you are okay with getting punched… but not with getting shot at."

Carmen opened her eyes wide in astonishment. He was right. Maybe that was why Nico was able to pull such insane strategies in such heated moments. Maybe he had been shot at so many times that it didn't make a difference to him at this point. However, this explanation of hers didn't convince herself completely…

The training to achieve her lack of fear of punches had been arduous, and somehow painful. In order to do so, Nico had thrown his fists at her every day, always stopping at a few millimeters away from her face, or stomach. Carmen was to suppress her natural reaction to it, or in other words, she was not to close her eyes or cover her body before this threat. Whenever Carmen complained about how useless this training was, Nico would always mention how those natural reactions limited one's array of decisions available when fighting, and he wasn't wrong. He made sure to prove it to her countless times, especially when he wouldn't punch her for real until he considered she was ready for it, and even then, he did it in a way that wouldn't hurt her. This mere fact bothered Carmen sometimes, that was, never to be taken seriously as an opponent. Yet, she never questioned Nico about it. Still, the Immigrant managed to read her mind, or probably just looked at her angry face, and answered that implied question. "Just remember why I can't hurt you… I mean, to hurt you seriously at least," he'd say out of the blue. "You gotta become unpredictable Carmen," he'd tell her as a piece of advice right afterwards, hammering this message as much as he could.

Again, with the action movie lines, she thought while rolling her eyes.

"I guess I'm not being *suficientemente* serious with this. The thing is, the only advantage we have over them is our unpredictability. No one is invincible."

"You talk too much, you know that?" Carmen said apathetically.

"Prove me wrong then," he taunted.

"How am I supposed to defeat the 'almighty Immigrant'? Whatever, I'd be proving you wrong, anyways."

Whenever they weren't discussing their philosophies or plans for the future, Nico would always challenge her from time to time, whether physically, or mentally, always encouraging her to question him at every step. It had become so monotonous and tiresome that Carmen often complained about these incessant, and seemingly useless, challenges. He was still an insufferable teenager after all...

"Try me," he taunted once again.

Carmen, now fed up with it, changed her stance to offense and attacked him. As usual, Nico wouldn't let her hit him, evading or blocking her every hit. Then, she would always end up in his arms in a tight lock that usually meant it was over. Nevertheless, this time she, having him behind her, tried to kick him in the groin. Nico evaded, but not by much. Soon afterwards, he released her.

"So? You happy now? You're invincible in the end... as always!" said Carmen sarcastically.

"The thing is... you almost made it," Nico said with a gentle smile.

"So?"

"You think that you can make it, and that's what counts."

Carmen looked at him, perplexed. "What?"

"You heard me. Such as yourself, others might also defeat me eventually," the youngster said calmly while sitting down on his cardboard about to perform his usual meditation.

"That's why I'll never return to Sanatorium to save more people or anyone else who might be chased by the Block," he said while taking deep breaths. Before Carmen could respond, he continued. "I made a promise to you that I will keep, even if it costs me my life, but that doesn't mean I'm not selfish. I'm just a human being, nothing else, nothing more. I'm no hero."

You might not be a hero… but you are my hero.

"And that's the reason why Death has come home," said the Black Cross as she approached the La Cruz mansion. "Death remains uncertain as well…"

Lights in the sky made their appearance as it all started to make sense. There was a military chopper in the area while agents, armed to the teeth, surrounded her former dwelling in the midst of darkness. Something was definitely being cooked inside, and it wasn't pleasant to look at. As soon as she caught a proper glimpse of one of said people, she immediately knew who *they* were. Nothing fancy this time, though. *They* were probably expecting her to be somewhere else, maybe looking for the Biologist's whereabouts.

"Death will claim the debris… beyond its inventiveness…"

She parked her vehicle on the limiting fence of her former terrain and jumped over it, falling inside the garden. Given that the patrol lights were still on, the Black Cross knew she had made the Block aware that they had company as she could hear them issuing orders among themselves to check on who had arrived at the scene. It didn't take long for two agents to approach her former vehicle with flashlights, and rifles, only to find traces of blood on the front passenger seat.

"There might be an injured officer around! Watch out!" said one of the agents in question.

As the Dire One got farther away from the car, she couldn't avoid recognizing her old place. The garden hadn't changed much, except for the occasional overgrown plants here and there. Her front garden had always been huge after all, its fresh air penetrating her lungs and the smell of wet earth reminding her of the vineyards during spring. And like vineyards, these new botanical additions in the garden meant stealth attacks would be easier to perform. The night was still young indeed, and smiling upon her new mission, especially since, like on *that* fateful night, the moonlight was almost nonexistent. Still, the agents were using infrared vision. Not that the Black Cross expected less. *At least they don't know I can see them perfectly in the dark*, she thought as she approached them, crouching among the bushes. *Their breathing tells me they are quite confident in their success… interesting…*

"All perimeter secured. I repeat, all perimeter secured. No hostiles inbound. Trash successfully trapped in the building. I repeat, trash successfully trapped inside the building. What are your orders, sir?" said one of the agents through a radio strapped to his chest, holding a rifle with a laser sight. "Do not engage? With all due respect sir but- I understand sir. Very well. Complying…"

It was clear who they meant by 'trash'. The only question that surrounded Carmen's head was: why would they not engage? From the way he spoke, it was evident that they had an overwhelming advantage in numbers, and weapons, and had rendered their prey unable to get out of the mansion.

The process to defeat *them* was almost always the same, as Nico had taught her long ago. The first step was crucial: that of locating every enemy nearby. *Twenty-seven heartbeats*, she counted. *This is way over the three-man rule… not that it matters much.* As she silently got closer to the mansion, she found it hard to discern anything in particular within it; she could tell there were several people inside, though. *Their heartbeats describe fear and despair… they can't be Block agents*, she concluded. *I have to hurry.*

"Aaahhhh!!!" one agent screamed out of nowhere, drawing the attention of his partners nearby. Soon enough, two agents went towards his position while aiming their weapons in all directions.

"Man down! I repeat! Man down!" said the first agent to arrive at the scene.

"What the hell happened down there?! Is the trash out there, too?!" said Alexander Pustakios, the commanding officer leading the operation from a helicopter through a walkie-talkie. "All of you have orders to shoot to kill! This is inconceivable for Frisks like us!"

"Sir... his head has been crushed against the ground..." replied the agent with a worrisome tone to his voice. "This might be..."

"Hmmm... it might be *her* of all people..." responded the commander, mostly talking to himself. "If that's the case, then be on the lookout. She must not escape! And-" he stopped when he heard an agonizing scream on the other side of the walkie-talkie, followed by an acute laughter. "Oh fuck... It is definitely her! Surround the location and shoot to kill!"

Contrary to what he had expected, the screams of agony only multiplied around the garden. Some of them didn't even get to scream or could only start to do so.

"What the fuck is going on?!" ranted the commander. "We are not supposed to fall like flies! All remaining agents! The Black Cross is on the loose! I repeat! The fucking Black Cross is here! Use maneuver B-12!"

The agents quickly formed circles, back to back, like defensive formations when men fought with spears and shields, aiming their laser sights all around them in groups of five. There were only three groups left by now...

"No sign of target! I repeat! No sign of target!" said one of the agents in command as he moved forward and rotated along with his group, trying to get out of the garden. The maneuver B-12 was quite precise, created in case of supernaturals with high physical capabilities. It had never failed so far.

"No sign of target here either! I repeat! No sign-aaaahhhh!!!"

"Impossible... only two damn groups remaining?!" the commander raged at the sight. "My name is not Alexander Pustakios if that monster is not captured or destroyed today!"

The remaining groups had simply stopped their movement, unable to tell where the demon would come from to claim their lives. And even then, their discipline would show as their legs didn't shake, their gaze remained calm, and their heartbeats unhesitant. Their grip remained fixed on their weapons searching for the monster, shooting towards the direction any sound that happened to travel to their ears could come from. There was one problem though: there were sounds everywhere in the garden, as if there was an invisible bunch of people walking around here and there. "If this damn garden wasn't so massive, we would've found you already bitch!" claimed one of them with a shaky voice. "You're just a coward taking advantage of her small forest!" he continued while shooting at several sounds that happened to appear out of the blue. "We won't die in vain! Come and prove us wrong! Now!"

The rest of the agents, inspired by his show of valor, kept on looking for her with increasing eagerness, walking towards the mansion's exit now almost out of the garden. "We made it! We made-"

These words, coming from that very agent, died off along with him and his group as the last remaining group, petrified nearby, watched with despair how the Black Cross fell from the treetops on top of him and his squad, crushing one more agent besides him at once with her wretched weapons, dancing in a fashion resembling ballet. She decapitated the other three by rotating her lethal partners in the middle of them and taking advantage of their circle formation.

"Shoot her down! Now!!!" screamed one of the agents in the last group alive. "She won't be able to escape our fire! We'll bring her down and live to tell the tale! Avenge our comrades!" he continued to rally the rest of *them* who started to show hope in their eyes. "We will defeat this evil monster and be forever remembered! For Panthea!"

"Die, you whore! This is where you meet your end!" the others responded. "We will defeat you!"

Or so they told themselves.

Once the entire group she was attacking had been annihilated, the Black Cross received the brunt of the projectiles shot by the nearest group as she ran towards them at her fastest speed, unbothered by massive amounts of wounds taking place on her body and laughing in insanity. Eventually, only clicks came out of their guns as they had emptied their magazines… and she was one mere meter away from them.

"Nooo!!! Someone help us! Please! Please!! Arghhhhh!!!!" were the last words of the last standing man in that group.

Pustakios couldn't believe his eyes, speechless before the massacre he had just witnessed. Among the trees, under the chopper's spotlight, there she was, her crosses dripping fresh blood from her most recent victims, looking at him with a mocking smile. Such a sight created a surge of anger that infused the commander.

"Surrender Black Cross! You have no way of defeating the mighty Block!" he challenged through a megaphone. After witnessing the slaughter, the pilot also made the chopper harder to reach for the monster. Just high enough to be out of harm's way. They knew who they were dealing with after all, unlike the police. A reason why the recent slaughter of their Frisk agents was deemed a humiliation.

The Black Cross only smiled maliciously in response as this barking of his could only mean that they wouldn't be an issue for her… or that she would get them later.

The commander continued with his threats through his device while the Dire One simply ignored him and ran towards the mansion's main doors. Expecting them to shoot her from above, she placed one of her crosses onto her back, like a giant turtle shell. Nevertheless, they didn't.

As she approached the entrance, she couldn't help smelling something… something similar to soap...

IV

"I STILL can't get used to that damn smell!" said the doctor while he prepared the syringe in question. Indeed, Doctor Rupert Stein, as he wanted everyone before him to mention his entire name when talking to him for the first time each morning, had a very bad habit which Martens would often point out as 'problematic'.

"Doctor Rupert Stein, sir, will you please record the steps and components of this experiment this time? Please?" begged Martens while rubbing her hands and watching her mentor mixing different substances and warming them in a test tube. "You know it goes against the organization's policy."

"Martens… do you remember who's in charge here?" Stein answered adamantly. And her answer was always the same.

"You, sir," replied Martens in resignation.

"Damn right! And you better not forget it!" continued Stein without taking his eyes off the test tube. "You already know why I keep my own policy, Assistant Martens."

Martens remembered then how much suffering she had witnessed in Stein when he had to kill lab animals, either rats or monkeys, sometimes driving him to the verge of crying. Sometimes he could become too depressed to even brag about being the head of the Research Department of the Block, which was admittedly his most favorite hobby. Thus, as the doctor had mentioned to her around seven-hundred and forty-seven times, "this was pure revenge against the organization for forcing him to do it," or that was how he liked to put it. As lame as this 'revenge' of his was to Martens, she knew she would never even dream of doing something of the sort. Getting kicked out of the organization would take just a single minor mistake on her behalf. It was clear that, unlike her, Stein could allow himself such whims as geneticists of his caliber were a rare find.

I wish I could become one, she often thought. *I just wished I could be one sooner…*

"You see all this Martens?!" he said, patting her on the back the first time she entered the lab as his new apprentice-assistant. "One day this enormous lab will be yours!"

Her eyes shone in delight at the presentation: the installation was top-notch, the latest in technology was theirs to use, and her salary was quite generous. "One day I will be known to the entire world as the savior of Panthea! As soon as we cleanse the country… we will cleanse the world!" he continued with a big smile on his face.

Afterwards, he would often talk about his family and how proud they were of him, especially his grandchildren Matthew, Judith, and Michelle. She had memorized their names within one week as Stein would spend entire afternoons talking about anything new they did, ranging from growing a bean plant in cotton to their commencement in quantum physics in kindergarten. As tired as she was of hearing those stories, she limited herself to smile back in response.

So, this is what having Frisk pride truly means, she thought in turn.

"You know… Michelle promised she'll make a macaroni castle for me if I made the breakthrough today!" said Stein enthusiastically with a smirk as he placed the contents of the test tube he had been working on all morning into a syringe.

"Then she better buy a ton of macaroni, sir!" encouraged Martens, smiling back at him as always, at least until her stomach growled. Working with the doctor tended to be quite time-consuming, without mentioning he was also time-absorbing, something Stein didn't seem to notice as he could work for twelve hours straight.

"I'm gonna get a sandwich, do you want anything, sir?" she said as she was opening the lab door.

"No... thanks... I'm on the brink of achieving the breakthrough I promised..." answered Stein, focused on his microscope with the syringe next to it. If Martens wouldn't have heard it six-hundred forty-four times in a row, she would've believed him. She actually had for the first twenty times, though. Afterwards, it was just a matter of habit. This time, however, he was especially excited since they would be getting a new specimen soon. A teenager of some sort who had escaped a dome near the border and that had been recently recaptured. That youngster had already been inspected and was being transported to their lab as they spoke. *Everything would be so much fun!*

Martens scanned her credentials and opened the massive armored doors, the only access point they had into the lab. Only the supervisor of the facility, Gerard Jones, besides them, was allowed to come in and out at will. Martens could easily tell that, if there was someone with a lot of patience, that would be Mr. Jones as he never questioned the doctor's methods, something she thought of as a bad idea sometimes. Still, she was sure the research they were doing would prove vital to the Block's plans in the near future. Sure enough, one pressing matter was the improvement of the soldiers participating in the invasion of the Middle West which was proving too hard for the present troops stationed there. Therefore, the government of the United Kingdoms of Panthea, and her Majesty Queen Anabelle III, required an urgent improvement upon its military. A new breed of empowered humans, or like Stein liked to call them, *supernaturals.*

Nonetheless, Martens was sure these beings had been in existence way before Stein had coined a name for them, as there had been many reports in the past regarding their presence. Most of them, if not all of them, were considered mere conspiracies by the common folk, herself included. This, however, was bound to change when she joined the Block. Supernaturals were now a common occurrence for her nowadays, even if they weren't for the rest of the world.

As the armored doors closed behind Martens, Stein pressed the plunger slightly in order to get rid of the air inside the syringe and looked down at the subject in question with unseen thrill and anticipation. He could still remember the happiness he had felt the day his right to perform his experiments had been granted. He couldn't thank enough the man who had made it all possible: General John Jacob Smith. A true patriot and a leading example for any Panthean.

In order to fulfill the general's high expectations, Stein was ordered to do something quite simple: he was to develop a serum capable of producing regeneration that would let the troops stationed out there, mostly in the Middle West, have an easier time in combat zones and more chances of surviving the ever-increasing attacks done by terrorists. Although this was Stein's first and main motivation, there was another reason for his fervor to the project: he had always regretted not being able to save his dog, Candy, whose breast cancer had crept into her spine. Said illness led her to not being able to walk and to her eventual sacrifice at the hands of her veterinarian. If he had created this serum way before, she would still be alive and well. He had never been able to forgive himself for that, to the point of never owning a pet again. In turn, he had promised himself that he'd make it this time. Therefore, he would create something that would change the world, not only for pets, but for everyone, forever.

Indeed, he had always imagined himself creating a serum that gave its subject a regeneration, so powerful, that it would make those affected by it almost invincible. In order to achieve this, he had tried different combinations of viruses with around three thousand subjects. While some of them would die right off the bat, others would develop strange mutilations or protuberances. Others remained unaffected, which in turn made them subjects to different experiments in another lab, in a different division. As Stein had never bothered to know how many research divisions there were in the Block, the ultimate fate of the survivors was completely unknown to him. No one working as staff in the facility knew, either.

"Here we go, little buddy... let's hope for the best!" said Stein as he injected a rat in a cage with the bluish substance. "On we go to change the world!"

His new serum, thanks to a newly engineered strain in the virus C81, had been able to successfully, and permanently, modify the genetic code of sample subjects. However, this strain alone didn't offer stable results. For instance, one of the subjects was now able to grow limbs out of any part of his body, while another had lost his sight. The results were never the same, even if the regeneration was still there to varying degrees. Additionally, said regeneration was way too slow, prompting the subject in question to be easily captured by an enemy during combat simulations. Nothing close to the invincibility he was looking for. Thus, he would relentlessly try adding a new element to the formula every day, or subtracting another, with similar results. *I am so close, and so far at the same time*, he often thought after witnessing any of those outcomes. The lab rats, similarly to humans, had also shown different traits with the same procedures, and this is what he hated the most. It greatly pained him to have to sacrifice such fine animals before trying it on humans when they had all those filthy non-Frisks all over the place. Even if this was a policy Stein disagreed with so much, he understood that getting rats was way easier than getting non-Frisks. Besides, his superiors argued that testing on rats was a necessary economic step as their little bodies took way less amounts of any substance required for any experiment, compared to humans. That was, if those 'people' were to be considered humans...

Being able to understand the logistics of this predicament was the only reason why his 'revenge' was so small in scale. After all, Stein knew perfectly well that the materials and resources used in his experiments were also extremely scarce and quite expensive, added to the mere fact of justifying the funds for his research, which was another matter entirely, was something he would never stop appreciating.

"Panthea will be cleansed! Today is the day we start taking it back!" he said as the new formula made its way into the rat's small body. A phrase he had repeated six-hundred forty-four times already.

His newest attempt was completely different from the ones he had thought of in the past, though. This time he had combined the C81 virus, not only with several components, but with the E49 virus, a virus that proved to be exactly what he needed given that it could modify its host's entire genetic code and, in turn, prompt the subject to age way faster than he or she naturally should. Being able to work with such a virus, dug up from the entrails of the Earth during the Ice Age, was also one of the reasons why Stein felt so privileged. After all, there was only one sample available in the whole world. Engineering it and producing it from a single mammoth corpse that happened to have it, frozen after thousands of years, had cost the organization billions of wollars.

It had to work! Or he might be in for a wild ride...

Absorbed in the task at hand, Stein hadn't noticed that Martens hadn't come back yet, even though half an hour had already passed. Although he would never admit it, he had grown accustomed to having her by his side whenever he was working on a new experiment, whether it ended in success or failure--mostly failure. So, it simply felt weird not having her around during such an important moment.

"W-what do we have here?!" he said, surprised.

His eyes had caught onto something within the cage. The rat in question had now red eyes and its former pink skin had turned brown. Its fur made it all the more difficult to discern its features as it had grown like that of a porcupine. A smirk appeared on Stein's face.

"Now... it's time to test this!" Stein said, his eyes glistening with the lights of the lab. "This time I will not fail! I swear!"

With a small gun, the size of his thumb, Stein shot the rat

in the head. His eyes widened and a big smile appeared on his face when he saw the result: the small bullet had been ejected out of the animal's body while the wound had closed completely without a trace at a record speed. It was too good to be true! He had been at it for twenty years without success! How could something so stupidly obvious have been the answer all along? How many men had felt the same way upon the greatest discoveries of all time? Now it was his time to shine! The savior of Panthea had finally awakened!

He was about to write down the necessary steps to produce the serum, as he hated typing, when the alarm hit off. The sound of it was too much to bear, so he put his noise-cancelling microphone headphones on. Then, he looked at the monitor in the lab, which showed the immediate outside with a car crashed in the entrance.

"What the hell is going on out there?!" complained furiously Stein over the emergency phone on the wall.

"There's an intruder, sir! Do not open the door by any means! Be ready for combat if necessary! This installation has been compromised!" answered the security officer in charge. "A civilian car has fallen into the complex and broken our doors! There are five casualties so far and the intruder is making her way into the facility! Please remain calm and don't open the doors and don't get out without proper escorts!"

"Very well... thank you..." answered the scientist calmly just to hang up right after. Then, he remembered. *Martens!*

She had been gone for forty-two minutes and seventeen seconds now! Maybe something had happened to her! She might have been just an apprentice, but she was also a Frisk sister. He wouldn't be able to bear watching her getting killed, so he waited by the door with his right hand ready to press the 'open' button.

"That idiot! She forgot her credentials again!" complained Stein grabbing her ID card from the table next to the doors. She had probably put it there after scanning it to get out. It was evident that she wouldn't be able to come back in without it. It was the eleventh time she had done so. How could a Frisk be so stupid was beyond him. Unforgivable, actually. Still, as a fellow Frisk she was bound to improve herself someday, and that much earned her the chance to be kept alive. Thus, he listened attentively, his right ear sticking to the doors' cold metallic surface. Then, he heard them. Faint and arhythmic knocks on the door. It was all so strange…

He had never heard any knocks at all on it before. Probably because there had not been any need to do so in the past. Subsequently, he continued checking the monitors which showed him that no one was around. Perchance Martens was in a difficult situation since it was possible she was hiding from the intruder and looking for refuge. Perhaps she had been the one knocking on the door as 'silently' as possible in order not to give away her location to the intruder and then had to hide from said intruder, which explained why she didn't appear on camera. Or more likely, Martens was just below the camera located on the top door frame, rendering him unable to see her. As Stein had started to relax upon considering such possibilities, despite the constant acute sound of the alarm, the knock appeared once again.

Stein had two choices: one, to obey the security officer and to let, potentially, Martens die out there; or two, to open the door and risk it, saving Martens in the process. Since Frisks would never abandon their own, the choice was obvious. They weren't like those filthy invaders, for sure. Thus, as instructed during his training in cases of emergency, Stein loaded his officially issued handgun. If it was Martens, the shot wouldn't kill her, but hurt her arm slightly. If it was the intruder, the enemy wouldn't expect such an attack, which meant that the possibilities of being able of shoot twice and killing this enemy were quite likely. *It's decided then*, he thought as he pressed his ID card against the scanner and opened the giant armored doors.

"Who goes there?" asked Stein, aiming his gun at the entrance as soon as the doors finished their loud opening. Finding no one, he realized it could be a trap and quickly commenced the procedure to close them. However, they refused to do so. A big black marble cross had appeared out of nowhere and was now stuck between said doors. They were now jammed. Stein found this event interesting, as those doors had a 200 MQu pressure coefficient. Whatever that had fallen there was supposed to be smashed by them.

"A supernatural..." concluded the scientist in a surprised voice as he stepped back, holding his gun at eye level. Shooting training given by the Block to its scientists wasn't the most efficient, but just enough for a precarious self-defence. Stein was aware of that, so he checked all around the aisle behind the doors by aiming his weapon, and yet no one appeared behind the thick cold titanium doors.

"Who the hell dropped this junk?!" Stein demanded out loud, sweat running down his brow. Where was everybody? Where were the agents who were supposed to protect him? The escorts should have arrived by now. None of it made any sense. Where was Martens? Was she okay?

Most importantly, would he be okay?

He couldn't forgive himself for having committed such a dumb mistake. Frisks didn't do that. Thus, he cautiously moved towards the object blocking the doors. The plan being to kick the cursed thing out, and allowing the doors to finish their course, sounded good enough.

He approached the object and pushed it with his right foot with all his might, in vain. The pressure, the doors exercised on it was way too powerful, added to the extreme heaviness of the object in question, was indeed a heavy predicament. It left Stein dumbfounded. In order to lift and throw such a heavy object with enough speed to catch the doors while closing was not humanly possible. Was this intruder an experiment that had managed to escape another facility?

Serums for superhuman strength weren't a novelty for the Block after all, as the results obtained proved them to be quite stable, unlike the regenerative ones. He had only seen one specimen who had been experimented on with said treatment. The boy in question had managed to survive but had ended up in a physical condition that left much to be desired. As for successful results that left the subject in a healthy status, he had only seen them in reports but had never witnessed them personally. So, this was now an alarming possibility.

"No way around it, I guess… I will have to stand my ground and wait for reinforcements while aiming at the door," concluded Stein as the cross was stuck in a way that one slim person would easily get through. Even if he were to open the doors and close them again, he heavily doubted he would be able to move the cursed cross out of the way. So, he kept looking at the doors and their new entrance… and there she was.

A pale-skinned woman with several injuries, in the form of bullet holes, present in her legs and torso. She was barely walking and seemed not to know where she was going. She was also carrying an identical cross to the one stuck between the doors on her left hand. Was she this dangerous intruder the alarm had sounded off for? No way…

"Hey! You there! Get outta here now!" warned Stein while still aiming at her. "And get your damn thing out of my damn door!"

The woman turned around, as if guided by his voice, and threw her remaining cross towards him, vertically, so that it fit in between both doors, rotating in mid-air towards the scientist. Stein wanted to move, but his legs wouldn't obey him. Probably because he hadn't expected this reaction from a weakened enemy. However, as the cross flew in his direction, he managed to shoot the woman in question, hitting her on the left side of her chest. From the way the bullet had entered her body, he knew he had punctured her lung.

You're going down, he thought as the cross crashed into him, taking him down to the floor. In turn, the woman walked slowly towards him through the mid-open doors. As she did so, she casually kicked the cross stuck between them. Contrary to Stein's expectations, the cross moved aside as if it were light as a speck of dirt. Once inside, the doors resumed their closing, just in time for the arriving agents to be kept outside of the lab. As Stein knew this was the end of her, he smiled at his first kill and tried to get up…

Then, he understood.

The cross had crushed his pelvis, to the point of almost amputating his right leg. He would be alive only for a few minutes as the blood coming out of his belly, which was promptly blocked by that same weapon, was also putting extra pressure on the rest of his veins. A stroke was likely to occur, or just plain death. He could only control his arms and neck, as well as his head.

In silence, he regretted his dumb protests against the organization. His damned method. His discovery was just inside his mind now as, even though Martens knew the basis of it, she didn't know what the latest addition to it had been. The addition that had turned it into a success, or that said addition was the only one left on the entire planet.

He cried in silence.

"Where am I…?" said the woman as she continued her approach. Her face seemed to have come directly from the underworld. Her hair and clothes were bathed in blood, as well as her crosses. She looked fearsome, like some demon who had just escaped Hell itself. The hole in the middle of her forehead made the sight the more interesting as Stein had never seen someone with those kinds of wounds still walking. Was she a walking corpse? Even if she was not, one thing was clear: she was a supernatural.

"You… you there… what have you done?" said Stein, trying to release himself in vain.

"I'm-" the woman couldn't finish her sentence. She violently fell to her knees, bumping into the desk nearby where Stein's newest serum was, to then fall completely face down. The rat raged inside its cage as it fell to the floor alongside the serum, still in the plastic syringe. While the cage bounced on the floor, jumping far away from her, the syringe remained close to her.

The woman tried to get up, however, her own body wouldn't allow such maneuvers. Her lack of oxygen, a product of her most recent wound, was taking its toll on her. It became clear to Stein that she was in her last moments. She would die in there, and so would he.

At least… she's a Frisk… like me… dying in her company… might not be a blessing… but acceptable… nonetheless…

On the other hand, he felt he was missing something else. Something he had yet to try before passing away. The sounds the rat was making inside its cage told him the answer: he would never have a chance of testing his breakthrough on a human body. Even if that meant one belonging to the so-called 'trash', he would've loved to see if he had truly succeeded. He would die never knowing if all his efforts had been in vain or not. It was too much to bear…

He often thought that he had sacrificed his family to complete his job. His wife and two sons had left his stead as they couldn't bear to have a father whose only priority was work. But that wasn't the worst of all: in the current situation, he would now also disappoint his grandchildren. He felt his chest starting to close at the thought as anything remotely similar to an achievement would also be soon gone. In the end, he would die like a nobody… like a fucking non-Frisk. His silent crying started to resonate with the lab walls. Why did it have to be like this? If he could at least…

Then, it hit him.

He had a test subject after all, closer than he would ever be willing to dream at a moment like this. Whether this Frisk woman in front of him died or not was of little importance. He had to see his experiment through as no one else would be able to replicate his formula as things stood. Maybe there was still hope all in all…

"You there… you're dying… aren't you…? missy…" whispered Stein, trying to keep himself conscious, "I can help you out… you… defy all logic… might as well… defy this… too…"

No answer came out. The woman was almost passed out while the syringe was now next to her arms. That mere sight was enough to provoke despair in the scientist's dying heart. He took a pen out of his shirt pocket and threw it at the woman. As the pen hit her right shoulder, she moved her head around in order to see him eye to eye, but she was probably blind at that point. He could tell she didn't know where he was given that she looked upwards when looking for him. Had that attack of hers been pure luck? Probably. He had been positioned exactly in front of the doors when she threw that damn cross at him. Maybe she had just lost her sight when he shot her. It didn't matter. She was too weak to answer him all the same.

"That syringe next to your left arm... it's my best and final work... use it... even if we're enemies... at least you're a Frisk... you aren't trash... I can die with that... use it... I want to see it come to... fruition... allow me to enjoy my... sacrifice... please..."

Besides... the Block is more than capable of capturing her if my serum is a success... and someone might be able to reverse-engineer my damn formula... I can only hope so much at this point... I got nothing to lose.

The woman moved her arms slowly, dragging them around the floor clumsily, as her body refused to obey her. Once she felt the syringe near her left arm, she pushed it so that it penetrated her forearm. Then, she stopped short, or rather, hesitant.

Stein hated this. Convincing people wasn't one of his strengths. "It's a regeneration gene... modifier... it'll heal you... use... it..." he continued, feeling his breath being taken away by death with every passing second. Nevertheless, despite its possible success in humans, he would never know if past observed side effects would also be present in his newest creation, such as sterility, insanity, among others that had appeared when experimenting on *trash*. He knew that said effects happened mostly due to the brain degradation caused by the Virus C81, which had not been completely cancelled by the formula. In the case of this new serum, red eyes and skin color change had been observed in the rat... changes that hadn't been observed previously, either...

As he didn't have much time left and felt his brain going

numb, as well as his mouth, he started to tap the floor with the little strength he had left in his fingers, wanting to scream but unable to do it due to the massive lack of air. This despair was more painful than the cross crushing his pelvis. He hated her guts will all his core, and yet, even he knew when to hate someone or not. To think that the mere fact of having to give his enemy his masterpiece would have made him commit suicide if the conditions were different...

This isn't the moment for childish thoughts... only trash is allowed to have petty conflicts such as those... not us, Frisks.

Thus, he kept insisting in a less audible voice. "Even someone with low intelligence... would be able to tell that... you're on your last moments... I don't think you have a choice... seeing you as... my last experiment being a success... will let me... die in peace... so... go ahead... use it... show... to the world... how superior... we... the Frisks... truly are!"

Carmen couldn't avoid feeling disgust, even though his words sounded mostly like random sounds in her weakened state. The mere fact that she should have to rely on and accept any sort of help from the Block would've made her puke had her body and mind been in a decent state. That substance near her arm was the product of countless human victims. Countless lives that had been forcefully stripped from all over the world. Although she no longer felt any guilt, she could still imagine it. Accepting it would also mean they had been right all along, that the barbarism they had done had been alright because she'd be pursuing a noble cause... that of saving Nico.

Nevertheless, and as disgusting as her decision would be, Nico weighed more in the balance of her heart. In her barely conscious mind, she thought of taking the cursed serum so that all those deaths producing it were meaningful, somehow. To let their cores rest in peace by carrying their will herself instead of a random Block agent. She knew, though, that that would serve just to sugarcoat the decision she had already made. Besides, even if it was a trap, she was about to die either way, so both choices, accepting it or rejecting it, sounded equally awful in her mind.

I have nothing to lose… either…

Still, the disgust this lack of choice of hers made her feel was annoying. However, what was more annoying was the fact that she couldn't grab the syringe in question, unable to close her grip around it regardless of how hard she tried. The needle would simply change place, or slide around the floor, escaping her grasp every time. It was impossible.

Nonetheless, Carmen had a moment of clarity, and, taking advantage of it, proceeded with her idea. Stein couldn't believe his eyes as she used a chair leg as an opposing surface that would serve as support for the plunger to be pressed against. It was as if there was something, or someone, guiding her agonizing movements. She then simply pressed her arm against the needle, now in position, and easily penetrated her skin. Even if it had struck a nerve, she could barely feel anything at this point. Moving her arm against the syringe with all her remaining might, she managed to inject the entire serum into herself.

"You… did it… you're… a… supernatural… after all…" laughed and coughed Stein, victorious. "A human… with skills… beyond… an ordinary one… we might be… enemies… you might… have… won… but… I get the… last laugh… you did… what I wan-"

Before he knew it, his being had stopped existing…

As his life vanished away, Carmen felt her blood turning into fire. Her physical pain, which she could suddenly feel again, and to a greater degree, could be observed from the outside as she convulsed on the floor, screaming with whatever energy she had left. The pain was unbearable. Her body kept punishing her for a few minutes until she finally passed out.

What is this…? what is happening to me…?

...

"Finally!" claimed Roger once the titanic door gave way to his diamond cutting tool. "I thought we'd never make it inside! I didn't think it'd take one damn hour!"

"You don't say…" replied Alex, his partner, also sweating like his triumphant companion. "What the hell happened here?"

"I'm afraid that's classified information," said an imposing voice behind them.

"Commander Jones!" said both of them in unison.

"Get ready to storm in. Weapons ready men!"

"Yes, sir!"

Martens remained beside them in silence, too scared to even take a glimpse of the scene. *If I had just been paying more attention to that breakthrough… everything could've been different… fuck!*

"Why did you have to continue with your damn protest sir?!" she asked the emptiness in front of her as her tears of sadness made their way to the floor.

"Don't blame yourself, Martens," said Jones, lighting a cigar. "This is just an example that we're far away from the perfection we seek as Frisks. To have this as part of our reality just means we need your research more than ever… this must never happen again."

"Y-yes, sir… I will not disappoint you!" answered Martens, brushing her tears away with her lab coat sleeve. "We will take that damn woman and use her for further experimentation!" she continued with a fit of rage to her voice and renewed motivation. "The Block will become the beacon of light every Frisk will ever look up to!"

Jones smiled sweetly at her resolution. "I hope so…" he said to then turn his gaze to the men. "We know, thanks to the surveillance feed, that the intruder was the one who killed Doctor Stein and that she injected herself with his newest creation. According to Assistant Lieutenant Martens, we know that this serum was supposed to grant great regeneration onto the subject. Additional side effects remain unknown as of now. Now, get in and watch out for any sudden moves on behalf of the intruder. She remains unconscious on the floor as we speak, according to surveillance. Our life scanners indicate she isn't dead. Just remember, you see her moving her eyelids, or anything, you shoot her head. Am I clear?"

"Yes, sir!"

Thus, the armed men entered the chaotic lab and placed themselves near Carmen, pressing their iron sights on her head. Martens tried in vain to enter the lab, stopping right at the door, while Jones entered the place right behind his agents. "Who the hell is this woman?" he asked, expecting someone to know the answer, calmly tilting the remaining half of his cigar.

"We have no idea, sir. She doesn't seem to have any sort of ID on her," answered Roger after a quick search, confused as the others. "Let me try the database... she might be an escaped test subject..."

Gerard Jones had never seen a picture similar to the scene in front of him in his entire life. The woman laid there, on her right side, crouched with her arms around her legs, and her knees close to her chin. Her skin had turned yellowish and her veins black and visible. Her hair was soaked in dried blood, like her former white dress. She had no shoes and no visible wounds. What the hell was going on? Stein also laid there, dead, with a smile on his face. His lab rat, on the other hand, was nowhere to be seen. Following surveillance footage, they knew its cage had fallen on the ground and broken into pieces. After all, glass cages were the norm in the facility. It was weird, nonetheless...

That was supposed to be reinforced glass...

"Until we know who the fuck this is, no one leaves the room!" ordered Jones as he strolled his way out of the lab. "Let the containment team handle this! Until then, just keep an eye on her, you hear me?!"

"Yes, sir!" answered the men, Alex and Roger, with a Block salute without interrupting their aim at Carmen's head. A Block salute looked as if they were about to cut the air with their right hand downwards. As Jones had heard so many times when training new recruits, it symbolized the rise of Frisk people in the world and how hard it was to maintain it that way.

I wonder how our Frisk agents would operate if they had their families on death row... like the trash ones... thought Jones as he reunited with Martens and accompanied her to the building's exit, looking at her tear-streamed face. *The containment team should arrive soon enough... you'll be missed Doctor Rupert Stein... of that much I'm damn sure.*

After Jones was gone, Alex grew uneasy. "Wait... I think I know her..." he crouched to check her face closer. "Oh Kothat... she's Carmen de la Cruz! The one who escaped from that asylum with that trash the boys just captured yesterday! Wasn't she there with him in that mansion operation?"

"No idea about that... not that it matters much now," Roger responded, showing an increasingly itchy trigger finger.

"Look man, I know how you're feeling, but we gotta respect the commander's orders. We must wait for the containment team to take care of her," Alex answered, patting his partner on the back smoothly. "I mean... it's not like I don't share your eagerness to put her down, you know? She just killed a bunch of good folks out there before getting here. I have the exact same reasons you have to kill this... whore. But, we gotta keep it professional. We Frisks are a superior race. We cannot act like savages. You'd do good to remember that."

"You know what...? I don't care. We can always study her damned corpse! This bitch must pay for daring to go on war against the Block! You know what?! Let's just say she woke up and attacked us! That's it!" replied Roger, excitement glistening in his eyes. "We had to kill her in self-defence!"

Alex thought it over for a second. "I mean... if she were trash, I would have seconded that... but she's one of us..."

Roger eagerly pressed his weapon's barrel against her left temple. "A traitor to the Frisk race is worse than trash!"

"Whatever. I'm not taking any responsibility for this..." Alex said as he turned around pretending not to see anything. The cameras had been shut off after the attack by Jones, so they had nothing to fear. Thus, the eager agent took the gun safety off while a big grin appeared on his face. He would avenge so many fallen brothers and sisters. He would set such a high standard for the Block! A role model to follow!

"Take this, whore!"

As his gun automatically cocked its hammer, the sound of it went straight into Carmen's left ear. It had been so acute, so cold, that it reminded her of something else... something horrible and terrifying...

Her slumber was finally over.

The agent shot his gun, yet the bullet only encountered the lab ceramic-tiled floor. The woman had moved her head away just in the nick of time and quickly picked up the strange crosses lying on the floor. The agent in question was now confused.

"Are you done yet? We got other things to-" said Alex as soon as he heard the shot only to stop short in his tracks at the sight. The woman was standing in front of them with two giant black marble crosses on each hand, looking at them with a strong intent. A killing one. Grinning. Her red eyes only showed utter derangement in her core. Her inhuman skin made her look like a creature they had only seen in horror movies, covered in dried blood and an almost destroyed dress. Somehow, she looked completely different compared to her sleeping peacefully on the ground.

"Haha... hahahahahaha... HAHAHAHAHAHA!" the wretched woman laughed insanely as the two agents remained unable to move, trying to assimilate what was going on.

"This is because of the serum she injected herself with!" said Roger, aiming at her. "She's a damn supernatural! She must not escape! Shoot to kill!"

"In the end, we didn't even need a damn excuse! I love my job!"

Their intense training had proved effective as their shots hit her head at the same time. "Oh yeah! We got you whore! Haha-" Roger had to stop his triumphant laughter, joining his partner's thunderstruck expression on his face, when he realized the woman was still standing there.

As if nothing had ever happened, they watched in horror as their bullets came out of her head and an insane regeneration took place. This, in turn, highlighted her malicious grin, with which she strolled towards them, calmly, taking her time. Enjoying their fear.

"Like life... Death also adapts..." said the Black Cross without relenting her pace. "While debris must disappear..."

"Fire at will! Fire at will!" ordered Roger's partner, as if he was in command. Even though they had dealt with supernaturals more times than they could count, they had never faced anything of the sort. Something so terrifying, and even more so since they had no idea about how to defeat someone with that kind of regeneration.

"What do we do?! She regenerates way too quickly!" screamed Roger, shaking to the core.

"We do what we must! What we've always done!" said Alex. "We shoot her back to Hell!"

This encouragement lifted both of their spirits as they rained fire upon the woman. Nonetheless, time and time again, their bullets would be expelled from the woman's body as more blood was drawn out of her numerous wounds. Wounds that were nonexistent half a second later. Thus, she kept a steady advance towards them.

Without realizing it, they had been stepping backwards while shooting. By the time they had emptied their clips, their legs wouldn't obey them again and their hands wouldn't be able to bring new magazines to their weapons.

"Please... don't kill us!" begged Roger, dropping his gun, and to his surprise, the woman stopped in front of them. One meter away.

"We can still make it!" said Alex in a moment of lucidity while producing a walkie-talkie from one of his pockets. "Need backup! Need back-"

However, he couldn't continue his distress call as he was struck down by one of the crosses hitting his chest, crushing his ribs and lungs in a single swing. Such a sight acted like a wake-up call for Roger, who finally got his legs to work and made a run for it. Then, he fell.

"Aaaahhh!!!" screamed Roger in pain, unable to feel his left leg. "FUCK!!!"

"Hahahahaha… HAHAHAHAHAHAHAHAHAHAHAHA!"

The demon wouldn't stop laughing at the slaughter she was making as she proceeded to dismember Roger alive. As Stein's corpse kept its eternal smile upon the scene, the monster looked at her hands once she was finished. They looked perfect and pure as not a single scar or blister could be found on them. She could see her veins standing out of her flesh, like a caravan of black cars against yellow asphalt.

Subsequently, the demon walked around the facility as if she owned the place. As she neared the exit, she came across a mirror wall whose sole purpose was to hide x-ray scanners for security purposes. Sometimes for experimental purposes. The fiend stopped and looked at said mirror. She seemed to be admiring her own body, looking at it from head to toe. Given that her smile never disappeared, one could easily assume she enjoyed her new looks. It fit her new self, after all. It fit the Black Cross.

On the horizon, beyond the facility's entrance, reinforcements started to make their appearance, coming her way and armed to the teeth. She smiled widely and devilishly at the sight. These men, led by Lieutenant Alphonse Havok, stopped in front of the main entrance and aimed at her. Upon seeing the wrecked state of the compound, they immediately took position and cover cautiously.

"You there! Raise your hands where I can see them!" yelled the lieutenant. "Lay off your weapon now!"

The beast simply laughed, laughed, and laughed before *them*. Then, she charged like she had never been able to before… for the very first time in her life.

"Open fire! Fire at will! Now!" ordered Havok. "Don't let her get anywhere near! Shoot her down!" he continued, trying to steel up his men in this situation. In all his experience, he had never seen anything of the sort. No one had, so far, been able to enter and run rampant in a Block facility. "This is your end!"

To think that they were simply responding to a distress call coming from the security monitor room, without much of an explanation, was beyond him. However, as experience had taught him, keeping the 'weird ones' far away, as much as possible, was the best bet, as well as avoiding all sorts of physical contact. Indeed, he hated these kinds of situations. The unexpected ones. Thus, the men fired upon the Black Cross as she danced towards them, moving quickly in unpredictable patterns as if dancing ballet while advancing steadily, a big smile appearing on her face. As the bullets made their way to her, either missing or hitting their target, the men didn't know whether to stay or run upon seeing her not affected in the least by her increasing number of wounds. Still, their weapons roared as the night gave way to the morning sun, looming on the horizon. A roar that could only be rivaled by the laughter that death itself was making in front of them.

"What the fuck is this?! We're not doing anything!" claimed one of the agents realizing the obvious. Indeed, their despair gradually increased as one hundred bullets might get into her body, and the same one hundred would come out of it right after. Her teeth would get pulverized by the lead projectiles, as well as her eyes and fingers. And yet, she would remain calmly dancing while they grew back as if nothing had happened to them.

She seemed to be enjoying this orchestra of death as the combined sounds of both sources, their voices screaming in despair and gunfire, were a spectacle for one of the greatest pleasures she had ever felt.

"She's not going down! SHE'S NOT GOING DOWN! WHAT DO WE DO?!" urged one of the agents as panic took over their minds. In a matter of seconds, their accurate shots had started to show evident deviations to target, hitting the walls behind her. Given that the inflicting wounds on her body became less consistent, the Black Cross stopped dancing and ran towards them.

"HAHAHAHAHAHAHAHAHAHAHAHAHA!"

Some of the men threw their weapons away and fled as if there was no tomorrow. The ones that remained, including the lieutenant, kept their attack going, in vain. One by one, tearing their flesh apart, mutilating them, and smashing them, were taken down by the Dire One. Their tendons snapping in front of their very eyes. Some of them, surviving the initial vicious attacks, would try to drag themselves out of the fight, as their legs were now part of the floor. Nevertheless, the Black Cross wouldn't show mercy as, once being spotted by the beast, their heads would also join their massacred legs, smashed into the ground.

"Life extinguishes under the bells..." said the Black Cross peacefully as she strode past the numerous corpses, closing in on the last survivor who couldn't run away even if he wanted to. There was something the Dire One wanted to test... Little did she know that this opportunity would repeat itself many times over.

"Please... spare my life... I got nowhere to go... PLEASE!" begged Havok. His left arm and leg had been crushed. He quickly looked around, hoping for help to be available near him... but he was the last one alive.

"Acknowledge parity in characteristics," she said in a neutral voice, standing in front of him.

Havok remained silent and confused as he couldn't understand her statement. Her mocking smile just rubbed it in on him, manifesting his current inferiority. Then, the way she looked down on him gave him a hint.

"Are you... asking me to... a-admit that I am... the same... the same as non-Frisks...?" he said in disbelief as if hoping to be wrong. Why would she ask that instead of any other more valuable information? What was she playing at? More importantly, what was the right answer?

He wasn't sure about the response he was about to issue. Unable to achieve any clear conclusion, Havok opted for the obvious. His voice was shaking as he pronounced his answer. "Yo-you're a supernatural-..." Then, it dawned on him after he remembered who the Block had just captured nearby a few hours ago. "Ar-are you talking about... that boy we j-just captured?" His face never shook away the expression of utter terror. His eyes, wide like saucers, could only look at the demon's crosses.

"The swain of death… as alabasters deride in scads… is unvarying from them?" said the Dire One, calmly.

At such a declaration, his face full of terror suffered a radical change: it was replaced by that of an angry beast. He had lost the fear of death he had harbored a second ago. Such a change in his personality slightly surprised the Dire One.

She had seen it somewhere before, though… she just couldn't remember where or when…

"ARE YOU OUT OF YOUR MIND?! HOW DARE YOU EVEN TRY TO IMPLY WE'RE EQUALS?! YOU MIGHT BE THE MOST HORRIBLE MONSTER I'VE EVER FACED AND YET WHAT YOU JUST SAID IS WORSE THAN DEATH! I'D RATHER DIE AND GO TO HELL THAN HAVING TO ADMIT I'M THE SAME AS TRASH!"

"Death will grant such a request…" In one swift move, she beheaded Havok by hitting him horizontally with her right cross. His ire became forever engraved on his face as his head rolled down the pavement.

"Unchaining the light will forever be the job of Death…"

V

OR SO SHE THOUGHT.

There were a bunch of smells inside, so many that she couldn't keep track. Still, the mere thought of so many supernaturals near the one whose smell brought some short-lived joy to her core scared her to no end. That, added to the fact that *that* one heart signal was going weaker with every passing second, prompted the Black Cross to locate the fainting heartbeat as fast as possible. She would no longer walk casually this time. Instead, she dashed towards the entrance and got inside the building with no resistance or obstacle: the main doors had been smashed open by something, or someone.

"The Black Cross has entered the building! I repeat! The Black Cross-" warned the commander in the helicopter through his walkie-talkie, however, he didn't finish his sentence when he was abruptly interrupted.

"Good," said a deep voice from the other side.

"Always so eager..." concluded the commander with a smirk as he pointed northwards to the pilot. "We're getting reinforcements. Don't go insane, yet. We need her alive..." he continued. The silence on the other end said all that the commander needed to hear. Then, the helicopter disappeared in the distance.

As for the Black Cross, she continued to make her way towards the group inside the mansion. Nonetheless, nothing made any sense past that point as the mansion halls almost blinded her with majestic light and supreme cleanliness. She couldn't believe her eyes as she had travelled back to a different time. A happier time. The servants were running around, working around the clock. The walls looked polished, shining in their cleanliness. The paintings brimmed in color. The tapestry was vacuumed and immaculate. The rich adornments were beaming with beauty. Carmen couldn't avoid walking slowly in order to appreciate the beauty she was beholding. And so, as she arrived at the main hall, she couldn't avoid admiring the two majestic stairs covered by an impeccable and magnificent red carpet leading to the second floor, and between them, the proud La Cruz seal. A seal she had never stopped to admire not even once in her younger days.

The seal told a story all on its own. That of victory, that of tragedy. Carmen remained there in front of it, embezzled by it, when the sound of a piano key stole her focus away. She quickly turned around and saw it. Her old piano lay there, looking back at her, shiny and elegant, inviting her to touch it.

Carmen approached it calmly, letting her right hand caress its keys, making them sound the way they had always had. Before she realized it, she was sitting down on its bench. She had also decided to play it for a little bit. Her father's favorite, *For Elsa*. The first song she had managed to get right, also the one she had practiced the most ballet dancing to. As her hands slid softly through the keys, the sound of the piano flooded her ears while her father smiled upon the scene.

Life is good again, she thought with a genuine smile of joy.

Pablo looked at her, spellbound by her beauty and skill, as Carmen continued and more servants came around her to admire their little flower in action, listening to her in utter silence and bewilderment. Taking her time, she slowly pressed the keys that ended the song, waiting for what she knew was the standard reaction of her surrogate family.

"Encore! Encore! Encore!"

Among them stood out Carolina, smiling upon Carmen approvingly and hugging her father, talking joyfully, prompting her heart to jump in jubilation. Being able to perform for Carolina couldn't make Carmen happier.

Still focused on the music, she looked at her hands. Young. Tiny. Marble-like skinned. The world was such a magnificent place! She could no longer stop! If Heaven existed, she surely was in it! This was too good to be true!

Then, she heard it.

"Help… me…" said a child, weakly, behind her. Carmen stopped short and looked over her shoulder. It was a kid that had been stabbed with a knife, deep into his belly. Blood had flooded his clothes. His face looking for help in deep desperation.

Carmen felt her whole body tremble as she left the piano alone and ran to him, pulling the small crowd of servants apart to pass through just to hold the boy in her arms. He looked at her, and upon seeing her face, he smiled weakly. Then, his eyes began to close slowly.

"I'm happy… you're here… with me…"

"Everything will be OK! I swear! Please don't go! I'm nothing without you!"

"Let's catch butterflies tomorrow… mom…"

"Juan Fernando! No…"

In a matter of seconds, the boy collapsed in her arms as Carmen cried inconsolably, feeling his heartbeat fade to silence, his warmth slowly going away and leaving utter coldness in its stead. Not content with that, his body started to dissolve into thin air.

"Why… why is this happening?! I can't stand it anymore!" she screamed as her hands held more and more emptiness. She closed her eyes and cried in pain. A pain that could only come from memory, so profound, that made her feel as if she had been stabbed in the heart. At the same time, Carmen couldn't understand what was going on as she looked at her hands, now bigger and older--bathed in blood.

"Help us…" she heard someone say.

She turned around just to find the servants gone. In their stead, there was her father and Eliana: him to her right, her friend to her left. While her father seemed not to have any sort of injury, Eliana had a big wound on her stomach. It looked like a shotgun shot that had gone through her torso so that the other side was visible. Also, flames enveloped her body, melting her skin and flesh ever so slowly. And, albeit her father had no wounds, he wasn't faring any better as Carmen could feel his life vanishing away. Both of them, trying to reach Carmen with their hands, unable to move forward, stuck to the ground as their legs melted into it like hot mercury.

Carmen ran towards them just to realize she wasn't getting any closer. This only prompted her to run even faster, in vain, as her loved ones continued their meltdown until they completely disappeared into the blackened ground.

"No… Why are you doing this to me?!" Carmen whispered in an almost inaudible voice. "I tried my best to help you… to protect you… I failed… I'm sorry… you didn't deserve this…"

As Carmen was trying to understand what was going on, she heard yet another voice.

"Help me…"

That of a younger man. Carmen looked at him terrified, as he was missing his limbs and bleeding like common cattle in a slaughterhouse. "*They*… killed me… why… have you… abandoned me… Carmen…?"

"Nico… no… no… NOOO!"

Then, Carmen opened her eyes. She was still sitting on the piano bench. She quickly looked around just to find herself alone in the main hall, bathed in shadows. Upon a closer look, she realized the hall was actually destroyed, so much, it didn't look at all like its former self. It didn't make sense at all. The entire place was rotten. The piano was also a piece of putrid wood now, as if excessive humidity had done an excellent job destroying what was once a beautiful piece of furniture. No sound would come out of its keys regardless of how much Carmen pressed on them. *What in the world is going on?* she wondered in surprise. In order for that to happen the mansion should've been abandoned for at least five years or so and bathed with express humidity. Even so, Carmen didn't remember the climate being so humid in the first place. There were even plants and mold that had made their way through the crimson wooden planks, which she had chosen herself at one point to embellish her household during its construction. It didn't make sense for her former home to be in such a deplorable state so fast. Unless…

"Aaaarrgghhh!!!"

A weird beast-like scream of pain came from the living room. The Black Cross jumped to her feet and instinctively followed it to its source, her heart racing as she caught wind of Nico's vanishing life. The one who had screamed was someone she didn't know.

"Death will prevail!" she said as her feet carried her as fast as they could in what felt like an eternity. The darkness of the mansion's halls and aisles, and the creaking of the floor increased her desperation as she kept looking for the victim. After visiting one room after another, she finally arrived at the scene in question. Then, she saw him.

A tall man, probably two meters high, with a bodybuilder aspect was standing on top of Nico's chest. The Immigrant, as she had feared, was unconscious under his boot, hardly breathing, blood coming out of his mouth. The giant on top of him smiled with great satisfaction, confident in whatever power he held over the teenager.

Albeit her anger was taking over her core, as the giant kept on pushing his enormous foot down on Nico's ribcage, she decided to go with caution. There were other people around them. A Rolve young man with an abnormally big head lay on the floor, bruises all over his body, holding a pistol aimed at the giant, trembling in terror. The giant wasn't even paying attention to him. Instead, his attention was set onto a Mizelas girl. Although this girl, also a teenager, was invisible to the naked eye, the Dire One could tell that she had been incinerated at some point due to her constant smell of burnt flesh. Besides, she could see her, although not with exact details, she was able to easily tell where her head, torso, and limbs were within the room. The Black Cross could also hear her steps surrounding the man in question at high speed, running in circles. She was probably looking for an opening to charge against him. And yet, even though the man wasn't even on guard, or a defensive stance, the Mizelas girl wouldn't dare attack him. Following her trail, Carmen's gaze stumbled upon another strange figure.

At the back of the hall, leaning against a wall, another youngster lay there touching his right leg while looking at the scene in complete anger; his leg was possibly broken. He had greenish scales covering him from head to toe, as well as a tail, and a mixture of human with crocodile-like features on his face. Maybe he was the one who had screamed a minute ago.

Right next to him, there was a raven-haired girl, passed out on the floor, who had Assan features. Assan people and Frisks were barely different to the Dire One's eyes, except for what was perceived as having slightly bigger eyes than Frisks, and mostly black hair. She didn't seem to be hurt anywhere, though.

Having done a proper reconnaissance of the 'battleground', the Black Cross' eyes went back to the Mizelas girl running in circles. Sure enough, it didn't take long for the teenager to notice her watching the scene. She bluntly stopped at the realization. Indeed, as Carmen's gaze went right into her eyes, she started shivering. At the same time, the Dire One noticed that that invisible girl's eyes were fixated on her dreaded weapons instead of her eyes, not knowing whether to attack her or not. One thing was clear enough, though: she and the rest of them weren't Nico's enemies. All of them shared a common sentiment when looking at that giant. That of utter fear. Their eyes had the same expression to them as the victims that had fallen to the Black Cross, while this huge man seemed to enjoy that very dread. She had seen his expression somewhere else as well… that expression of malice…

Such a mixture of relief and outright dread… thought the Black Cross at the discovery. *There's another monster… other than me…*

There was also something else unique to this monster: a smell she had never felt before. None of the youngsters in the mansion had a smell similar to that of melting wax. As the smell of blood and guts didn't disgust her, she found it strange that this one did.

"Submit trash! Submit and I promise you won't suffer… much!" said the giant while laughing out loud, fully confident of his victory. "Accept your place as the piece of shit you are! Hahahahahaha!"

The man grinned maliciously as he removed his foot from his Nico's chest, crouched, and took him by the neck, lifting him with his right hand. The Giant was clearly doing it in a careful manner, and judging from his movements, he was containing himself quite a lot in order not to break the neck he had in hand.

"We'd rather die!" claimed the invisible girl in a defiant voice, her eyes emitting fury like magma from a volcano in eruption. Still, on the side of caution, the Black Cross hadn't moved at all from where she was, at the entrance of the hall, facing the Giant's back. She kept watching as the Mizelas girl decided to ignore her crosses and to focus on the Giant instead, continuing her running around and getting ready to attack. It seemed that this man hadn't detected death itself, yet.

"I was hoping you'd say that, trash! Hahahahaha!" he answered while staying in the same position, Nico's neck at his mercy. "Come at me already! I'm getting bored!" he taunted while putting some pressure on Nico's neck, visible by how deep his fingers had gone into his flesh. Thus, after quickly changing her running patterns, the invisible girl went slightly behind his right shoulder and launched a punch to his face, just to get grabbed by the neck all the same.

"Aaagghhh!!" the girl screamed, her invisibility abandoning her as the Giant's left hand exercised pressure.

"Nice! Nice! So, trash like you can activate your powers at will! Hahahahahaha! That's a first for me! I definitely cannot drag you dead out of here!" continued the man mockingly as he now held both youngsters up in the air. "Let's play a game!" His face was covered in eagerness as he crashed the teenagers' heads against one another, just enough to make the girl faint-- just enough not to break their skulls. He was a monster after all, even in his consideration for his prey.

"Heave Ho!" he said as he threw his victims onto the nearest wall. Both teens crashed against it and fell, next to the Rolve youngster, limp onto the floor, their bones cracking at the feat. Nico's heartbeat was almost extinct by now while the girl's was also starting to fade away.

Carmen could barely hold herself together, barely able to wait before attacking him. Her grip around her crosses' handles was tightened to the point of having her hands bleed. Before, attacking the Giant meant that he could've evaded her swing, and, because he had been standing on top of Nico's chest, he could've also crushed the Immigrant's ribcage in the process. Whether by accident or not, it was too high a risk to take. When he had Nico by the neck, a similar outcome would've been possible: had he detected her before she could connect a hit, or had he been hit successfully by her weapons, he could've broken Nico's neck in a reflex response, either way. Both results were not favorable. Now, with Nico relatively safe and out his reach, it was the Dire One's turn.

Keeping herself at his back, the Black Cross charged against him at full speed, as silently as she could, taking advantage of the fact that he had started walking towards the Immigrant as if the world around him didn't exist. Once she was half a meter away, she crouched and gathered all the strength she could muster into her left arm. As she was about to swing, she caught a glimpse of his face.

He was smirking and looking at her out of the corner of his eye.

Thus, she quickly hit him in the chin with her left cross with all her might in an uppercut motion, like a baseball player who had just scored a home run. The attack seemed successful as he went out flying towards the wall opposite to the one where Nico had crashed on and fell to the ground. His neck had been slightly elongated while his lower jaw had been pulverized.

He was down for the count and the Black Cross had to make the most of it. Judging from past experience, he would be up and running soon enough. And yet, that wasn't what worried her the most.

Why did he smirk at me? she thought. *I guess that can wait… there's something more important right now.*

She looked again into the big-headed Rolve's eyes. He was still trembling in fear, aiming at her with his gun, seemingly unable to tell if she was an enemy or ally.

"Don't get any closer!" he yelled while his hands could barely keep the aim steady at the Black Cross. "Y-you'll regret it! I swear!"

Nico was barely breathing now, his life hanging by a thread. As Carmen felt sweat roll down her face, the Giant's bones had started to make cracking sounds. Sounds well known to her by now. Attacking him again where he laid would only stall him for a while longer, however, she had no idea what other abilities he could possess. Had she been alone, caution would've been the least of her worries. For all she knew, the Block could have set that giant to blow up.

I must get Nico out of here…

"Alone can Death replay what was once fulfilled…" she said as she looked up and spotted an old chandelier hanging above her head, remembering that this was the only piece of decor she had managed to bring from Estú that had belonged to her former home. A treasure her father had always boasted about. It was still intact, lustrous and beautiful. Its twenty candle-like light bulbs were still in place, glistening in golden colors. Once her eyes were done admiring it for the last time, she threw her right cross upwards, making it fall from the ceiling and breaking into a million pieces. From it, she tore off one light bulb, so that she held half of it in her right hand. To everyone's surprise, she made a deep cut with it into her left arm, the bulb looking now like a micro saw, peeling off her skin and slicing her tendons. As she did so, she collected some of her blood into this improvised recipient.

"Have my brio... utilize Death's offering... vanish from Death's den..." Carmen said as she threw the broken light bulb onto the Rolve's hands, who caught it by instinct and, in turn, dropped his gun.

"I guess y-you're sayin' th-that w-we should get outta he-here, r-right?" the Rolve youngster answered, still unsure of what she could possibly be saying. Nonetheless, Carmen could tell he had understood what the message was, just not the intention, which was a first as it usually went the other way around. "Alright, it'll be done," he said more confidently as he picked the pistol up from the floor and put it into a holster he had in his pants. Then, he stood up and went towards Nico, being extremely careful not to let a single drop of Carmen's blood spill.

The reptile-looking youngster also stood up, struggling to step with his left leg, and limped away putting the Asan and Mizelas girls on his back while the Rolve one managed to get Nico on his.

"*Gracias*," said the Dire One, smiling gently at the big-headed youngster.

"Farewell... *pequeño*," she then continued as she saw Nico and his companions disappear from her sight through a broken window. *Fortunately, we're on the first floor*, she thought as she later placed herself between the fleeing teenagers and the Giant, who was already walking towards her.

"That was a nice display... Black Cross..." he said while cracking his neck back into position in what looked like a total overhaul of his bones. "I'd never imagine that the so-called Dire One was so… beautiful…"

The Giant walked around her as if trying to get past her to get to the window, from which the teens had escaped, and continue his chase. Nevertheless, the Black Cross would do just the same and keep herself in front of him, blocking his way.

"You should join us… we're the better race… the final victors!" he proposed, his face breathing eagerness and illusion. He seemed completely convinced that what he was saying was the truth. "You're one of us! It's nature itself that has decided that the infamous Black Cross is a Frisk as well! Hahahahahaha!"

"Death doesn't exist acting as slaughter," the Black Cross answered as she kept walking in front of him, preparing for battle, tension rising in her arms and legs.

"I don't know if you speak like that for fun or due to brain damage, but that doesn't change the fact that I've always wanted to meet you. I thought it would've been easier to make you understand that your rightful place is among us. I guess you need further convincing," he replied as he finished accommodating his neck and stopped walking. "I'm surprised you managed to deal all this damage to my body. Scratch that, I'm more than surprised… I'm impressed," he continued while granting her a wide smile, mockingly.

He has been aware of my presence from the moment I stepped into the mansion… he knew I was going to attack him… he purposefully received my swing to measure my strength… concluded the Black Cross as the giant kept grinning at her, as if enjoying her inner wonder.

"Still wondering how I survived it seems. It mustn't happen often… right?" he said to the Dire One's surprise as he strolled towards her in a calm fashion. "The look on your face says it all… maybe I overestimated your prowess… either way, my name is Ian Griffin, nice to meet you. But for you, you may call me the same way all that trash that recently ran away with their tails between their legs do… you may call me Massacre."

His excessive tranquility was somehow irritating to

Carmen. He was the first, besides the Biologist, to show no fear at all of her. He even scratched his nose and yawned from what she could tell was true boredom.

"My job consists of hunting down trash… like the one you just let escape… and to take it out… in both senses of the word…" he added, his speech in complete calmness as he casually cracked his knuckles. "It's truly unfortunate that you had to make this harder on yourself… you mayn't agree with us… but that's just a matter of time…"

The Black Cross looked into his eyes and grinned maliciously in response. "Slaughter might have borne the storm… twofold might be dicey…" she answered as she raised her crosses to shoulder level, blood drops falling onto the floor from them. "The cruor of the remorseful is seldom squandered… after all… it is Death's turn to reverse that."

Massacre laughed at his heart's contempt. "Oh, is that so? You truly are something else," he sneered as he posed his body into a ready-to-run position, touching the floor with his right hand and his left knee. "Let's begin, Black Cross. Show me what else you can do!"

His attitude might have been irritating, but it had also given some information away. His demeanor, his sheer size, and the strength he had displayed when toying with the youngsters, with no wounds or visible marks of being attacked, meant only one thing…

I won't be able to beat him… will I?

For Nico's sake, she would have to try to do just that. Besides, the single fact that this man would defeat her and continue his chase for the Immigrant right after was simply bound to happen. Buying time for Nico was all she could do.

I'll lose, won't I?

As he got closer and closer, his steps shaking the entire room, the Black Cross started to wonder questions she had never thought of up to that point. *How many times can I regenerate?*

Massacre simply smiled at her while his body covered itself on scales popping out of his pores. Scales similar to the ones found in crocodiles… similar to the ones she had witnessed on the reptile-looking boy…

At this point, nothing else matters… bring it on!

To Massacre's surprise, the Dire One dropped her right cross on top of her right foot, smashing it into a bloody pulp. The pain, reflected on her face, produced a wide devilish smile instead of a scream. This, in turn, changed the look on her face entirely, provoking Massacre to smile as well.

"Hahahahahahahahahahaha!!!" she laughed as she picked up her cross, allowing her foot to heal.

"I see what you did there… you erased any doubts you just had about this encounter… fascinating…" he mentioned as he observed her placing both crosses at shoulder level once again. Her foot had healed completely in half a second from an utterly crushed state, prompting a sarcastic gasp from the Giant. "Who would've thought that when they say that once you go to Friornia your life is changed forever…? they were right!"

"May any of slaughter's lapses be anted dearly…"

VI

"I DON'T THINK SO," said Mark when they finally arrived at the deranged woman's final destination. "I-it's not possible…"

"Well… you're seein' it with your own eyes, partner," said Josh while opening the door and walking near the cliff, hardly visible with the darkness of the night. "That's why normally we don't chase a suspect for so long! Now she got us to the damn Grand Pit!"

"Quite a big hol', isn't it?" said Mark, joining him overlooking the cliff. "But, why did she come al' the way here? None of it makes sense…"

"I wish, for once, that this woul' be just some damn drug trade or somethin'," replied Josh, starting to get back to the car. "I don't think there's much else we can do, pal."

"Who would've thought she'd run down the cliff without a doubt? Her car… I mean, the stolen car from that institution is down there but she's not," continued Mark, also going back to the car. "We must report this. This is no stuff we can handle alone, partner."

"I mean… this isn't even our jurisdiction," added Josh as he took over the steering wheel. "The rangers are in charge of national sanctuaries after all… and sure as hel' those boys wil' need backup…"

Both officers closed their respective doors and left the

place. Just as they had issued their report concerning what they had seen, they received an order to go to the scene of an accident over the radio. It seemed that another vehicle carrying living beings, the kind of which hadn't been specified, had had a problem with its brakes and fallen into the Pit. Given that there could be survivors, they were to rush to said place.

"What on Earth?!" claimed Mark as soon as they found it. The van in question had been going on the same road as them. However, unlike what the reports informed, it had not fallen into the Pit but had simply flipped onto its side along the pavement. As its back doors were open, and no one was around to explain anything, or to file the pertinent documentation, both officers could only take a guess. There were no bodies around, either, and it seemed as if this vehicle had been opened from the inside, given that the doors didn't show any signs of forceful aperture or damage. Whoever had done it had had access to its respective keys.

Upon witnessing the scene, Mark returned to the patrol and turned it around, followed by a skeptical Josh. "What on Earth are you doing pal?!" protested Josh. "Our duty is to-"

"I don't care, partner..." replied Mark as he accelerated away from the flipped van. "You saw what that woman did to those folks at that buildin'... first that, and now this... I don' think I can take this shit anymore..."

"We must go back to the site of the accident or-"

"My wife has been naggin' me all year lon' to get funds for Christie, you know... she's about to enter college... I want to see her grow... I just can't die here, man... you got that?!" barked Mark in a fit of rage and sadness to Josh's surprise. He could see a lonely tear come out of his left eye. "We're leaving, understood?"

"Ok-okay, partner, whatever you say..." concluded Josh as they rode back to the city.

As the officers disappeared amidst the forest near the Grand Pit, several Block agents descended the canyon and scouted its very bottom. All of them, wearing infrared visors and assault rifles, their standard equipment.

"That damn trash cannot be far! He has a bullet wound in his leg damn it! Find him now!" commanded William Styler as his men and women dispersed all over the place like ants. "Hernandez! Come here!"

"Yes, sir!" Hernandez greeted with the usual Block gesture, his eyes trembling before the commander.

"I heard it was you who let that trash escape... the details are quite... interesting... what the fuck were you thinking? Heh trash?!"

"I-I-I-I c-co-could n-not s-st-stop him! I swear for my mother!"

Styler took a handgun out and aimed at his forehead. "You can tell her that yourself." He then shot right through his skull. "Hey! Patel! Take this trash out of my sight!"

"Yes, sir!"

Styler put his gun away and looked at Hernandez's corpse. "Hopefully your younger brother will do a better job at this. I hate to be put in charge of a bunch of trash... so much expected failure... whatever." As he sighed, he heard sounds coming out of his walkie-talkie. "Any news? Over."

"Yes, sir! We found him! He's limping southwards! We should get him soon!" informed the man on the other end. "It's just a matter of time! Over."

"Very good, Westley! Over and out," congratulated Styler. "Of course, it had to be a Frisk the one who did it!"

Then, another voice came from his walkie-talkie. "Westley? Any more news? What-"

"Help us... please..."

"Swanton? What the fuck is going on over there?! Over."

"A demon... is... killing us... help... no... nooo... nooooooooooo!!!"

Swanton's voice fell silent completely as the buzzing sound of the walkie-talkie took its place. Styler put his walkie-talkie away and took his gun out, checking if he had enough ammo. "It seems that we were followed... only a supernatural could do this to our agents..."

Then, like a domino effect, the squads near Swanton

started to send similar messages to Styler through the same means. Those squads were supposed to be patrolling the north of the Pit. "Comrades and trash! Come here!" ordered Styler to his nearest units. "We have a supernatural attacking us from the north. We are yet to know the details for his or her origin or abilities. Until then, we're to stick together in Rho formation. Now!"

His agents obeyed him, accordingly, placing the Frisk agents in the center of a circle formed by the non-Frisk agents. Four Frisk agents usually protected by ten non-Frisk ones. Then, they waited. None of them were nervous in the least. In other words, they were mostly unaware of what was really going on, or if the enemy was a supernatural or not, or if this enemy was more than just one person.

"Fortunately, I managed to train these suckers in tension management... it seems it paid off... oh well..." murmured Styler to himself as he observed all around him. It was just a matter of seconds now. He had mentally calculated how far away was this enemy of theirs and how long he or she should be getting to them. "I can't wait to see who the fuck that is!" he mentioned as he closed his eyes in satisfaction when he heard the first screams of terror from a squad nearby. "He's here!"

Notwithstanding, the screams of agony had a completely different effect on the rest of his agents.

"N-n-no..." said one of them, now trembling to the point of dropping his gun to the floor. "W-what is going o-?" He couldn't finish his phrase as Styler shot him through the heart.

"Anybody else?" taunted Styler. "No one? Good... Ready yourselves! Here he comes!"

An acute and mocking laughter now echoed all throughout the Pit. It belonged to a female. Styler found it interesting that it sounded motherly and deranged at the same time. In response, he aimed his gun at the direction said laughter was coming from.

"C'mon! Don't take so long!" pleaded the commander sarcastically as he and his forces prepared for the assault, most of them still trembling in their shoes despite his warning.

Nevertheless, the agony of screams ended, and heavy silence made its appearance. "Now… where could she have gone-"

Styler was abruptly interrupted when a black marble cross fell on top of the Frisk agents in the middle of a nearby formation, crushing their ribs to a pulp and making the surrounding agents scatter. The cross had fallen with such a strength that it had sunk into the ground, along with some body parts. The rest of the agents looked around with their laser sights.

"Enemy spotted! Shoot her now!"

Nonetheless, as the sun rose on the horizon, along with the demon in question, Styler spotted her holding another cross in her right hand. He smiled at the realization that, by running with the emerging sun behind her, his forces were forced to take out their infrared visors which bought the enemy additional time without any projectiles going in her direction. This feat also hid her physical features. Nonetheless, there wasn't much they had to think about regarding the next course of action.

"Fire!" ordered Styler, joining in with his agents, raining bullets onto the woman in question. Her laughter and the lack of visible progress regarding the damage they were doing to her body made some agents drop their weapons and run away, being killed soon enough by the commander himself. "Fucking trash! Don't let her get any closer!"

Still, this attitude of theirs only worsened as she started to dance ballet among the shootout, as if she was using the bullets as a pacing method for her dancing. Even performing a *fouette* while approaching them.

"This is ridiculous!" concluded Styler at the sight. "Shoot her hands! The crosses are the source of her power! She's already lost one! Go go go!" he ordered as he started to do just that. *If she had other sorts of power, she would've slaughtered them with her bare hands, or with different moves… those fucking things must be the only lethal aspect of her fucking being!* Styler analyzed. However, to do just that proved to be hard to do as her body spinning made it too difficult to aim at her small hands. Styler realized she had figured out that her mocking of his agents wouldn't improve her assault on them any further, which prompted her to increase her approaching speed, stopping her ballet steps and racing towards them.

"Here she comes! Shoot her straight on! Now!" insisted Styler, predicting her to attack them in a group-by-group fashion, his voice starting to shake. "She clearly has no idea about military tactics! This battle is ours! You hear me?! Now shoot her-"

Styler couldn't finish his words.

He simply looked down realizing the demon had thrown her remaining cross at him, taking advantage of the kinetic force she had created with her running, and killing him alongside many others who were between him and herself. The force she had used had been strong enough to separate his lower and upper body, as well as that of her other victims. Only the legs and the guts coming out of the lower stomachs of those unfortunate agents were left for the rest of them to see. Some of them had managed to be simply hit on the side by the cross' patibulum, getting only their livers or stomachs ripped out, dying in the process.

"Commander… commander?!" yelled one of the agents far away, unable to see what had happened to his senior officer. "What do we do now?!"

As confusion reigned in the Block lines, the monster ran through the path of corpses she had created and recovered her weapon, now redder than before. As the rest of the agents didn't know what to do, or who was next in line as commander, they ran away *en masse*. However, their retreat wasn't fast enough as the demon started to chase each and every single one of them, picking up the first cross she had thrown in the process. A process she had recently mastered.

Now it was the echo of her scared victims propagating throughout the Pit instead of her laughter. With her frenzy seeming to never end, the last of the agents was taken down when her right cross fell onto his back and crushed his spine horizontally. Right afterwards, her maniacal laughter stopped when she heard a voice coming from one of the walkie-talkies belonging to a dismembered Styler's corpse.

"We got the bastard, sir! He won't be walking anytime soon! Haha...! sir?"

The woman in question crushed the walkie-talkie with her left cross, regardless of it still attached to Styler's severed body. Then, she ran as fast as she could southwards. On her way there, and in order to have a better sight of where her heart was guiding her to, she climbed onto a vantage point overlooking the massive canyon. It was then that she saw him.

He was done for.

"Where the fuck you think you're going, trash?!" said one agent while kicking the Immigrant on the right leg. Given that the teenager had been shot in the other leg as well, the pain he was enduring barely allowed him to keep himself conscious. "C'mon! Get up, motherfucker!"

The Immigrant tried to get up, fruitlessly. His legs were burning. His pain was too much to bear, both physically and mentally. His usual white pants were now red bathed in his own blood. And so, the agents laughed out loud at every attempt he made to get back on his feet, even more so when looking at his face painted with powerlessness and rage. Indeed, the Mizelas boy had been surrounded by six agents, all of them aiming at him with assault rifles, one by one hurling insults at him. Even if he managed to lift himself a little bit, an agent would come to kick him in the face and get him back down to the ground. Their wide smiles showed how much they were enjoying it.

"What's wrong, trash?" taunted one of them, pushing the teenager down with his left heel to his back. "Trying to escape your superior masters?! Hahahahaha!" he continued as he approached the fallen Immigrant and continued his course by punching him in the face. "If you, fucking worms, would understand our dreams... if you could fucking understand anything at all, you would just submit! You would all submit like the inferior beings you are!"

The Immigrant wiped out some blood that had come out

of his mouth, guessing it was due to the agents having kicked his stomach repeatedly. His eyes could merely be kept open, and yet, it didn't matter. He was, as usual, an insufferable teenager.

"Is that all you, assholes, can say?" Nico taunted back while trying to get up once more, helping himself with the nearest wall of rock. "Why don't you come closer and say it again... to my face...? Or is talking... all you Blockheads are good for?"

If I do die here... the very least I can do is to choose how I do it... and not them... I just wished... I could see... you... again... he thought while showing a confident smile to his attackers.

In response, the agents approached him and started beating him up in unison, by kicking him mostly. Nico could only grit his teeth and clench his fists in response, not even trying to cover himself from the incoming blows. His consciousness seemed to be vanishing as pain took over more and more territory within his body. He even tried to punch back some of these feet impacting his head to no avail. Even if his punch landed, it was so weak it looked more like a baby's kick. Even when trying to grab their ankles, he would simply receive more kicks to the face as well as stomps on his hands. He didn't know how many bones were still intact, if there were any. Barely able to see, due to the blood coming out of his head blurring his vision, he realized some of his fingers had bent backwards.

I'm sorry... papá... mamá... I won't be able to save you... I failed you... and Carmen... even though it was a short time... I wish I could've said how much I love you... so many, many more times... I wish I could've taken advantage of the chance you gave me by sacrificing your life... I have failed you as well... whatever happens now... at least I know that... our destiny is the same...

The youngster noticed how his heart had started to relent its beating. He would be joining Carmen soon. He could already see her face when he closed his eyes, even hear her voice. She seemed to be yelling at him, screaming his name, trying to reach his hand.

"What the hell?" said one of the agents. "Who's there?!"

Somehow, the sound of her voice made the thrashing stop as he no longer felt limbs hitting his body. Being barely able to open his eyes, he realized that the agents seemed to be looking everywhere for the source of said sound he had assumed had come from his head. They were aiming their rifles right and left, up and down, as uneasiness had grown into their hearts. Even the dying Immigrant could tell.

After that, the sound of a rock falling from above and hitting the ground shook them to their very core. The Immigrant couldn't understand what was going on as his senses no longer worked as intended. So, he hadn't realized that what had just fallen was not a rock. Sure enough, one of the agents had been smashed into the ground by a big black object in a way that his head had joined his feet in an unnatural fashion. His torso, legs, and arms had been ripped apart so that it looked like the fallen object had cut right through him.

He never knew what hit him.

"What the fuck is going on?! Who the fuck is she?!" screamed one of the agents. As Nico began to slowly lose his consciousness and was no longer able to open his eyes, he could still hear the agents, although more and more distantly. Their trembling voices, their words shivering in horror. With his ears shutting down as well, he could only draw one conclusion. *Whatever this is… as horrendous as it might be… you earned it…*

An acute laughter had shut down their voices altogether, added to a loud human growl of anger. Then, everything went black.

When he opened his eyes, he was in a strange place. After rubbing his eyes, trying to check if he was seeing properly, he could tell this place looked like a cave made from flesh where he could float at will. He was naked and his body didn't feel heavy, like usual. Unsure of what to do, his instincts told him to swim towards a light shining at the end of this cave. Notwithstanding, he stopped. He realized there was no pain there, no despair. It felt like… the days of old…

"This is so warm… and comfortable… I wanna stay here…" he said as he let himself go, floating in nothingness.

"Nico! Nico! Don't go *pequeño*… please don't go…" said a voice from within the light. "I love you… so much… so much…" the voice kept going, calling him towards it.

"I feel… so good… I don't wanna leave…" replied Nico, dreamily.

"I beg you! Please come back! Come back to me!"

As the sound vibrated through the living chamber, the Immigrant's memories passed before his eyes. From them, a smiling woman appeared, along with two old people. Then, he remembered.

"Please work! Please! Please!" said the voice desperately, more distant now.

"I… I still have something to do…" Nico realized and resumed swimming towards the light. Nevertheless, as he approached the exit, a red liquid streamed from it, showering him in turn, some of it entering his mouth and dragging him back to the bottom of the cave.

Still, the youngster wouldn't give up, swimming against it with all his might. No matter how many times he felt tired and hopeless, the voice kept giving him strength. A voice he recognized and that made him smile. When he least expected it, he got out.

I made it! he thought as he was ejected from the cave.

He slowly got back on his feet and looked around. Looking behind him, the cave was nowhere to be found, just a seemingly infinite field with flowers of all colors and sizes. Contrary to what he had expected, stepping on them with his bare feet didn't produce him any pain. Thus, he stared at the horizon, wondering… when a voice called him from behind.

"*Pequeño*…"

Nico turned around with a smile on his face when he saw her. She was there, still wearing her pristine white dress, smiling back at him. No wounds on her body. No signs of violence. Her eyes glistened in happiness.

Nico jumped towards her and hugged her with all the

strength he could muster. He didn't care if he harmed her or not, he just wanted to make sure this would never end, that he was finally meeting her in another world. In the afterlife.

"Carmen… I missed you so much… I'm so sorry… *perdóname*… I failed my promise to protect you…" he said in a voice that sounded like a mixture of sadness and happiness, tears cascading down his cheeks. "I'll never leave you alone! We will-"

He was about to kiss her lips when he stopped completely.

Carmen's face had suddenly changed. Her skin had turned yellow. Her veins had become visible, black like petroleum beneath her skin. Her hair had become messy and dirty, covered in blood clots. Her tidy white dress was now torn, stained with mud and blood. Her eyes had become crimson red. Nonetheless, that wasn't what terrified Nico the most.

Her smile.

He couldn't tell what it was, but there was something disturbing about it. He felt as if that smile had something horrifying behind it, something he didn't want to know…

"Carmen… is that you?" he said as he hesitantly stepped back. "I-is that really… you?"

Carmen simply looked back at him as the flowers around them started to wither and the sky was swarmed by black clouds. All that remained was a nightmarish ashen land where no life could ever come to.

"W-what is going on?! Who are you?!" demanded Nico nervously while looking at all the death happening around him and stepping back.

"*Pequeño*…" said Carmen as she stepped closer to Nico. "It-it's me… Carmen…"

"No… what have you done with her?! You can't be her! Monster!"

Carmen looked down and started walking towards him, unable to meet Nico's gaze as he kept stepping back trying to escape her, while blood started to seep out of every footprint she made on the ground. As if she was producing wounds on the field just by existing. Nico had to cover his nose as the smell of death, mixed with blood and flesh, became too much to bear for him. However, the strongest smell came from Carmen herself. Nico, unable to help himself, puked in utter disgust.

"Get away from me!" commanded Nico furiously as the blood coming out of the ground had started to take the shape of mutilated corpses sprouting everywhere. Still, Carmen insisted and kept going towards him.

"No… no… GET AWAY FROM ME!!!"

The devilish smile upon Carmen's face vanished. She now showed an expression of shock with her right arm extended towards Nico, trying to reach him, meeting his eyes as she stopped dead in her tracks. It seemed she had finally decided to obey Nico's orders.

Nico also stopped stepping back, looking at her more carefully and seemingly less disturbed. She lowered her arm and looked down again. If it weren't for the neutral expression on her face, Nico could've thought she felt some remorse or guilt. Nevertheless, he could hear her heartbeat, telling him that she wasn't affected by any of the flesh and blood surrounding her.

"Just… who are you?" Nico insisted, staying where he was.

Two black marble crosses fell from the sky and landed on near each of Carmen's hands, also bathed in blood.

"I don't know who you are… and I don't wanna know… but I refuse to accept that you're Carmen! You can't be her! A monster will never be her!"

The woman in question picked up her crosses and turned around. Not saying another word, she disappeared in the distance. Nico could only observe the landscape as the mounds of flesh and rivers of blood followed her wherever she was going, also vanishing in the process. With her completely gone, he sat down in lotus pose, closed his eyes, and focused on keeping his mind blank.

Several thoughts and memories came to his mind while he

felt how his veins were slowly being set on fire. Unlike before, he started to feel pain again while his blood bid throughout his body. Life coming into him in a fashion he could've never imagined.

Then, he opened his eyes.

"Where… am I?" he wondered as he slowly got up. "This looks like a cave… what happened?"

Once he reincorporated, he realized he felt like new. Could all that beating by Block agents have been just a bad dream? He wanted to believe so seeing that his wounds were gone. He had no blisters, not the slightest sign of suffering violence. It didn't make any sense. However, his pants had two tears on them, one bullet hole on each leg, and were still stained in red.

At the sight, he quickly tested his body, not fully convinced, by throwing some punches into the air, and even punching his leg where the bullet holes had been. The pain produced from it was the standard three times more painful. "Just… how?"

Nico could only formulate several theories as to how this could have happened while he prepared himself to leave the cave. "Maybe this is an experiment, too, but I doubt it. The terrain is way too large and I could escape. This is just not *their* style… then how?" he said to himself as he walked towards the sunlight at the exit. As the sun almost blinded him upon leaving, he was forced to cover his eyes with his right arm. Once his eyes got used to it, he watched his surroundings and realized he was still in the Pit. Everything seemed so peaceful, birds nearby singing and the fresh breeze filling his lungs… until acute sounds of sirens in the distance entered his ears.

Several lights also made their appearance far away. "The Block must have sent reinforcements, I gotta move or they'll get me," he whispered as he started to accelerate towards the direction opposite to where the lights were. At the same time, he was able to judge, by the position of the sun, that he was in the southern part of the Pit. "They'll never guess I'm going Eastwards… or at least I hope they don't."

Over time, and after hiking for a while, Nico eventually

got out of the Pit and stopped for a lift in the middle of the road. With no one picking him up, he strolled into the forest nearby. *I can't stay out in the open for so long*, he thought. With the trees starting to become more frequent and numerous around him, Nico was able to finally rest a little bit by sitting down on a fallen log. As he recovered his breath, he felt cold and put his hands inside his pockets. "What's this?"

From inside his right pocket, he produced a folded piece of paper. It was quite small. He then unfolded it and saw, on one side, the expenses he and Carmen had paid when they had ordered ice-cream in Las Esbirras. "This receipt… I would've never guessed it was here…" he said as a smile appeared on his face. After a moment of reminiscence, he turned the small paper around and found a message written in red ink that shook him to the core, prompting him to briefly sorrow in silence.

I'm sorry *pequeño*
We'll see each other again
Someday
I promise

Nico folded the receipt and placed it back into his right pocket. He then quickly brushed away a lonely tear coming out of his left eye with his right hand and proceeded to continue his path. He couldn't tell when this message had been written. Maybe it came from the time when they got separated at the ice-cream store shooting, but that didn't make sense. She didn't have the time, nor the will, to do it during that moment. His memory was a blur and wouldn't help him.

"This message… why would she promise me this back then? Besides, it smells like fresh blood… Unless… no… that's impossible…" he concluded, shrugging his shoulders and breathing deeply. Still, his mind wandered into nothingness, and while doing so he tripped and fell on his face. Fortunately for him, he managed to put his hands on the ground before making an impact, avoiding major injuries in turn. He then got up, and as he was doing so, he realized something had fallen off his hair. "What in the world? What's this?" he said as he picked up some sort of red particles with his left hand and looked at them.

"Dried blood clots? What…?" he wondered.

Then, he smiled.

Epilogue

And so, did Massacre.

"Is this really all there is to you?" he said, mockingly. "Keeping me away from you by rotating your cross like a damn chopper propeller? I expected more…"

Effectively, the Black Cross was only keeping him away from her at a small radius, keeping the other cross near her chest to attack him if he managed to come close, her smile still unyielding.

"Alright then, let's practice something…" sneered the Giant. Right afterwards, he disappeared just to reappear behind the Dire One. "Peekaboo!"

The Black Cross turned around and he received a cross to the face, which sent him flying and crashing into a wall. Still, instead of continuing her attack, the Dire One kept her defensive stance as Massacre got up once more, with a wide smile upon his face while he showed that his right arm had been the one to receive the blunt force of the attack. It now had a new joint in its middle.

"As I suspected…" the Giant concluded as his arm rearranged itself and regenerated, his bones cracking loudly and echoing within the decaying mansion. "Just like me, your eyes are sensitive enough to detect invisibility. This night will be quite promising!"

Thus, he renewed his approach, this time not turning invisible. Instead, he simply ducked when approaching the rotating cross and chain, evading its swings as the Dire One lowered her arm, and the rotation, to hit him. Once out of the cross' reach, he tackled her with his left shoulder, in turn, throwing her into a wall and burying her body into it.

Then, the Giant approached the Black Cross in an extremely slow fashion as her bones cracked back into place, and her wounds disappeared under renewed muscles and skin. Upon seeing him getting closer, she struggled against the bricks she was stuck in until she got out of the wall. Of course, she never stopped smiling devilishly at him. Afterwards, she pulled her crosses back to her thanks to her chains and threw her weapons against him, who easily dodged her attacks again.

"Unfortunately, I can't hide my disappointment… you're… too weak!" he said while scratching the back of his head and evading her blows at the same time. "Maybe it's my fault for having such high expectations…"

With that said, Massacre ran to her and caught up to her in a matter of seconds, not giving her a single chance to defend herself, and punched her in the face. This buried her back into the same wall to the point of making it through to the adjacent room: the main hall. The Dire One fell on her back amidst the debris, the La Cruz seal observing her thrashing from her right. The Giant made his appearance by coming through the same hole he had just made with her, making it bigger.

"In the end, that's all you are… just a damn woman," he continued with increasing disappointment in his voice. Massacre grabbed her by the head with his right hand and squeezed slightly, prompting some blood to come out of it, streaming like jets onto the floor as her skull started to crack. "Toying with you isn't even fun without a challenge, you know?!"

Seeing her lack of response, he sighed. "Whatever, you're still of great interest to us, so I'll have to capture you alive. Such a pity that trick of yours of playing dead doesn't work on me."

As the Giant crushed her head slowly, she kept on smiling maliciously with her remaining teeth behind his hand. Massacre yawned, nearing the brink of boredom, to then throw her against the farthest wall, like a baseball pitcher, causing her head to almost explode upon impact and her clavicles to dislocate to a visible point. Her arms hung like used rags.

"C'mon! Do something woman! I want a tale to tell the others when I defeat you!"

The Black Cross' body rearranged itself as she stood up once again, her devilish grin also back with her once her teeth grew back. "Incom-mersh are par-ra-rallel to t-the slaughter'sh kin… debrish is secondary…" she said as her jaw came back into place.

As she expected, the Giant's face changed from peaceful to that of utter anger. The Dire One raised her partners to shoulder level, waiting for him to charge. Nonetheless, his face went back to normal as quickly as it had gone angry, to her surprise.

"Nice joke you got there!" he said while winking at her with his left eye, pointing both of his indexes to her. "You know? unlike the rest of my brothers, I don't get angry… I know our superiority it's a fact."

Upon hearing that, it was the Black Cross who charged towards him to his surprise. In response, Massacre evaded her swings once again, even if these had increased speed.

"This is so easy…" he mentioned, with an even more disappointed voice when he counterattacked by punching her in the stomach as she jumped on him, crosses on top of her head. This act alone made her puke blood as she was sent flying towards one of the four big pillars of the hall. Said pillar burst into pieces upon impact.

The Dire One stood up as soon as her spine was back into place. This time, her grin didn't emanate only insanity, but also utter confidence. "Slaughter doesn't manage to induce Death's cessation…" she said in a neutral voice.

Massacre didn't waste any more time and charged against her again. Nevertheless, the Black Cross threw one of her partners to the pillar across the room, getting it stuck in place, and pulled from her chain. This, in turn, pulled her out just in time to evade the Giant who ended up crashing into the main stairs. Likewise, Massacre quickly cleaned the debris off his body and rushed towards the pillar she had just arrived at to tackle her at full speed. The Dire One jumped out of his way, so that he went through that pillar, destroying it in the process.

"*¡Olé!*" she said mockingly as she fell on her back on the floor.

"Why wouldn't you surrender? It should be obvious by now that there's no way you can defeat me, Black Cross," protested Massacre after shaking the dust off his shoulders, without the slightest sign of irritation. The Giant looked at the window from which the youngsters had escaped from through the hole in the wall. "You know that that trash is long gone. Even if I went after them right now, they are out of my reach... You're just wasting my time now."

Massacre touched his nose in slight annoyance as the Black Cross got up once more and positioned herself in a defensive stance. "If you possess the same skills I have, you should know how far away they got by now. We're just wasting time here, and you're not even entertaining me. If you weren't Frisk, I would've crushed you outta existence a long time ago. Don't push your luck."

"Death and slaughter are Xenox... *lusus naturae...*" she said in an increasingly tired voice, unable to lift her crosses to the same height as before, her hands slightly shaking. "Death would rather be no more..."

"So, monsters, eh?" mocked Massacre while closing in on her at a slow pace this time. "Whatever floats your boat. I don't care. I'm taking you with me now. Time's up. That trash isn't gonna hunt itself, you know?"

Unlike before, the Black Cross ran across the hall towards the center, near the destroyed stairs and away from Massacre's grasp.

"Whatever you're planning now isn't going to work... now be a good pet and stay the-"

The Dire One rotated both of her crosses as soon as she got to the middle of the hall while laughing in insanity. "Luxuriate in Death's gambol..."

Massacre couldn't avoid staring in embezzlement at the spectacle in front of him, his eyes shining in admiration. And so, after two rotations, she crashed both of her partners into each of the two remaining pillars supporting the hall, destroying them in the process. As soon as she did so, the entire ceiling started to crack open and to fall upon its recent visitors.

Now I realize… I was never complete…

"So, this was your plan all along… heh…! smart woman-" said Massacre while putting his right palm to his face, smiling compliantly, when he got interrupted by the falling debris as the whole structure came down on top of their heads.

…

"That was… exhilarating!" exclaimed Massacre when he emerged from the rubble, rubbing his eyes, trying to get used to the sunlight of a brand-new day. Next to him, there were twenty Block agents aiming at him, unsure of what they were witnessing. Once they recognized him and his scale armor, they lowered their weapons. The Giant shook off the dust off his head and shoulders and walked towards them as his scales disappeared into his skin.

"Where's she?!" he demanded his comrades. "Where's the Black Cross?!"

"Sergeant Griffin, sir! We were unable to find the subject! The corpse doesn't appear anywhere in our heat scans or radar! We don't know how she escaped! We deeply apologize for our fail-" the agent couldn't finish his explanation when Massacre snapped his neck with his right hand.

"FUCK!" he said as he walked away among the rest of the agents saluting at him in the Block fashion. "Why didn't they send Frisk agents to this operation?! FUCK!"

"Actually, according to the mansion blueprints, she might still be here," said Anthony Mascherano, another agent who had approached him, pointing at a location on a map-like document and showing it to Massacre. "It'll take at least five hours to dig it out and reach her."

"Interesting… but, five hours? Really? Such a pity. Oh well, good job! Off we go then!" Massacre said after patting him on the head. "Of course, it had to be a Frisk who noticed such an important detail!" The Giant simply walked towards a helicopter they had brought.

"Sir, aren't we going to hunt her down?" asked Mascherano, astonished.

Massacre boarded the helicopter by sitting down on its door and letting his legs hanging, ignoring the question.

"Alright, everyone! Retreat!" ordered Pustakios, already on board through his trusty megaphone. "The invading trash has gone southwards according to our trackers! We got a job to do, you hear me?! This time we got Sergeant Griffin to help us with this mission! Those bastards won't get far!"

I'll let you go this time, Black Cross… you're lucky I got no time to lose with you… the trash you let escape has a higher priority than you, after all… besides, letting you alone with my men is the same as granting you free kills, thought Massacre as he observed the collapsed mansion further and further away as the helicopter carried him upwards. *You still haven't outlived your usefulness, yet.*

Then, he smiled in satisfaction. *You will appear sooner or later anyway… I hope sooner…*

As the helicopter vanished in the horizon, and the agents rode their vehicles out of the La Cruz mansion, a yellowish right hand emerged from the nearby chapel's floor…

I've always wanted to meet her…

I've heard stories… more like I've made them up.

When I found that old box in the attic, as I ditched my action figures, some memories came to me. Memories I had thought long forgotten. Happiness in all its might, shining so bright with blinding light. Like day, it finishes when darkness comes.

I never forgot her face… full of ill intent.

I wish she was watching me, though, and not… that thing…

Whatever I've become…

Wherever she is…

Deep in my heart, I'm certain of it.

Despite all those who said it would be impossible, my hope never wavered. On the contrary…

I'm sure that I'll see you again, mother.

About The Author

Omar D. Rios

After more than 20 years of writing for fun, and studying different fields, Omar decided to launch his universe into the public sphere. This is but the first of many entries of what will be known as the Kallpa Magnaverse. He claims that he'll have to live up to 150 years to complete his catalog.